# REBEL

## A LEGEND NOVEL

# MARIE LU

PENGUIN BOOKS

PENGUIN BOOKS

UK | USA | Canada | Ireland | Australia
India | New Zealand | South Africa

Penguin Books is part of the Penguin Random House group of companies
whose addresses can be found at global.penguinrandomhouse.com.

www.penguin.co.uk
www.puffin.co.uk
www.ladybird.co.uk

First published in the USA by Roaring Brook Press
and in Great Britain by Penguin Books 2019

001

Text copyright © Xiwei Lu, 2019

The moral right of the author has been asserted

Book design by Elizabeth H. Clark
Printed and bound in Great Britain by Clays Ltd, Elcograf S.p.A.

A CIP catalogue record for this book is available from the British Library

HARDBACK
ISBN: 978–0–241–43644–8

INTERNATIONAL PAPERBACK
ISBN: 978–0–241–43647–9

All correspondence to:
Penguin Books
Penguin Random House Children's
80 Strand, London WC2R 0RL

MIX
Paper from
responsible sources
FSC
www.fsc.org    FSC® C018179

Penguin Random House is committed to a
sustainable future for our business, our readers
and our planet. This book is made from Forest
Stewardship Council® certified paper.

*To those charting their own paths*
*and those who make it possible for others*

Let us never forget the pain that our ancestors have suffered and are still suffering all around the world. Let us never forget the struggle between global tyranny and democracy that led us to found this free nation of Antarctica, where every person has the chance to work their way up from nothing, and where technology, not human ego and error, governs how successful you can become. Our Level system may seem like a game, but it is far more than that. It is a tool used to help us each live the life we deserve. And it will become the reason why Antarctica is the greatest nation on earth.

**STATE OF THE UNION**
THE NATION OF ANTARCTICA
2050 AD

# ROSS CITY

ANTARCTICA
2142 AD

# EDEN

IF YOU ASKED ME TO TELL YOU ABOUT MYSELF, I'D say first that I like to understand things.

I always have. Ever since I was a kid, I've been a tinkerer—prying apart old gadgets and laying out the innards of a broken radio or clock or toaster, delighting in the puzzle of making something new out of something old. It doesn't have to be a human-made machine, either. I love watching ants march in a line to a bit of food, take it apart, and carry it single file back to their hill. I love the way flowers bloom and then wilt, how you can preserve them forever just by pressing them between the pages of a book.

I like figuring things out, the how and the why.

My mother once called me her little alchemist, told me she believed I could turn rust into gold, and that I would ramble on about every little detail that makes up something until I ran out of breath. I skipped the last few semesters at my high school to become one of the best students at Ross University of the Sciences, the top-ranked college in the world, and I'm about to graduate with an advanced degree after seven years, which should have taken ten. I've already got an internship lined up back in the Republic, and in a couple of months, I'll be headed there for an orientation session.

But most people don't know me like this. Instead, they'll say:

*This is Eden Bataar Wing, Daniel's younger brother.*

That's who I am to others.

I understand why, of course. I may be a star student, good at figuring things out . . . but my brother is Daniel Altan Wing.

Ten years ago, he was known as Day, the boy from the streets who led a revolution that saved the Republic of America. His name was spray-painted on buildings, his profile drawn on both rebel pamphlets and wanted posters. He went from being a notorious criminal to a national hero in the span of a year. There are documentaries about what he did during the war between the Republic and the Colonies, about all he had sacrificed. For his country, for me, he had nearly died.

Yeah. It's kind of hard to top that.

After the war ended, we moved here to Ross City, Antarctica, and during that time, I finished school and Daniel became an agent in the Antarctican Intelligence Service. Daniel, at least, is eager to leave our past behind. But that doesn't mean anyone has forgotten his name or his face. There are still times when we'll get stopped in the streets, or when I'll overhear people murmuring as we pass by.

*That's Day, Daniel Altan Wing, a legend. And that's his little brother, Eden.*

Over the years, I've let this become the version of myself that everyone knows. Eden, the little brother. Not Eden the tinkerer, the inventor. They don't know how I'm drawn to understand things, or how I've had nightmares almost every night since the Republic's war ended. No, my identity is permanently tied to my brother's, regardless of what I do or think.

I don't tell most people who I am. I don't talk about the questions that run through my mind or the nightmares that keep me awake at night. People instinctually know to avoid someone who carries a weight on his chest as heavy as mine. So most who know me just see the quick smile and the earnest face and hear the breathless, rapid-fire chatter about the inner workings of a machine. They don't see the boy who startles awake at the sound of fireworks popping outside, convinced that it's the thunder of gunfire as soldiers break into our home. They don't see the boy who forces himself to stay up one more hour just so it means one less hour of calling for his mother in his dreams. So it means not feeling embarrassed for still not being over her death.

I like to show my bright side because it puts people at ease. *Eden, who's going to be just like his brother when he grows up.* Not even Daniel seems to get who I really am. When I pretend I'm okay, it makes my brother happy. And when he's happy, I can believe that I am too.

But at night, my dreams are filled with scenes of the Republic. They seep into every corner of my vision, all the good memories and the horrific ones, blending together so thoroughly that sometimes I can no longer tell one apart from the other.

Does Daniel have nightmares? If he does, he's never mentioned them to me.

The Republic, my past . . . these are things I haven't been able to figure out. To understand. Maybe that's why I ended up applying for an internship back in Los Angeles. Because I miss it, because I want to make it better by turning the Trial stadiums into hospitals, universities, and museums.

But also because it haunts my dreams, those old streets and faded memories. Because I can't stop thinking about it in the quiet and the dark. The brother that Daniel and I lost. The mother we will never see again. The father I never knew. Their ghosts walk my sleeping world, calling me back home.

I think about the Republic all the time. I wonder what it was like when I was small. I mull over and over the few broken memories I have. I read every article about the Republic that I can find. It's the hole in my past, the part that makes no sense to me, and I'm obsessed with understanding it. I need to comprehend what happened in my childhood. How I managed to survive one of the darkest moments in our history.

But maybe that's stupid, you know? Because, sometimes, it's impossible to understand something. Sometimes things don't happen for a reason.

The family we lost. The war that engulfed our lives. There is nothing to figure out, there is no how or why.

Sometimes things just *happen*.

\* \* \*

To understand Ross City, my home, you need to tour it in two separate halves. Let's start with the Sky Floors, where Daniel and I live.

Ross City is the capital of Antarctica, one of the most advanced nations in the world. Compared with the Republic of America, it's an absolute utopia. Its towering skyscrapers are stacked to the heavens, sealed securely inside a biodome that keeps temperatures comfortable and simulates a regular day-night cycle during the long summer and winter months. Don't ask me how it works. I've searched online for years and worn my brother down with questions about it, but it's still a fascinating and somewhat frustrating mystery to me.

Daniel and I live in one of the wealthiest sectors—the Sky Floors, the top half of the skyscrapers where there are sunlight and stars and fresh air, where the buildings are interconnected like a web by long walkways covered in green ivy. Up here, each floor is made up of luxury homes, shops, fancy restaurants, schools . . . not a single crack in the pavement, not a flower or shrub out of place. A kaleidoscope of massive virtual commercials and murals lights up each side of every skyscraper, all the images in a constant state of rotation. Looking out across the city from up here is like staring out into a rainbow sea. In the winter, the skies light up with the aurora australis—the southern lights—and paint the nights with brilliant bands of turquoise and gold. In the summers, the biodome simulates the night for us, and we get the same effect with virtual displays.

To people who have lived here all their lives, this is a completely normal neighborhood perched high in the sky. To me, it's a multicolored wonderland—as alien a place as the Colonies of America.

And it's where I am now—at Ross University, on the top floor of Building 23 in downtown Ross City, where I'm currently trying to figure out the best way to sneak out of the complex before everyone else gets dismissed from class.

I peek my head out from my lecture room and into the empty halls. The university is a neoclassical wonder of a place. Antarctica likes to pay homage to grand civilizations of the past, like the Romans and the Egyptians. I never learned about those societies back in the Republic. I didn't even know what *neoclassical* meant until recently—it's not something my old homeland ever showed anyone, what buildings used to look like in the days before the Republic existed. So the university is full of light-filled geometric spaces and straight columns currently adorned with moving virtual murals designed by students in the Art majors, and when the halls are as quiet as they are right now, you can hear the fountains outside the front entrance. Beyond that, walkways link this floor to the same floor of nearby buildings, so that it all looks like a honeycomb of interconnected bridges.

A few other students wander the school's halls, but otherwise, I'm alone.

Perfect.

I wait a second longer, then lower my eyes, hoist my backpack higher on my shoulders, and walk in the direction of the main entrance as quickly as possible. If I'm lucky, I won't bump into anyone I know until I make it outside, where my friend Pressa should be waiting for me.

Virtual images and text hover over parts of my view, changing as I go. There are titles like ORGANIC CHEMISTRY and THEORETICAL PHYSICS above the classrooms. A virtual Level hangs over the head of every person in the hall. LEVEL 64. LEVEL 78. LEVEL 52. Interactive virtual buttons drift above the potted plants lining the halls. They say:

WATER | +1 POINTS

Other buttons hover over the classrooms.

ORGANIC CHEMISTRY FINAL

A | +100 POINTS

B | +50 POINTS

C | +10 POINTS

D | –50 POINTS

F | –100 POINTS

All of this—the labels on the classrooms, the points you can earn for watering plants or taking tests, the Level that each of us belongs to—is part of Antarctica's Level system. Everyone in Antarctica has a chip embedded under their skin, right behind their left ear. Through that chip runs a technology that overlays virtual images over your vision.

It tracks what actions you make throughout the day. It assigns you a Level based on those actions. And then that Level floats over your head, so that everyone can see what it is.

Everything you do here earns you points that go to your Level. The more good things you do—score well on a test, help someone cross the street, and so on—the more points you earn toward your Level. The more bad things you do—cheat, steal, pick a fight—the more points you lose.

The higher your Level, the more privileges you're allotted. At Level 7, you earn the right to use the city's public bus, train, and elevator stations. You're allowed to rent a home.

At Level 10, you're permitted to shop for fresher produce, as well as eat certain types of foods and walk into certain restaurants.

To even set foot up here, in the Sky Floors where Daniel and I live, you need a Level of at least 50.

This is how Ross City uses its Level system as an incentive. It's meant to encourage people to do good and discourage them from being bad. Apparently, it's the fairest government ever designed, created after Antarctica realized that the rest of the world was stuck suffering in the same cycles of tyranny and dictatorships over and over again.

I mean, I'm from the Republic. I get what Antarctica's going for.

But as I hurry down the halls toward the entrance, all I can think about is that, no matter how virtuous the system is, some people just don't care to be good.

Sure enough, a familiar voice behind me makes me cringe.

"Hey, it's Wing. *Hey!*"

*Damn it.* I swear under my breath, shrug my shoulders, and pick up my pace. My glasses slide down my nose as I hurry. I push them up nervously, accidentally smudging one eyepiece a little with my finger. Despite Antarctica's advanced technology, the chip in my head can't fix my eyes—which were damaged by the Republic's plagues long ago—so glasses are still a part of my life.

Behind me, the voice only gets closer. Now I can hear the beat of other footsteps accompanying it.

"Hey, Wing, slow down. Where are you going in such a rush?"

Alan. Emerson. And Jenna. It's too late to avoid them. So instead, I take a deep breath and try to look calm as they come up on either side of me.

We're all the same age, except they're undergraduate seniors, whereas I'm in the graduate program. The first, Emerson, grins as he slows down to match my stroll.

"You're always heading out in such a rush," he says, putting a casual hand on my backpack and grabbing the top strap of it. He pulls me back.

I shrug, keeping my eyes straight. "Just meeting a friend," I reply. To my relief, my voice stays even and lighthearted.

"Your friend?" Jenna says on my other side. "Pressa, right? The assistant janitor?"

My friend Pressa doesn't attend the university. She doesn't have a high enough Level. Instead, she manages all the floor bots that sweep around our halls, cleaning them every morning and afternoon.

I hear the sound of my backpack unzipping behind me before I can respond. "You're amazing, Wing," Alan, the third student, marvels in false admiration. "All our books are downloaded into our virtual systems, but you still carry physical science books around?"

Emerson takes one of the books out of my bag. "That's because he doesn't use them for studying," he says, flipping the book open.

I snatch my backpack away. "Be careful with that."

But he's already shaking the book. Out fall delicately pressed flowers—goldenrods, bluebonnets, fragile winter lilies—that I'd carefully placed between the pages.

I suck in my breath at the sight, then drop into a hurried crouch to pick them up. Already, several of them have come apart from the fall, leaving their ruined petals strewn on the marble floor. My cheeks redden as I hear a couple of snickers above me. The light sheen of sweat on my nose makes my glasses slide down again, and I push them back up, hating the awkward gesture.

"I didn't know you were such a talented florist," Jenna says.

I try to ignore her and pick up the rest of the dried plants, then place them back into their pages. Now other people in the halls are looking at me as I work. I love flowers—their colors, their fragility, the way they grow, the way they smell. I was going to dry these out and put them into frames. But I'm too embarrassed to say it.

Pressing flowers isn't the kind of hobby that boys are allowed to take up. It's not the kind of interest that gets you friends. My brother would probably never be caught dead doing this.

"Need some help?" Emerson asks me, stooping down to my level. As he bends down, he intentionally steps on the flowers still on the floor.

A surge of anger pierces through my calm, and I shove him backward. "Get off those," I snap at him. But the flowers are already ruined.

## ACCOSTING CLASSMATE | –10 POINTS

The text pops up over my view before I can stop myself, and the negative points glow red in my account.

Emerson gives me a mock look of shock. "Oh! Sorry—I didn't see where they were." He holds his hands up. "It was an accident. Don't get too rough."

This is how they treat me every day. It's a careful kind of bullying, one that doesn't trip the Level system. They're not saying anything obviously cruel to me. They're not pushing or shoving me. So the Level system doesn't catch it, doesn't deduct points for harassment.

Emerson hands my book back to me, then pats me twice on the shoulder. "Well, hope you have a fun time with the janitor." His voice stays friendly and warm. Yet another way he tricks the Level system. "If you see your brother, tell him I said hi."

Jenna brightens at the mention of Daniel. "Tell him I said hi too."

The last time Daniel came to see me at the university, Jenna had blushed bright red and giggled all around him. Emerson and Alan had peppered him with questions about what it was like being the champion for a nation. Daniel, as usual, kept his answers polite and distant, but it didn't change how I felt standing there on the sidelines.

I stare at the dried flowers in my hand, feeling like an idiot. How

would Daniel do here, at Ross University? He was never the studi-
ous type, because he never had to be. Daniel is *Day*. He can run up
the sides of buildings. Evade the police. Jump through a fourth-story
window.

Me? I'm the nerd with bad eyesight who likes building things and
framing flowers. When I speak, my voice is higher and softer than my
brother's. He is the hero who never has nightmares anymore. I am
the odd, quiet one that he still treats like a kid.

I shove the crumpled flowers in my backpack, then crush them further by dropping my book into the bag on top of them. Anger simmers
beneath my skin, along with embarrassment.

"Hey!"

Pressa's at the front of the entrance, leaning against a tree and
waiting for me. Her face is round and smooth and light brown, the
shape of her eyes slender, and when she gives me that easy smile, one
of her teeth is endearingly crooked.

Her smile vanishes immediately at the look on my face. "What
happened to you?" she asks as I approach her.

I got to know Pressa when I started showing up early at school
every morning to work on my inventions. I helped her speed up her
work by installing additional code into the cleaning bots. We've been
hanging out ever since. In a university full of hostility, she's been a
lone comfort.

I think about telling her everything that just happened. If anyone understands what it's like to deal with some of these seniors, it's
Pressa. But the words lodge in my throat, refusing to come out. Real
men don't press flowers into their books. They don't spill their inse-
curities to their friends. Daniel certainly doesn't tell me about all the

things that happened to him in his past. Real men suck it up and change the subject until their hearts wither to dust inside them.

So I fold the words back into my mind and smile instead. "Nothing," I reply. "Just glad to be out of class."

She gives me a sidelong glance, as if she doesn't really believe me, but she doesn't push me further. Her arm loops through mine. "Still want to head to the Undercity?" she asks me.

I nod as we head toward the elevators. "I've been ready all day," I reply.

She grins and gives me a wink that she knows always improves my mood. "Good. Because there's a drone race happening later this week, and at least a hundred thousand corras waiting to be won. I figured we should go enter our bets."

Drone racing. Gambling. These are dangerous activities in the seediest part of Ross City, but it's the one place where I feel good about myself. I grin back at her, admiring the way her bobbed hair forms a straight line with her jaw. Then I unhook my backpack from one shoulder and reach into it. I pull out a small, circular tube.

Pressa's mouth forms an O as she studies it. "Is that what I think it is?" she whispers.

I smile a little. "If you're thinking it's a drone engine, then you'd be right," I reply. "I've been working on it for weeks." Good thing Emerson didn't dig any farther than my dried flowers. "This time, we don't have to just place a bet. We can enter the race."

Pressa shakes her head and grins. "Sometimes I wonder if you belong up here in the Sky Floors," she says. "You have way more in common with the rest of us down below."

I don't answer her as we head into the nearest elevator and start making our way down. Maybe she's right. I don't fit in up here, in the Sky Floors where everything's perfect until it isn't. My heart belongs to the lower floors, the part of this place that hosts things like drone races and gambling. The part that Ross City doesn't advertise.

The Undercity.

# DANIEL

EDEN'S NOT PICKING UP HIS PHONE AGAIN.

I tap off the virtual ringing icon in my view, swear under my breath, and try calling him one more time.

Maybe the connection's bad. I *am* currently in the pockmarked streets of the Undercity, after all, perched in the shadows on top of a crumbling neon sign overlooking a crowded street. This is the lowest rung of Ross City, the ground floor, where sunlight never reaches and where neon signs advertise the rusty jumble of cheap storefronts lining either side of the road.

It's not like this is the best place to make a call to the Sky Floors.

No answer again.

I take a deep breath and try not to be annoyed. When we first moved here to Antarctica, I promised myself that I'd never lose my temper with Eden. He survived a goddy revolution. He lost our parents and nearly his life.

He's my little brother. And nothing would ever be worth getting angry with him about, as long as he is alive and healthy.

Still. You'd think a kid could get around to calling his brother back now and then. Maybe he's hanging out with classmates. I don't know much about who he talks to these days. Last time I visited him at school, he seemed friendly with some seniors named Jenna and Emerson—but they're headed into their finals for the year. That means he's going to be out more, doesn't it?

The concept of a university, of taking exams without real consequences, is so foreign to me that trying to figure out Eden's life nowadays gets me nowhere. June would probably understand him better. I wonder for a moment if I could use this as an excuse to call her, get her opinion on how Eden might be feeling.

My thoughts always wander to June. I fiddle idly with a paper clip ring on my left hand, try to force her out of my head, and call my brother one last time.

He doesn't answer.

I sigh, give up, and turn on the geolocation tracking on him. That's another feature of Antarctica's Level system. You can at least find out where someone is.

"Any sign of her?" a voice comes on in my earpiece. It's from my AIS co-agent, Jessan.

I let Eden's geolocator keep searching and instead focus back on my job. My eyes scan the bustling marketplace below me. "Not yet," I mutter.

Jessan sighs over the line. "She's late. Maybe she's not heading out today."

"Give her a few more minutes, yeah?"

"Fine." Jessan hangs up, and I go back to my watch.

It's a good thing I'm crouched in the shadows here. People always recognize me, for one reason or another. My face is the one they've seen before on the news, on the wanted posters that used to plaster every goddy JumboTron back in the Republic of America.

Now it's the one that appears whenever you've committed a crime against Ross City. It's the one you see right before I arrest you.

My name used to be Day, the boy from the streets of the Republic. The fugitive who unwittingly started a revolution.

Now, though, I'm Daniel Altan Wing, of the Antarctica Intelligence Service. My job is to hunt down the worst criminals in Ross City. Here, apparently, I'm the law.

Pretty ironic for me, yeah?

Unlike other AIS agents, I'm kind of a fluke. I grew up in the grungy, broken streets of Lake. I stole and fought and scraped by with the worst of them. I used to be the most-wanted criminal in the Republic, a street rat who somehow got the credit for making a government crumble and rebuild itself. I know what it's like to live in the worst places in the world.

Most of the others I work with didn't grow up like that. Certainly not my co-agents, Jessan and Lara. They're Antarcticans, born and raised here in the glitzy, hyper-advanced, technological wonderland of Ross City. So they tend to treat me with a sense of curiosity and awe.

*What's it like*, they ask me with wide eyes, *to live in a world like the Republic?*

I usually shrug off the question. Life in the Republic is a nightmare that I'd prefer to leave in the past.

If anyone from my Republic days saw me now, they'd probably laugh. I don't look anything like how I used to—my hair long and tied back into a knot, my cap secured tightly to obscure my features, my clothes worn and grungy from the streets. Now I'm wearing a sharp black suit and sleek black collar shirt and polished shoes, and my hair's cut short and wild. I still can't get used to it, so I run my hands through my hair all the time. By the end of the day, it looks like a goddy disaster zone.

I wonder what June would think of me. Then again, I wonder what she'd think of a lot of things.

My leg's starting to fall asleep, so I shift my crouch and keep waiting. Today, we're down here tracking a woman who works for Dominic Hann, one of the most dangerous criminals in the Undercity.

Me, Daniel Altan Wing, tracking a criminal. Sometimes the thought makes me want to crack up.

But Dominic Hann isn't anything like me. He isn't some kind of vigilante fighting for justice or for his family. He's a killer, cold and merciless.

In the past two years, Hann has become the most notorious name in the Undercity's crime circles. He's left bodies hanging in the middle of intersections, gutted and mutilated. He runs illegal racing rings down here. He gives out loans to anyone not living in the Sky Floors, to people with low Levels who are desperate and hungry, and then comes for them and their families if they can't pay him back with double the amount.

No one who's crossed paths with Hann seems to want to talk about him. It's been hard to gather info.

Some people ask me why I chose to work in such a dangerous job after everything that's happened to me. I'm not sure, actually. Maybe it's because the thought of someone terrorizing the poor down here reminds me too much of my past. Maybe it's because this is the world I know, and crossing paths with danger is something I'm good at. Not that I like being familiar with all this.

The Undercity is a far cry from the gleaming luxury of the Sky Floors. This is where the poorest people in Ross City are. Spilled garbage and rusted scooters stripped of parts litter the intersections down here. Crowds of people stream by underneath me like a tide of ants.

Through my vision, I can see their virtual Levels hovering over their heads. LEVEL 6. LEVEL 10. LEVEL 14.

My gaze settles on a few homeless people crouched against the walls, begging idly for spare change. Level 0 hovers over their heads. People with Level 0 have no rights at all. They can't rent housing. They can't take the trains. They barely have the right to rest in the streets.

You can work your Level up, of course. That's the whole point of this system. Over time, some people in the lowest floors have been able to level up into the Mid Floors and get access to better food, housing, and transportation. But pulling yourself up that way takes an overwhelming amount of work. Most never make it out.

Ross City is still a better place than the Republic's ever been. What advanced nation doesn't have some poverty? At least these people have never been subjected to the Republic's Trials or the Colonies' stifling corporations.

But as far as I've seen, no place in the world treats their lowest rungs well. That's why I hate being in the Undercity. It's too much like life in Lake, going hungry and sleeping in alleys. Every time I come down here, I end up having nightmares.

People may think of me as some kind of shining hero. But honestly? All I really wanted in the first place was to protect my family.

Suddenly, I tense. My posture straightens. My gaze fixates on a woman who has just emerged from the bodega underneath my neon sign. She glances furtively behind her, then merges into the crowd with a shrug.

I tap my ear once. "Time to go," I say to Jessan, then hang up and rise.

I shrink farther back into the shadows of the building, slide off the neon sign, and start inching along the second-story ledge. Down below, the woman's moving surprisingly fast. If I wasn't specifically tracking her, I would have lost her in the crowds.

My feet move with the assurance of someone who's done this a thousand times before. I hop between ledges to another building, then another, my figure never emerging from the shadows. My fingers search instinctively for the next crevice in the walls to grip.

Up ahead, the woman turns down a narrow side street and makes her way through a food market. I stop short of the turn and cut instead through the back side of the buildings, then shimmy down from the second-story ledge to land in an alley leading out to the market.

Smoke from open grills lingers in the air, layering the street here in haze. I keep the woman's light-brown hair in sight as I hurry from one alleyway to the next. At least the people here are so preoccupied with hawking food that none of them notice a ghost slipping behind the stalls, a shadow moving among them.

Gradually, I edge closer. The woman looks back every few minutes, like clockwork. After a while, I kick off against the wall in an alley and move up to the third floor. My speed picks up. A series of laundry lines connect the next building with the one I'm currently on—I step onto the line, crouch to grab it with my hands, then use my momentum to swing down to the second floor.

Now I'm just a few paces behind her. Her movements are quick and nervous, as if she's sensed that someone may be watching her. My eyes flash briefly to the buildings around me. Jessan and Lara should be on their way, too, closing the trap around her.

The woman abruptly darts into what looks like a dead end. I hop into a second-floor balcony and swerve around the corner of the block after her. When I reach the alley, I see her about to slide through a narrow corridor at the end of it—but Jessan's already there at the other side. She steps out of the shadows, wearing the exact same black outfit as me, and points a gun at the woman.

The woman whirls around to try and run back the way she came, but I'm already there. In one move, I leap from the second-story balcony, grab the edge of a sign, and swing myself down.

I land right in front of her and pop up onto my feet, my hands in my pockets. "I don't think so," I say.

She throws a punch at me, but I step to one side and easily dodge her. Cuffs are already in my hands—as she stumbles past me, carried forward by her own momentum, I seize one of her arms and pull it behind her back. I snap one handcuff against her wrist, then the other.

"Alexandra Amin?" I say through gritted teeth as she struggles against my grip.

She doesn't answer, but there's a desperation to her moves that betrays who she is.

I allow myself a small smile as Jessan and Lara both approach me now. Jessan sighs and claps her hands together, while Lara runs a hand across the smooth, tight bun knotted high on her head.

"About time," Jessan mutters as she places a call to the AIS's headquarters. "This one was elusive."

"Keeps our jobs interesting, yeah?" I reply to her with a lift of my eyebrow.

Lara barks out a laugh at that.

We've been tracking this woman for a month. She'd reportedly been Dominic Hann's personal assistant, gathering info for him and helping him run messages down here in the Undercity. Our intel on her told us she grew up with him and was about his age.

She's a lot younger than I thought she'd be. I remember the rumors about Dominic Hann himself, supposedly the youngest crime lord in Ross City, and wonder what other gossip about him might be true.

This will bring us one step closer to hunting him down. I start to recite the woman's rights to her.

"You have the right to be judged before a court of Antarctican residents in addition to the Antarctican Level system. Before you stand trial, you have the right to—"

She twists around in my hands and gives me a wild, terrified look. "I have a daughter," she whispers to me. "Her name is Ashley Amin. Don't let Hann punish her because I've been caught. Please."

I blink, taken off guard. "Nothing will happen to your family," I tell her. My voice turns low and steady. I can hear the fear in her words. "I promise you. We just need your help."

That's when I notice a light foam building at the edges of her lips. Her skin has turned ashen and sweaty, and I realize the trembling of her limbs isn't just from fear. She turns those wide eyes back on me again. Her gaze sears straight through me.

"Don't let him hurt my daughter," she gasps, foamy spittle flying. "Don't let him." She keeps repeating the words deliriously.

I curse and glance at Jessan. "Call for help," I say. "She's poisoned herself." Jessan taps on something in her view without hesitation.

My stare whips back to the woman. I shake her once as her eyes start to glaze over. "I'll protect your daughter. Where can we find Hann?" I demand. "What's his next project?"

The woman's head lolls to one side. Nearby, Jessan is calling for an ambulance.

"Drone races," the woman finally whispers, her voice so quiet now that I barely catch it.

"Drone races?" I say. "Where?"

But her eyes roll back, and she goes limp in my arms. I shake her again, but her body has stopped trembling. When I touch my fingers to her throat, I can't find a pulse.

I'm no stranger to dead bodies, of course. I'd seen my fair share ever since I was a kid—after all, I'd been left for dead myself by the Republic and had to crawl my way out of a lab's mortuary when I was ten years old. I'd played dead for years on the streets of Lake, had seen my own mother and brother slaughtered, had witnessed plenty more deaths when the war broke out in earnest between the Republic and the Colonies.

But that has never numbed me. Every time I come face-to face with death on this job, I feel the same sickening despair settle deep in my stomach. The same sense of repulsion and grief.

*This is my fault.* I shouldn't have questioned her so severely. I should have checked to make sure she wasn't swallowing some kind of poison. I should have stopped her.

Now she's dead, and we're left with barely a thread of info about Hann. I lay the woman on the ground and slowly push myself back onto my feet as Jessan and Lara pat down her lifeless body.

What kind of man is Hann, to inflict such deep fear in his assistants that they'd rather kill themselves than be captured? What would Hann have done to this woman if she'd lived?

The blare of the ambulance arrives at the alley's intersection, and in a daze, I look on as two people clad in white rush to the body. Lara walks up to me and folds her arms.

"Drone races, eh?" she asks.

I nod. "If anyone finds out when the next one is," I reply, "don't let them shut it down yet. We'll be there, if Hann's going to show his face."

Lara nods. "Too bad about this one," she says, shaking her head. "I felt a little sorry for her."

"We wouldn't have to feel sorry for her if the Level system was fair," I mutter.

She sighs in exasperation. "Not this again."

"People like this work for Hann because they don't have a choice."

"Hey, you want to argue about it, take it up with Min."

Min Gheren, the AIS's director. I've brought it up before—not that anyone wants to hear it. So I just shrug and give Lara a sidelong look. "If you actually think that'll do any good, I'll talk to her. I'll even dress in a costume and do a skit."

We watch as hospital workers cover the woman with a cloth. At least bodies here are treated with some semblance of respect. A memory flashes through my mind, the old trauma of waking up in a sea of bodies, of dragging myself out while clutching my bleeding, ruined knee that had been experimented on.

"Are you all right, Daniel?" Jessan asks me as she peers at my face. I hadn't even noticed her come up to me.

"I'm fine," I reply, shaking the memory off. Already, I know what my dreams tonight will be about. The sooner we can get out of the Undercity and back to the Sky Floors, the better. I can't stand this goddy place anymore.

As we turn around and start to head back to the main street, a virtual alert pings in my view. It's a floating icon of Eden, with a glowing green circle around it. When I tap on it, a map pops up with a location dot.

Guess the system's finally tracked my brother down.

I stop short, then narrow my eyes to study it more closely. "Oh, hell no," I mutter to myself.

Beside me, Jessan frowns. "Hell no what?" she says.

The location dot's blinking not far from where we currently are. Eden's not hanging out up in the Sky Floors at all. He's here in the Undercity.

# EDEN

If you've ever been to one, you know why. Basically how it works is that a total of a dozen racers, who each brings their own flying machine, compete in races that take place all over the Undercity. The drones zip through the air and along the narrow, crowded streets down here, going fast enough to kill a person or destroy the side of a building. They have no permits to fly. They don't get permission to set up a trail through the streets. The gambling that happens over them is all cash, so the government can't tax or trace it. Still, it's an exciting sight. People will gather to watch them shoot by until the Level system catches on—*promoting disruptive behavior!*—and the police come to break it up. Even then, it can be hard to pinpoint exactly where the race's starting point was and catch those responsible for organizing the whole thing.

Pressa's been gambling on the races for years. Several months ago, she told me about them, and I went with her to watch a race without telling my brother about it.

I loved them immediately—the homemade ingenuity, the way the drones are usually pieced together haphazardly out of spare parts, some of them sleek and small and fast, others large and heavy and menacing. They tear down the streets at a hundred miles an hour, and when I watch them, I can't help but be impressed that something so fast and dangerous can be made just by putting together metal scraps from the Undercity's junkyards.

Now Pressa and I emerge from the elevator onto the grungy ground floor of the Undercity and head toward where she lives, a tiny, ramshackle apartment above her father's apothecary.

"How's your dad feeling today?" I ask Pressa as we pass through a food market on our way there. "We're not bothering him, are we?" We move in and out of the smoke from open grills. Over each food stand hovers virtual text telling me what they're serving. My system automatically translates some of the foreign text into English. KEBABS. SUGAR CANE JUICE. CORN SOUP. FRIED DOUGH.

Pressa shrugs, trying not to look concerned. "Don't worry about it," she replies. "He's having a pretty good day today. He's probably downstairs in the apothecary right now."

Technically, her father's apothecary is as illegal as the drone races, although Ross City's too lazy to do anything about it. If your Level is below a 7, you're not allowed access to regular health care. Antarctica claims it's because if your Level is that low, you can't be trusted not to use the drugs for illicit purposes.

So Pressa's dad runs an apothecary where he sells all kinds of dried herbs and natural medicines that are unapproved by the authorities. It's not really the best option for the poor, but it's better than nothing.

Pressa stops on a smaller street branching away from the market-place, then guides us through the maze of graffiti walls and cracked ground before we finally emerge on a different street.

Her father's apothecary sits on the corner of this intersection, its window barred with rusted iron and its door ajar. It's a dingy and dirty place, the kind of shop you'd never see in the Sky Floors, where you can have things like toothpaste and shampoo and medicine delivered right to your doorstep just by saying the items out loud.

But the sight of the apothecary still makes me smile. The lights on inside give it a warm glow. As I step in, the familiar, medicinally sweet smell of licorice fills the air. Next to a potted bamboo plant, a lucky porcelain cat sits on the checkout counter, its painted face bobbing back and forth. The aisles are crowded with shelves of cardboard boxes, each with something scribbled on them in Chinese—raw aconite for treating arthritis, ginseng, ephedra stems, rhubarb roots. On and on.

We make our way to the front counter, where an old man's chatting with several customers. Beside him is his assistant, a lanky boy named Marren, who's helping to fill a paper bag with various herbs. The customers pat the man on the back, then wish him well before they leave.

Marren sees us first. He waves, then gently taps the old man on his shoulder. The man's head jerks up—he peers around the store before his eyes settle on us. He breaks into a smile.

"Well," he says, giving me a wink as Pressa slides over the counter to give him a kiss on his cheek. "It's the skyboy. How are you, Eden?"

I smile. "Doing well, Mr. Yu," I reply. "Pressa says you're feeling good today."

"Did she, now?" The man raises a graying eyebrow at his daughter. "You don't think I always feel good?"

She just rolls her eyes at her father. "Never seen such a sickly guy in so much denial."

Mr. Yu gives me a mock-pitiful look. "My daughter wounds me every day," he laments. Pressa gently punches his arm.

He does seem stronger than usual today. His back is less hunched, and his skin looks like it's got some color in it. Pressa says he has a disease that has been slowly eating away at his muscles, but it's the kind of thing that you need a Level of at least 25 for in order to treat properly at a hospital.

The herbs Mr. Yu sells don't do his condition any good. That's why Pressa gambles. The amount of money she needs in order to get illegal doses of the medicine that'll actually save her father is so exhorbitant that even Daniel doesn't make enough to afford it.

"What brings the skyboy down to the Undercity this time?" Mr. Yu says to me.

"Eden's going to show me how he put together his latest gadget for his Robotics class," Pressa tells him as she takes my hand and drags me away from the counter.

Mr. Yu brightens at that. "Oh! Great!" He gives me an approving nod as two more customers come into the store. "You know I always appreciate you sharing your Ross University classwork with Pressa. Keeps her out of trouble down here."

I'm not the best liar, so instead I just give Mr. Yu as toothy a smile as I can manage before Pressa drags me through the apothecary's back door. By the counter, her father turns his attention to his new customers as they all greet one another enthusiastically.

"Mrs. Abesman!" he exclaims, giving her an affectionate hug. "It looks like my aconite tonic is working wonders for your arthritis. No, don't worry about paying me back right away. Take your time. How's your son?"

His voice fades away as we exit out into a back alley.

"Are you ever going to tell your dad how you're getting some of his medicine?" I ask Pressa as we walk.

"Are you out of your mind?" Pressa replies over her shoulder. "You know how he'd react if he knew about the races?" She turns briefly around to make a mock face of horror. "*I've spent my entire life trying to protect you from the dangers of the Undercity! You don't understand how dark it can get. They'll bleed your wallet dry. They'll kill you!*"

"I mean, he's not all wrong."

Pressa shrugs and keeps walking. "Listen, if you don't learn to take your chances down here in the Undercity, you'll get walked all over. Besides, it's not like we have much of a choice. Dad's Level isn't gonna get any higher."

Her voice turns harder at this. She knows there's nothing I can say in response to that, so I don't. What right does a privileged skyboy have to tell Pressa about what they should be doing in the Undercity? Besides, I know what it's like. The rules are different when you're poor.

"What are the details of the drone race?" I ask instead as the street we walk through narrows. Here, the graffiti gets denser, paint layered over paint until the walls are blanketed with it.

Pressa pulls out a wrinkled, folded piece of paper from her pocket and shoves it at me. I shake it open and read it.

## DRONE RACE

### SEMIFINALS AT MIDNIGHT

### 8 RACERS, 8 DRONES

### CASH ONLY, 100 CORRAS BET TO ENTER

Pressa glances quickly back at me. One side of her lips tilts up in a smirk. "You still thinking about entering your own drone in this?" she asks.

Races like this are never strict. If you show up with a drone last minute and impress the organizers, they'll add you into the heat. I nod, then pull the circular engine out of my backpack again and hold it between us. "I want to test the efficiency of this engine, anyway," I say as I hand it to her. She curiously turns it over in her hands.

"What's it do?" she asks.

My words turn eager. "I'm trying to get it as close to a perpetual energy machine as possible. See this battery? It's double the efficiency of the battery that runs my Sky Floor home and ten times as powerful, so I'm going to retrofit it onto a drone, and it'll shoot the whole thing forward up to two hundred miles per hour—"

She looks at me skeptically. "Get outta here."

"Numbers don't lie. If it works like I think it will, I'll design a bigger version to help power buildings in the Republic."

"Already getting ahead of your internship, aren't you?" She raises an eyebrow and shakes her head at me. "You and that bleeding heart of yours."

"You're the one willing to risk your life for your dad."

She shoves me, and I laugh at her. Then she gives me a questioning look. "Won't you risk losing your internship if you're caught racing down here?" she says. "Your brother's gonna kill you if he finds out what you're planning, you know."

Daniel. The mention of him clouds my temporary good mood. "He's not going to know," I say with a shrug. "Even if he did, he's not going to be able to stop me."

Pressa and I stop in front of a tiny shop crowded with people. She raises an eyebrow at me. "Listen, I'm serious. Your brother's an AIS agent. That's not nothing. If he tracks you down at a race, he might bring other agents with him and arrest people left and right. I can't afford that kind of hit."

"He's not going to stop us," I reply firmly. "Now stop worrying about him, and start fantasizing about what you'll do with a hundred thousand corras when we win."

Pressa searches my gaze, then decides against arguing. "*If* we win," she says.

"*When*," I insist again.

She grins at me, then looks back at the crowd as everyone pushes toward the front of the shop. Here, there are no virtual overlays. It's too dangerous to run drone races on the Level system. So at the front of the shop stands a tall man so lanky that he looks like a moving skeleton. He's taking cash bets from people and writing them down on paper.

Pressa has no qualms about waiting around patiently in line. She shoves her way forward just like everyone else, snapping at people who are putting in their bets too slowly. Finally, she gets to the front and takes out a wad of cash from her jacket.

She shoves it at the tall man. "A thousand corras," she says to him, then nods at me. "On this guy."

The man eyes me skeptically. "Who the hell are you?" he grunts.

I swallow, then raise my voice to match Pressa's confidence. "I'd like to enter as a racer," I say.

A look of amusement crosses the man's face. He somehow has the grace not to laugh at me. Instead, he just shrugs and jots down a note in his book. "You got a drone ready?" he says.

"It'll be ready by the time the race happens." I take a deep breath.

He doesn't ask for more info. If I can't follow through, we'll be the only ones who lose money, anyway. He pockets Pressa's wad of cash and nods at me. "You're in," he says. Then he loses interest in us and waves at the crowd behind us. "Next."

We both step out of line as the people behind us push forward. Judging by how many bettors there are, this is going to be a big race.

When we manage to get out of the throngs near the shop and head back the way we came, Pressa nods at me. "I'll be at the race tonight about half an hour before it starts," she says. "You can't be late, all right? My money's on you, and if you're late, they'll start without—"

"Have I ever been late to a hangout with you?" I reply.

She smiles a little at that, then steps closer to me. Her hand brushes my arm. "No," she replies. "And I expect you to keep it that way."

I put both hands over my heart and flutter my lashes once at her. "You know I love you," I reply.

She rolls her eyes, but her smile doesn't waver. "I gotta go help my dad at the shop. See you later, skyboy."

I watch Pressa go. The hairs on my arm where her hand touched me stand on end, making my skin tingle. Somehow, it's easy to lose track of time when I'm with her.

It's late afternoon already, and with the heavier foot traffic down the narrow street, I can tell that workers here are on a break between shifts. The food markets are crammed with people, all busy wolfing down a bite of burger or pastry or sandwich before rushing off to their next jobs. I shove my hands in my pockets, already lonely without Pressa's company, and start heading back toward the nearest station, where an elevator will take me back up to the higher floors.

Wandering around the Undercity as a skyboy would be a scandal if word of it got out beyond Pressa and Daniel. The university could expel me and strip me of my degree. The government might even confiscate my passport, making me lose my internship in the Republic.

Still, I can't help myself. If only I could feel this comfortable up in the Sky Floors.

I make my way through the throngs until I decide to take a shortcut through an alley. The instant I turn into the alley, though, I know I've made a mistake.

Someone is standing at the opposite end of the narrow path. When he sees me coming, he straightens and starts walking in my direction.

Behind me echo footsteps. I keep my head down and continue walking, but a sixth sense tells me that someone has noticed me. Maybe it's because I don't walk like everyone else down here. Maybe it's something in the clothes I'm wearing.

As the man reaches me, he casts me a quick glance. Then his eyes dart to the space right over my shoulder.

It's all I need to see.

*Thieves.*

I suddenly break into a run. The man beside me stiffens in surprise, then whistles to his partner to go after me. His footsteps pound the pavement behind me. I don't look back. I just keep going.

But he's too fast for me. One second, I'm nearly to the end of the alley. The next, a rough hand grabs me by the collar and sends me flying backward. My back slams hard against the wall, and then there's a hard blade pressed against the skin of my throat. I find myself staring into a pair of hard eyes.

"Well," he says, smiling as his friend saunters up beside him. "Got us a skyboy."

I try to struggle, but the man's got at least fifty pounds on me. A buzzing sound of panic seeps into my thoughts. I have to get out of here.

That's when I hear his voice.

"One more time. I dare you."

It comes, as it usually does, from somewhere up high, echoing against the alley walls. I turn my head up. He's perched on a second-floor balcony. One of his legs is dangling idly over the edge, and the crisp black shirt he's wearing under his black suit is lazily buttoned, the collar half up and half down. His blond hair is short and disorderly.

It's my brother. Daniel. His eyes are trained on my attackers. And right now, the smirk on his lips is the dangerous kind.

I groan and hang my head. *Oh, hell.*

# DANIEL

**THE WOULD-BE THIEVES DON'T WAIT AROUND.**

I see their eyes dart to me—not even to my face, but to the tell-tale black suit I'm wearing—and instantly, fear washes over them. They know exactly who I work for.

"Let him go," one of the thieves snaps to the other.

The man holding Eden's collar releases him, then sheathes the knife he was carrying. The two of them start sprinting down the alley. One of them chances a glance back at me, then shudders and speeds up.

For a second, I think about chasing them down. Jessan and Lara are still here—I could call them and tell them to track those two men with the Level system's geolocator and have them arrested the instant they're cornered.

But I've already had a woman die in my arms today. My strength for dealing with the Undercity's crimes is pretty exhausted.

Instead, I turn my glare down at my little brother. My smile feels like a line drawn in stone against my face. "Well," I call down at him as I shift my footing against the balcony. "You told me you were going to stay late at the university, yeah? Fancy running into you down here instead."

Eden doesn't look relieved that I've saved his ass. He shoots an irritated glance up at me and crosses his arms over his chest. "You followed me?" he says incredulously.

I'm not about to tell him that I tracked his location. "Don't flatter yourself," I reply. "I had real work to do down here."

Even though he's a lanky young man now, his wavy blond curls darker than they used to be, his eyes slender and pale, his glasses perched against the same kind of angular nose that I have—all I can see is the version of him that's still a small boy. The boy I once thought I'd lost to the Republic. The boy who had stumbled out of a hospital room, blind, calling my name. The boy who had sat with me on a cool tile floor and held my hand as I fought through an illness that almost killed me.

The boy I'd bled to protect.

He doesn't say a word as he pushes away from the wall. I pull my shades back over my eyes, swing down to the first floor, and fall into step beside him.

"Are you going to tell me anything? Or do I have to start?" I say to him.

He doesn't even look at me. "Why? Are you going to tell me what job brought you down here?"

I shake my head. "You know I can't talk about what I'm doing."

"Then I guess I don't have much to say."

I sigh as we fall into an uncomfortable silence. When we'd first moved to Ross City from the Republic, Eden had still been small, and he'd been happy to follow me everywhere I went. But over the past few years, our conversations have turned into this, in which neither one of us really knows what to say to the other.

"Have it your way," I say, at last, as we cut through the main food market. People make a wide berth for us when they see my black suit. "What were you doing down here?"

"Nothing."

"Nothing," I repeat, shooting him a sidelong glance. "I mean, that's why people come to the Undercity, of course. To do nothing."

Eden glares at me. "Are you extra sarcastic today because you haven't been on a date in a few days? Have you finally seen every girl in the city?"

"I'm being serious here."

His expression darkens. He looks away from me and picks up his pace. I try to ignore the whispers that follow us.

*Look at his suit.*

*It's the AIS.*

*Don't stare.*

"You were here to see that girl, yeah?" I say, after another long silence. "What was her name? Pressa?" We've left behind the worst part of the Undercity, and up ahead, I can see the station with the elevators leading back up to the Sky Floors.

Eden shrugs, but I can tell from his reaction that I'm right.

"Her father's running an illegal apothecary, you know," I go on. "I've actually told the AIS not to intervene because it would shake up their community too much. But—"

At that, Eden's eyes flash at me. "Is that a threat? Are you trying to tell me to stay away from her because she's a dangerous influence? Are you using her against me or something?"

"No, I'm trying to warn you so that you and your friend don't end up crossing the AIS. I only have so much influence in the agency."

"Thanks. But I don't need your help with Pressa. Isn't June coming to town tomorrow? Why don't you worry about that instead?"

His casual mention of June stings, and he knows it. June—the person who changed my entire life, the one who lingers so strongly in my mind that I can't bring myself to stay in a relationship with any other girl for longer than six months—will be in Ross City tomorrow, accompanying the Elector Primo as he visits us to discuss a trade deal between the Republic and Antarctica.

Suddenly, I'm very aware of the paper clip ring around my finger.

I try not to let him see how vulnerable her name makes me feel, and I shift the topic back to him. "I'm not mad at you," I say in a level voice. "You know that, right?"

I look for a reaction on his face, but all I get from him is more stony silence. We reach the elevator station. As we walk under its entryway, a pleasant *ding* sounds, the indication that our Levels—me, Level 87; Eden, Level 54—are high enough to allow us to use this transit station. Behind us, a man at Level 26 tries to sneak in behind us. An alarm beeps, and he's stopped by an invisible force field.

I halt in front of a private elevator made specifically for AIS agents to use. It approves my account, and I scan Eden in as my guest.

Finally, as we step into the elevator and it seals us inside its cool, glass interiors, I turn to face my brother.

"You gotta give me something here, Eden," I say. "Or do you seriously not trust me with anything anymore?"

Eden studies me. "Why aren't you mad at me?" he asks.

I blink. "What?"

"Why aren't you mad at me?" he says again. There's an edge to his voice. "You caught me wandering around the Undercity, the most dangerous place in Antarctica. I lied to you. And now I'm not talking to you. You should be furious."

"You *want* me to be angry with you?" I narrow my eyes at him. "What good does that do?"

"It would be something," he snaps. "An emotion, at least."

I take a deep breath. "Listen, I know it's been rough. You don't talk to me about what's happening at the university, so I don't know what it's like—but I've been able to read you since you were a baby. You've seen happier days."

"I'm fine," he replies, in a way that tells me he's obviously not. "And I'd be a lot happier if you didn't chaperone me all the time."

"I don't chaperone you all the time."

"You tried to call me nineteen times in one hour. Was that just for casual chitchat?"

"All you have to do is answer the phone once, you know."

"It's not your business where I go during the day."

"Everything you do is my business. I'm in charge of you."

"You indulge in your life. Let me indulge in mine."

"Is that why you come down here? To pretend you're something you're not?"

"That's what you think?" Eden asks. "I go to the Undercity to play at being poor?"

"I'm saying I hate it when you put yourself in danger when you don't ever *have* to."

"Maybe our definitions of danger are different."

"Excuse me if I thought you looked like you needed some help back there."

Eden's gaze pierces me. "You tracked me with the geolocator, didn't you?"

I hesitate for just a fraction of a second, but it's long enough to give him the answer. He makes a disgusted sound and turns away. "I thought I disabled it," he mutters.

I swallow my rising annoyance. Disabling a geolocator should be impossible, so of course Eden was figuring out some way to hack it.

"The city'll fine you for that if they find out," I tell him. "How many times are you gonna make me cover for you?"

"Like you've always been a law-abiding citizen."

Behind his glasses, Eden's irises have their faint purple tint in the light, the color that never entirely faded since he recovered from the plague. It's my constant reminder of what it was like to almost lose him, what it could be like again if I'm not careful.

"I used to break the law because I had to," I say coldly. "What are you breaking it for?"

Eden turns to face me fully. "You want to know the real reason I was in the Undercity today?" he says. "Because it reminds me of Lake. When I walk down there, I'm home. All that smoke and grease and grime, the rags and barred windows . . . I feel safer down there than I do anywhere else in this city. When I'm there, I think of John and Mom."

I can tell there's more he's not telling me, but my temper sharpens at his mention of our mother and brother. "How about you don't bring them into this?"

But Eden doesn't stop. "Sometimes I think you've forgotten

where you come from. When you're in the Undercity, it's like you can't wait to leave it behind."

He has no idea how wrong he is. How often I used to do exactly what he's been doing. I try to remind myself that Eden never saw the way I used to wander aimlessly down the streets of Lake. Back when I'd first been accepted into the Republic's inner circles, when I was working with June but still felt like an outsider at all the Republic's goddy balls and banquets . . . I'd walk the quiet streets of my old neighborhood and take in the rust and the grime. The humble homes and dirty coasts.

But Eden doesn't remember that. He was too young. He doesn't understand what it's like to crawl your way out of that kind of life, to want to keep your younger brother from ever having to see what you've seen, endure what you've endured. I took him here to get him *away* from Lake. But he keeps ending up down there anyway.

And I get it. The corner of my heart that's still Day, the boy from the streets, begs me to explain that to him.

Instead, I say, "It's because I don't ever want to walk those streets again. That's our past, not our future. We didn't move all the way here just to go back to that. And yet you're in the Undercity every other week."

Eden crosses his arms over his chest. "I can't spend an hour away from home before you ask where I am. I can't stay out a second past midnight before you come searching for me. Soon I'll be working for the Republic. Remember? I have a life that's completely separate from yours."

"Forgive me if our past has made me a little paranoid about your safety."

"Daniel." For an instant, Eden's voice softens. "I know. Believe me. But it's not up to you to watch my back every second of my life. You can't always know where I am. I'm not twelve years old anymore."

"Well, to me, you'll always be twelve."

Eden flinches as if I've hit him. I suddenly notice that he's been arguing eye to eye with me. When did Eden get so tall? Has it really taken me this long to notice? Then the initial sting leaves his expression. He looks away from me and out through the glass, back down at the Undercity far below us.

The elevator finally reaches our floor. Eden steps out first and doesn't look back. "No need to follow me," he calls over his shoulder. "I know the way home. Or did you want to supervise me through the front door?"

And before I can protest, he's left without me, his figure fading down the hall.

# EDEN

**DANIEL DOESN'T COME HOME UNTIL LATE THAT** night. I'm in my room, working by lamplight on my perpetual engine machine, when I hear the alarm ding over our front door, followed by a pleasant, automated voice over the speakers installed into our walls.

*"Welcome home, Daniel Wing."*

Out in the living room, I hear my brother take off his shoes, then the sound of the refrigerator door opening and the pouring of a glass of water. Instinctively, I breathe a sigh of relief and relax my shoulders. Then I turn off my own tracking of his geolocator. My brother may be overly paranoid about me, but he's the one with the dangerous job that he never talks to me about. How many hours has he worked today? What kind of mission is requiring him to pull these late nights?

I don't leave my room to greet him. Our argument from earlier still rings fresh in my mind, and I'm not about to be the first one to cave. Instead, I hunch lower over my machine and keep working, half listening to Daniel in the kitchen. He seems to drink his water, then sets the glass down with a clink and opens the fridge door again. I'd pulled his dinner out of the freezer and into the fridge to thaw. He wouldn't have remembered to do it earlier, and he won't remember now that he never did it.

It's one of those small things left over from our Republic days: his spotty memory. He remembers things that happened when we were kids, or from decades ago. But sometimes he can't recall a place he was just at several minutes earlier. Or a name. A face. A task.

Physical reminders can sometimes help trigger a lost memory for him, and occasionally I'll catch him just standing there with a thoughtful frown on his face, struggling to place the feeling of déjà vu that a familiar street sign or narrow alley has awakened in him.

He takes daily medication for it and runs several programs on his Level system that pop up constant reminders for him. I try to make up for the rest of the times when things slip through the cracks. But it makes his job doubly precarious. I have enough nightmares about him never coming home. So I keep a constant eye on his location and his daily habits.

*Well, to me, you'll always be twelve.*

The words make my temper flare again, and I go back to working on my perpetual energy machine with a vengeance.

It's a smooth, elegant design, a small ring of a battery that I now fit with a coil of wire around it. Beside it sits my drone, which I'll soon attach to the engine. The race notice from Pressa sits folded in my pocket. I check the time—nine o'clock. Just a couple of hours left before I head off to see her.

A light knock sounds against my door.

I don't respond. Daniel knocks again, and I half expect him to call through the door for me to open it. But he doesn't. I can almost picture him standing there, leaning casually against the frame, his shirt rumpled and a plate of food in his hand.

When I was little, we'd leave our doors open and I'd go back and forth all the time, peppering him with questions until he'd tell me to leave him alone. But that was back when I felt like I knew him. Then he took this AIS job, and now spends all his time keeping his secrets. So I keep mine.

The knock comes a third time, but I still don't answer. Finally, his footsteps turn away and he heads off into his own room.

I try to concentrate on attaching the new engine to my drone. When had we stopped really talking to each other? Why is it so hard for him to understand me now? How can he possibly go to the Undercity for so many missions and not feel the same pull to it that I do? Hadn't he grown up in Lake too?

It just reminds me of why I don't tell him about my nightmares, the way I cringe at loud noises or tremble over little things that remind me of the past. My brother had gone through worse than I had, and somehow he seems to have come out of it relatively unscathed. Functioning. Practical.

But things linger in my head. They don't go away.

Maybe he's right. Maybe I really am still a kid who doesn't know how to move on.

An hour ticks by slowly. Finally, I finish attaching the engine and test the drone by hovering it quietly over my desk. It's a sleek design inspired by a Colonies jet that had once been flown by a girl named Kaede, who carried my brother and June Iparis across country lines during the heat of the Republic's war. The wings are swept and narrow, the shape of the drone so sleek that it resembles a needle. The engine underneath it glows a faint blue, humming serenely.

From the other room, I don't hear anything. Daniel must have gone to bed by now. After a while, I get up and leave my room without a sound. Then I peer over at his door and give the handle a try.

It's locked.

He's probably fast asleep already, in a perfectly made bed. Where my room is a mess, his is always tidy. Something about Daniel's years on the streets has made him more careful with his stuff than I am. Everything is always in its place: computers and devices arranged neatly on his desk, his bed made without a single wrinkle in the blankets. He has few mementos from our life back in the Republic on his shelves. A dangling pendant from our father, always polished. Medals and badges from the Republic are all put carefully away into a box. He doesn't display them openly.

I turn away from his door and head back into my room. With any luck, he won't hear me leave and he won't notice when I come back. I turn off the lights in my own room, then put the drone away in my backpack and start throwing on my jacket. The patterns from the city lights outside stretch against my ceiling. Everything's silent and dark. All I can hear is the crowd of thoughts in my head.

Finally, I'm ready to go.

As I turn to head out the door, a motion outside stops me.

I pause in the darkness, then grab my glasses from my dresser and walk over on silent feet to the sliding glass door that leads out to the long balcony that wraps around our home.

My vision at night has never quite recovered from the Republic's experiments, and there is a faint halo around the lights glimmering outside from windows. But I can still make out my brother crouched precariously on the ledge, his face turned out toward the massive city.

This would be a terrifying sight to anyone else. The way he's sitting, Daniel looks like he could plummet to his death at any moment. But instead, he is perfectly balanced and at ease, one elbow propped up against a raised knee, his other leg hanging down over the side of the balcony, the foot pressed flat against the railings. With my blurred vision, a glow of light from the skyscrapers behind him outlines his figure in blue-white.

Guess he's not asleep after all.

I wonder what he's thinking. Whether or not he still has nightmares like I do. What he sees when he gazes out at Ross City. Surely, he can't walk through the Undercity on his sweeps and not think about where we came from. He can't possibly pass those ramshackle vendors, the people who huddle in the alleys, and not think of his days struggling to survive.

Maybe he's thinking about seeing June tomorrow. A needle of guilt pricks me as I remember how I'd brought her up to him earlier in the day. He'd switched the topic back to me so quickly. But that's the thing about him now. He'll spend all his time digging into my life without ever telling me anything about what's going on with him. I don't even know if he's still in love with her.

There used to be a time when all I wanted to do was talk to Daniel. Now I don't know what I want. For him to understand me, I guess, except that seems impossible.

I watch him until he stands up on the ledge, turns, and hops back down. He disappears back inside his room.

A call from Pressa comes in. I accept it, then answer in a hushed voice, "Hey."

"Hey." She sounds breathless and excited. "Looks like you're officially on the racing roster. You still in for tonight?"

For just a second, I hesitate.

I made a promise to Pressa, said it right to her face. But Daniel is still an AIS agent.

If the AIS ever gets a whiff of how Pressa really makes her money, how she's been paying her father's medical bills by betting on illegal drone races, she'll be jailed and her Level flattened before I can take a breath to speak for her. Even Daniel doesn't have the kind of power to save her.

I fold the drone notice back into my pocket and hide it away. The Undercity. The danger and noise and chaos. The need for it to fill my mind and push everything else out.

"I'm heading down now," I confirm. "Meet you at midnight."

# DANIEL

IT'S A COLD NIGHT, BUT I DON'T MIND THE STING of the air against my skin. There's something familiar about the wind against my face at a place high above the city, where I can see everything—the pulse of the hundreds of floors below me, the menagerie of bright lights lining the walkways that connect each high-rise, the flickering of virtual notations over people shuffling by below. Tonight, the skyscrapers nearest ours have a set of virtual murals of the ocean overlaid against their walls, of bright corals and rainbow-hued fish swimming between each building. As I look on through the augmented-reality system installed in my chip, a virtual whale colored neon turquoise and pink glides lazily in the air between two skyscrapers, its massive body materializing out through one wall and into another like a ghost.

I admire the moving art in silence.

Back in the Republic, I would climb to the top of a building and look down at a scene of haze and dirt, concrete and steel and red banners and metal waterwheels. At night, there would be patches of the city that were completely dark, areas where they cut the power to conserve it for military use. I have fragments of memories about those rolling blackouts, nights when Tess and I would light a roll of trash as a torch to navigate the pitch-dark alleys. It was a place that always seemed broken.

All I see here is a sea of eternal lights and colors. Yet, somehow, everything still has a feeling of precarious balance—like this whole goddy city's sitting on a neglected, crumbling foundation, teetering on the brink of something sinister.

*Dominic Hann.*

The AIS has been tracking him for so long, and yet we still have no good leads. Not even a public sighting of him. The only thing I know for sure is that he's got some powerful friends and a lot of spies. No doubt he knows that we're after him, and he's found a way to keep out of our sights.

I check my messages again in my view. No new updates from Jessan or Lara. No luck hunting down where the next drone race might be happening in the Undercity.

I run a hand through my hair and try not to remember the feeling of that woman's body going limp in my arms, her head lolling to one side as the life left her. Every time I close my eyes, I picture the foam flecks at her mouth and feel the weight of her. The memory makes me shudder. I'm too afraid to see her in my dreams.

It was easier when I had an enemy I could face: the old Republic, the military jeeps and the airfields and the plague patrols, those shining epaulettes and black boots. Not that I'm itching to go back to living on the streets anytime soon.

The thought reminds me of Eden, and I look instinctively over my shoulder toward the darkness of his room. At least he can get some sleep. Maybe in the morning I'll be able to catch him before he heads off to the university and get a few words in with him. A part of me itches to check his location again, just to make sure he's where he should be—but Eden's outburst from this afternoon makes me pause. I force myself to leave him alone.

Instead, I look up to the few floors above our apartment. Tomorrow, the Republic's Elector and his entourage are going to land on the Sky Floor of a nearby building. June will be with him. It'll be the first time I've seen her since I bumped into her on the street in Batalla a month ago.

A knot of excitement and fear tightens in my chest. I look to my side and imagine our meeting, picture her standing here beside me and leaning against the railing. My memories have been so shattered since I left the Republic, and for years I couldn't even remember who June was at all. I'd only see a nameless girl in my dreams, her long, dark ponytail swinging behind her, and wonder how I could never seem to catch up. I'd study the paper clip ring around my finger, something I've always worn since I left the Republic, and try to remember why it mattered so much to me.

It wasn't until I saw her in the Republic a month ago, purely by accident, that fragments of her in my memories came rushing back to me. That I remembered June was the one who'd give me that paper clip ring.

That time, we'd shaken hands, and there had been tears in my eyes. We smiled over dinner with Tess and made awkward conversation. I walked her back home. I made jokes and she eased into them. Every gesture, every question, and every laugh from her triggered old memories that I thought I'd lost. She was the flint lighting sparks in my darkness, illuminating a history that I can just barely see.

That was the last time we spoke. She hasn't contacted me in the month since then, and I haven't reached out either. I don't know why I'm terrified to call her again. Maybe it's the fear of those sparks of memory returning to me.

But tomorrow, I'll see her again. So every idle moment I have, I find my thoughts drifting to her.

I clear my throat, then pretend to look over at her and smile. Even this practice session makes me nervous. What the hell do I say to her?

"Fancy running into you again, yeah?" I murmur to myself, feigning the casual, flirtatious tone I try to have around her. I shake my head. I don't want her to think I'm an idiot. "Seems like we're always bumping into each other on the street," I rephrase, but grimace. I try out a few other phrases.

"Welcome to my new neighborhood."

"If you need a guide around the city, I'm pretty free today."

"Any plans with your Elector tonight, or can I steal you for dinner?"

I scowl, embarrassed and grateful that no one else is around to see me talking to myself. I've never had trouble talking to a girl before. Why am I working myself up into such a panic?

I shift my footing against the ledge and start reciting things I've been working on telling her all week, memories of us that I've been working hard to recollect.

"Remember the time when you taught me how to fight?" I murmur to an imaginary June beside me, a sly grin on my face. "You had a fever from being Patient Zero for a plague, and you still beat me up."

Honestly, the memory is vague for me. Most of them are. I remember the fight, recall June teaching me how to space my footing and how to protect my chin. But I don't quite remember where we were, or why. I don't remember what happened after she tripped me. There was a long, dark tunnel. Sweat beaded her brow.

If I mention it to her, she might help me fill in the gaps of that memory.

"Or the time when you wore that scarlet dress? You were the most beautiful person I'd ever seen in my life. Still are."

That memory, too, is like a blurred photo. There were glasses of champagne and glittering chandeliers. There was the vision of June in that stunning red gown, her hair clipped high and thick on her head. We stood in a room lit only by moonlight, and for some reason, I'd walked away from her. Why would I ever do that?

I recite other fragments of memories. Her face, wet and glistening, as we crouched in a raging storm. Us, huddled together under a burlap sack in a rolling train car. Me, kissing her, pulling her to me, brushing strands of hair away from her face. Me, painstakingly twisting a pair of paper clips together and giving the ring to her. Her, doing the same for me in return.

There are a million pieces of us scattered through my memory, moments tiny and insignificant to everyone else in the world except for me.

I fall into silence and go back to staring out at the city. Suddenly

I'm aware of how small I am against its backdrop, nothing more than a shadow in the night, lost in the sea of lights.

Maybe she doesn't remember any of this, either. Maybe it wasn't worth remembering. I look down, gathering my courage, taking in deep breaths to undo the knot coiled tight in my chest.

It doesn't matter. If anything, it'll have been worth it to tell her that I know we had something special.

# EDEN

I DON'T KNOW EXACTLY WHEN DRONE RACING started. Decades ago, I think, in some other country, during a time when a game had supposedly taken the world by storm. All I know is that when Pressa first took me to one of the matches—when I saw the drones' colorful streaks light up the air—I was hooked.

Now I pull my hood farther down over my head and hurry through the night markets of the Undercity. Where the Sky Floors of Ross City are awash in virtual murals, the scenes down here have the grit of reality. At this hour, everything is bathed in neon—flickering red and yellow signs hanging over crumbling stores and barred motels, trails of neon bulbs dangling over the menagerie of market stalls that are still as crowded as they are during the day. Everyone keeps their head down as they shove their way through the smoky streets. No one pays attention to me.

Tonight I'm passing through the area of the Undercity that's usually teeming with criminals. Conmen. Gamblers and thieves, drug dealers and mafiosi. The Level system starts to break down here, where the majority of people have hacked accounts. Numbers and names don't float over most heads. And when violence and murder break out, there are no points deducted, no alarms sent digitally to the police.

This is where you go if you need to take out a loan in a hurry, to temporarily bring your Level up high enough to be allowed to use a bus, or to buy medication that's off the official market. People down here will do it for you, hacking your system so that you Level up—but for an exorbitant price. If you can't pay that price back after your Level goes back down to normal . . . well, a lot of desperate people go missing all the time, their disappearances uninvestigated by an uninterested country.

I double-check my account. Hacking the Level system is no small feat, but it helps when your brother works for the government and you've occasionally glimpsed how his account is set up from the inside. So tonight I've got my Level turned off and my identity randomized, and when you glance over my head, you don't see: EDEN BATAAR WING, LEVEL 54. Instead, it reads: ELI WHITMAN, LEVEL 5.

For all I know, though, Daniel's found a way around that and is following my location again without telling me. I glance over my shoulder, as if I'll see him tailing me somewhere in the crowds.

As I turn a corner and hit a darker section of the Undercity, where people with flattened Levels shelter along either side of the streets in rows of tents, I start to feel nervous. Even though I'm dressed in my subtlest clothing, stares dart my way and eyes seem to pierce my back. Something about my demeanor—the hunch of my shoulders, or the way I push my glasses up, or maybe just the fact that I know I don't belong here—makes me stand out.

Maybe I look like a pawn again, and someone's going to come at me with a knife and rob me. I shove my hands into my pockets and lower my head farther. I should have asked Pressa to come with me instead of agreeing to meet her there.

As I get closer to the drone race's starting point, I start to notice crowds of people lining the sidewalks here and there, standing around and waiting, as if for a parade. Money exchanges hands, and excited murmurs fill the alleys. I can tell people are toggling their virtual settings so that they can follow the race through their chips.

The streets get more and more packed until I'm squeezing my way through the throngs. Finally, I stop before what looks like a run-down bar, so tiny that I can barely squeeze through its grated door.

The inside of it is lit with scarlet-neon light. People pack around a bar, behind which a woman leans, eyeing me.

I clear my throat and give her what I hope is a calm look. "Serving any red whiskey tonight?" I ask her. It's the current password I'd found in my searches.

For a second, I think I got it all wrong, because she doesn't react. She just stares at me as if I don't look like the right type of person to be here.

Then she steps around the side of the bar and nods for me to follow her. We walk to the back, where a bathroom door is locked tight with a sign over it that reads: OUT OF ORDER.

She scans a finger in front of the door. It cracks open.

She nods for me to go in, but doesn't make a move to follow. I give her a quick smile, then step past her and head into the darkness beyond the door. It closes behind me. I'm in some sort of dark, enclosed space. All I can see for a moment is a faint, glowing green light on the door handle. My heart thuds, and I feel a hint of claustrophobia.

Then the ground beneath me shudders. A neon-green light washes over the space, and the wall in front of me slides open with a rusty creak. I pull my shirt up over my nose as the smell of sewage threatens to suffocate me.

I step out of the makeshift elevator into a square plaza fenced in by four skyscrapers, lit by flickering neon lights against the walls and a haze of crimson fog. Pounding music and a roar of voices hits me.

I don't know what I expected to see. Neon-red bulbs dangle by the thousands from building to building. Vendors selling savory buns and fried meat on sticks jumble near the edges of the square. The walls are lined with lattices of steel support beams, and a giant circuit breaker hangs near where I came in. This looks like it used to be an elevator station under construction at one point that then got torn down and abandoned.

People are packed so tightly into the space that any disaster—a fight, a fire—would turn this place into a death pit. But no one cares. They all gather around a circular clearing in the middle of the plaza, where the racers for tonight are now lining up and preparing their drones.

A giant virtual countdown hovers over the middle of the plaza, turning in my view to match wherever I move.

DRONE RACE: SEMIFINALS

FIRST HEAT COMMENCES IN 10:00 MINUTES

Right below it is the list of racer names for the first heat, updating as each racer checks in to the space.

My false name is up there.

### ENTRY 9: ELI WHITMAN

For a moment, I freeze up. The people around me look like they've been coming to races like this forever. I, on the other hand, must look like the easiest mark that ever stumbled into the Undercity. My palms start to sweat.

**Pressa,** I send out a message. **I'm here now. Where the hell are you?**

Eventually, I catch sight of a stand where people are registering their drones. I walk over to it, trying to ignore the way others are staring at me from the corners of their eyes.

The man behind the stand gives me a skeptical look. "Drone," he says.

I swing my backpack to my front and unzip it, carefully removing my drone model for him to inspect. He raises an eyebrow at my design. It looks unlike anyone else's here, with its small, slender shape and the glowing engine attached to its end. I stand back and wait as he holds it up this way and that.

"A little runt of a drone, eh?" he mutters. Finally, he nods at me. "Patron?"

I frown. "A what?"

He raises an eyebrow. "Every racer needs a patron. We need assurance that you can pay for any damage that you cause. Unless you got ten thousand corras lying around, and can be your own."

Pressa hadn't mentioned anything about a patron. "I don't have one yet," I start to say, glancing around for any sign of my friend, "but I'm on the roster to race. If you look—"

But he's already shaking his head at me and handing the drone

61

back. "You must be new here," he says with a laugh. "No patron, no race. I don't care where your name is."

"But if you just let—"

Any sympathy for me now leaves his eyes. Annoyed, he waves for me to exit the line. "There are people behind you," he barks, gesturing for the next person to step up.

"Wait!"

I slacken in relief as Pressa emerges from behind the gamblers and heads to the table. As usual, her persona down here looks completely different from what I'm used to seeing of her at the university and her father's shop. She's in a long wig, for one—bright blond, a startling contrast from her black, bobbed hair—and sporting a pair of fake pink glasses that make her eyes look abnormally large. She flashes a frown at the man.

"I'm his patron," she says, taking out a sealed envelope and sliding it over to him.

He seems to recognize her, because he grunts in acknowledgment before tearing the envelope open. Inside is a stack of corras, clean and crisp. He holds them up to the light, then nods and pockets the envelope.

"You're official," he says to me, and barely a few seconds later, he nods up to the racer names displayed in the rotating virtual menu. Over my head, a blue light goes on, indicating me as one of the entries. As if in unison, people around us turn to look at me.

"Do you wait in a corner and just watch me until I look like I'm about to do something stupid?" I mutter to Pressa.

She smiles at me and loops an arm through mine. "I don't have to wait around very long for that," she replies. "You're welcome for saving your ass."

"Where'd you get ten thousand corras?"

She shrugs. "Not important. Been saving up. If your drone's as good as you say, we'll earn it back after the first race." She peers curiously at my backpack. "Care to show me what you got?"

Up on the wall, the countdown has moved down to three minutes, and most of the standing area around the clearing is packed. I can already see the racers lining up in the center, some of them doing last-minute tinkering on their engines.

As we reach the other racers, I show my drone to Pressa.

Compared with the other models here, it's easily the smallest, maybe the tiniest size that could qualify for these races. But it makes up for any fragility with speed. The engine coils in a perfect circle underneath the drone, and when I flip it on, it glows with a faint blue light.

Pressa makes an impressed sound at it. "Pretty design," she says, admiring its swept wings. "Efficient. Can it survive a hit, though?"

I shake my head. "If one of the others bumps into mine, it's game over."

She gives me a withering look. "I thought you said it was amazing."

"I don't intend on letting anyone get close enough to touch it."

She throws up her hands, but I can see the light in her eyes, the hunger for how much we could potentially win. "All right," she concedes. "I'm trusting you."

Overhead, the neon-red bulbs dim, brighten, and dim again, alerting the audience that the race is about to start. I squeeze through the throngs until I'm standing to one side of the arena, on the side closest to the other racers.

One minute until the race begins. Like the rest of the crowd, I reach a hand out in front of me and toggle my virtual-sight settings. To watch the entire race unfold, you log onto a channel being recorded by a default drone that follows the official racing drones. Its footage will play before your eyes as the drones zip through the Undercity's streets, as if you're racing along right behind them.

I try to keep a calm expression as people in the audience stare at me, murmuring under their breath. Adrenaline pumps fast in my veins, dulling the thoughts that usually plague me when things are too quiet, and I smile. All I can concentrate on is the thought of winning the race. This, in its own way, is freedom.

Ten seconds before the race starts. I see Pressa moving through the crowd with her head ducked down, trying to be discreet. At the same time, she sends me a message that appears in white letters before my eyes.

**Good luck, skyboy.**

The other drones lift up into the air, the hiss of their engines filling the space.

As the audience chants uproariously for their favorite picks, I quietly turn on my drone and warm up the engine. In my view, I see its stats go live, a scroll of virtual blue letters and numbers in the side of my vision.

The lights overhead flash once, brilliantly. At the same time, a loud pop like a gunshot echoes from the speakers overhead.

The race has begun.

Every drone darts forward. A huge cheer goes up.

I toss my drone into the air. It glints once. The engine hums into high gear.

"Do your thing," I murmur at it. Then I wave my hand once.

My drone turns in the direction of the others and jolts forward. Suddenly, in the center of my vision, a live feed from the channel appears as if I'm actually riding *on* my drone. I focus on the video now, steering my drone into the alleys of the square that will lead out into the streets. As all of our drones zip out into the city, they leave behind them virtual trails of bright colors.

From the side of the square, the announcer gives a whistle. "Keep an eye on Entry Nine!" she exclaims. "That's a pint-size drone with an engine unlike anything I've ever seen!"

A burst of cheers and boos comes from the audience. I just grit my teeth and continue. Through my view of the channel, my drone arcs hard around a street corner, narrowly avoiding a collision between two others as it skips ahead. People walking in the streets glance up with startled gasps—two auto-trucks almost hit each other as the drones cut through an intersection. Onlookers who had been gathering through the city in anticipation of the race cheer loudly.

I dart a glance at the crowds in the square where I'm standing. Pressa's nowhere to be seen.

One of the other drones swivels in midair and swings sharply toward mine.

I barely dodge it. My view whirls as my drone tumbles, diving low until it's skimming right over the ground. It almost crashes right into the steel post of a food market vendor. People on that street scream as my drone clips in between jumbles of legs before it finally emerges back over the street.

"Close call!" the announcer shouts. "Entry Nine almost didn't make it out of that one!"

Another drone guns for mine, attempting to ram it out of the street path. I turn my drone's nose up. It shoots high into the air before it arcs down, several paces ahead of my attacker, faster and more stable than any drone should be going.

Now people standing around are looking at me with startled curiosity. I'm moving my way steadily up the ranks now as the engine builds in strength. There's an audible shift in the audience as people start to take notice of how my drone is performing.

A larger drone edges dangerously close to mine. One of its wings scrapes against the edge of my wing. I careen wildly away from the others and go spinning out of control. Cheers and gasps go up.

*Pull straight*, I tell myself frantically. *Pull straight!*

The engine stalls for a split second before it roars back to life. I push it as hard as I can—and the sheer momentum forces my drone's center of mass to steady itself again. There's an ugly tear along its side, but it still dives back into the fray.

We're almost three-quarters of the way through the race map now. Only a few more streets to go before all the drones arrive back here in the plaza. Near the beginning of the map, several police drones have activated, their sirens flashing as they struggle to keep up with the racers.

My engine heats up until I can see the blue glow of it hot in the edges of my vision. I focus on the turns. Another drone tries to take me down. The ones ahead of me are forming a barrier. But I force mine up, its body arching over everyone as it sails onward, engine glowing, passing them up one by one.

The finish line approaches in a blur. I can hear the buzz of the drones as they come back around into the plaza where we are. The other drones are behind mine now. I smile in the clear, my drone edging on—until it finally hurtles across the last marker hanging over our heads. It wins by a good length.

The crowd around me bursts into chaos. There are enraged gamblers shouting at the announcer to throw the game. Others are already calling for bets on tomorrow night. I steer my drone back to the plaza, navigating it to my side before shutting its engine down. It lowers itself carefully to the floor of the clearing, then turns off as I pick it up and put it in my backpack. Other racers around me shoot me ugly glares while they each collect their drones as they come hurtling back one by one into the plaza's center.

I can't help smiling a little. I may not have my brother's charisma or cool factor or resilience. I may not be able to find my footing at my university. But in this—in making things, in finding a way to create something that works—I know I'm good. I know I can win.

A rough hand suddenly grabs me by the back of the neck. Not something I'd expected to feel as the winner of a drone heat. I feel myself lifted right off the ground and shoved roughly forward as a flashlight beams right into my face. Glowing spots explode in my vision. I put my hands up instinctively to block the light.

"Eli Whitman," a woman snaps at me. Beside her, a man is holding Pressa firmly by her arms.

It's the tense look on Pressa's face that chills me.

"You funding this race with counterfeits?" the woman asks me. As she does, she tosses Pressa's envelope of corras to the ground.

"Counterfeits?" I manage to say.

Pressa shakes her head. "I didn't know they were counterfeits," she argues. "They were approved right at the window! Your own guy held them up to the light. Someone's framing us."

But the woman just glares at her. "This race is forfeit," she announces. A roar erupts from the stands—outraged gamblers who'd bet on me, smug viewers who'd lost money on the race. "You need to repay in real corras right now, plus double for a penalty."

Pressa glances at me, warning me to stay out of this, before folding her arms across her chest and looking at the woman. "And if not?" she says.

"Did I say that was an option?" the woman asks, and the man grabs Pressa's arms, pulling them back so hard that she screams.

"Hell on earth!" my friend spits out. "I didn't know they were damn counterfeits! Let me go, and I'll get you your real money, I swear it. Or cut it from our winnings. We all know who won tonight."

They don't look amused by her words. For an instant, I think about bringing up my own bank account—but anything I send them down here will be tracked to my real identity. They won't accept something that isn't untraceable cash. "Come on," I start to say to the man and woman. "She already said she didn't know. *I* didn't know. I'll withdraw from the race, okay? Let her go. We'll come back with the money in an hour."

Pressa curses at me. Her eyes are wide with anger. "Shut up, Eden," she snaps. "I'll handle this. Don't withdraw!"

But they're not listening to either of us anymore. The man starts dragging Pressa away—and in his hand, I see the glint of something sharp and metallic. Ice grips my heart in a vise. *They're going to kill her.* Already, the audience—excited at the thought of blood—have risen to their feet, their shouts reaching a fever pitch.

"I can pay," I start to shout. Even though I don't know what I'd do to stop them, I lunge forward, ready to yank Pressa out of their arms if I have to. "I can pay!" I say again. "I have the money in my account. I just need a way to get it to you untraced. Please, I—"

Then, without warning, the plaza goes quiet. It's as if a switch just turned everyone off.

The woman and man halt too. Pressa blinks, as confused as everyone else. I look around, trying to understand what has just happened.

Everyone has stopped to stare at a figure that has appeared from one of the other halls with several men on either side of him. He waves them off. Then he's walking toward us, and as he goes, anyone around him quickly steps aside, lowering their eyes.

The figure is a man, and at first glance he doesn't seem like much to look at. He is slender, even delicate, and young, his skin so pale it catches the red hue of the bulbs overhead, his hair thick and midnight black. His suit's perfectly tailored and neatly pressed. He moves with surgical grace. His gaze is fixed easily on me, but there is something about his expression that makes me shrink instinctively away.

I can sense the way this man's presence tightens a noose around the air, the way it makes the entire audience just a little bit tenser. This is someone that everyone here fears. Pressa and I exchange a quick, uncertain glance.

The man nods at me. "I'll be this boy's patron," he says, his gaze going from my backpack to my face. "So I suggest you start preparing for the finals tomorrow night."

My first impression of him is that he seems too young to have such an effect on everyone else around him.

I mean, my brother is Daniel—I know what it looks like for a young person to be revered. But this is different. This guy isn't that much older than Daniel, but the ripple of his presence through the crowd almost feels like a living thing.

He stops in front of me and nods now, extending his hand. His expression seems kindly, almost *fatherly*. "That was an excellent race," he says. "Your drone is impressive."

"Thank you," I say, not knowing what else to do.

When I take his extended hand and shake it, he leans in close to me. "Your name's not Eli Whitman, is it?" he whispers.

A shiver of terror crawls down my spine even as I try to lie. "It is," I say.

"Don't be afraid," he adds. "I'm not saying this as a threat. If we're going to work together, we need to trust each other. Right?"

Then he leans back and, before I can respond, smiles and raises his voice so that those around us can hear. "Let the girl go," he says, nodding at Pressa.

The man holding her back releases her immediately and steps away. Just like that. It's such an instinctive reaction that I could swear it was as if the newcomer could control his mind.

Pressa rubs at her wrists as she glances quizzically at my patron. He folds his hands behind his back in the silence. "I'm going to cover the ten thousand corras for this young racer," he announces, repeating his vow so that everyone can hear. "To me, it's beyond a doubt that he won this race. Does anyone question it?"

Just a few moments earlier, everyone had been up in arms about my win. Boos had filled the square. But now the silence is deafening. No one even dares to look directly our way. They just glance at their neighbors and then down at the ground.

He smiles briefly. "Good," he says before looking back at me. There's a rasp to his voice that reverberates from deep in his chest, the kind of sound indicative of some long-festering condition. "You'll be paid for your first win," he says to me. "As your patron, I'll take my share from what you've earned."

As soon as he says this, someone steps forward and motions for me to stretch out my hand. I do as he says, then look on in stunned silence while he counts out a thick wad of cash into my hand, an amount directly proportional to how much of a long shot a bet on me was. I look down at my hand, numb.

One hundred thousand corras.

Beside me, Pressa stares in shock at the amount. Neither one of us has seen this much money all together in our lives. Not even Daniel gets paid like this.

The man seems pleased with my reaction. "I think we're done with this race." He holds a hand out in front of him, suggesting that we take a brief walk together. Already, everyone around us has made a wide berth for us to pass. "Can I ask you a few questions?"

My instincts tingle with warning and confusion. I don't know what to make of him. All I know is that he may have just saved Pressa's life, and mine too. "Sure," I say as we both fall into step with him. He guides us down one of the alleys branching into the plaza. Everyone makes a deliberate point to ignore us.

"What should I call you?" I ask the man when we're somewhat alone in the alley.

"That depends," he answers with a small smile. "What should I call *you*? Because you're not Eli." He glances at Pressa. "You, I've seen at the races before. Pressa, is it? Your father runs an apothecary in the center of the Undercity. Hardworking man." He nods respectfully, and Pressa's lips twitch with a surprised smile.

"Thanks," she mumbles.

The man turns back to me. "My name is Dominic," he says, then pauses for a moment. I can't tell if he's honestly thinking or if he's just trying to give me the impression that he is. "Your brother," he finally adds, "works for the AIS."

A rush of fear washes over me. Pressa gives me a quick, alarmed stare. Underneath all of that, I also feel that familiar undercurrent of resentment, of being identified only in relation to Daniel.

The man named Dominic must have read my expression well, because he continues, "And you are a top student at Ross University of the Sciences. You're graduating a year early, with honors. I've seen your name in the news for some of your college designs."

Now this surprises me. I *have* been in the local news before for my science experiments, but no one has ever really commented on it. I frown at the man, unsure whether to feel wary or flattered. "Why do you know so much about us?" I ask.

"I make a point to know about everyone participating in the drone races," he says as we walk. "It's just good business."

Business. Is this man a sponsor for the entire race? He certainly had no problems blowing ten thousand corras to be my patron. Warnings buzz louder in my head at his words. I think about how far we are from the elevators that will take us back up to the Sky Floors. We'll have to at least humor him for a while longer.

"Thank you for sponsoring him, er, Mr. Dominic," Pressa says for me, breaking my hesitant pause.

He waves a hand at us. "No need to thank me," he replies. "Your prize money will more than make up for my investment. Smart move to enter the race tonight." He raises an eyebrow at me. "Where did you learn to make an engine like that?"

I shrug, unsure how to answer. "I've been working on its design ever since I was a freshman," I reply. "Drones just happen to be a cool way to test it, and earn us some money in the meantime."

Dominic nods. "I've never seen an engine like yours before," he says, and the impressed note in his voice is so genuine that I can't help but feel a little proud. "You can apply this engine design to powering anything?"

I nod. "Anything."

We reach the end of the alley. Here, the narrow space opens back up to a main Undercity street. "Well, this is where we part for the night," Dominic says. "You have my word that no one will bother you as you both head home. I expect to see you tomorrow for the finals." He gives us a small smile.

"Wait—" I start to say. There's so much left unanswered. Who the hell is he? What does he do in the Undercity? What's his level of involvement in the drone races?

But he's already swallowed by shadows as he heads back down the alley. Pressa and I are left standing in the middle of the busy street with our winnings, people streaming past us in both directions.

We stare at each other in bewilderment.

"Dominic," I mutter at her. "That doesn't ring any bells for you, does it?"

She shakes her head. "Beats me. But you got your patron." Then she steps closer to me and gives me a grave look. "You don't have to do this. If you bow out, you won't have to repay his patron money.

He'll get it returned. If you're uncomfortable with this . . . well, you live in the Sky Floors, anyway, and . . ."

She trails off as she bites her lip.

I think of Pressa's dad, his fragile frame and his weak voice. How much he needs his medicine. My gaze lingers on her dark eyes and heart-shaped face, and I realize that her nearness is making my cheeks warm.

It's true that I don't know what I'm getting myself into. But whatever I'm in, Pressa is too. What might happen to her and her father in the Undercity if I don't show up for the final race?

"I'll meet you after classes tomorrow," I tell her instead. "We can talk about it then."

# DANIEL

THE NEXT MORNING, EDEN'S GONE BEFORE I EVEN have a chance to see him. I walk out of my bedroom to see his door already flung open, revealing the mess of his bed and his pile of clothes on the floor. His dishes are already in the kitchen sink.

Figures. It's the last day of his exams, anyway, so maybe he had to head out early. I remind myself of this, trying not to let his absence bother me as I freshen up and pull on my suit.

On any other day, I probably would give in and track his location, just to make sure he's where he says he is. But today, thankfully, there's something else to distract me.

June's coming into town.

The call pops up in my view right as I head out the door. "Hope you slept well, Wing," Jessan says. "The Elector and his party are scheduled to land at AIS headquarters in an hour. You on your way yet?"

"Stepping out the door right now," I reply.

There's a pause on the other side, followed by Jessan's amused voice. "You sound more nervous than usual. Could it be because of someone on the Republic's plane?"

I scowl at her laughter. Everyone here knows about my past with June, apparently. Who knew a bunch of foreigners were always watching the news about us and fabricating their own ideas about two fugitives on the run?

"Your mind's playing tricks on you, sweetheart," I reply, trying to keep my voice nonchalant this time. "I'll be there in ten minutes."

"Sure, sure." I can hear Jessan's smile in her answer. "It's okay if you're distracted today, you know."

"I'm not distracted."

"Yeah, *that's* a convincing statement. I've lost count of how many times you've asked about when the Republic's going to visit us."

"*Ten minutes*, Jess."

"Right, okay. See you soon. And if you have trouble finding words after you see Miss June Iparis today, just tell us—"

I roll my eyes and hang up the call before Jessan can keep going.

But as I walk alone to the elevators that will take me several floors up and twenty buildings over to where the AIS headquarters are, my thoughts keep wandering to June.

It's not like she's here just to see me. She'll be accompanying her Elector, guarding his safety while he meets with Antarctica's President. Maybe she won't care much about whether or not I'm there. All the notice she gave me, after all, was a quick text message several weeks ago to let me know that she'd be in Ross City.

But I don't care. The image of her lingers in my mind as I step into an elevator. For all that I hate Jessan's teasing, I haven't been able to stop thinking about June since I found out she was visiting.

My dreams last night were an exhausting blend of nightmares—some about the shadowy Dominic Hann I've been pursuing, some about Eden's safety . . . and some about June.

Visions of June uninterested in seeing me today. Of her turning away and heading back to the Republic's plane. Of her being polite and distant. We've seen each other only once after a decade apart. What if we've changed too much? What if we're just not meant to be?

\* \* \*

The AIS headquarters is a lavish spread of offices accompanied with a landing pad on its top floor. During my time here, I've seen all sorts of world leaders touch down to talk to our President while several of our AIS agent teams follow along.

But this time, June is going to be accompanying the Elector. It leaves me that much more on edge as I head up to the top floor to join the rest of the agents.

Jessan and Lara are already here, out of at least a dozen agents who have gathered into two lines leading up to the landing pad. A series of barricades separate them from the rest of the floor, where a barrage of reporters are already waiting, their cameras clicking away at our agents.

I frown when Jessan gives me a humored smile. At least Lara approaches me with a more serious face. She swipes her fingers through the air, as if downloading something, and then moments later, I get a message from her that pops up in my view.

"We tracked down the rough location of a drone race that

happened last night," she tells me as I fall into place beside them. "It was somewhere in the northeast quadrant of the Undercity."

I hear an edge to her voice and look up at her. "And?" I ask.

She hesitates. "And," she replies, "I heard that Dominic Hann himself was spotted at the semifinals yesterday."

My thoughts waver momentarily from June to Lara's words. I look sharply at her. "He was there? In person?"

"Apparently. I wouldn't believe it if I wasn't sent some footage."

She shares another file with me. When I pull it up, I see a video clip set at the start of what definitely looks like a drone race gathering, of someone addressing a young man as *Mr. Hann*. He greets one of the racers that I can't make out. I frown as I watch the video again. The man looks just barely older than me, but even with the poor quality of this video, the ripple effect he has on the audience is unmistakable.

I watch the clip again, trying to make out more details of the square's surroundings. But the video is way too dark and grainy. "No location pinpoint yet on exactly where this happened?"

"No, but we're checking out the streets to see if we can find something recognizable."

"Good." I nod at Lara. "We'll find our way to the finals tonight," I tell her.

Our conversation cuts short as a blast of wind hits us from somewhere high above. When I look up, I see a plane materialize through the clouds, lowering itself through Ross City's biodome to hover over our landing pad. Its tail is painted in streaks of black and red. The Republic's colors.

The Elector and his team are here. *June* is here.

All our conversations stop as the elevator to the top floor opens now, and out step President Ikari and his personal bodyguards. He straightens as he walks down the pathway toward our landing pad, a serious smile on his face. Around me, the other agents all stir to attention. I do the same. My heart starts to race. Overhead, the roar of the Republic's jet engine drowns out all other noise.

I've mouthed off at country leaders, blown up airships, and survived being shot—but I'll tell you this, I've still never felt more cracked than I do right now, minutes before the Republic's Elector touches down. The wind whips my hair back as we wait, until finally the jet rests in the center of the pad's circle.

I'm walking out toward the jet's landing ramp before it even completely unfurls. Across from me, Jessan and Lara watch for my command. As camera flashes go off behind us, I point them to the opposite side of me, then pull a fourth agent to join me before motioning for the others to stay with the President. Then we get into formation on either side of the ramp and wait as a silhouette appears at the jet's open door.

I haven't seen Anden Stavropoulos, the Republic's Elector, in person since I left for Ross City. He looks older than I remember, even compared with his interviews on TV, but there's a comfort in his gaze that wasn't there before. A confidence in his position that he didn't use to have.

The cameras go into overdrive. I look back at the reporters, surveying the audience carefully before studying the windows of the skyscrapers on either side of us.

Then I turn to see to those emerging behind him. There's his expected bevy of bodyguards, same as our President's, as well as his Princeps-Elect, Mariana. On Anden's other side is his fiancée—Faline Fedelma, a new presence in the Senate, and the same girl who had once taken me to a banquet in Denver.

Behind me, I can hear murmurs from the reporters as they frantically take photos of the recently engaged couple.

"—had been dating for several years before they made it public—"

"—match well, with her poise and—"

"—heard that Commander Iparis congratulated them—"

The mention of June's name thuds through my heart. I keep my position, but my body still leans slightly forward as I search for her.

Then she's stepping out too, with her guards trailing her down the ramp.

Commander June Iparis is a vision—gold epaulettes shining on her shoulders, gold threads looping down the sides of her sleeves, her cape long and dark, crisp white gloves shining as she keeps one hand permanently on the hilt of a gun at her waist. As they walk, she's already gesturing wordless instructions to her men, assigning two of them to one side of the Elector and his fiancée, two to the other.

Her head is held high, her gaze steady and unwavering.

So many things have changed about her since the first time we met. She was a girl then, full of anger and grief; now she's a woman, poised and mature and sure of her place in the world.

But in some ways, she hasn't changed at all. I still watch her in the same way I did the first moment I saw her on the streets, when she stepped into that Skiz duel ring. I still marvel at that glint of fierce intelligence in her eyes, how awake and alive and invincible she seems. I am still entranced.

Her eyes are searching too. They stop when they settle on me.

It could be my imagination, but there's a slight blush on her cheeks right as she passes me. I have to remind myself not to break out of my formation. Then she's sweeping by with her soldiers, and I'm closing our ranks to follow behind them, and the roar of the press consumes us all as the Elector shakes hands with President Ikari.

As they pose for photos, I make my way through the crowd behind June, who is standing off to the side with her soldiers. She nods once at the sight of me, then looks away to pay attention to the Elector and the President's conversation.

I try to concentrate on guarding my President too. But my thoughts whirl like a storm through my head. Was there really a time when I could instinctively know her thoughts? When we had such a comfortable rapport with each other that we could share anything? Or have we always had this strange chemistry—where I have no idea what to say to her, but would do anything to be near her again?

I must have lingered too long on these thoughts, because one moment we're standing separately and watching over our world leaders . . . and the next, we're closing ranks behind them and walking next to each other.

"Agent Wing," June says with a tilt of her head and the arch of a slender eyebrow.

*Damn.* She can still make me weak with a single, searing gaze.

"Commander Iparis," I reply, forcing myself to stay formal and polite. Her eyes dart away for a moment and she clears her throat. We don't say anything else. Instead, we keep walking in an awkward silence, keenly aware of the other's presence.

Finally, when the two men start to head down the walkway and we follow in the wake of their entourage, June turns her head slightly toward me. "When are you free?" she asks.

My heart lifts at her question. Maybe she's been looking forward to seeing me too.

"Tonight," I reply. "After the President's meeting, I report back to the AIS headquarters for a while. I'm out at sunset."

For the first time, she looks directly at me. "Would you like to have dinner?" she asks. "It'd be nice to catch up."

Our words are formal and stilted. Is it because it's been so long? Because we're older now? I give her a nod and try not to sound too eager. "I'd like that," I reply.

She smiles a little. It softens everything about her, and I find myself wanting to lean in and pull her to me for a kiss. At one point in our lives, that had been something I could do naturally. Now? I feel like I'm stretched tight between two poles, unable to breathe.

"Great," she says, and her voice stays formal. "Where should I meet you?"

"Tell me where you're staying," I answer in a low voice. This time, I'm unable to keep the pull out of my reply. "I'll come to you."

Her cheeks turn pink, and I find myself wondering how I managed to bear ten years without her in my life.

Then the President and the Elector are shaking hands and moving toward the elevators to head downstairs, and we're all following along with them. Our units are about to diverge.

My heart beats rapidly at the thought of meeting up with her later. All I can do is give June a slight bow. "Commander," I say to her, then wink once and turn away to join the rest of my fellow agents.

* * *

Sunset in Antarctica, of course, isn't really sunset at all. It's a simulation created by the biodome encasing Ross City. Still, it doesn't make it any less beautiful, and by the time I meet up with June in front of the hotel where the Elector is staying, swaths of pink and purple are streaking the sky.

Their hotel is perched on the highest floor of a luxury skyscraper, a property that covers ten floors from the top down, with each of its walkways connecting to other skyscrapers adorned with lush, potted trees and strips of grass. From up here, you get a view of the entire twinkling upper half of the city as it dips into the clouds.

I'm perched in one of the trees lining either side of the hotel entrance when I see June emerge from the lobby. She's changed out of her formal military uniform into a sleek, comfortable shirt and coat, her tall black boots pulled over her jeans.

My heartbeat quickens as she looks around for me. This angle, looking at her from a perch somewhere above, is so familiar. It's how I'd first seen her, after all, with her hands on her hips as she challenged Kaede to a Skiz duel. I admire her for a moment, then step off from the branch and land lightly on my feet before her, my hands in my pockets.

She almost startles, but her expression turns amused an instant later at the sight of me. "You still like making your entrances," she says.

I grin, relieved at her reaction. "Only for you, yeah?" I reply.

She laughs. "And still as insufferable as always, I see."

Insufferable. Was I that bad? I think back, trying to pinpoint a specific moment when I might have been insufferable to her.

At my expression, she just laughs harder. "It's fine," she says. We pause for a moment, shuffling awkwardly, before she continues. "So. Where are you taking me?"

Even as we do this shy dance around each other, I can see poise in every line of her body. She seems like she has her entire life together in a way that I might never be able to do. I wonder if I should be acting more mature around her, so I give her a polite nod and start guiding us down the walkway.

"Someplace where we can catch up properly," I reply.

Everything about her here feels both right and strange. The way her hair occasionally swings enough to brush my shoulder. The slight distance we keep between us when we walk beside each other. Even the way we keep trying to talk at the same time.

We take a seat at a restaurant at the highest point in Ross City, overlooking almost all the myriad skyscrapers. I can pinpoint exactly when the sunset fades into evening because the color of June's hair shifts from a warm, dark brown to a midnight raven's black.

Maybe this moment doesn't affect her in the same way. I can't be sure.

"How's life treating you in—" we both say over our plates, then stop and laugh.

June continues when I stay silent. "You seem like you're enjoying Ross City," she says.

It's not entirely true, of course. But I shrug and smile. "Can't complain," I reply. "I gotta say, it's been a hell of an upgrade to sit in a place like this, looking out at a view like that." I nod toward the stunning cityscape.

June gives me a wry grin. "I guess that means you're not planning on moving back to the Republic anytime soon."

"Well, I might for a while. Eden's got an internship set up in Batalla. But the Republic's still an idea I'm not sure I can ever get used to." I pause, suddenly unsure if I should stay on this topic. Is it too sensitive to bring up between us now? My thoughts return abruptly to the argument I'd had with Eden, the way we'd left things hanging and unfinished. "You know how it is," I decide to say instead.

June watches me in a way that makes me feel like she knows I'm keeping something from her. Then she looks away and out at the city. I'm quiet as I feel my heart sink. June is Anden's most trusted officer. Someday, he may appoint her to lead the Republic's entire military, to help restructure the whole country. She's not leaving it behind anytime soon. If I want any chance of being in her life, the Republic is where I have to go.

Can I do that?

Immediately, I'm embarrassed at myself for my reaction. I have no hold or right on June's life. We're not dating. I don't even know if she wants to. That old feeling between us now roars back to life in my head—that maybe there are just too many things that have changed in our lives for us to find a way back to each other. Or that maybe she's just too good for me.

On the surface, I smile at her. "I hear rumors that Anden's going to tap you to be First Commander someday."

At that, she returns my smile. "Oh? Has that been circulating on the news here, or are you just asking around about me?"

I shrug and lean back against my chair, trying to hide my blush. "I ask around about a lot of people," I say defensively.

When she doesn't laugh, I drop my façade and ask, "Are you okay?"

She hesitates before she turns back to face me. Those dark eyes of hers fixate on mine, and I find myself feeling that strange sense of imbalance again, like I can never get my footing around her. "This isn't you, Daniel," she says.

I frown. "What do you mean?"

"This." She looks around at the pristine restaurant, full of marble floors and white pillars, waiters in polished uniforms carrying silver trays. "You don't feel like you're comfortable here."

A flash of déjà vu hits me in that moment—suddenly I'm remembering another restaurant from another time, when we sat across from each other and June asked me why I never told her about the illness that almost took my life. That took part of my memories.

I lean away from the table. "It's not like I haven't been here before," I reply, feeling embarrassed. "Everything in my life is now this—the polished floors and high ceilings, the newness. I like it. I'm as used to it as you."

She shakes her head. "I'm not trying to insult you," she says, leaning forward on her elbows. "I just . . . want to let down my guard. Like you want to. Don't you?"

*Let down my guard.* That's when I notice, with some irritation, my stiff back and straight posture. Of course June had sensed my anxiety and my forced politeness. Had I really forgotten what it was like to be around her, how she'd always manage to figure out every-thing and everyone around her with a few quick glances? If I could look into her head right now, I know I would see organized lists of observations and reactions.

But that's what makes us different. She can figure me out in an instant, but I can't do the same back.

A waiter approaches us and pours us some more sparkling water. I remember how long it'd taken me to even understand the *concept* of sparkling water. My gaze lingers on the bubbles rising now in my drink. Across from me, June's eyes rest on the paper clip ring looped around my finger. It's catching a glint of light right now that makes it shine, for just a moment, like a rare gem. She gives me a hesitant smile, and my entire heart tightens with hope.

A place where we can let down our guard. Where we can find our way back to how we used to be.

Suddenly I perk up and give her a quick smile. "I know a place. Come on. Let's get out of here."

At that, June's entire demeanor changes. Her eyes light up with a warmth that I recall from our younger days, and a brightness fills her face until all I can do is stare at her, completely entranced.

"Sounds perfect," she says, already pushing away her chair.

It's winter down here, and the biodome's simulation has started to disappear, giving way to the sheet of glittering stars overhead. I lead June across a walkway toward an unfinished skyscraper. It's far at the east side of Ross City, in a development complex that has never been finished. Now the skyscraper stands alone and unoccupied, a strange dark structure among the others that are lit from top to bottom. Ivy has crawled all over it in the year since it was abandoned.

"Watch that step," I say over my shoulder to her as I climb up the side of it into an open window. She follows close behind.

We land in a bed of lush vegetation and ivy, flower buds shut for the night against the cracks in the floor. Overhead, past the green trails hanging from the open ceiling, ribbons of southern lights dance across the blanket of stars.

"This might be the only quiet place in Ross City," I tell June as we sit on the edge of the building and look out at the never-ending sea of lights. "Sometimes I come here to think."

June has her eyes turned up to the stars. She can't see them like this in the Republic, and the serene wonder on her face is breathtaking. "About what?" she asks.

I tear my gaze momentarily away from her. Down below, the floors vanish into slants of shadows. "I wonder if coming here to Ross City was the right choice," I say. "For my brother. For me."

June turns to me. "It seems like it's treated you okay," she replies.

"Maybe. But I can feel Eden's discomfort with our life. He's drawn to the streets of his past—he spent less time there than I did, so he's curious about it in a way that I'm not. Sometimes I can feel him pulling away from me and back toward the Republic."

At that, June nods stiffly. There's a look of understanding on her face. "Are you afraid of the Republic?" she asks me.

"Maybe. I don't know. When I think too long about the past, I get nightmares. I lose my appetite. That sort of thing." I shake my head. "I don't think Eden gets the same. If he does, he doesn't talk to me about it." I look at her. "And you?"

June hesitates as she gazes at the sky. Finally, she says, "Do you know the real reason why Anden came here to see your President? It's because the Republic needs money."

"Money?"

"We're deep in debt. Anden's trying to rebuild everything—fixing the infrastructure in the poor districts, tearing down the Trial stadiums, replacing them with new buildings. It all costs far more than we have. So he's been trying to make deals with as many countries as he can." She pauses. "I'm glad. It needs to happen. But protests have been happening too. There are times when I look out at the Republic and feel afraid. Afraid of where we came from. Afraid of what might happen in the future. Nothing ever feels secure, you know? I'm so used to our lives falling apart that it makes me nervous when it hasn't happened in a while."

Her words hint at a part of myself that I haven't revealed to anyone in years. It's the part of me that still looks across Ross City and expects to see everything crumble. It's the version of myself that wakes, gasping, from a nightmare of me back on the streets of Lake. I'm not the only one afraid of my past.

I reach out to touch her hand with mine. The warmth of her skin jolts through me, both new and familiar. "I know," I tell her gently. "I remember enough about that time."

She smiles sadly at me. "Do your memories still haunt you like they used to?"

"It's not all back, but I remember most things now. Sometimes there's a peculiar slant of light or the scent of smoke in the air, some small lingering thing that reminds me of something I can't quite place." I shake my head. "It's like a dream of a different life."

June turns to me. Her hair is shorter than it used to be, cut straight to her shoulders, and now I find one of those lost memories tugging at the edges of my consciousness. My fingers combing through her hair, my whisper against her ear.

She can tell I'm struggling. Nothing has ever slipped by her. "Near the train station that evening," she murmurs, "when you said you remembered me and shook my hand, what was it that triggered that first thought?"

This part of us, too, feels stuck between being an old relationship and the beginning of something entirely new. I smile and look away. "The light in your eyes," I reply. "Not everyone has the ability to draw people in with a single glance, June, but you have a very specific glow about you. Even if I hadn't known you, I would have stopped and looked back. I would've introduced myself."

June's silent for a while, her eyes lingering on me, and I feel suddenly shy under that searing gaze. In the month since that fateful moment, we haven't seen each other again. We haven't chatted. A part of me doesn't even dare believe that she's here right now, in front of me.

There are so many pieces of our story that I still can't recall. My time in the Republic's prisons feels like a blur of blood and chains, an overwhelming sun and an all-consuming pain in my leg. I barely remember any of our time in the Colonies that June claims we experienced. There are important people missing, faces wiped clean.

For a long time, that included June.

On impulse, I move nearer to her and touch her arm. I half expect her to stiffen and move away, but she doesn't. Instead, her breaths turn shallow, and she allows herself to lean closer too, until we're close enough to feel the warmth emanating from our bodies.

I want to ask her how she feels about me. But that old fear returns, that maybe she's come all this way to tell me that we're best as only friends. She's about to move, I live in a different country, and neither of us is anything except busy.

*I remember that I loved you*, I want to tell her. *I'm in love with you. I love you still.* But the words don't emerge from my lips. They stay buried, trembling in my throat.

For a moment, I think this may be as close as we allow ourselves to get.

Then June moves before I can say more. She leans toward me, stopping a hairsbreadth away from my lips.

I can't hold back any longer. I close that remaining distance between us—and my lips touch hers.

And everything inside me breaks, every barrier and hesitation and insecurity, it all shatters as the feeling of her with me crashes through my chest. I wonder if it will be like this every time we touch. Everything in me wants to press us against the wall and kiss her harder, to make up for all the time we've lost. I want her arms to wrap around my neck, pulling me down to her. I want her so badly. All the questions unanswered between us—*What do we do? Where do we go from here?*—fade away, leaving only the sharp present, her body warm in my embrace.

But I force myself to stay in the present, our kiss suspended in this uncertain zone between us, part of it a reunion, part of it a possibility that maybe this is as far as we can ever take it.

A pending call appears in my view, interrupting the rush of this moment. It's from AIS, followed by a message and a map.

*Crime scene in the Undercity. Come immediately.*

Could there ever be a worse time for my job to get in the way? It's almost as if life *wants* to keep us apart. I sigh and send a quick message back.

*Emergency? Did we find the drone race location?*

*Yes, it's an emergency. And no, we haven't yet.*

I whisper a silent curse.

June senses the break in the moment and pulls away. We're both breathing heavily, dizzy from the rush of being so close.

"You should go," she says, even though she doesn't know what the message had read. Like everything else about me, she can probably sense that it's something significant.

I don't want to. I want to stay here, watching a star-filled night sky with her. The ache of being away from her for so long, the twinge of fear that, if I leave her side, I won't be able to make my way back to her again, swells up in me with an overwhelming force.

Maybe she's waiting for me to make the first move, to reach out and keep us from stepping apart.

*You should go.*

Those are her words, not mine.

Maybe I am misreading everything from her, then. I feel myself tearing away, my feet taking a step backward from her and letting the distance between us cool. I can't tell if she's disappointed or surprised. There's so much that I'm unable to read about her now.

"Can I see you again?" I finally say.

She nods. The politeness has returned to her smile, the distance to her posture. But at least she doesn't turn away and leave. At least she looks like she still wants to stay here and linger. That's something, isn't it?

"When are you free?" she asks.

*When are you free?* My heart lifts. "I'm attending the gala in honor of Anden's arrival in a few nights," I reply. "Will you be there?"

"I'll be there," she answers. My heart hangs on to her every word and gesture, every tiny step between us as I try to read her the way I once used to. She gives me a faint smile. "See you at the party."

# EDEN

**I TOSS RESTLESSLY IN A SERIES OF NIGHTMARES.**
My mother, getting shot over and over again. Me, locked in a glass
cylinder in a forever-rocking train car, weeping and waiting for someone to let me out. The blurry haze that blankets my vision after the
plague finishes with me. The man named Dominic steps out of that
haze to talk to me. Drones zip by overhead as I run down strange
streets, searching for a family that isn't there. It all swirls together
into one long, endless dream.

I wake in a panic, as I always do. I spend the rest of the night
pacing in my room, scribbling down more engine ideas to distract
myself, until the first light of dawn appears.

Then I head off to the university before Daniel's even awake.

The final day of exams passes before me in a blur. I finish my tests
early, even though I'm exhausted, and hurry out into the school's halls
as fast as I can in an attempt to avoid talking to anyone.

The halls are still pretty quiet, but some of the other classes have
already let out, and a steady stream of students are making their way
down the halls and out of the university. I walk down the path alone.

My shoes echo against the tiles. Simulated afternoon light from out-side the city's biodome is streaming into the halls, painting every-thing in gold.

A few loud voices drift to me from somewhere up ahead. I stiffen, slow my walk, and listen more closely.

*Damn.* Emerson and his crew.

He's laughing his head off at something that Jenna has said, and from the sound of it, they're hanging out at the end of the hall, block-ing the entrance of the university.

I stop in the middle of the sunbathed hall and try to figure out an-other way to leave the campus. On a normal afternoon, there would be two other entrances and exits in this building. But because of to-day's finals, I know the back entrance is already locked. I think about trying the side entrance to see if it's open, but it doesn't connect to the elevators that lead back down to my floor. I'd have to take a long, meandering route down to the Mid Floors in order to get back home.

Maybe I'll be lucky today. It's the last day, and he must be in a good mood, too busy celebrating with his friends to notice me slip-ping out of the university.

I hesitate there for a moment too long. In that instant, I hear his voice suddenly turn in my direction, followed by a shout that echoes down the hall. "Well!" he shouts. "Looks like the Wing boy's out early, as always!"

My palms break out in a cold sweat. Emerson chuckles, the same sound I always hear whenever he's thought up some new way to mess with me. I curse under my breath, then whirl around and start walk-ing toward the side entrance.

But I can hear him catching up, along with the laughter of his friends. My eyes dart to the timer floating in the corner of my virtual view. Other students won't get out for another fifteen minutes.

I'm only halfway down the hall before an arm grabs the back of my shirt and forces me to turn around.

Emerson's cheery brown eyes are staring straight at me. He grins. "What are you in such a hurry for, Wing?" he says.

My eyes dart to the two behind him. Jenna and Alan smile back at me.

*It's the last day you'll ever have to deal with them,* I tell myself over and over again. *Just get through this.*

So I shrug out of his grasp and mutter, "I'm late to meet up with my brother."

Alan grunts in surprise. "I thought you and your brother weren't talking much these days," he says.

"Doesn't he have another brother?" Jenna pipes up.

Emerson's face lights up. "He did! But I think he died in front of a firing squad." He shakes his head at me in mock sympathy. "I remember seeing the leaked video of that online."

*John.* I still in Emerson's grip. My heart freezes. Emerson senses my tension and knows he's hit a nerve, because the edges of his lips tilt a little in grim satisfaction.

I've never seen the video of John's death before. But I've read enough descriptions of it in the news to visualize it. It happened in a prison courtyard with high stone walls and a dirt floor smeared with dark stains. Republic soldiers dragged in a struggling figure and chained him in place against one of the walls. John's execution, when he had taken Daniel's place so that Daniel could escape.

I can't breathe. The world around me—their laughter, the footsteps of hundreds of students—sounds muffled. I don't say a word.

Emerson, Alan, and Jenna are all staring at me, daring me to look away from them. "Poor thing," Jenna says, her voice dripping with just a little too much sympathy to be genuine. "Are you okay? I'm sorry. I didn't mean to bring him up."

The Level system doesn't penalize them for talking about my oldest brother. The tech still can't tell the difference between a hard heart and a bleeding one.

*John.*

I am standing in front of my brother's broken body, and I'm delirious on a gurney as the Republic drags me away, and I'm calling for my mother as a soldier lifts his rifle to her head. The anxiety crowds my mind and swells to the surface.

*The way John would walk with me to school. The way he stayed up struggling to read by candlelight.*

Emerson leans so close that his nose almost touches mine. "It's okay, skyboy," he says, just loud enough so that others can hear. He pats my shoulder. "Why don't you let it out? You can cry—"

One second, his face is an inch from mine—the next, he's on the ground, and my fist is smeared with blood from his broken nose.

The students around us scream, some in delight. *Fight!* The word ripples through the hall, and suddenly people are pressed in a tight circle around us. In my view, a red warning flickers, followed by:

INSTIGATING A FIGHT | −50 POINTS

I couldn't care less. I swing down again. Emerson is so surprised by my attack that I manage to catch him on the chin again. Then his weight is overwhelming me, and he shoves me off hard enough to send me skidding across the ground. Still, he doesn't attack. He doesn't want the Level system catching him fighting back.

"Skyboy's grown a pair, eh?" he says instead, his voice sharp. I struggle to my feet. My hands scrape raw against the ground. "Look at you, attacking someone unprovoked."

I scramble to my feet and swing blindly for him again. Then people are prying us apart, and someone is shouting something in my ear.

"Hey! It's okay. It's okay."

The voice belongs to Pressa. She's still in her janitor uniform, and her hands are on my shoulders, shaking me. She looks up at the crowd around us. "What the hell are you all gawking at, anyway? Don't you have places to go?"

The heat of the fight's over, and the crowd's already losing interest. As they scatter, Emerson dusts his shirt off and gives me a grim smile. So this is going to be how we part ways forever.

Pressa helps me to my feet. "Are you out of your mind, attacking someone like those guys on the last day of uni? You're gonna get more point deductions, you know, if his parents file charges and the court agrees with them."

But the memory of what had happened to John is burned too deeply into my thoughts for me to care. I swing my bag back over my shoulder and start stalking toward the exit again. "What does it matter, anyway?" I mutter. "If the system's rigged from the start?"

Pressa doesn't argue with that. She sighs and rests her hand on my arm. "You don't have to explain it to me," she says, her gaze distant.

"Someday, we're all gonna get out of here. Find adventure and happiness somewhere else."

In gratitude, I touch her hand in return. At least there's one person in my life who seems to understand, and of course she's from the Undercity.

"You sure you still want to go to the drone race finals?" she says as we step out through the university's double doors. "Maybe tonight's not the best night for you to head down to the Undercity. Take some time and cool off, you know?"

But cooling off is the last thing I want to do. I'm always the one cooling off, shaking free. The thought of John's execution plays over and over again. I have to go. I *need* to. If I don't, my mind will burst.

"No," I reply. "I'll be there."

# DANIEL

MY HEART'S STILL HAMMERING FROM MY EVENING with June by the time I step out of the elevators and into the streets of the Undercity. My lips still burn from our kiss. A million thoughts run through my mind, and I find myself cursing silently at everything I did.

What a goddy idiot I am. Why didn't I just tell her exactly how I felt? What kept stopping me in the moment? So what if she doesn't feel the same way? Am I such a coward that I'd rather not know?

I sigh, indulging in my bad mood as I shove my hands in my pockets and hurry through the grungy streets. If I let myself, I could almost pretend that I'm back walking through Lake at night. Maybe nothing's changed at all since June and I first got together all those years ago.

By the time I arrive on the scene in the darkest district of the Undercity, there must be at least half a dozen AIS drone vehicles blocking the intersection, their flashing lights painting the buildings in alternating washes of red and yellow, adding to the mess of colors from the neon signs hanging overhead. Jessan and Lara are already here, and when they spot me, they wave me over with grim faces. Some distance away, I see Min Gheren, the AIS director, talking in low voices with some of the police. She and I exchange a brief look of greeting.

"What took you so long?" Jessan asks me as I approach them. "You in the middle of a date or something?"

I glare at her as we walk. *Yeah. Only my first kiss in ten years with a girl I'm crazy about.* "Something like that," I mutter back. "What happened here?"

"You'll see," Lara interjects from my other side.

The street is crowded with curious onlookers, and police and AIS agents alike keep telling people to get back behind the barricades. The pockmarked street is littered with broken glass, and burn marks against the sidewalks and the walls tell me there was some kind of explosion here. Already, the name hangs unspoken in the air—I can see it in the tense faces of my fellow agents, the way they're taking extra precautions. This is Dominic Hann's work.

Then we reach the crime scene, and I halt in my steps.

In the middle of the intersection lies a body laid out so purposefully that there's no question this was intentional. It's been sliced open. The face is unrecognizable. Beside me, Jessan and Lara look away from the vicious wounds that lace the corpse. I look on, my heart beating rapidly. An ugly flashback emerges from the dark corners of my mind now, the memory of bodies piled next to me as I woke up among them, terrified and in pain.

The memory is so vivid that I barely register Min coming over to stand beside us. Her lips are folded into a grim line as she studies the body with us.

"It's him, yeah?" I say to her in the beat of silence that follows. "He did this?"

Min nods toward the telltale red handkerchief tied to the corpse's ankle. "And he wanted us to know it," she replies.

The kind of cruelty that Dominic Hann inflicts on his victims is so sharply reminiscent of what the Republic used to be like, what Commander Jameson used to do, that I feel an ominous weight on my chest. This isn't just the work of a sadistic criminal. This is manipulation, someone trying to send a message. Someone threatening the city with his power.

"Who was he?" I ask as I bend down beside the body. "Do we know yet?"

Lara nods. "A councilman in the President's inner circle."

This stops me cold. The President's inner circle. My eyes go back to the mutilated figure before us. Most of Hann's past attacks have been against people who couldn't repay his debts, but an act like this is bold beyond belief. Had this councilman owed him money too? It's possible. But this isn't a regular citizen. He had bodyguards. All kinds of security attached to his account.

If Hann was able to do this to a prominent councilman in a coordinated attack, then he's not only growing more confident, he's got more connections in powerful places than I thought.

"How did it happen?" I ask.

Jessan runs me through what they already know: that the councilman had gone missing earlier today; that he'd been driven here and dumped at the intersection still alive; that he had then been set on fire. I wince at each graphic detail. My attention goes briefly to people sitting on the curbs now, being interrogated by the police.

Probably nearby storeowners, some who might've witnessed every-thing happening.

"And they still managed to get away?" I ask when Jessan finishes.

She shrugs, and Lara nods at the scorched walls. "They seem like they struck fast and hard. It's not their first time at this game. It's just the worst one yet."

I run a hand through my hair in frustration. "But what does Hann want?" I mutter to no one in particular. "Money? Revenge? Do we have any evidence? What does he get out of killing a councilman, aside from all of AIS descending on him like a horde of wasps?"

"No idea, but there was a theft tonight at the East City Labo-ratories, where a rare energy coil was stolen. No confirmation yet on whether or not these two events are related in any way, but the timing is unusual enough that it's worth noting."

My eyes go back to the pitiful remains. We're going to be the ones to deliver the news to the family.

Min is looking at me with a thoughtful expression. She turns to Jessan and Lara, then gives them a terse nod. "I need you two to gather some more eyewitness accounts," she says. "Go on. Let me have a word with Daniel."

They don't hesitate. As they head off, Min turns to me and low-ers her voice. "I know that look, Wing," she says quietly. "What's going through your head?"

"That this all looks familiar," I reply, my eyes still settled on the body.

"The wounds?"

I shake my head. "The political escalation. Up until now, Hann has stayed in his realm, punishing anyone who fails to pay their debts to him or loses a gamble or is a part of some rival gang. But this is different." I cross my arms. "He's prepping the people."

"What do you mean?"

I give her a hard look. If there was ever a time to bring the topic up to her again, it's now. "You know how I feel about the city's Level system. I remember what it's like to be part of the lower class when we're pushed to our limits."

At that, Min makes an exasperated sigh. "Daniel. You know my answer to this argument already."

"Then don't ask for my opinion," I say. "But I'm warning you— Hann isn't a fool. He knows that the number of poor down here is growing, that more people aren't able to raise their Levels and can't afford to feed their families. You got flattened Levelers setting up entire rows of tents down here. Hann knows that. He's already instilled a proper amount of fear in the Undercity—people here are intimidated by him. But he also shows them enough mercy to make them love him. Now he's attacking the city council. Prominent politicians." I point at the body. "It's not a coincidence that Hann decided to put this body on display down here instead of hanging it up in the Sky Floors, where they live. He knows how much the people down here hate the Sky Floor politicians. He *wants* the people down here to see. To know who's really running their city."

Min gives me a skeptical look. "You're insinuating that Hann wants to stage a coup?" she asks incredulously.

"I'm saying that's a real possibility," I argue back.

Min shakes her head in frustration. "Hann doesn't have that kind of power. You're telling me he's going to try seizing the capital of the most advanced nation in the world?"

"A nation that's still too young," I argue back. "That can topple just like anything else."

She rubs her temples in irritation. "Give me something I can work with. I'll never be able to convince the council that this is even a remote threat."

Her expression makes me want to scream. These cracked Antarcticans have never lived through a revolution before. Their country is barely a few decades old. They have no idea how fragile this entire system is. Everything always seems like it's going fine until suddenly, one day, it's not.

"All of you think this place is invincible," I snap. "You don't see the poison bubbling under the surface, that's been here since day one."

"What do you propose we do, then?"

"Find a way to Hann's side. We've had no luck hunting him because our relations with the Undercity are so poor."

"And how are we going to do that when we don't know the first thing about him?"

I smile grimly. "I've got some insight into how a notorious criminal can be caught by someone from the inside. She did it by becoming someone I could trust. But you need to tell the President that this system is unsustainable. We're setting the Undercity up for a revolution, and I don't even think they're wrong to do it."

Min still looks unconvinced. She shakes her head. "The President's not going to like me bringing up this conversation again," she says. "You know how much he supports the Level system."

These Sky Floor bastards always try to maintain order by giving themselves all the advantages. Eden's words linger in my mind, along with his disgust at my working for the AIS.

*Sometimes I think you've forgotten where you come from.*

But I was never the same as someone like Dominic Hann. Hann is a killer.

"You don't have to talk the President into taking it down," I reply. "Just tell him how much his own life is at risk. Hann isn't going to stop at killing a councilman. President Ikari is the prize at the top, and if he wants to stay alive, he needs to do something to quell this."

Min's eyes have gone cold again, but she doesn't dismiss my words. Instead, she nods at me. "Go join the others to gather eyewitness accounts," she says. "We'll talk again later." She doesn't wait for me to respond before walking away with her hands in her pockets.

Jessan comes up to me as I watch the director go. "I think we're narrowing down where the drone race's final is happening," she says to me, sending me a virtual map of the Undercity.

"Yeah?" I answer.

"Yeah. It might be the same place as the semifinal. We've pinpointed a few scattered crowds idling on the sides of the streets. Looks like they're waiting around for drones to pass through."

"Then it's happening very soon."

She nods. "It's too hard to track the drones, since they move so fast. We can only rely on the gathered crowds."

"Once those spectators catch on that they're being watched, they're going to scatter in a second." I force myself to turn away from the crime scene. "Show me where the crowds have been spotted."

As I start to follow Jessan away from the crime scene, I bring up my directory of names and instinctively pick out Eden's account to send him a message. But he's offline again, the tracker on his system disabled. Barely a day since our argument, since he almost got a knife to the stomach down in the Undercity, and he's already at it again, off to do hell knows what. I sigh. What do I have to do to force him to stay put—tie him down in a chair?

*Maybe he's back home*, I tell myself. *Or out celebrating, as he should be.* Today had been his last day of classes, after all, and he could be out with his friends, laughing his head off in some Sky Floor bar.

If I track his location and find him again, he'll know. And *that* won't get me anywhere with getting him to open up. I take a deep breath and try to ignore the nagging feeling in my gut.

But all that swirls through my mind are memories of the days when Eden was lost to me, when the Republic had taken him somewhere and I had no idea where he was. All I remember is seeing him stumble forward through the ash and fog of war from the hospital, and me scooping him into my arms.

Screw this. I give in to my worries, then tap on the icon for Eden's location. My AIS privileges let me bypass permissions, so that I can track him without his consent.

A small loading icon swirls in the center of my vision as my system traces him.

Ahead of me, Jessan pauses to bring up a virtual map between us. "See?" she says. "We've noticed hints of drone spectators crowded along these locations. It's not much evidence to go off of, but it puts the rough estimate of where the race is happening tonight right . . . here."

She points to a spot on the virtual map.

At the same time, my system finishes tracking where Eden is. His location dot appears, bright red, over almost the same spot where Jessan is pointing.

I blink, then frown and shake my head. "Hang on a sec," I mutter, reloading the geolocator. "I think my system glitched. Show me where the race is on the map again?"

Jessan brings it up again, while Eden's location also refreshes.

This time, there's no mistaking what I'm seeing. A sudden wave of dizziness sweeps over me. Eden is exactly where Jessan's finger is pointing.

He's down here in the Undercity. And he's at the drone race.

# EDEN

**THE SEMIFINALS OF THE DRONE RACE MAY HAVE** been crowded, but that was nothing compared to tonight.

People squeeze into the already-tight plaza until it's fit to burst. Those who live in the dilapidated apartments surrounding the square watch from their windows. Some of them look like they've charged money for other spectators to come watch from their balconies, because there are packs of people dangling off the side of the upstairs ledges, their legs swinging. Shouts fill the air.

Apparently, word has spread through the underground circles that a last-minute entry surprised everyone and won the first heat last night.

Now I crane my neck, looking through the crowds for any sign of my new patron. Beside me, Pressa keeps my drone tucked securely under her arm and pushes us through the throngs. She impatiently brushes strands of her blond wig from her face as she goes.

"Hey, move out of the way!" she snaps at two large gamblers blocking our path. "You wanna bet on last night's champion or not? Then let him through so he can set up!"

Barely five feet tall, and yet the people move aside for her, letting her cut a swath through the crowds. I admire the way she throws her shoulders back, and I'm grateful to follow in her wake.

In the center of the square, the virtual display hovering over the space now shows both a countdown clock to the race and a list of tonight's contestants. Half of the racers have already gathered on the line. I notice a few glances cast in my direction—but this time, the racers look wary. When I meet their gazes, their eyes dart away.

An uneasy feeling churns in the back of my mind. There's something about the man who became my patron that has reverberated through this space. In some ways, he reminds me of Daniel—he has a natural-born charisma. I think about how he seemed to recognize me in a way that most others never have. And his interest in my drone's engine . . .

Pressa nudges me, jolting me out of my thoughts. She nods toward the crowd. "There he is," she murmurs.

His presence is undeniable. The crowd parts without question for him as he makes his way to the plaza's clearing. Unlike many down here, he's dressed in crisp, almost harsh attire, whites and grays underneath a long black coat. Premature silver peppers his hair and stubble. He seems imprevious to all the commotion around him, and indifferent to those watching him walk.

When he sees me, though, he quickens his steps.

"Good to see you here, Eli," he says to me, resorting to my false name. His eyes dart to Pressa, who still has my drone under her arm. "And all ready to go."

"Almost," I reply. "What happens tonight if we win?"

"If we win, you get a pot ten times larger than the one from last night." Dominic smiles. "That's why we're all here, isn't it?"

"And if we don't?" Pressa asks.

The man doesn't seem concerned. "If you don't, I'll stay your patron." He glances at me. "There's promise in that engine you built. We can do a lot with it, beyond entering it in illegal races like this. I think you're destined for more."

*Destined for more.* I can't help but feel that same sense of pride welling up in me again. Daniel spends his days worrying more about whether or not I'm alive than what I've been working on. The other students at my university couldn't care less. But Dominic's words make me stand a little straighter.

"Sounds like a plan to me," I say to him.

Dominic glances up at the virtual countdown hovering over us. We have five minutes to go. "Then you'd better get to it," he says to me, and before I can ask him anything else, he's turned his back to me and stepped toward the crowd.

Here and there, I notice guards in suits watching him, paying attention to his every move. It's an unsettling contrast to the easy way he talks to me.

Then they're calling my name to the line, and I return my focus to the race. Pressa's arms are folded tightly over her chest, and every muscle of her body is pulled taut. She steps closer to me as if to give me a good-luck hug, but stops short, so that we just idle there, with a narrow sliver of space separating us.

Somehow, I get the sense that she also thinks there's more to winning this race than meets the eye. But for now, that's my job. And if we win, Pressa's father can get all the medication he'll need for the rest of his life.

Pressa nods at me. "Good luck," she says, flashing me a brief grin. "Not that you need it."

I don't know why I feel compelled in this moment. Maybe it's the flush of her cheeks, or the fear pumping through my veins at the thought of losing this race. But I suddenly lean toward her and, when she doesn't back away, give her a light kiss on her cheek.

"I'll do my best," I say. It's amusing to see a look of surprise on her face for the first time. Her eyes are bright and wide.

Then she smiles and shoves me toward the racer lineup. "Yeah, you better," she calls over her shoulder as she heads back into the crowd. I watch her go until I can't distinguish her from the mass of onlookers.

The red lights overhead flash again. Everything in the space tenses. I turn my view onto the channel that will follow the track of this race, then brace myself in the line and turn my eyes to the starting path.

Then the starting sound goes off. My drone flies out of my hand to hurtle forward, nearly lost in the blur of others. Cheers explode from the audience.

I tune out the mystery of my patron. I tune out what Pressa might be thinking about me or where she is in the crowd. I forget about my brother. All I do is focus on the track.

My engine, now warmed up, moves faster than ever. It glows a fierce blue-white as it curves around the end of one alley branching off from the square, clipping past two other drones to take an early, easy lead before vanishing around the intersection.

From the stands come shouts of surprise—but unlike at the semi-finals, there are no grumbles. No angry calls at me. It's almost as if Dominic has stopped anyone from wanting to antagonize me.

Drones close in from behind me, seeking to knock me out or catch me off guard from both sides. But I'm too far ahead now, and they can't catch up. We hurtle through the narrow streets of the city—past one intersection, then another, through a food market, down an alley winding around a series of smoke-spewing factories.

This time, I'm better at steering my drone. It zips sideways through a small crack in a wall, narrowly staying on track while cutting short the race path by a hair. One drone manages to close in behind me. I veer my drone up, tricking it into following me, and then suddenly dive down toward a busy street of stalls selling fabrics and pots. At the last second, I pull my drone level again. But the one following me can't do it fast enough. Its wing catches the side of one of the stalls, and it goes careening out of control, smashing into the side of a building in a shower of sparks and metal.

The people on the street let out startled cries. It's all I get to see before my drone leaves the scene behind to dart through the rest of the track.

There are no other challengers that come close this time. My engine churns faster and faster, its glow intensifying. My heart feels like it's close to bursting. This is exactly how I'd envisioned it working. It's perfection.

The entire race felt like a blur of seconds. Then I'm already hurtling back toward the square, leaving a trail of virtual neon blue on the race path behind me.

My drone zooms back into the square, winning by a handy two

lengths. The crowd explodes. I can feel hands slapping my shoulders hard. A ringing fills my ears as the plaza catches the fever of a hot race. Everyone is on their feet. Vaguely, I register Pressa shoving me in excitement as my name appears at the top of the rankings again.

The rush of the win is so strong that I feel dizzy from the glow of it. I close my eyes, relishing the feeling, not wanting it to end. Everything is a haze around me—the roaring stands, the virtual numbers hovering in the center of the arena, shifting in real time as they declare me the winner.

Then the red lights in the plaza flicker. The audience looks up, momentarily confused. They're supposed to flash only when the race begins and ends. Delayed reaction? But right as I think it, they flash again—then flicker out completely.

I blink in the new low light. Everyone breaks into a buzz. Already, some people start making a beeline for the exits as whispers lace through the crowd that the event's been compromised. *The police are here! The guards are coming! Clear out!*

Somehow, my eyes catch a movement that's all too familiar to me—the sight of a silhouette high up against a wall, perched with perfect balance. I see the figure against the massive circuit-breaker board that I'd first seen situated at the entrance to the plaza. Even though I can't make out anything but his outline, I recognize him immediately.

My brother is here.

# DANIEL

USUALLY, WHEN I'M IN THE UNDERCITY, I'M DOING a sweep with my fellow AIS agents. I've definitely shut down illegal gambling and drug operations and all sorts of other cracked businesses before, as well as closing down unauthorized, makeshift elevator stations built out of old sewage tunnels.

But tonight I'm alone, masked, and hooded. I look like one of the hundreds of gamblers that roam this place.

It's obvious that this side of the Undercity is the worst side—rows and rows of tents line the walls along the narrow, dark streets, and vendors stand outside forlorn, empty shops, watching me as I pass their storefronts.

Here, in this outfit, I go back to my Lake routine—hunched shoulders, listless gaze. I'm careful to keep a lookout for anything suspicious while at the same time not making eye contact with anyone. It seems to work okay. People think I belong down here, someone who's clearly used to walking rough streets. But it still puts me on edge.

I didn't come to Antarctica just to return to living like a street orphan.

What the hell is Eden doing down here again? The thought rings through my system like a warning bell. He's the smartest damn kid in his entire university. He's got an internship waiting for him back in the Republic. He's got friends. He's got everything he needs.

Why is he here? Why can't I understand him? Why won't he talk to me?

His location now takes me to a small, unremarkable bar. The bartender gives me a hostile look. This kind of place should be intimidating for most people unused to being down here, but I've seen plenty worse than this.

"What's going on in there?" Jessan says over our line.

I observe the bartender's posture, then everyone else in this space. "My guess is we need a password to get through," I whisper. "Can you scan the outside perimeter for anything behind this building?"

"Looking now," she says. I step out of the bar and into one of its narrow side alleys.

At first, it looks like any other dead-end street—a narrow space packed with garbage bins and wads of trash strewn all over the place. But when I walk closer to the back wall and run my hand along it, it feels thin and hollow. On the other side, I hear the sound of raucous cheers. There hadn't been a doorway to this in the bar, at least that I could see. This is some kind of shoddy, makeshift wall separating the main streets from a hidden space.

I glance up to see where the back wall ends. It extends up maybe five or six floors, a crumbling brick surface bordered on either side by dilapidated apartments.

A familiar sight to a runner.

I sprint toward the wall, then skip up several steps to grab the second-floor ledge of the building next to the back wall. In a few seconds, I'm pulling myself up and jumping to grab the third floor's balcony railings. The exertion sends a familiar thrill through me. This was how I survived in the Republic.

It takes just a moment for me to get to the top of the back wall. The cheers coming from the other side suddenly turn deafening. When I get my first glimpse over the wall, everything looks bathed in a hazy glow from strings of red lightbulbs.

I find myself staring down at a clearing packed full of people. There must be at least a thousand people crammed into a space that's probably meant to fit less than half that number. They crowd around a small clearing in the center of the square, where a line of racers now stands with their drones.

Eden's location in my view now flashes as it signals he's very near. And sure enough, when I take a closer look at the racers, I see him.

His familiar blond hair, his glasses, his wiry, lean frame.

My brother's a drone racer.

I lean against the wall, in danger for a moment of losing my balance. Maybe I'm just making up what I saw—maybe I'm so intent on finding Eden I'm hallucinating.

But when I take another look, he's unmistakable. It's him, along with his friend Pressa, who's in a long blond wig and wearing a smug look of satisfaction.

Not only was Eden in the race, but judging from the way everyone's gathering around him, he won.

That's when I notice the other man. He's standing before both Eden and Pressa, his face hauntingly recognizable from all the internal AIS reports I've seen.

*Dominic Hann.*

I can't believe my eyes.

Dominic Hann has killed hundreds. He's committed some of the most gruesome murders I've ever seen—some that make even the worst of the Republic's crimes pale in comparison. The image of the body in the streets is still fresh in my mind. I think of the sheer terror on the faces of the witnesses we were questioning. Even the act of hunting for him is considered dangerous. You don't want a man like this setting his sights on you.

Dominic Hann doesn't attend races like this. He rarely appears in public when he can just send his underlings in his place. He's one of the most elusive figures terrorizing the city. AIS has glimpsed him only a few times, with nothing but a grainy photo of his face to prove it.

And yet, here he is, standing in front of my brother, a thoughtful smile on his face. As I look on, Hann says something to Eden that I can't make out.

The blood in my veins chills to ice.

I force myself to stay calm, blending into the shadows, while the audience below gapes at the exchange. Before him, Eden stays frozen, unsure what to say in response.

*Walk away,* I urge him silently. *Turn your back. Run.*

Except my brother doesn't. He smiles a little at Hann and then says something to answer him.

I feel like I'm back in the Republic again, looking on helplessly as the soldiers take my family away.

Why is Hann talking to him? What does he want with him?

But even as the questions flood my mind, I know the answer by instinct. It's because Eden made the best drone here. His nimble hands have built a machine so remarkable that it caught Hann's interest. That it beat out all the experienced racers. That it *won*.

I've never doubted Eden's talents, but have I still been underestimating him?

Everyone makes room for Dominic Hann as he steers Eden back toward the center of the clearing. Hostile looks linger on my brother. If it weren't for Hann's presence beside him right now, he might already have a knife in his back.

A surge of panic hits me. I have to do something.

My hand lingers by the gun at my belt. I'm not as good a shot as June, but I've gotten pretty good over the years with my AIS training. From here, I might be able to take out Hann with a single shot to the head.

But Eden would be the most immediate suspect. The new kid, suddenly here when Hann's killed? I don't know how many of the people in this audience are Hann's spies and bodyguards, but I do note that there are some whose eyes sweep the audience instead of focusing on the racers. If I managed to kill Hann, his men would shoot Eden dead before the body even hit the floor. And there's no guarantee I'd hit Hann. What if I missed?

I grit my teeth and force myself not to draw my gun. Instead, my gaze goes up to the red bulbs dangling over the space. I follow the trails of lights until they end next to the walls, the sides of which are supported by a lattice of thick, steel beams. An enormous circuit breaker sits against the wall that would have led back into that small bar.

I straighten a little from my perch on the back wall. In the shadows, I know I look like little more than a moving silhouette, and no one seems to notice me as I swing to the crisscrossing steel supporting one of the side buildings and pull myself soundlessly up onto the lowest horizontal beam, then the next one.

I keep climbing until I reach the circuit breaker. The wires connecting all the ceiling's bulbs bunch together here in the upper corners. Aside from those bulbs, this clearing is lit only by the weak light coming from the surrounding buildings' apartments.

I pull a knife out from my boot. Down below in the clearing, Hann pats my brother on his shoulder.

The sight's enough to send a shudder deep through my bones. I slash once through the red bulbs' wires.

The entire space plunges into darkness.

No time to waste. I turn on my system's grids. In the chaos, a series of thin, neon-blue virtual lines light up over my view, showing me where to go and where people are. I swing down from the beams one at a time, as fast as I can. My feet hit the ground in seconds. Then I'm bolting into the crowd, shoving past people as I seek out my brother.

I reach him. In my grids, he looks like a sickly green animation.

He lets out a startled shout before I clap a hand over his mouth. Then, without a word, I pull him with me and run. To my overwhelming relief, he doesn't resist. He just follows me.

We dart through the crowds to one of the narrow alleys that other people are running toward, one that dead-ends at a nondescript shop, then leads out into a main street. Everyone around us jostles past, panicked that the clearing is being raided.

Somewhere behind us are Dominic Hann and his men. But I don't dare look back.

"You followed me down here," Eden snaps at me as we go. In the darkness, his eyes glitter once, livid. He doesn't have a clue how close he came to death.

"You don't understand," I say. "That man was Dominic Hann."

At that, Eden blinks at me. "So?" he asks.

"So," I answer grimly, "you have no idea what you've just gotten yourself into."

# EDEN

**DOMINIC HANN.**

Daniel says his name again as we sit back in our apartment. For the first time since I can remember, he tells me about one of the missions that he's working on. Apparently, he's been on the trail of this guy for months.

He tells me that Dominic Hann is wanted for at least a dozen murders and has probably committed many more that have never been linked to him. Undercity victims indebted to him, unable to pay back their money. People who have crossed him, whether on purpose or accidentally. And now councilmen, given the murder that happened tonight.

"And there you were," my brother says, pacing in front of the couch where I sit. "Having a conversation with the deadliest murderer in Ross City like you two were goddy friends."

"He just wanted to profit off my winnings," I say, trying not to show my shaking hands. In my view, I can see messages from Pressa coming in, each more frantic than the last. **Your brother was there!**

she's exclaiming. **Are you home? I'm back at my dad's shop. Every-thing just went pitch-black! Are you all right? Eden?**

**Can't talk right now,** I quickly message her back. **Tell you later.**

"Right." Daniel flashes me a look. He seems even more annoyed as he notices I'm messaging while he's talking. "Because that's all a notorious killer needs, a few extra corras in his pocket."

"He liked the design of my drone, he offered to be my patron so that he could see it race, and he pocketed a bunch of money for my win. He never seemed interested in hurting me." My voice turns urgent, as if I'm trying to convince myself too.

I try to picture Dominic as a ruthless killer. But his calmness still lingers in my mind, the way he understood me with a single observation, more than my brother does right now. The contrast between these two thoughts makes me shiver.

Daniel stops right in front of me and sighs. "Eden, I know you don't know what it's like to truly live on the streets. I've worked my entire life to make sure that never happens to you. I know you don't understand a lot of what happened tonight, or what made it so dangerous. But—"

His tone makes me recoil. *I know you don't understand.* Like I'm still ten years old. Like I don't know what the hell I'm doing with my life. "Don't talk to me like that," I say.

He frowns at me. "Like what?"

My temper starts to boil over. "Like *that*," I say again as I get to my feet. "This isn't a conversation or a discussion. We're not even having an argument. You're lecturing me."

"You were down in the Undercity again! In a drone race! Do you have any idea how dangerous that is?"

"Then scream at me!" I insist. "Tell me how you can't believe I did what I did tonight! Anything's better than your pity!"

"I don't pity you!" he yells. "My life would be a lot easier if you weren't disappearing off to the dregs of this city every night!"

The Undercity is nothing but a pit of filth to him. When had he changed so much? "If the agency you work for wasn't so tyrannical," I yell back, "Pressa's dad wouldn't need to be a millionaire just to survive. We wouldn't need to gamble on the races. And I wouldn't have to explain myself to you as if I were talking to a damn stranger."

Daniel just shakes his head. "You don't get it," he mutters. It's all he resorts to, turning me back into the little brother.

But we aren't brothers here. He's my father, and I'm his son. The feeling of distance, along with the fear of everything that happened tonight, now threatens to smother me.

In disgust, I turn away. "When I leave for the Republic," I say, "maybe it'd be best if you didn't come with me. You should just stay here."

Daniel winces, and I feel an urge to take it back. But instead I turn from him and head to my room.

Behind me, Daniel raises his voice. "Wait, Eden," he calls out.

I pause as he hurries to my side. "Please," he says, taking a deep breath.

"What?" I mutter.

He hesitates and his gaze hardens on mine. "Fine. Go to the Republic by yourself."

He's letting me go? I narrow my eyes at him. It surprises me how his comment cuts me. But my pride refuses to let me show that. "Fine," I repeat.

Daniel winces again, as if he'd been hoping I'd say something different. But we each stay on our own side, no longer able to understand each other. It's like I'm looking back at someone I haven't known since I was a baby.

Then I turn away again. This time, Daniel doesn't stop me as I head into my room and close the door between us.

\* \* \*

"This won't take long. You may feel a little buzz."

Beside me, my brother folds his arms and turns his mouth down in a concerned scowl. "Go easy," he replies to the woman. "He's never used this system before."

I grit my teeth at his familiar condescension and ignore him. I'm standing in the middle of a circular room at the top of the AIS headquarters with Daniel, a half-dozen other investigators, and the woman who had just spoken to me—Min Gheren, the AIS director herself. Glass windows stretch from floor to ceiling and curve around the chamber, giving us a stunning view of Ross City.

My eyes dart briefly to the endless plain of skyscrapers outside, each interconnected by webs of walkways. From up here, you can't see the Undercity. It's like it doesn't exist at all.

I jerk back to the scene as one of the others in the room comes up to me and presses a thin metal bar against the back of my ear, where my chip is installed. "What are you doing?" I ask the director.

She fixes me with a piercing stare. "Mr. Wing," she says to me, and Daniel shifts uncomfortably nearby, "it was right of your brother to inform AIS of the fact that you crossed paths with a man we've been struggling to track down for months. You need to understand that Dominic Hann never appears at gatherings like the one you attended last night. He does not need to show his face when his underlings can do the job for him. So imagine what it means that your performance *so* interested him that he decided to speak to you in person."

The director pauses, then looks to her side at Daniel. She gives him a stern nod. "Tell him," she says.

Daniel looks at me. His gaze is cool and calm this morning, like we didn't have our argument the night before. "AIS has a system where we can replay and pull your memories up as a virtual scene," he explains. "It's all stored away on your chip. When we activate your system in here, it allows us to see the memory as you did, while trying to pick up on clues that you may not have noticed."

I exchange a silent look with my brother. He doesn't say more, but there's a difference in the way he stares back at me. He's not angry with me anymore; he's afraid.

"Sounds like a plan," I say.

The director gives us both a nod of approval. Then she waves a hand before her. A virtual screen hovers between us. From the way Daniel's turned his head toward it, I can tell that it's visible to everyone else in here too.

ALLOW MEMORY ACCESS TO LAST NIGHT?

I take a deep breath. "Granted," I reply.

The screen disappears. A strange tingle starts at my temples, sweeps up to my head, and then all the way down my body. I shiver.

The world around me takes on a blue tint. The chamber, the glass walls, the floor and ceiling—all of it fades away, leaving me and the others standing against a black backdrop. I sway, dizzy at the sight.

Then a scene rushes into place around us. It's everything that happened the evening before, just as I remember it—I see myself walking through the tiny bar and stepping into the makeshift elevator. The rusted interior of the elevator shaft appears all around us, like a weird reenactment of the scene in which Daniel and AIS agents are also heading down with me. We stop at the bottom. Then we follow the memory version of myself out into the same hall, stopping ultimately out in the underground arena, where the countdown is on the wall and the drone race is setting up.

"Pause," the director says beside me.

The scene around us halts abruptly, like a movie stilled in three dimensions. The waving arms of the audience freeze, their voices go suddenly silent, the countdown stops.

Min walks around the scene, studying the walls and the crowd. Daniel waves me forward, and I walk uneasily through my frozen memory with him. My brother stops before one of the halls on the other side of the room, where my memory of it goes a little fuzzy. It translates as a grainy view before us.

Daniel points to one of the halls. "Dominic Hann came out of there," he says to the director. It's something I hadn't seen in the heat of the moment.

The director nods before she shifts to analyzing the crowd. We walk through the scene again until we reach the center of the arena. She points out a face near the front of the audience. "There," she says. "One of Hann's men. They were running this show."

Daniel calls for the scene to continue. As if in a dream, I see my-self with my drone, then everything that happens in the race.

"Pause." This time, Daniel says it, and my drone halts in midair. He nods down to the corner of my memory's scene, where the blur of the audience's faces is. He points to the man that the director just called out as one of Dominic Hann's people.

The man isn't watching anymore. He's standing up, exchanging a few words with someone else as his eyes dart toward me.

The race continues. We halt the scene several more times when-ever my view returns to show Hann's person. The man walks out with another associate as the race ends, and they disappear into the hall that Daniel pointed out earlier.

Then an hour later, halfway through the second heat, I see Hann emerge.

Daniel sucks his breath in, while Director Min lets out a low whistle. Her eyes veer to me. "So," she says, "Hann came out to the race specifically to see *you*."

Even as I hear her words, the scene continues to play, and I see the virtual version of Dominic Hann walk up to me. The unease that ran through me then—the instinct that told me this man was someone unusual—now washes back over me.

He looks so realistic that, for a moment, I genuinely believe he's in the room with us. I take an unconscious step back as he approaches me. The virtual world around us shudders and blurs, and a haze fades the images around us.

Daniel steps toward me. "Pause. Clear," he says, his gaze on his director. The scene halts, and Dominic Hann and the Undercity fade into white before the AIS chamber comes back into view. "Give him a rest. His emotions are interfering with the quality of the memory playback."

"I can do this," I say to him.

But the director's not paying attention to Daniel anymore. Instead, her stare is fixed on me. She narrows her eyes. "What were you doing down in the Undercity, Mr. Wing?" she asks me. "You know drone races are strictly banned."

She's going to dock my Level hard for this, I know, but in this moment, I hardly care. My lips tighten into a line. "I don't think it's relevant to why you needed me here," I reply.

She raises an eyebrow at me and glances at my brother. "Well, I see where he gets his attitude from," she says wryly to him before returning her attention to me. "We'll need to pull an earlier memory from you, of how you heard about this race and what sent you down there."

*Pressa.* If the director digs as intimately into that memory as she did to my journey down to the Undercity, she'll have AIS agents questioning Pressa in no time.

I cross my arms and frown at the director. "You said you just wanted my memory from last night. I didn't authorize anything beyond that."

"You are obliged to aid us in this investigation as we need it. That includes your past memories, including your thoughts and any dreams you might have had recently."

My nightmares. And suddenly I can feel those haunting dreams of mine creeping up in the back of my mind, a faceless mother and a desolate Republic street, details I've never been able to fill in. The AIS system shudders around me as it tries to re-create the images popping up in my thoughts. *No*, I think, trying to hold back. Fear rips through me. *I don't want to show them.*

I half expect Daniel to agree with her, to turn to me and insist that I answer her question properly. But he takes a step toward his director. "You're not digging into his other memories," he says. His voice is calm, but I can hear the familiar undercurrent of steel in it.

And, for once, I'm grateful.

The AIS system around me cuts off abruptly, along with the emerging whispers of my dreams. I let out a shaking breath.

The director turns to my brother with an exasperated look. This isn't the first time he has disagreed with her. "Watch that tone, Agent," she says.

He shakes his head. "Doesn't change what I'm saying, ma'am."

The director looks like she's ready to reprimand him—but then she sighs and looks back at me. I hold my breath. "We'll comb through the rest of the Undercity memory you've given us," she finally says. I exhale. Before the relief can linger, though, she adds, "But that doesn't mean your involvement on this case is done."

Daniel speaks up again. "Director—"

"Stand down, Agent," she snaps, and Daniel quiets into a scowl. She looks back at me. "You are the first person in months to get a glimpse of Dominic Hann, let alone direct access to him. When I tell you that this man does not just let you play a single game with him, I mean it. Hann likes to get what he wants, and he's clearly expressed interest in you."

She forces my memory to continue playing, and we watch the final moments go down before she pauses at the end of the race, right before the lights cut out, when Hann has risen from his seat. I didn't notice it myself—but in that final moment, he had his eyes fixed on me as he murmured something to his associate. They were getting ready to approach me.

The director places a hand on her hip. "I'm willing to bet anything that he was about to make you an offer to join him. It's not the kind of offer you can turn down."

The thought makes my stomach recoil. Daniel stiffens beside me.

"Enough," Daniel says.

Min ignores him and focuses on me. "Our proposal is this: We need you to draw him out. We will track every movement you make. If you lure Hann out into a space where our agents are ready for him, we can take him down before he can escape."

My face pales. Daniel steps in front of me, his arm instinctively pushing me behind him as he'd done when I was still a kid. "You want to use him as a mole?" he snaps. Now the real anger is out.

"You are an agent for the AIS," the director snaps back. "And right now, Eden is the sole link between us and the man we've been hunting." She looks back at me. Even though she is stern, there's a pleading glint in her eyes. "I am not going to force you to do something you're uncomfortable with. This all depends on what you decide. But you are the closest thing we have to a lead, and it's an overwhelming one. We are going to do everything in our power to keep you safe."

"But we can't guarantee that," Daniel adds.

"Do you run this agency, Wing?" Min says coldly to him.

He just shrugs. "I'm willing to do a lot for this agency," he replies. "But handing my brother over to a killer is not one of them."

Her eyes narrow. "This isn't a game. There are a lot of lives at stake here."

Again, others are deciding my fate, not me.

"What do you want, Eden?" Daniel suddenly asks me.

I look at my brother. All I wanted to do was help someone out—I didn't expect to find myself here, caught in a web between two enormous forces. I turn back to the director. "Give me some time," I finally say.

She nods. "You have until morning."

Daniel mutters a curse under his breath and turns away. He nods for me to follow him. The tension in the room feels thick enough to cut, and I wonder how many times he's had confrontations like this with his director.

When my brother escorts me out of the room and we are alone in the hall, he reaches up to disable my system's records. He turns his own off too. Then he leans close.

"Eden," he says in a low voice. "Don't do this."

His voice is so worried that it even cuts through my resentment. "Your director's going to be disappointed," I mutter.

"That's my job. Yours is to steer clear of Dominic Hann. Your interaction alone has given us more clues than we've ever had." He's silent for a moment. When he glances over his shoulder through the windows, out at the city, I glimpse the fear on his face. He turns back to me. "This isn't like the war, Eden. This isn't saving the Republic from the Colonies. We didn't leave the Republic behind just for me to throw you back into a snake pit."

I look at my brother. "*You've* been in this snake pit for months, and I had no idea. You never breathed a word about any of this to me. You put yourself in danger every single night while I stay home and wait, hoping you come back from whatever the hell you're doing."

He looks exhausted now. I think back to how I saw him perched on the edge of his balcony the other night, his gaze settled on the city before him. I have nightmares, but I wonder for the first time if maybe he does too, if they're worse.

His voice hushes. "Let me deal with AIS," he says again. "But promise me you'll stay away from the Undercity. Let Hann forget about you. He's still a busy man with plenty of other businesses to attend to. Maybe a racer isn't going to be his top priority." He takes a breath. "Maybe it really is like you said. He just wanted a quick win."

I meet my brother's steady gaze. "I promise." I don't add what I want to say. *Even though you can't do the same.*

The director's suggestion lingers in my mind. If I don't help them out, my brother is going to continue his hunt for Hann. And if even half the reports I've heard about the man are true, then Daniel's walking straight into the snake pit he's trying to keep me away from.

# DANIEL

WHEN YOUR KID BROTHER HAS CAUGHT THE
attention of the most notorious criminal in Ross City, it's hard to
concentrate on anything—even a gala thrown in honor of the Republic's Elector.

Several nights later, when I head in full black tuxedo to Ross
City's Hall of Philosophy for the gala, my mind is still swirling
around what Eden's memories revealed at the AIS headquarters.

Long blue banners stretch vertically down the sides of the skyscraper, all the way from the top floor to the lowest rung of the
Sky Floors, where we and other guests are mingling on the outdoor
walkways. Above and below us, the rest of the city's floors shim-
mer in a sea of lights. Overhead and beyond the biodome, a snow-
storm is raging, but when the flurries pass through the biodome,
the warmer atmosphere turns them into rain. The air smells clean
and cold.

Director Min Gheren is here, along with several other high-
ranking members of AIS. Now she finds me standing on one of the
ivy-covered walkways leading into the Hall of Philosophy, staring

up at a virtual projection of the Republic's flag on the side of the building. With her is Anden Stavropoulos, the Elector of the Republic.

"I believe you both already know each other," the director says as they approach me. "But a greeting is in order, nevertheless. Elector, this is Daniel Altan Wing, one of our most promising young agents in the AIS. Mr. Wing, the Elector of the Republic."

Anden doesn't look too different from how I remember him—a tall, composed young man with grave green eyes and a regal tilt to his chin. He seems more relaxed now, though, as if he's finally been able to step into his position with comfort.

I give him a respectful bow of my head. "Elector," I say.

Anden smiles at me and repeats the gesture, even though I don't think it's protocol to do so. "In the Republic, he has a longer title than that," he says to Min. "He's still well known within all circles as the boy who saved a nation. I'm indebted to him."

Me, the savior of a nation. It's still a bizarre idea. Listening to the Elector talk about our shared history gives me a strange, light-headed feeling. I try to think back to that blur of time, when I was known as Day and when the Elector and I had a trust in each other so thin that June was really the only one who held us together. My memories of those few conversations I had with Anden are spotty, but even then, I remember the way I'd feel every time I saw him standing in some fancy hall with June standing at his side as his Princeps.

"You're indebted to no one, sir," I reply to him now. "The Republic's thriving because of you."

"Ms. Iparis has always spoken of your humility," he says. "It's as intact as ever."

June. The mention of her name warms my cheeks. It hadn't been that long ago when she and Anden were still in a relationship. I remember seeing it rotating on the news over here. "Well, if June's saying it," I reply, "I'll take it as a compliment."

Anden laughs quietly. "We'll welcome your brother when he returns to the Republic for his internship."

"Thank you, sir," I say.

The Elector bows to us both again. "If you'll excuse me," he says, turning back in the direction of the hall. "I need to have a word with the President. It was good to see you, Mr. Wing," he says to me. Then he leaves me with the director.

I let out a breath.

"Thought you were off duty today," Min says.

I nod to her. "Would've been," I reply. "Somehow I got an invite to this thing."

"Yes, well . . . I'm assuming it has something to do with Ms. Iparis."

I scowl when Min notices the blush on my cheeks and gives me a small, sidelong smile. Then she steps closer and lowers her voice.

"Has Hann reached out to your brother in any way?" she murmurs.

All of my worries come flooding back anew. "Not yet," I reply. "And honestly, it'd be great if he never did."

Min frowns. "I know you're unhappy about your brother getting involved in this Hann investigation," she says. "But he's the closest link we've gotten in a year."

"We'll find another way," I say. "We got a sighting of him, didn't we? We're hunting down more info about the race itself too. Hann's going to show up again if there's another race."

"Not if your brother's not there," she replies. Then she turns her entire body toward me. "If we get a lead, I expect to see your brother cooperate."

"And if he doesn't?"

"I think you'd prefer that he does," Min says. "This isn't a request, Daniel. This is an order."

I lean over the side of the walkway and stare down at the dizzying height. "I don't do well with personal threats, Director," I say through gritted teeth.

"Good, because neither do I." Min starts to walk away. "So let's make sure it doesn't come down to that."

I watch her go, feeling a sense of helplessness that I haven't felt since the Republic was at war.

The rest of the guests seem like they're starting to stream inside the hall, but I stay where I am, in the solitude and the rain. At least I'd had Tess on my side when I used to live on the streets of Lake. Here, I feel alone.

"You're not heading in?"

June's voice comes from one side of the walkway. I jump, straightening, and look over to see her approaching.

My words jumble in my throat and fail to come out. Tonight, she's in a floor-length gown of scarlet and black, the skirt billowing with floating fabric in a fanlike pattern. Whenever she walks, she looks like she's gliding on air. Crystal drops sparkle on her ears.

I realize that she's still looking at me, and force myself to stop gaping and turn back toward the main Hall of Philosophy. "I thought I'd get some fresh air before I had to head in," I say. "What are you doing out here? Isn't the Elector expecting you inside?"

She comes to stand beside me and gives me a brief smile. "He's deep in conversation with Faline," she replies, nodding toward the hall. "I think he'll be fine on his own for a while."

June, who always seems like she's put together and has everything under control. I give her a tight smile, wishing I could feel the same way, instead of this awkward sense of uncertainty around her.

"Something's bothering you," she says after a while.

"Is it that obvious?" I reply.

She glances sidelong at me. "Well, I like to pride myself on how well I can read the details of everything around me."

I laugh a little at that. "Yeah, I seem to remember you having a knack for it."

She smiles, then turns serious. "Care to share any of it with me? You look like you could use someone to hear you out."

And again, there she goes, predicting me. I hesitate, wondering whether I should embroil any more people I care about into my business. "Work's been rough lately," I finally decide to say.

"Rough like how?"

I sigh. "I think I'm starting to understand why you acted the way you did when I was first getting to know you. When you worked as an agent in the Republic. Working for a country you didn't agree with, staying loyal even if the cause was imperfect. It was almost easier to be from the streets. At least all the right choices were obvious there."

June's silent for a moment. Rain pours down the sides of the archway above us, forming a makeshift waterfall. "It's not easy being in a gray zone," she finally replies. I notice with gratitude that she doesn't ask me the sensitive details of what I'm involved in. "Maybe you should think about a line of work in something less dangerous. Finance, perhaps."

"Why?" I straighten the lapels of my suit and puff out my chest. "Is finance a hot look on me?"

She raises an eyebrow. "I thought we were talking about making the right decisions."

We smile a little, then lapse again into silence.

"Not here," I whisper after a moment. "It's too sensitive to talk about in public."

June's expression never changes. She smiles like I'd just murmured something intimate to her. But when she replies softly, she says, "My place, then, after most of the festivities are done."

* * *

It's almost midnight by the time we finally leave the gala.

June's staying in a penthouse across from the Elector's suites on the top floor of their hotel. As we enter the space, the security system greets us both by our names. I watch the light shift against June's back as she removes her heels and walks on quiet feet toward her bedroom.

I lean against the kitchen counter and let myself admire the main chamber, trying not to think about June changing out of her dress in the other room. Our President definitely spares no expense in making sure foreign leaders here have a full sense of how well Antarctica's doing.

I walk over to the long glass windows overlooking the black ocean. I'm still staring at the view when June emerges from her room.

Her hair is down now in soft waves against her face, and she has changed into a comfortable wrap that drapes silken against her figure. Her eyes are liquid dark in the night, as mesmerizing as I remember.

Hell. She's still the most beautiful woman I've ever seen in my life.

Was I ever able to relax in a room with her? Or was I always like this—my heart beating rapidly in her presence, every sense of mine attentive to her and ignorant of everything else?

She seems to notice my sudden discomfort, and for a moment, we just stand stiffly apart, not knowing what to say.

"You look nice," I end up blurting out. Immediately, I regret it. Could I have thought of something dumber to say? Probably not.

She clears her throat, unsure what to say back. I curse inwardly at myself. Way to make her uncomfortable.

To my relief, she flashes me a small smile. "Thanks," she replies. "Always the flatterer, even when things are going wrong."

Another shard of a memory comes back to me in that moment. We're sitting side by side, passing a bottle of cheap sea-grape wine between us and squinting at its sour, salty aftertaste. I don't know who she is, and I don't know what I say to her. But she's so beautiful and strange. Our lips touch.

The memory fades, and I find myself back in June's hotel room, blinking at my recollection. Beside me, June tilts her head curiously.

"What did you just think about?" she asks.

I hesitate, then look down. "I remembered something," I reply. "About us, before."

At that, she brightens. "A memory?" she asks. "What was it?"

I glance at her with a bashful smile. "The first time we kissed."

June's lips quirk, and a little laugh escapes her. She looks away too, out the windows at the black ocean and the lights of the city. "Do they come back to you in pieces like that? Your memories?"

"Yes. Specific things will trigger new memories. Most of the time, they're just fragments. I remember kissing you, for example, and the bottle of wine we were passing between us. But I don't remember exactly where we were, or who else might have been nearby then. I don't know what I said to you, or you to me. I just remember . . . the feeling of being near you. As if it were from a different lifetime."

June closes her eyes for a brief moment, as if soaking in the memory herself, before she looks at me again. "We were on the streets of Lake, and you didn't know who I was yet. I didn't know you were Day. It was right before everything unraveled."

Before everything unraveled between us. Now I remember. It was before my mother died, before the Republic arrested me. It was the beginning of being forever linked with her.

I turn back to her. "But nothing's unraveling for you now, yeah? You seem really happy these days," I say.

She smiles a little. "I am," she replies. "Tess is still doing well. You know she's been promoted to head doctor of her hospital? I see her often. Pascao and I hang out constantly. Life has settled into a nice routine, and it made me realize how much I missed having that." She nods out at the city. "Some sense of balance. Of normalcy after the war. Isn't that strange?"

Normalcy. Routine. I find myself smiling at her, content to know that she was content. Then I wonder if my presence in her life—and all the chaos it currently has—would disrupt all of that for her.

Maybe I've always been the reason for the unraveling of her life.

She looks at me. "And yours?" she asks. "What has your life been like?"

I shrug and look away, reluctant to break this peaceful moment with my problems. "Good," I reply. "Great, actually. Sometimes I still can't believe I live here, in luxury. I'll never have to spend another day fighting to survive in the streets."

June hears the hesitation in my answer. "But you're fighting *something*," she says.

For a moment, everything in me resists telling her. But June steps closer to me and forces me to face her head-on, then crosses her arms. "Tell me," she says, her eyes dark and warm.

Her presence is overwhelming in every sense. I have to tear my gaze away from hers in order to think straight.

Finally, with a deep breath, I start to tell her. I mention the missions I've been running lately in Ross City, the man I've been hunting down. I tell her about the hierarchies of this place's skyscraper tiers, how the Leveling divides the classes, how even though it's all more fluid than anything in the Republic, it's still as imperfect as anything else in this world. I tell her about the murders of anyone who has been unable to pay their debts to Dominic Hann, and the seedy underground of the Undercity.

Then I tell her of Eden's involvement, how he has entangled himself in something so much more dangerous than he knows.

June frowns. "You weren't afraid of Dominic Hann before Eden met him," she says, studying me.

"He was a job before then," I reply, "until I saw the same culprit from our crime photos walking up to my brother. And now the AIS wants Eden to join the investigation, to lure the man out of hiding."

June doesn't answer right away, but her eyes are steady. They steady *me*. Somehow, in the midst of everything going wrong between Eden and me, her presence is a comfort in the dark. I don't feel alone confessing all this to her.

"You still know Eden better than anyone else," June says after a while. "He's your brother. You've protected him all your life, and I know he understands that."

"It's my protection of him that seems to have pushed him away." I run a frustrated hand through my hair, ruffling it. "I used to think that nothing in the world could ever divide us. But then Eden grew older. He's changed, maybe for the better. But there are things he doesn't tell me now, and I don't know how to guess what he's thinking."

June smiles. "You'll never be able to guess what he's thinking," she replies. "Metias always tried with me, you know. He never really succeeded, but we'd still been linked. You and Eden have a bond that's unbreakable. No matter what he isn't telling you, he still loves you more than anyone else in the world. I know it. I've seen it."

*Metias.* The brother that June had lost, the death that had, fatefully, brought us together. I search her gaze and find grief there, but also a sense of peace. "He practically raised you," I say gently. "I wish I could measure up to that. I've tried being a good father figure for Eden, but . . . sometimes I wonder if he's worse off for it."

"You're afraid for him," June says. "That he wants to help in this investigation of a dangerous criminal."

"I'm always afraid for him," I reply.

There's a deep understanding in June's eyes. "You've helped Eden come into his own as a person. Everything about him is modeled after you, in the best way. Don't you see that? But, Daniel, he's not a helpless child. He'll resist every attempt you make to insulate him from the world. Let him in a little. Let someone else offer their shoulder to you. Maybe he's pushing away because he loves you, because he worries for you just like you worry for him."

"I know he's not helpless," I mutter, shoving my hands into my pockets. "But the AIS isn't keen on his safety. No one is. I'm the steward of that."

"I wasn't talking completely about Eden's safety. I was also talking about yours." A slight furrow creases in June's brow. "Something you never seem to be as concerned about as you should. Others worry for you too, you know. You would do well to acknowledge that."

Her rephrasing instantly sends a stab of guilt through me. "I'm sorry," I admit, turning my eyes down. "I'm just worried for him." Outside, the southern lights have begun their evening dance, painting the sky in ribbons of turquoise and white. "Hann isn't going to forget about him. He's probably got his men investigating the power outage I triggered down in the Undercity. He's not going to let Eden go that easily, not when he seemed fascinated enough to come out of hiding to see him race."

June shakes her head. "Eden hasn't changed at all, has he?" she says quietly.

At that, a smile sneaks onto the corner of my lips. "It's the best and worst thing about him. He does things that shake entire structures of society. He finds himself at the center of everything, without ever trying to do anything other than help someone. Sometimes I wonder what John would think if he were still here, how proud he'd be of his kid brother." I grimace a little. "I just wish it wasn't always something that could get the damn kid killed. Sometimes it's noble. Sometimes it's just stupid. It's a fine line."

June smiles gently at me. "Noble. Sometimes stupidly so. At the center of everything because he's always trying to help someone. It sounds to me like he takes after someone I know."

I grin a little at that. "I did what I had to do."

"You do what you believe is right. Always. And doing what's right tends to be hard."

I look at her. "You aren't exactly a conformer yourself, Ms. Iparis," I say, turning to face her directly now. "I think the Republic has a few things to say about that."

She smiles again and looks away from me to the view beyond the window. I know she's thinking about her brother now. "The Republic's changing slower than I would like. Anden's doing his best, but the politics of it all makes me impatient." She runs an idle hand through her hair, and the gesture reminds me of another forgotten memory, of her fingers through her shining ponytail, the hair hanging long past her shoulders.

My thoughts return to her life, and how she has learned to steady it. I clear my throat awkwardly and stare down at my hands.

"Hey," I say quietly. "Can I ask . . . what made you and Anden decide to end things?"

June's quiet, and for a moment I think I've overstepped. But then a faraway look crosses her face. "I don't know how it gradually fell apart," she finally replies. "But there was one early morning that changed everything. I remember it because the light coming in through the window was so beautiful, the purest light I'd ever seen, just painting a golden stripe against my arm." She smiles a little at that. "I got up, walked to the window, and admired the most stunning dawn I'd seen in a while. And you know what? All I could think about was that I didn't want to share that moment with him, because I didn't think we would be admiring the same thing. And then I wondered whether that was strange, to not want the person I loved to be beside me." She looks down. "I think both of us already knew, though. I moved out pretty soon after that."

I don't really know what to say. All I can think about is that I would've given anything to share a moment like that with her. But I don't tell her that. "I'm sorry it didn't work out," I finally answer.

She gives me a wry smile. "Hopefully not too sorry, though."

Her words send a ribbon of wild hope through my veins. I laugh in embarrassment, afraid to think about the possibilities between us. "Okay, fine—not that sorry. But I'm glad you're both still friends. You're the one who pushes him forward, anyway. He'll always take your advice. You can see it in the way he's always turned toward you, waiting for your opinion."

"Yeah, well," she replies, "my advice isn't worth much if we can't act on any of it. He's doing his best." We're quiet for a few seconds.

"Even after everything we've gone through," she adds, "after all the war we've both seen, there are still so many things wrong. The work never really ends, does it? It just shifts to something else."

My gaze wanders to the glow of the city against her skin, to the soft waves in her hair, to her dark eyes. "Maybe," I say softly. "But there are constants to anchor ourselves to." I hesitate, almost too afraid to say it. "And you are mine."

We're very close now. June blushes, and my heartbeat quickens. I can't remember whether I felt this exact way when we were young, whether moments like this felt like an electric current humming beside me. I can't imagine reacting any other way to her.

"Daniel," she whispers. "I . . ."

I hold my breath, wondering what she might say. Terrified to guess.

This is the moment when I'm going to close the distance between us again. When I'm going to kiss her, when she's going to pull me with her to her room.

But then I sense a slight hesitation from June. She holds back, afraid, pulling the string between us so taut that I can feel it ready to snap.

And I freeze. I clear my throat. I step away.

The air between us seems to sigh in disappointment. All I can hear is the conversation we had that night when I saw her at the train station, about everything that had happened to us in the past.

Are we ready? Is *she*?

I don't know if this can ever last. I don't know if I am the catalyst for all that might unravel in her life, the one who might end the normalcy she's earned for herself. I don't know if we are meant to be.

Maybe she's thinking the same.

June speaks first. "I have to check on the Elector," she says. "He must be heading back from the gala soon."

I nod, looking down. "Of course," I reply. "I better get back too, to do the same with Eden."

The electric tension still hovers in the air, but there is too much space between us now. So I give her a smile and a bow, then turn around and head out of her apartment.

# EDEN

THAT NIGHT, AS I HEAD INTO THE KOMODO CLUB with Pressa, my thoughts still linger on the replay of my memories at the AIS headquarters. Pressa tugs on my hand, leading me deeper into the chaotic space. But even the flashing lights and pounding music can't quite drown out my thoughts.

Maybe Daniel's right. It's possible that someone like Dominic Hann would cut deals like mine with lots of people. Maybe if I stay away from the Undercity, he'll shrug off our encounter and just be content with the rounds I'd won him during the drone race.

The AIS director's words echo in my mind. *You are the closest thing we have to a lead.*

I might be their best chance at capturing Dominic Hann. Daniel himself has been hunting the man for months. If I stay away from the entire situation, my brother will keep heading into the Undercity. He'll keep putting himself in danger until he gets him. Didn't he go deep into the same drone race pit that I was in? How many more situations like that before his luck runs out? Will there be a day when he doesn't come home?

*"Eden!"*

Pressa's voice cuts through the music and my thoughts. I blink and look down at her. She's holding a drink out at me, and her lips are pursed in concern. "Are you sure you want to be here?" she says. "We don't have to be at the club. Want to head to a diner instead?"

I shake my head and take the drink from her. "No, I'm fine," I shout back. "Let's stay." I take her hand in mine and lead her closer to the stage.

If we weren't hooked up to the Level system, there'd be no one onstage. But with our systems running, we can see virtual performers dancing up there, fantasies of people with wings hovering in midair, mermaids sitting on giant spinning hoops overhead, all surrounded by a ceiling of virtual ivy and swirling clouds. It's a mesmerizing scene.

I force myself to stare at it all until it seems to consume me. Everyone around me looks dressed up in some kind of virtual outfit. They're colorful, even grotesque, and I'm grateful for the distraction as I join Pressa in a dance to a feverish song.

Here, she always lets herself go. Now she flashes a smile at me as she twirls. "We're no longer in Ross City," she exclaims. "We're somewhere far away. I'm leaving the Undercity behind!"

I smile at her as she moves to the beat of the music, trying to sink into the fantasy with her. As we dance, she wraps her arms around my neck and I put my hands at her waist, pressing her close to me and feeling the thud of the music rush through us.

She tilts her head at me so that her bobbed hair falls in a sheet against her chin. "You're looking for something," she says, pulling me close enough to shout in my ear. "I can tell. What's on your mind?"

I haven't told her yet about my talk with the AIS. Instead, I just shake my head. "The race," I reply, my words almost lost over the beat. "And who was sponsoring it."

I half expect her to laugh it off and tell me not to worry so much. But instead, Pressa nods, a thoughtful frown on her face. "Keep this identity on whenever you leave the Sky Floors," she finally tells me. She nods to the fake name and Level hovering over my head. "I've crossed paths with men like that before. They don't play around, but I don't think you've done enough to warrant them going after you. It might not be worth their while."

I can't tell if she really believes everything she's saying. But it's similar enough to what Daniel had told me that I feel a pinch of relief. I nod. "Right. Not worth their while," I repeat, trying to take comfort in it.

She gives me a smile and goes back to dancing to the rhythm. "Try to relax tonight, all right?" She pats my shoulder. "You've graduated! Soon you'll be off to the Republic!"

Maybe it's my imagination, but I see a flash of sadness cross her face even as she exclaims it. *Soon you'll be off to the Republic!* And Pressa will stay behind here, trapped in the Undercity. A pang twists my heart at the thought, and suddenly I'm very aware of how close we are. Her hair, smooth as silk, brushes the skin on my arm.

"Not *that* soon," I shout back, trying to sound nonchalant about her answer. Trying to ignore the flutter that she's started in my chest.

Pressa brightens a little at that, and the spark in her eyes is enough to make me forget that maybe our friendship won't last forever.

In the mess of wildly dressed dancers, I see a shadowy figure. It looks straight at me before it vanishes again into the throngs.

I slow in my steps and frown, then rub my eyes. Neon colors swirl around me in a haze. Am I seeing things now? I shake my head, then smile at Pressa and go back to dancing.

A few minutes pass. Then the shadow appears again.

This time it's closer, and off to my left, but it's distinctly the silhouette of a man, gaze pointed straight at me.

I freeze and whirl to face him. It's there for another moment, long enough for me to catch my breath and nudge Pressa. I point in its direction. "You see that?" I gasp out.

"What?" Pressa looks toward where I'm pointing—right at the moment the figure disappears into the crowd again. "The dancers at the edge of the stage? Those are real people, not virtual figures. I hear if you want to go up there, you have to—"

"No. There was a shadow standing there." I blink several times, as if the figure will reappear. "It was a man looking right at me. I saw him over on my right earlier." I whirl in place again, scanning the crowd.

Pressa tenses too, sensing the change in my energy. But there's nothing to show her now. Everyone around us is still in the throes of the beat, laughing and shouting and pumping their fists in the air. No sign of a mysterious figure.

I rub my eyes. "Never mind," I mutter. Pressa leans closer to me with a concerned look. I just try to give her a grin. "I think I'm just exhausted from everything that's happened."

She looks unconvinced. To her credit, she looks across the crowd again, just in case she'd missed what I was talking about. Then she turns back to me and takes my arm. I try to take solace in the warmth of her touch. "Come on," she says. "Let's head to the lounge, cool off a bit."

I nod numbly and follow her off the dance floor. We jostle past bodies all around us as we head out of the main atrium and into a narrow side hall.

I do a double take as we pass the lines at the bathrooms. A figure in dark clothes is leaning against the wall, and as we go, I swear he turns his head to follow us, his gaze penetrating. I look directly toward him. But I just see a group of giggling girls and boys, trading some secret among themselves.

My heartbeat starts to quicken. Dominic Hann's men can be everywhere at once. He's murdered people in the Sky Floors before. What if he's here right now? Are they watching me?

But even as I think this, a part of me scoffs at how ridiculous it sounds. All I can remember is the genuine interest in his eyes and the charisma in his words. Hadn't he been so supportive of me? Why would he want me dead, if he seemed so interested in what I could make?

We reach the lounge. Pressa forces me to sit down, then grabs me a glass of water from the bar. "You look like you just witnessed a crime," she says as she hands me the glass. "Everything okay?"

I take the glass and don't stop drinking until the water's gone. My eyes scan the room, searching for a shadow. Maybe I'm too tired to be here. Maybe it's too much noise and too many people. "I think I need to go home," I whisper, my eyes darting from person to person.

Pressa nods. "Okay."

She gets up, and I follow her gratefully. The colors swirl around me, making me light-headed. Maybe the shadows are nothing but my own anxieties, or maybe I'm even lost in a nightmare. I've had dreams like this, where I'm stuck in dark hallways and trying in vain to find the exit. I keep looking for the shadows.

My thoughts keep lingering on them. *Dominic Hann's men*, the whisper goes in my head.

It's stupid. Why would he waste time following me around?

But as I stumble out of the club's exit with Pressa, I see one last glimpse of dark figures behind us. There are two of them, both silhouettes with hands in their pockets, and their eyes are trained on me.

Virtual figures, I tell myself. They're not real. I turn back around and hurry out with Pressa. But the sight haunts me, and I keep looking over my shoulder the entire way home, expecting to see them following close behind.

And even though I don't quite believe it, the nagging whisper in my head keeps talking to me.

*They're coming for your brother. They're coming for you.*

# DANIEL

BY THE TIME I RETURN TO MY APARTMENT, MY thoughts still swirling around what had—or hadn't—happened with June, Eden's still gone to who knows where. I step in through the doorway, expecting to hear the security system's usual announcement of my name.

But there's nothing.

I pause in the entryway, glance up at the speaker system, and then frown at the screen embedded against the entry hall. "System's rebooting again," I mutter, then flash my hand against the screen and watch as it lights up blue, resetting all of its features.

But something's off in the apartment. I look around again, warier this time. Everything seems like it's in its place; Eden's shoes are still clustered haphazardly near the doorway, and his dirty dishes are in the sink, left in a hurry as usual. Dim light spills across the floor.

But the place doesn't feel empty like it should. I step into the center of the living room, trying to pinpoint exactly what's bothering me. There's a hint of something foreign in the air—a faint cologne, maybe, or the scent of a mint that neither Eden nor I buy.

My eyes go to a shadow stretching behind me.

It's not the shadow of the kitchen counter.

Every hair rises on the back of my neck. *Someone's here.* I whirl around, but it's too late—there's a woman in a black suit standing in front of my door. For a split second, I think she's an AIS agent—but she's not recognizable, and she's not wearing our uniform. Another presence moves behind me.

I duck, managing to dodge out of one lunge for me—but then another set of arms catches mine, forcing them behind my back. How many people are in here? I bare my teeth, ready to spin around and attack. But a damp cloth is shoved over my mouth. The overwhelming smell of chloroform invades my senses.

I fight wildly to escape it, but whoever's holding me is easily double my size. Before me stands a figure blurred by my motions. I recognize the neat trim of his beard and the tint of his glasses. He smiles at me.

"Daniel Altan Wing," he says. "Well. I'm really going to cause a stir in the city this time."

It's Dominic Hann.

*Eden. Where is he?* But my senses are already starting to cloud over. My movements turn more labored. The lingering, relentless stench of chloroform triggers some old memory this time of the Republic's labs, and I feel a sudden rush of panic—I'm ten years old and back at the Trials again, have failed again, and the soldiers are putting me under, cutting open my knee and injecting poisons into my eye, leaving me for dead. I am going to wake in a pile of corpses. The panic surges through me.

*No. I'm not going back to that.*

But I can't fight out of this darkness. The world closes in around me.

In a last, desperate act, I bring up June's account in my view. Then I message her. I don't even get a chance to say anything—all I get to send her is an empty few seconds of static.

We aren't what we used to be, but we know each other enough to sense when something's gone wrong.

It's all I have the strength to do. The last thing I see is the silhouette of Dominic Hann standing over me, giving a command to his men.

Then the darkness settles in, and I don't remember anything more.

# EDEN

DANIEL'S NOT ANSWERING MY CALL. NOT ONLY that, but the call doesn't go through to his account at all—I just get an automatic message telling me to try again later.

I frown as I head away from the nightclub and back home after parting ways with Pressa. It's a beautiful space, a walkway between two skyscrapers that's been transformed into a lush green landscape, full of roses and willow trees and vines that crawl over the side of the walkway's glass barriers to hang down to the floor below. Now in the middle of the night, it's quiet, with only the occasional late partier heading back home.

Maybe Daniel's still out with June. It would be the only reason why he's not returning my calls.

The only reason I want to think about, anyway.

The memory of the figures in the club is still fresh in my mind, along with Daniel's worried eyes and ominous warnings. Here, in the upper echelons of the city, it's hard to dwell on the fact that I'd just been in the Undercity days earlier, face-to-face with a notorious killer. It's so serene here. All I can hear is the trickle of water from a central fountain on the walkway.

*It's nothing*, I reassure myself. *Daniel's fine.* There had been a warning this morning, anyway, about a solar flare that might knock out transmissions for the next few days. Maybe service is just bad right now.

Another automated message comes onto my view right as I reach the elevator station that will take me back up to my floor, telling me again that Daniel's not available.

I pause, my eyes fixating on the glowing red outline of the hovering text box. It's true that Daniel's been on missions before that have required him to keep his system powered completely off . . . but he's always given me warnings about that in advance. And after our meeting at AIS yesterday, the timing on this seems off.

A knot tightens in my stomach. I don't know for sure, because an error message is hardly a reason to panic about something. But the knot is a familiar one. I remember it from childhood, from the nights when Daniel was still fighting his illness—of how I'd stir awake to see a blurry image of him hunched on the edge of his bed, his face pointed down at the floor and his lips tightened into a wince.

And even though a part of me keeps repeating *Solar Flare Interference* and *AIS Business* to myself, the knot still feels the same.

Something's wrong. I know it without confirmation, without hearing Daniel saying it to me.

I bring the error message back up. "You better have a good reason for this," I mutter at the message under my breath. With a sigh, I try to shake off my growing sense of unease.

The elevator station is empty tonight, and for the first time in a while, I'm the only one heading up fifteen stories to my floor. The music playing in the lobby echoes against the empty floor. I swallow, the knot in my stomach twisting into something painful.

It's going to be okay, I tell myself as the door finally slides open and I step in. My thoughts whirl as the elevator rises silently. Daniel's going to be at home, and he's going to be wearing that annoyed expression he always gets as he asks me why his messages weren't getting through to me.

Then, abruptly, the elevator stops ten floors shy of mine—and a man and a woman in suits step inside.

I stiffen immediately. Both of them are looking at me.

"Do you need something?" I ask.

The woman gives me a terse smile. "You're Eden Bataar Wing, yes?" she asks.

I realize I don't have my name displayed over my head right now. "How do you know?" I reply.

The man gives me a nod so courteous that it seems mocking. "A pleasure," he says. "My employer, Mr. Hann, would very much like to extend a cordial invitation to you for a meeting with him tonight."

Mr. Hann. Dominic.

The name hits me like a hammer, and the wind is knocked out of me so hard that for a moment I can't respond to him. The knot pulls tighter. *Something is wrong something is wrong something is wrong.*

"I—" I start, then stutter to a halt from the dryness in my throat. "I can't make it tonight," I try again.

The woman smiles at me and puts a hand on my shoulder. It feels ice-cold. "Mr. Hann would very much like to make it worth your while," she replies.

I'm trembling now. Through the elevator's glass windows, the walkway to my university disappears far below me. I shake my head, wishing I could come up with a clever reply. "I'm sorry," I say instead. "I have some homework to finish up, and I need to work on an engine—"

The man doesn't wait for me to finish repeating my pitiful lie. He waves a hand subtly in the air, and suddenly a video screen appears between us.

It's a feed of someone following Daniel as he leaves a hotel room. June's, most likely. The video trails him down through the Sky Floors as he takes the elevators, his hands casually in his pockets, his silhouette familiar. There's a small, lingering smile on his face. He has no idea someone is watching him.

Every hair rises on my neck at the sight.

Daniel steps inside our apartment. The alarm system doesn't greet him in its usual way. The door starts to slide shut behind him, but the video feed follows him in. Whoever it was that was trailing him got into our apartment.

The feed cuts off.

As if on cue, I get an incoming call from June that appears in my view. When I don't answer, her voice starts playing automatically. "Eden," she says. "This is June Iparis. I just received a blank transmission from Daniel, and I can't seem to call him back. Is he with you? Where are you? Eden?"

The knot in my stomach turns to stone. The world around me hazes at the edges. The echo of *Something is wrong* fills my mind until I can hear nothing but its shrieks. All this time, my brother had been the one worrying about *me*, and I'd been stupid enough to believe that that meant he was invincible. All this time, I'd never thought about what might happen if things were the other way around.

"Mr. Hann would like to insist on seeing you tonight," the man says to me now. "You'll be very pleased to know that your brother will also be in attendance."

# DANIEL

**I'M BACK ON THE STREETS OF LAKE. I DON'T KNOW** how the hell I got here.

My boots splash in dirty puddles as I hurry down the familiar roads near my old home. The metal of my artificial leg feels so cold that I think it's encased in ice. All the homes on this path are boarded up, their doors sprayed with red Xs, and the silence roars in my ears. My lips part and I try to call out for someone, anyone—but when I try to utter a sound, nothing comes out. It's as if the world had been muted.

*Daniel!*

Except there's a familiar voice. I whirl instinctively in its direction to see a line of Republic soldiers standing along the end of the street, barricading it. Behind them, struggling to get to me, is my older brother, John.

Overhead, along the horizon, the ominous black silhouette of a Colonies airship approaches, and with it comes a field of distant screams, like a swarm of locusts rushing in my direction. The ground in the distance is obscured with dust. John is trying in vain to break through to me, and I am pushing through thick air as I struggle to run toward him.

He reaches his hand out; I do the same. Just a little farther . . .

And then the distant screams draw close, and suddenly we are engulfed in a dust storm, shrieks whistling all around us. A bright light overhead grows steadily brighter until it makes me squint. I call out John's name over and over, but he doesn't answer. It's too late to save him—but where's Eden? I have to—

I jerk awake, trembling, sweat trickling down my forehead.

The light overhead turns into a blinding lamp. I blink away tears in my eyes as the world gradually sharpens, my dream turning blurry around the edges. Already I'm having trouble remembering what I saw, but John's outstretched hand, his blue eyes mirroring mine, remains clear.

It's been a long time since I've dreamed about the Republic like this.

The next thing I realize is the throbbing of a dull headache. My limbs feel sore and bound. My gasps are muffled behind a tight gag, and as I become more aware of my surroundings, I realize that I'm tied firmly to a chair. The chamber around me is luxurious in its sparseness—thick, monochrome rugs and clean-cut sofas, the wallpaper a minimalistic gray and white.

It takes me a moment to pinpoint exactly what's off about the room. There are no windows.

"About time," someone says, and I turn my head slightly, wincing, to see a man in a suit sitting on a couch beside me. There are others stationed near the chamber's door too.

The man tilts his head at me and speaks again. "He's awake now. What do you want us to do?" He's talking to a superior, I realize.

There's silence, followed by a few grunts of agreement from him and the nod of a head. Then he settles back against the couch to wait again.

"Mr. Hann thought we might've given you too much chloroform," he says to me. "Good thing you pulled through, saved us all a load of trouble."

*Dominic Hann.*

Eden. Have they taken him too? A rush of terror courses through me at the thought, and suddenly the gag feels like too much, and there's not enough air in the world for me to breathe.

*Calm down,* I tell myself firmly. They had wanted Eden. It's probably the entire reason why I'm here. And if they have me as collateral, it means Eden is alive and likely unharmed, if possibly held against his will.

*Alive. Unharmed.* It's all I want to know.

I stare at the man for a while before studying the room again. There's no obvious clue of where exactly we are, and as expected, my system has been powered off, with nothing but a warning blipping in the corner of my view. Wherever this place is, it's nowhere I can connect online.

One of the others near the door leans back from the wall and strolls over to me. She looks bored. "How long do we have to stay down here?" she mutters as she reaches me and bends over to inspect my face. "I didn't sign up to be a babysitter."

"You'll stay until you're told otherwise," the man replies in exasperation.

She smiles slightly at me. I glare back at her. "So this is the world-famous Day," she muses. "He's even younger than I thought."

Then she directs her words at me. "You don't look like you've lived through a war, kid."

Too bad this goddy gag is in my mouth, or I'd be able to answer her. Instead, I meet her gaze steadily until it seems to unnerve her. She shoves my chin away so roughly that I have to catch myself to keep the chair from tipping over.

"What the hell are you looking at?" she snaps, then straightens and crosses her arms.

Behind her, one of the other women by the door sighs. "Leave him alone," she says. "We're not supposed to touch him."

"Or what? He was staring at me." The first woman scowls.

"Just wait until the others head down to get us, all right?" the man on the couch says with a sigh. "It's not like he's going to do anything or get anywhere like this."

Head down. We're probably somewhere in the Undercity. My head pulses with pain again, and I wince, my thoughts scattering. *Leaning against the wall at midnight, being wheeled down a hospital corridor in a gurney, collapsing to the floor of a train.* Bright fragments of memories come back to me now, along with a phantom pain of what I'd once gone through.

I'm suddenly filled with a rush of anger. I did not live through a revolution and take my brother all the way to Antarctica to be strapped down by some stupid mob boss who somehow thinks he's important. I did not come here to be intimidated by a bunch of trigger-happy trots.

*The AIS's communication system.* If I can get close enough to one of the guards, I can try to tether my system to theirs, get a connection going—if only for a second. Had June received my last message?

I have a vague memory of trying to send her a call with nothing but a few seconds of static, but I can't be sure it ever reached her. Or if she knows that it means I'm in trouble.

I jerk hard against my bonds. The chair clatters forward, scraping against the tiles.

To my satisfaction, all my guards startle at my movement. I smile a little behind my gag. Haven't lost my touch yet.

"Stay still," the man on the couch orders me, his frown deepening. He looks reluctant to come to me, though, and his hesitation just makes me more reckless.

*Or you'll do what?* They can't kill me if I'm supposed to be collateral. They need Eden to stay compliant and do what the boss says. So I push harder and bang my chair loudly against the floor. My hands wring behind my back.

"Damn it all," the man hisses between his teeth as he finally gets up and walks toward me. He smacks me once in the face and then grips my chin hard. "Stay still, unless you want your fingers to go missing one by one."

Idle threats. I stare fiercely back at him. In his eyes, I can see that what he'd said earlier is true. Hann had instructed them not to touch me, and it bothers this man right now to be forced to discipline me.

*Link.*

I send out the command on my system with my mind, and it catches his nearby account. A loading circle spins in my view. *Attempting to connect*, it says.

The man shoves me roughly back away from him. The connection attempt stalls.

I pretend to choke on my gag, coughing uncontrollably. At first the man laughs, smug at the thought of my suffering—but when I keep going, putting on a show of struggling to breathe, his smile wavers a bit. One of the women nods at him.

"Readjust his gag, for chrissakes," she calls out. "Don't want him choking to death."

The man grimaces but does as she says. He comes over, pauses in front of me, and unties the gag from my mouth.

I instantly lash out at him. My teeth close down hard on one of his fingers.

He lets out a yell and shoves me back so hard that I topple over with my chair. My body hits the ground with a painful thud and my head rings from the impact. The coppery taste of blood lingers on my tongue. Above me, the man stalks around in a circle, swearing up a storm, his hand cradling his bleeding finger. In rage, he spins around and kicks me hard in the stomach.

It knocks all the wind out of me. I gasp, my eyes widening at the blow.

"Goddamn little AIS shits," the man shouts down at me, spitting once on my face as the woman hurries over to force the gag back on over my mouth. Behind her, the man snaps his fingers impatiently, shouting for servants to come clean up the spots of blood on the rug.

I just squeeze my eyes shut and act like I can't hear anything he's saying, because at that moment my connection starts up again.

*Link successful.*

The warning in the bottom of my view disappears, replaced with a glowing green circle. I'm online.

"Tell Hann to hurry the hell up so we can move him," the man barks as he wraps his finger in gauze. "I have better things to do."

This link won't hold for long. I don't waste another second. As I lie on the floor, I think a command to my system. *Location.*

My system can't seem to pinpoint my exact area, but it does give a general read for where it thinks my signal is coming from, and a map appears, displaying a top-down view of the south side of Ross City.

*Send to AIS,* I think.

The system sends the map. The upload speed down here is slow, and the progress bar inches along.

But before the message can finish sending, the man steps far enough away from me to sever our link. Everything in my display vanishes again, replaced by the blinking red warning.

*Damn it.*

The first woman yanks my chair back upright and shoves me against the wall. My curled hands hit the wall wrong, and I let out a muffled gasp as the ring finger of my right hand breaks. Searing pain lances up my arm.

She hears the snap of my bone, then smiles at the pain on my face. With a toss of her hair, she leans down and bends so close to me that our faces nearly touch. "Next time, that finger's coming off," she murmurs.

I keep my eyes down until she steps away. Behind her, the man I'd bitten is impatiently waving in a couple of servants dragging buckets of soapy water and brushes to wash my blood off the rugs. They look scared.

Then the guard who I'd bitten hits me across the face again, this time hard enough to send my head slamming into the wall.

Everything goes dark.

# EDEN

**THEY LEAD ME INTO A PRIVATE ELEVATOR STATION.**
Then they blindfold me.

I tremble in the familiar darkness. Their hands firmly on my arms, their low voices, the faint lurching of the elevator—every bit of it feels like the Republic again, those terrifying moments when I would lie inside a glass cylinder, rocking along with the train car, unsure where they were taking me. I couldn't see anything. The world looked like nothing but a blur of strange shapes.

I've never spoken to my brother about those days when we were first separated. There's too much to say, and it all bleeds together into one continual nightmare. Screaming at the searing pain of injections. Lying exhausted in a pool of my own vomit. Shaking uncontrollably from fever. Feeling like my body was on fire, like I would die. Shrinking away from horrifying hallucinations. Feeling cold, stiff corpses lying beside me. Being moved over and over again, without being able to see.

In the first years after it all ended, I was a child who could push it away. But the darkness of those moments have clawed back year after year into my dreams. And now I have returned to that same place, reliving the nightmare of being forced into the dark.

*My brother.* The image of his unconscious face, his closed eyes, and gagged mouth haunts my vision. The thought of where he might be now is almost more than I can bear.

I can't tell how long we stay in the elevator. Too long. Then their hands are gripping my arms again, and I stumble out with them. They shove me onto a seat, and a moment later we're moving again, this time forward instead of down.

Finally, after an eternity, we stop. They shove me out roughly and sit me down onto what feels like a couch of some kind. The darkness over my eyes shifts as one of them unties the knot at the back of my blindfold.

They lift it away. I squint in the sudden light.

I'm in a luxurious living room that looks like it's part of an estate, except that there are no windows. The couch I'm sitting on—all the furniture in the room, actually—is severe in its elegance, all clean, rectangular lines and muted colors. The lights embedded in the ceilings fill the room with a cooling glow.

And standing before me is Dominic Hann himself, dressed in a tailored shirt and trousers. He smiles as my eyes meet his.

"Eden Bataar Wing," he remarks, scrutinizing me. His voice is as rough and grainy as I remember, as if he suffers from some kind of chest infection. "Your brother has quite the reputation."

Always known in relation to Daniel, even down here. I narrow my eyes at him and clench my teeth. "What have you done with him?"

"He's safe. I didn't bring you here to terrify you, although I've been told it's a bad habit of mine." Hann steps toward me, and that's the first moment when I realize that he isn't *physically* in the room with me. His figure is slightly translucent, and as he moves, I see his shoes pass through the thick surface of the rugs.

*Too afraid to be in the same place as your guards?* I want to say archly to him, but the thought of Daniel captured somewhere here keeps my retort at bay. Instead, I say, "And what's the point of all this?"

He pauses beside me and sits down on the couch, as much as a hologram can sit. I can see the cushions through his body. He coughs forcefully enough that his shoulders hunch from the force. When one of his guards gives him a questioning look, he waves her away with an impatient hand.

"You're a Sky Floor citizen," he begins when he's cleared his throat enough. "There are few in this country who can enjoy a more luxurious lifestyle than yours. And yet there you were, in the Undercity, risking your level and your reputation in order to enter a drone race." He looks sidelong at me. "What brought you down there?"

I can't help the sarcasm that rises now in my voice. "You went to all this trouble just to ask me why I was down in the Undercity?"

Hann smiles. A couple of his guards smile along with him, and when he laughs, so do they. "There's a spark in you," he says, genuine fondness in his voice. "You're made for our world down here. I don't attend Undercity events. I haven't watched a drone race in years. There's no reason for me to show my face and risk my own safety for an event that my guys are going to bet on for me anyway. So why do you think I showed up after one of them told me about you?"

"My drone," I answer without hesitation.

He nods, pleased, and some small part of me feels oddly complimented by that. "You told me you built all of that yourself."

"Where are you going with this?" My anger is starting to triumph over my fear. "Are you going to tell me what you want or not? Where's my brother?"

Hann leans back in ease and ignores my questions. "I looked up your files. Seems like you're a star student at Ross University. And yet, here you are, coming down to the Undercity week after week. That's not the typical behavior of a Sky Floor kid with their entire future ahead of them."

"You didn't bring me here to be my therapist."

At that, Hann laughs. His guards join in. "No, I didn't. I brought you here because I think you are the kind of talent that I see only once in a generation."

"Show me my brother," I demand. "Then we can talk."

"Rest assured, he is safe, and I will do you the favor of keeping him that way." He leans forward to rest his elbows on his knees, then regards me with a piercing gaze. "But this is not about him. I'm not interested in your brother. This is about you."

His words are hitting some part of me that yearns to hear it. *This is not about him.* If Hann is trying to manipulate me, he's going to be smart about it, I warn myself. He understands exactly what my weak points are.

Where is Daniel? What has Hann done to him?

The man frowns at my expression. "You're not used to hearing that, are you? That you're the focus?" He rises from the couch. His hoarse voice is oddly gentle, with that same warmth that had drawn me in when I first met him. "Come with me, please."

As he steps out of the room, he snaps his fingers once without looking back at me. At first, I think his guards will drag me up and force me forward—but instead they bow as they approach me, then nod for me to follow Hann out of the room. I hesitate, afraid, but then start walking.

We head out of the room and down a narrow hallway. As we make several turns, the clean walls and elegant corridors vanish, making way for a smooth concrete floor and steel walls and ceilings. Here, they usher me into what looks like a train inside a tunnel.

This must have all been salvaged and renovated from an old, abandoned part of the Undercity.

We ride in silence for a few minutes before the train comes to a gentle halt. Then we step out into a hall that opens up into a vast, cavernous space.

I balk at the sheer size of it. It looks like a factory filled with halls of identical machines, each of them blinking blue in unison. There must be millions and millions of them, and when they're all stacked together like this, they look dizzying. Overhead, sheets of cold white lights shine down on the building.

Giant vents run along the ceiling, and tall steel beams tower up in rows. In the center of the room, though, is a large, circular structure that looks like some strange combination of steel and glass and . . . twisted, fractal mesh. Like something halfway between machinelike and organic. It has a soft blue glow about it. Surrounding it are metal supports, and in the center is a large, circular platform where several workers now stand. The platform's floor changes to a smooth, dark metal, and my boots clank against the new surface as I step onto it. A couple of the workers look up to see us enter.

"You are getting exclusive access here, Eden," Hann says to me as he strides toward the structure. "This is a world-class engine I'm building, so I suppose you could say we have similar interests."

"What does it do?" I find myself asking, momentarily over-whelmed by it and resenting my own curiosity.

"You answer none of my questions, and you expect me to tell you anything?" He smiles at me. "The drone you built for that race, it had a perpetual engine?"

I look at him. "Close, yes," I reply, surprised that he knows. "It's powered by a combination of tech and biology."

"The microorganisms in it feed off the heat that the initial engine blasts generates, and create more energy of their own." Hann nods. "I recognized the glow that your engine was giving off. Now, I know you are planning to head back to the Republic of America and begin an internship there." He shakes his head. "But I think it's a waste of your talent. Stay here, and you'll find yourself designing much more interesting things than hospitals and museums."

I bristle at his backhanded compliment. "I don't consider it a waste of time."

Hann gives me a crooked smile. "I had to fight my way to where I am today. I knew my worth, that I was destined for more than just staying on the lowest rungs, running errands for someone else. You're destined for more too. How about you apply that skill of yours to working for me?"

I stare at him incredulously. His machine looms beside us, its light casting a faint glow against my skin but not against his hologram. "You're offering me a *job*?"

"I never shaft my talent, Eden. You'll be paid handsomely. More than anyone in the Republic would offer you, I can guarantee it. Any-one you love and care for will be taken care of."

"Like how you're taking care of my brother right now? Like how you had your guys show me a video of someone following him home?"

He shakes his head. "My methods are unconventional. It's a result of the world I operate in. But I'm not interested in hurting your brother, Eden. What good would that do me, when I'm trying to earn your trust? Cooperate with me, and your brother will be released unharmed, with no knowledge of where he was held, and he and the AIS can go back to hunting me like they always do."

*If you lure Hann out into a space where our agents are ready for him, we can take him down before he can escape.*

The AIS director's words come back to me now, haunting in their premonition. I'd refused to do it, but now the choice has been taken out of my hands. Now I'm down here, and my brother is in real danger, with no promise that AIS will be able to find him in time should I refuse or displease Hann.

I turn my head back to the towering machine, to its soft glow. On a small scale, my engine was able to turn the drone into one of the fastest racers I've ever seen. What is this engine for? What is Hann planning to do with it?

At this very moment, Daniel is somewhere down here, wondering whether I'm still alive.

Hann sighs when he sees my hesitation. "When I was younger," he says, "I lived in the Undercity with my family. My mother once sent me on an errand to buy groceries in a part of the Undercity far from our home. That's what happens to single-Level folks who don't qualify for the good stores, you see? We have only a few shops to choose from, and the only one with what we needed was on the other side of the city. I got lost on the way there, and ended up in an alley where I witnessed an attack.

"I hid behind a trash bin and watched several people holding down a man. His attackers all had knives. The man they held down was sobbing, apologizing for stealing a crate of canned food." Hann glances at me. My heartbeat quickens. "Do you know what they did to him?"

Is he telling me a story from his past, or is he threatening me? All I can see is the blurred edges of my vision, the sharpened focus on this criminal. All I can think about is the way I'd crouched beside my brother on the floor of our kitchen years ago, holding his hand as he fought through the pain in his head.

The way he'd screamed and collapsed. The way I'd shouted for an ambulance. The bright lights of the hospital.

Hann looks grave at my pale expression. "Some of us aren't born with the luxury of a good childhood. Isn't that right, Eden? Some of us know what it's like to carry a burden on our shoulders for the rest of our lives, something that no one can understand except those who have experienced it for themselves."

And in spite of everything, I find myself drawn to what he's saying, like he knows me from the inside out. I wonder what had happened to Hann in his past, and why he sounds like he has a chronic condition of the chest or the lungs. He looks so sharp and proper now. It's impossible to imagine him as a young boy hiding behind a trash bin.

"I'm not trying to hurt your brother," Hann says quietly to me now. "But I know talent when I see it, and I don't like wasting it. Your brother is only my way to you. You don't have to work for me forever.

If you don't like it, I swear that I will let you leave. And your brother will be unharmed."

In this moment, I am a small boy again, and every word Hann says brings me back to the dark years, and I hear John's shouts in my mind, I hear the shaking of my mother's voice, I am strapped down to the gurney and being taken away from my family. I am blind, helpless against the onslaught.

So I hold up my hands, and when I speak, my voice comes out quiet.

"Leave him alone," I hear myself say. "Don't hurt my brother."

Hann frowns at the tears blurring my vision. "And in return?"

"We can talk about what I can do for you. Just talk, no guarantees. All right?"

He doesn't answer at first. All he does is give me a steady smile. "A good start," he says.

# DANIEL

I CAN'T REMEMBER HOW MANY HOURS OR EVEN days might have passed. The lack of windows down here is disorienting, and a lack of water is making me weaker than I should be. Guards change rotation around me.

I don't know if it's because I'm just delirious now, but I find myself continuously thinking about June. This time it's a recent memory, of the night when Tess first set up a dinner between June and me.

I'd seen June walking toward me at a train station in Los Angeles, right after Eden had finished interviewing for his Batalla Hall internship. Eden and I had been in a good mood that day—he was chatting up a storm beside me, explaining all that he wanted to do, while I'd walked quietly and listened to him, grateful that we were walking down the streets of a peaceful Republic. Then I'd looked up and seen *her* heading toward us.

It'd been the briefest, most significant meeting of my life. A glance, a flash of a memory. Her dark eyes had locked for a second on mine, and I'd stopped in the middle of the path, overwhelmed by a sense of nostalgia. I'd looked back at her, and then decided on a whim to introduce myself to her.

June Iparis. A girl I'd loved for a long time. Someone who, despite the flaws in my memory, I'd managed to hang on to all those years.

That night, we sat down in a restaurant at the top of a newly constructed Republic building. Tess and Eden sat across from us. I sat next to June, trying to figure out what to say to her.

I asked her how Anden was doing. Word was that June had been in a long relationship with the young Elector, that they had even moved in together.

"We're not together anymore," she told me. There was a small smile on her lips as she said it, as if she was embarrassed to tell me. I didn't know what to make of it, but I knew to smile back.

"Ah," I tried to say. "I just got out of a relationship myself."

We spent the entire dinner stumbling through our words. Tess found it so entertaining that she kept throwing questions our way, forcing us to bring up specific memories from the past.

Afterward, we walked together in the late, quiet hours of the Ruby sector. The air had the clean chill that comes after a good rainstorm, and we steered carefully around the puddles that dotted the streets. June stayed a small distance away from me, and I did the same. We walked as if we'd just met each other. In a way, I guess we did.

When we finally reached her front door, I faced her with my hands in my pockets, trying to find a good way to say goodbye.

She gave me a small smile and tilted her head. "You're not staying in the Republic, then," she said. "You're heading back to Antarctica soon."

Everything in me wanted to ask her to come with me, so that I could show her the new city where I lived. But I held back because she held back. "Tomorrow morning," I answered. "Eden needs to finish his degree before he comes back here for his internship."

"Are you going to move back here with him?"

I shrugged. "I don't know yet. My work is in Ross City. But I'll come here, at least for a little while. I'd rather not leave Eden alone."

She nodded. "Don't worry. He'll have friends in town."

I smiled at her. "That's a relief," I replied, taking a step closer to her. She didn't pull away. She leaned toward me too, with such an earnest expression that it took everything in me not to kiss her right there and then.

I looked down. "I was wondering . . . ," I started to say. "Tess told me that when you came to the hospital ten years ago, to see me off to Antarctica, you didn't mention who you were. I didn't recognize you, either. It was the worst of my memory loss, that year."

June hesitated, her eyes far away for a moment, and then nodded. "That's true," she replied.

"Why'd you do that?" I shook my head. "Just thank me and walk away without telling me your real name? Why'd you let me go?"

June stayed quiet. Then she turned to me and said, "I once made a promise to myself that if it meant it would help you survive, I would never step back into your life." She smiled faintly. "And you did survive. So I kept that promise."

For me. She had done this, made this sacrifice, for her heart as well as mine. I closed my eyes for a second, overwhelmed by her gesture, and then looked at her again.

"Are you happy here, in the Republic?" I asked her.

She shrugged. A rare uncertainty came into her gaze. "Yes," she said after a pause. "We've had such a time together, haven't we? I still don't know what it all means. But you have your life in Ross City now. And I have mine here in the Republic. We're moving forward and leaving our past behind."

Up until that moment, I would have broken down at her feet and pulled her in for a kiss. I would have wrapped my arms around her and let myself fall madly back in love with her.

But her words pulled me up short. *You have your life in Ross City now. And I have mine here in the Republic.*

It was true. We were completely different people now, living completely separate lives. We had just sat through an entire dinner and barely managed to exchange a handful of sentences with each other. My memories of her were still so fragmented, a million broken shards of a once-intact window.

She had been the one to let me go.

Did she ever love me as fiercely as I loved her? How fiercely *had* I loved her?

I didn't know if she read the hesitation in my gaze first, or if she just reacted the same way I did. But she seemed to retreat from me then too. Her smile was guarded, as if she was also afraid of being hurt.

"Perhaps," she said, "we can find a way back into each other's lives. Perhaps we can be friends again."

Friends. It would be a start, at least.

I pulled back my desire to kiss her, the way I wanted to obsess over every detail of her—the darkness of her eyes, the curve of her lips, the thick length of her hair that I remembered running my fingers through. I pulled it all back and let it close, safeguarding those emotions for another time.

"Friends again," I said, nodding in agreement.

She smiled at me, genuinely smiled, and it brightened her face so much that I wanted to remember it forever. I stretched out a hand to her. She took it. We shook once before pulling each other into a farewell embrace.

"Travel safe tomorrow," she murmured to me.

I let her go reluctantly. "Tell me if you're ever in Ross City," I replied.

And I stepped away from her. I let her go this time. I turned my back and forced myself to walk away. It was our first night together after ten years apart. This was as large a step as we could possibly take. *Friends again.*

Maybe we could find our way back to that friendship space. Then, and only then, could we have a chance for more.

It would be another month before we saw each other again.

\* \* \*

The delirious memory came into focus and then faded away, focused and faded again, ceaseless and repetitive. I don't know how long it's been. Days? If they kept withholding water from me, I would die down here. Did June get my message? I don't know. My head lolls to one side as I dream of water, of rainstorms and summer pools and rivers.

*Your past is always a part of you,* June had said to me during our last conversation in her apartment. *Just as it is a part of me.*

I let her words play over and over in my thoughts. I think of how right it'd felt to be beside her. I think of her dark, steady eyes, her beautiful face. It clears my mind, forces me to think.

I'd spent ten years pushing that old part of me away, carefully boxing up every piece of it, every nightmare and horrible memory and moment of grief and hate and rage, had started here in Ross City as if we'd always been here. That I'd only ever been Daniel.

But June, as always, is right. Boxing that past away hasn't stopped it from creeping into my mind. And if I'm going to get out of here alive, if I'm going to get Eden out of this and pull him through his trauma, if I'm ever going to see June again, I need to remember that I'm still the boy from the streets. The boy who could raise hell.

That I'm Day.

# EDEN

**"I KNOW YOU'RE HUNGRY."**

I glare at Hann. I'm standing at the door to his Undercity estate's dining room, with two of his guards behind me. He's sitting at the opposite end of a round table, observing me with his hands tucked casually into his pockets.

I'd spent most of the afternoon at the construction site, helping them integrate my drone's engine into their own. The structure they're working with glowed a pulsing blue the entire time, casting its light against my skin. I can still see the rhythm of its color whenever I close my eyes.

The entire time, Hann had looked impressed with what I'd done.

Now he frowns at me as I stand swaying in the doorway. "Are you refusing to sit down because you're worried about your brother?"

"I mean, it's not like I've forgotten about him or anything," I reply, a little too sharply. "I've helped you as much as you wanted me to."

The man pauses to cough his heaving, sickly cough. Then he sighs and glances at the guards behind me. "Leave him here."

The two guards exchange an uncertain look with each other, but it's only for the briefest moment. Then they're bowing their heads in unison to their boss and stepping back. I hear the door close behind me, sealing me in with my kidnapper. The guards are probably standing watch on the other side now. I hadn't heard any footsteps echoing away from us.

Hann motions for me to take a seat at the table. "You'll do your brother no good by just standing there. Sit down, please. Eat something. You're going to need your strength, no matter what you do."

He acts like this is a completely normal day for him. How large is this underground estate? I try to remember the distance that I'd walked today, then guess at how much more space there might be down here. What if he's not keeping Daniel here at all, but at some other location?

When I still don't move, he gestures again toward the seat.

Behind me comes a faint knock on the door. I step aside as it swings open, this time letting in a cook bearing two silver trays. She hurries past me to the table, places the trays at each of our place settings, and then bows to Hann like all the others. She doesn't even bother looking at me as she steps out of the room.

Whatever the food is, it smells delicious. My stomach rumbles in spite of itself. I hesitate a while longer. Then I finally walk over to the table and slowly lower myself into the second chair.

Hann lifts the cover off of his own tray. "I've been told you're a vegetarian," Hann says. "Your dish has been adjusted to your tastes."

His words send a chill through me. *How does he know that?*

"Thanks," I mutter, the word thick with sarcasm.

"I can tell you're no stranger to tense situations," he says. "I'm guessing that's from your days back in the Republic."

I watch him as he lifts a forkful of steaming fish to his lips. "I had my share of moments," I finally reply.

He looks up briefly at me from his meal. "I can respect that. News about what was happening in the Republic back then was sparse, but I followed it. It was a worthy cause, what you and your brother fought for."

I narrow my eyes at him. He's baiting me, praising my brother while he keeps him locked up in some other room. "What does someone like you know about what we went through?" I say.

"Your family survived based on the whim of your government. Isn't that true? Your brother was someone like me. An underdog. A rebel. A wanted criminal. I understand, more than you know, what it means to be under the authority's thumb."

"Except my brother fought for the people," I reply. "And as far as I know, you sound like you take advantage of those down here in the Undercity."

He doesn't look offended by my words. Instead, he bows his head and smiles grimly. "I *am* one of those down here in the Undercity," he replies. "What happens down here has directly affected me all of my life."

"What do you mean?"

"I don't think I've been very fair to you," he says. "You are, understandably, worried about your brother. And while you've told me many things about yourself, you still don't know much about me. So I'm going to make a deal with you."

"What kind of deal?" I mutter.

He puts his fork down and laces his fingers together, then gives me a steady look. "I'm going to let your brother go," he says. "If you finish helping me install your engine on our machine."

I wasn't expecting him to say *that*. "You're what?" I blurt out.

"I'm going to let him go," he repeats. "I told you that none of this was about him, and that my only interest in him was to find a way to get to you." He holds a hand out at me. "But here you are. You've demonstrated your talent already by what you've done here." He leans back in his chair. "So I'm going to do what I promised myself I would. I'm going to release him."

He must be lying to me. It doesn't make any sense for him to let Daniel go, not when he could keep using my brother against me. "How can I even trust that you'd do such a thing?" I ask.

He nods. "Because I'll show you," he replies. "I'll send you a live feed of him being released."

I shake my head, confused and wary. "I don't understand."

Hann sighs, then leans against his armrest and regards me carefully. When he speaks again, there's a strange tinge of sadness in his voice. "You remind me very much of my son."

"Your son?" I ask.

"Like I said. You've offered so much about yourself. It's only fair that I now tell you a bit about me. It's the only way we'll build trust around each other." He regards my question. "So let me enlighten you about where I came from."

Everything about him now—his grave expression, the sudden exhaustion in his eyes, the weight on his shoulders—seems serious, and instinctively, I feel myself leaning forward to listen.

"I grew up down here," he says. "In the Undercity, just like your friend Pressa. My mother and father worked a tiny stall in the markets, selling fried skewers. I remember running in the dirty streets, just like you, weaving through the crowds at the markets, helping my parents until the late hours of the night. Like you and your brother, I grew up learning how to fill the holes in my pockets with things I could steal from others. I had to, you see. We could barely feed ourselves."

Something strange clicks in my mind. For an instant, I see John circling before me, as tall and rumpled as I remember, his hands burned from his factory shift. He slaps a stolen coin from my hands and kicks the money into the gutter. *Don't ever do that again*, he scolds me. *The next time, that money will come with street police at our door. It's never worth it.*

I shake the memory away, my stomach churning uneasily. My eyes dart for a second to the corridor behind us, where two guards stand now, and then go back to him.

"I married into the Undercity too, you know," he continues. "I loved my wife, and we had a son that mattered more to us than anything else in the world."

*Loved. Had.* The mention of his son again.

"Except he got sick." His eyes flatten at that. The rasp in his voice trembles. "So did I. It was a common side effect in our neighborhood, located so close to the factories on the outskirts of the city. The smoke from the factories turned my son's lungs black and shriveled. His grades fell in school, and his Level fell because of that. I began to cough blood." He pats his throat once. "The infection in my lungs cost me my job. That lowered my Level further. They punish you for not working, you know. This government. And the lower my Level fell, the harder it became for me to qualify for work."

There's a brief silence from him. "So my wife took out a loan with the illegal businesses that run down here, made a deal with them in order to pay for our son's illness. She agreed to something we couldn't possibly pay back."

"What happened?" I whisper.

"I came home one day to find her body in our ransacked apartment."

His words make my chest tighten. He says it so calmly and quietly that I can tell it's something he's used to saying. Suddenly I see the soldier—*Thomas, his name was Thomas*—lifting a rifle to my mother's head. John lunges in vain against the guards holding him back. June holds out a helpless hand in an attempt to stop him.

"They left a note, demanding payment by threatening our son. So I did the only thing I could. I offered to work for the gang, to pay off the debt." He's silent for a moment, the weight of it hanging between us in the air. "It didn't matter, in the end. My son died a couple of months later."

*He could be lying to you.* But I swallow hard, feeling sick at his story. There is nothing that feels false about these words.

"I don't blame the Undercity," Dominic Hann says, snapping me to the present again. "People are businessmen. They step in when no one else will. There's a need for services like illegal loans down here, for the people forgotten by your government." He points up at the ceiling. "No, I blame this entire damn system, the Levels and the floors and the hierarchy of this place that made it impossible for us to get out of our predicament. I blame the fact that the President sells the Undercity the dream that, if they only worked hard enough, they too could Level themselves up to the Sky Floors. I blame the fact that the dream is a fantasy."

It's as if he's having the exact same conversation I'd had with Daniel. The Undercity has no choice but to be the way it is. I find myself staring back at Hann with a confused look, trying to understand how a ruthless, notorious killer can make so much sense. Can grieve a family he had lost, just as I'd lost mine.

"Is it still true, though?" I manage to say at last. "The things you've done to people here? You killed that councilman the other night. You—" I swallow hard. "You've murdered Undercity citizens in the same way that your own family was murdered."

"You want to play a game?" he says coolly. "Play it down here, where there are no rules at all. Then it's fair. You do what you have to do to survive. Everyone knows what the game they're playing is. There are no unfulfilled promises, no special favors. It's just business here." His eyes harden. "*That*, I can work with."

I look for that taunting edge in his expression—but Dominic Hann looks genuine now, his eyes lit up in earnest as if trying to convince me of his words. And for an instant, I can see him rising up the ranks of this dangerous world, drawing people to him with nothing but his own resolve.

*Like Daniel.*

The thought is so startling that I shove it away in fright.

"And if someone doesn't want to work their way up like you?" I say through gritted teeth. Every hair on my skin feels like it's standing on end.

His cold ease has returned. "Few don't," he replies. "Why wouldn't they, when the system's decks are stacked against them anyway? Surely you, of all people, can understand that."

"Stop comparing me with you."

"Why not?" He leans toward me. "You're instinctively drawn to this place. This is where you feel at home, *down here,* where you can keep all those memories swirling in your head at bay."

I wince. In spite of everything, I find myself struggling to breathe, impressed that this criminal—this murderer—has figured out secrets about me that my own brother hasn't been able to understand. He knows me better than Daniel does. His words pierce straight through me, as if he could see the dreams that swallow me whole every night.

"You can't understand why your brother is no longer in the same place you are," Hann adds. "Hadn't he been just like me, made his entire reputation off fighting for the people? But he's left behind that dark place from his past. Now he works for the government, helping to enforce this system that's crushing us. Working to dismantle what people like me are trying to do."

He's trying to turn me against my brother, convincing me of something I've always disliked—his work for the AIS, his siding with this government that is crippling its people. And if he were saying this to someone else, maybe it would even work. I see Daniel's face, his worried expression. I think of the way he'd argued with the director, how he'd railed against this system. He doesn't support the Level system, either. But it doesn't matter. He still works for the AIS.

Hann sips from his glass. "So you see, Eden," he says as I hesitate, "I'm not trying to force you into anything. But what I *am* saying is that I think you're a better fit down here than you think. Even if you left—even if I let you go or you escaped . . . you'd come back. You belong here."

*You belong here.* A part of me wonders if this is what he tells everyone before he kills them. But another part of me . . . knows he's right. Because I *do* keep coming back.

"What is the machine that you're building, then?" I finally ask him. It's the question that has been waiting on the tip of my tongue. "What does that have to do with anything you've just told me? What exactly am I helping you to do?"

Hann gives me a pointed look. "Finish installing your engine today," he says, "and we can run a blank sample test. Then you can see for yourself."

*  *  *

When we head out after dinner to the construction site, there's no hint at all on Dominic Hann's face that he had revealed any weakness to me. Instead, he seems cool, almost cold. There's none of the weight and the anguish that he'd let me witness when he told me about what happened to his family. I wonder whether he's genuinely confiding in me.

"How much longer?" Hann asks me now as he walks over to where I'm working.

I look up at the structure. The new engine I've installed is mostly in place now, the new pieces expanding on top of the original drone engine I'd built so that it can conduct enough power for the whole machine. The rest of Hann's workers are already securing the final pieces.

I point at one end of the machine, the portion that's supposed to send some sort of signal out. It's all I've managed to puzzle out about what the whole thing does. "They're installing the last piece now," I say to Hann. "This signal needs to be amplified more than you thought if you plan on making it hit the entire city. So I needed to make sure it gets that boost."

Hann studies the engine I've made closely. "And this will work," he says, lifting an eyebrow at me.

I wish it didn't. But everything else about the machine was already in place. All it needed was enough of a power boost. And my engine has given him that.

My silence is the answer that he needs. He smiles in approval at me, then straightens. "I want to see a demonstration of it, then," he says. "Send out a blank sample of a signal."

Of course he wants to test it. I glance to where his guards are watching us, then back to the machine, where one of his workers comes over to start programming in a blank sample to test the signal.

"You look nervous, Eden," Hann says to me as I watch them work. "It's as if you don't believe in the capabilities of your engine."

"It works," I reply, but there's a slight tremble in my voice. Is he really going to free Daniel if this works? I think back to everything Hann had told me about himself. If I fail at this, will Hann kill me? It's all part of his business, after all.

We wait until the programmer has finished inputting a sample signal. It's fast, the work of a moment. I watch carefully as he does it, observing the chip he places on the machine and then the info he swipes right onto the system. He steps away from the machine, then nods at us.

"Ready," he says.

Hann nods. "Good." We all take a step back from the machine. "Send the signal out."

The machine's coil begins to glow. At its bottom, my drone engine, now with its power amplified, glows a bright, brilliant blue.

Maybe everything I'd calculated is incorrect, and my engine will fail the machine. If that happens, what will he do with Daniel?

For a moment, nothing happens. I hold my breath, waiting.

Then a pulse comes from the machine. It ripples out in a wave of vibration that tingles through my body. On the machine's monitor, the entirety of Ross City lights up with green dots, millions of them.

When I look over at Hann, his eyes are bright and focused. A smile plays on his face.

The signal works. I can see it written all over his expression. And in spite of myself, I feel a wild surge of pride at what my engine is capable of. This is the first real test of something I've made, and Dominic Hann—of all people—is the one who gave me the chance to do it.

My delight makes me recoil in horror.

Hann glances at me and nods. "You're pleased," he says. "And it goes beyond your desire to protect your brother."

I'm too afraid to say anything back.

He studies me curiously. "Could it be because, deep down, you believe in everything that I've told you before?"

"You promised me that you would release my brother if this worked," I say through clenched teeth. "How good is your word?"

"Don't ever question my word." Hann looks to his side and nods once. Two of his guards don't even hesitate for a breath. They bow immediately, then leave without a word.

"I want to see it," I say. "On a live feed, like you told me."

"Done." Hann turns back to me. "Any other requests?" he asks.

My palms are slick with sweat, and my heart shivers with each beat. There's the final question I have, the one that Hann hasn't answered up until now, and that I'm almost too scared to ask.

"What's the signal for?" I say, my voice coming out like a hoarse whisper. "What does your machine do?"

Hann smiles sidelong at me. I look back up at the machine. My gaze settles on the screen full of green dots.

And suddenly, I know. The Levels that had crushed his family, the system that had forced his mother's hand. The points, the game that runs this city.

I know what this machine is going to do.

It's going to take down Ross City's entire Level system.

# DANIEL

MAYBE IT'S STILL THE SAME NIGHT AS WHEN I WAS having my illusions of memories about June. I can't tell.

My lips crack from thirst. My eyes can focus only on a gray line of sparse embroidery along the edge of the floor's rug. The guards near the door shuffle their boots against the floor.

They sound like they're about to switch out. The two women are still here. There are other guards now too, just arrived, and in the exchange between them, I listen for clues.

"The boy's been working on the site," one of them says in a low voice. "He's good, from what I hear."

"Yeah?"

"It sounds like Hann has really taken to him."

Another sighs. "Great. But what about us? How long are we going to sit around with this one?"

The woman shrugs. "As long as it takes."

*As long as it takes.* Through my thirst-induced weakness, I attempt to concentrate. Are they trying to break Eden? Has he not already offered his help?

I close my eyes, trying to stave off the nausea that bites at my insides. My hands twist quietly behind my back. I've been tightening and loosening my hands against the ropes for hours now. My wrists are scraped down to the flesh, and I can feel the blood trickling wet down my hands, probably soaking crimson into the rope fibers. But it's not for nothing; the rope has loosened slightly since I first started working on it. Another couple of hours, and I might be able to slip a hand through one of them.

After that, I don't know what the hell I'll do. But I'm used to taking crises one step at a time.

Near the door, the women switch out with two male guards. I see them turn their heads in my direction, but my figure stays limp against the chair. After several long minutes, they lean idly away and against the doorframe. My last round of guards make their way down the hall outside that I've never seen, their boots echoing against marble.

I listen closely to them until they fade away. It takes a long time. How big is this place? The hall they walked down seems to continue forever, and only after long seconds have dragged by am I no longer able to hear their echo at all.

My wrists keep twisting. The pain of it makes me clench my jaw, but I fight to keep the grimace off of my lips. The metal of my artificial leg cuts cold through my pant leg as I keep my ankles crossed.

The new guards don't pay me any attention. They must have been warned about the way I bit the first man, but they haven't seen it, and as far as they're concerned, I look pretty harmless.

My wrists keep twisting. Fresh blood flows down my hands. I can feel it dripping silently down my fingers to the rug behind me. The slickness of it makes my hand slightly more mobile within its bond. I tug slowly, careful not to show my arms at work.

The bonds loosen a fraction more. Just enough.

I stop twisting and pull one of my hands gently against the frayed bond. My thumb and pinkie finger are squeezed together as I tug as hard as I can. At first, the bond doesn't give, and the ropes cut hard against my already-damaged skin. I let out a quiet, shaky breath. Then I pull harder.

Finally, the rope gives a little. The tight bond edges closer to the rim of my knuckles. I keep working it. By the door, one of the guards casts me a casual glance.

I stop moving for a moment and keep still, my eyes still focused on the ground.

He nudges his friend and says something about me in a low voice. They laugh. Then they do what I'd hoped, going back to their positions.

I give my hand one determined tug, ignoring the pain.

This time, my knuckles finally squeeze past the rope, and my hand comes free.

I don't dare react. My arms stay firmly locked in place behind my back. But my freed hand searches for the knots tying my other hand down, and quietly I start to work on that.

My second hand loosens, then starts to come free.

By the door, one of the guards looks in my direction. This time, instead of glancing away again, his gaze lingers. I stop moving for a moment and shift uncomfortably in my chair, letting myself look like I'm settling back into a restless sleep. But through the slit of my half-opened eyes, I can tell that he's not looking away.

Then he pushes back from the door and starts heading toward me.

For some reason, this triggers a flicker of a memory. June, standing at the door of an underground bunker, approaching me and motioning for me to get up. Her hands brush my waist, my chest, my chin. She positions me for a fight, then teaches me how to view my opponent. She throws a purposeful punch and shows me how to dodge and counter.

I try to hang on to this wisp of a memory even as it starts to fade. Over the years, I've learned to hold my own in a fight, have fought back the urge to run and replaced it with the bracing of an attack. And now, as the guard steps toward me, I can feel my muscles tensing, my hands instinctively tightening into fists.

The guard stops in front of me with a frown. Then he starts moving to look behind the chair.

My second hand slips free. I move.

He shifts toward me in surprise—but I'm already in motion. I snap to my feet in an instant, then swing the chair up. The guard has only a moment to bring his arms up in defense before the chair catches him in the side hard enough to send him sprawling onto the floor.

I don't wait. Instead, my eyes fall on the gun at his belt. I lunge for it. He kicks out at me.

The other guard runs toward me now. I manage to get my hands on the gun, but the first man's leg kicks up at me. *Better to let the gun go instead of falling.* The thought flashes through my head and I snap backward, giving up on grabbing the weapon. I race toward the entrance.

But I'm weaker than normal right now, and my swinging of the chair has sapped more of my energy than I thought. I stumble in my steps.

One of the guards catches up to me and points a gun at me. Gritting my teeth, I thrust the chair at him. The chair leg hits him in the face—just enough time for me to whirl and dart out the door. I'm temporarily in the open.

Running—now *that* I can do. The hall before me is long and narrow, cutting through several rooms, and I race down it. At the end of the hall stand a couple of guards who don't yet realize I'm coming. I won't be able to go around the bend, but there's a window against this wall. The first window I've seen.

The guards at the end of the hall turn toward me for the first time. Behind me, the others let out shouts. A bullet pings near my leg.

My breath runs shallow. The lack of water holds me back. Spots appear in my vision as I go, but I force myself to push back against it all.

As I reach the second set of guards now trained on me, I slide against the marble and turn my feet at the last instant. I lunge for the window, my bloody hands nearly slipping against the windowsill, but they catch, and I'm swinging myself through the window and out of the hall.

One glance out this window tells me that this building is entirely underground. High ceilings rise multiple floors over me. The complex is sprawling. And far ahead, I see what looks like a construction site and part of a large, circular machine.

*Eden.* My heart lurches. The guards had said he was working on some *site.* Was that where it was?

It's all I have time to see. Then I'm twisting my body up, my boots pushing off against the windowsill and propelling me up toward the roof. My hands catch the edge of the roof and pull me up. I land in a firm crouch. Below me, I can hear shouts coming from inside. A spotlight starts to sweep across the estate.

This must be just one of Hann's many hideouts. How many other places does he have? I duck behind a chimney as the spotlight sweeps close. My eyes narrow. As if bred out of years of muscle memory, my body knows exactly how to avoid the light, thinks it's in Batalla Hall again and trying to find a way out. Thinks it's on the Colonies' airfield again and searching for a way to get close to their parked fighter jets.

I dart across the roofs. The construction site nears.

Then a bullet scrapes the roof nearest me. It misses me—but it chips the roof tiles hard enough to shatter them into fragments. My boot catches in just the wrong way against the breaking tiles.

I slip.

My hands scramble to grab the edge of the roof, but they're too slippery with blood. I tumble off and to the ground.

Immediately, I try to scramble up again, but now a guard has reached me.

*A Republic soldier, seizing me as a bullet shatters my knee. My scream, hoarse with rage and grief.*

The memory is like a flint in me, lighting up the dark. A vicious growl rumbles in my throat, and I whirl on the guard, catching him hard in the jaw. I hit him once, twice—

—and then my strength gives way again, and I fall, dizzy from the exertion.

The guard stands over me. Several others rush to join him. I look back down to the ground and realize that I'm not sweating at all. There's no water left in me.

That's when I hear one of them say something above me that I swear I must have hallucinated.

"No," one of the guards says to the others. "Let him go."

"Hann's order just came in. We're to take him back up to the surface."

I look up, thinking that maybe my weakness has left me too delirious to think straight. They're letting me go.

I must be dreaming.

But then they're taking me by the arms and dragging me up and throwing something dark across my eyes. I struggle with all the strength I have left. I'm misunderstanding what they're saying, I tell myself. That's the only way this makes sense. They're not going to let me go. Hann has ordered them to kill me instead.

But I wait for the bullet through my head and it doesn't happen. My feet drag against the floor. My consciousness is flickering in and out now. I can't even tell when I'm awake and when I'm gone because, in this suffocating darkness, it's all the same.

*Eden.* I have to find where they're keeping him. My mind struggles to remember the path we're taking.

I don't know when they drag me into what seems to feel like an elevator. All I can do is try to remember how long we're in it. *Five seconds. Fifteen. Thirty.*

My mind starts to fade. The guards' voices above me are still talking, barking sharp orders at one another, but I can't tell what they're saying anymore.

I have to find my brother.

And then, suddenly they're gone. The hands holding my arms vanish, and I crumple to the floor. It feels like asphalt, cement. The darkness lifts from over my eyes, and I suddenly see myself lying on the street somewhere in the Undercity, the smoke from nearby food stalls hazing the air.

AIS agents are here. They're everywhere. The red dots of their guns are shining on me, and their shouts are deafening.

*Hands in the air! Hands in the air!* For an instant, I feel like a criminal again.

Then someone is shouting. *"Stand down!"* It's the AIS director, Min. Her voice echoes against the concrete walls, forcing the guns to lower in a tidal wave. *"Stand down! It's Daniel. Stand down!"*

Pushing through their ranks, too, is June. Her eyes lock on me and never steer away. I must be dreaming now. I lie where I am, the edges of my vision slowly fading into black, while she bends down beside me, her hands touching both sides of my face. Agents swarm around us.

"We're here," she's saying. Then she raises her voice to those crowding around us, the authority in it returning. "Get back. Give him room. He's injured!"

They listen to her instinctively, parting around us like a school of fish. I close my eyes, savoring her presence beside me. "They've got him," I whisper through my parched lips. "Eden."

June says something else. I think she's ordering me to relax, that paramedics are going to take me to a hospital. I strain to understand what she's saying, but her voice sounds muffled now. It's still the loveliest voice I've ever heard. I want to stay awake to hear it.

And then everything is a blur of ambulance sirens and a chaos of other voices. June is nearby, holding my hand. Through it all, I keep looking back at where I'd come from. My thoughts blur together as I try to make sense of everything.

Hann ordered them to release me. They'd let me go. Why would he do that?

What does he want with Eden?

Where has he taken my brother?

# EDEN

**DOMINIC HANN KEEPS HIS PROMISE TO RELEASE** Daniel.

I watch it numbly on a live feed in my view that night. My brother's figure is undeniable—he's tied down to a chair in some other part of this estate, struggling against his bonds. As I look on, he gets into a scuffle with the guards, and somehow—miraculously—breaks free. Shouts echo as he slithers out of a window with others on his tail.

Sometimes it's easy to forget that my brother used to be the master of avoiding the Republic's soldiers. I'm dizzy with the speed at which he did it. How would he even know the route to get back up to the surface? But it doesn't seem to matter. He keeps moving, even though he stumbles occasionally. I watch him go, my throat so dry that I gag.

He almost makes it on his own, even without Hann's generosity. But then he stumbles. That's when the guards approach him, and I think for a single, terrifying moment, that I'm going to witness them kill Daniel right there on the spot.

It will be what had happened to John, all over again.

But instead, I hear one of the guards say, "Let him go."

He shakes his head and orders the others to pull Daniel to his feet. To my disbelief, they throw a bag over my brother's head and start leading him away. They take him up an elevator, then leave him in the streets of the Undercity. The last thing the feed shows is the AIS finding him and swarming to him. Among them, I think I see June Iparis.

I don't know what to make of the entire scene. I don't know why Hann would agree to do such a thing.

Daniel's free now. He's going to come back for me, that I know with a dead certainty and a wild hope. He's going to find where they've taken me and pull me back to the surface.

But if Hann succeeds in what he wants to do, I don't know if any of that matters. I've now witnessed what his machine can do when powered with my engine. It's one of the most spectacular and terrifying inventions I've ever seen.

Ross City is about to crumble.

# DANIEL

I MUST HAVE BLACKED OUT BETWEEN THE TIME
June and the AIS found me and when I arrive at a hospital, because
I don't remember getting out of the ambulance. I don't recall going
up in an elevator or traveling down a hospital's corridors.

All I know is that when I wake up next, I'm in my own bed, my window overlooking a blanket of clouds shrouding the glittering city.
It's nighttime now. The dizzy weakness I'd felt before is now gone,
and I feel awake and alert, rehydrated, and as good as new.

When I look to my side, I see a girl asleep against the side of my
bed, her head buried in her arms. Her dark hair spills behind her in
a shining blanket.

It's June.

She suddenly stirs, sensing that I'm awake. Her eyes dart first
around the room, doing a quick sweep, probably sizing everything
up in the way she always does to make sure we're okay. Then her
gaze settles on my face.

She lets out a long breath. "Hey," she whispers, getting to her feet.

I give her a small smile. "Hey," I reply.

She puts a cool hand against my forehead. "I don't know how much longer we would have taken to get to you if you hadn't sent that message. You looked pretty bad when we first found you."

"They still have Eden," I say. "Did you and AIS find anything about him?"

She shakes her head, her lips pressed tight. It's the expression she gets when her mind is spinning, and I find myself remembering snippets of other memories, of when we were escaping the Republic. "No," she says. "But AIS is trying to track him based on the general area where you were."

"They were underground," I reply.

"Is that where Hann was stationed in a hideout?" June asks.

"A hideout is an understatement. It looked like an estate buried under the city. I don't know how many other spaces he might have like that. But he has a construction site there. A machine."

"Do you remember anything about the route they took you through?"

I shake my head. "They had me blindfolded the entire time. The area beneath the Undercity is a maze of old tunnels and abandoned elevator shafts. It'll take weeks to get down there and do a proper sweep. We need to find a different way."

Had Eden heard that I'd gotten out? Does he know that Hann had intentionally let me go? Did he have anything to do with that— had he made a bargain with the man?

Immediately, I start trying to get out of bed. That's when all the soreness of my captivity hits me. I wince, looking down at my bandaged wrists.

June gets up in the darkness and pushes me down. "You're not going anywhere," she says sternly. "Strict orders from the doctor. Everything you need to do, you can do from the comfort of your bed, okay? Your director said she'd contact you in the morning, and we can go from there."

"What about you?" I ask. "The Elector? He—"

"—is well aware of the situation," she says. "Anden sends his regards and concerns." June leans closer to me. In the night, her eyes shine like dark marbles. "This is big news in your inner circles, apparently. The President wants to be kept updated on what happens with Hann."

I slump back on my pillows and clench my teeth in frustration. I made a promise to myself to keep Eden from harm, but I've failed to do it again. Nightmares from the Republic come rushing back now to haunt me—Eden, being taken away for experimentation; Eden, blinded and weak; Eden, left to die during the war with the Colonies.

Now he is in Hann's grasp, and I have no goddy clue what the man wants with him.

June puts a hand on my shoulder. Her warmth is the only thing that breaks through my whirlwind of thoughts. "We're going to find him," she tells me. "He's a smart boy, and he's going to take care of himself. Your job is to be sure you're strong enough by morning to tackle all this. There's nothing you can do before that. Understand?"

I look back at her. "How long have I been out?"

"A day," she admits.

"And you stayed here?" I ask softly. "The entire time I was out?"

A flash of fear glints in her eyes, then fades. She looks away and out my window. "I was afraid," she murmurs, "to lose you."

And again, I find myself thinking about what she'd said during her first night here, when we shared a kiss. When I realized how much her life had moved forward and settled into place.

She looks back at me. "What's on your mind?" she asks me. "I can always tell by the weight in your eyes."

"I'm thinking about how I'm the catalyst for chaos in your life," I answer. "And how sorry I am for it."

"Don't be," she replies. June sighs and looks down. "We've always been each other's catalysts, haven't we?" she says. "I don't think we would have met if we weren't. And sometimes I find myself pulling away because I want to end that cycle for you, as if that might somehow solve it all."

I think of the way June pulls herself away from our intimate moments. It's the exact same thing I do. I lean closer to her, letting my hand brush hers. For an instant, I think that she might pull away . . . but her hand lingers in place, and she stays where she is.

I know that fear she mentioned. That terror of not knowing what might happen to us next, of what could go wrong if we opened our hearts completely to each other. I'd bled the last time I allowed myself to love her, and she had bled the same.

But still, I find myself tightening my grip around her hand, then pulling her closer. She turns to face me in the night.

The fear still grips me, and the words I want to say still stutter to a halt in my throat. But this time, all I can think about is what it was like to live without her for a decade.

When I open my mouth this time, the words finally spill out.

"I don't deserve having you in my life," I tell her quietly. "There may always be pain and grief that follows me, even here, in all this

Ross City luxury. Maybe that's the way it goes in life. You don't deserve to share that pain." I take a deep breath, trying to quell my fear, the rising tide of all the darkness that still haunts me from the Republic. "But I think you do deserve to know the truth of how I feel. Because even if we can't be together in the end, I would like you to know."

June's eyes are glossy against the blue-gray light filtering in from the windows. "And what is that?" she whispers.

"That I love you," I whisper. "That I've been in love with you for years, even when we were separated. *Especially* then. I've lived with you in my life, and I've lived without you. No matter what kind of fear I feel in the possibility of us being together, the fear of being away from you is something I don't think I can bear." I look down, shy to meet her gaze now. "I have nightmares of losing you again. All the time."

There. My heart is ripped open and exposed before her. All the uncertainty that had plagued me before now roars in my mind as I wait for her response.

Maybe this was all a mistake. I shouldn't have told her this. It's too soon.

Then June draws nearer. "I never had a chance to tell you, before you and Eden left for Antarctica, that I love you too. So fiercely that it frightens me." Her voice trembles.

*I love you. I love you.* I have never heard these words from June before, and now they fill my heart to bursting, making me whole in a way I never knew I could be.

She smiles a little, and now I see that her eyes are moist. "Even if we don't know where we'll go in the future, perhaps our lives were always meant to collide again and again. Perhaps we are forever meant to be each other's catalysts."

*Forever.* It's a word I've never dared to use with June. Maybe there is a chance for a forever in our lives.

"I've looked over my shoulder for a decade," I whisper, "wondering what it was that was missing in my life. Turns out, all this time, it was you."

Then I lean close, and this time, I kiss her.

She nearly collapses into my embrace. Her lips are so soft and familiar against mine, everything that I've missed in the years we've been apart. Our conversations together may be awkward and polite, and our presence around each other stilted and distant . . . but *this*, this feels right in every possible way.

She belongs here, in my arms, and I belong here, giving my whole heart to her.

A deep hunger rises in me. This time, I don't waste a second. I wrap my arms tightly around her and push her back against the bed. My skin prickles in pleasure wherever she runs her fingers. She runs her hands through my hair and sighs contentedly against me. Her waist, her slender neck, the curve of her hips . . . I shiver at the warmth of her. Everything about her is like a fever dream. I want to preserve this in time for us. I want a million more of these moments.

She unbuttons my shirt. I pull hers over her head. My fingers run across new scars on her, here and there, a healed scratch, an old raised bruise. She is older, as am I, and we are different now than we were. I love her more for it, wish I had been able to share in all of it with her over the last few years. She kisses my cheeks as I fall into her. Her hands slide down my back. I shudder at her every touch.

The rest of the apartment is silent. Outside, I hear the passing of airplanes. Somewhere in the distance, music is playing. Millions of lights twinkle beyond the windows and against the night, each one a different life, a different moment from ours.

But tonight, we let ourselves stay entwined together, as if everything will remain as perfect as this moment. As if this could be our future.

# EDEN

I DON'T KNOW WHEN HANN PLANS TO UNLEASH the real signal. All I know is that Hann finally comes to see me again in the makeshift chamber that he's offered me at the estate.

I jump a little as he enters the room with two of his guards.

"I don't mean to startle you," he says to me now, holding up both of his hands. Then he nods at the guards. "You're no longer needed," he adds. "I'd like a word alone with Mr. Wing."

The guards do as he says. They step out, and the room is suddenly just me and him.

Hann sits down in a chair across from me and leans his chin on his hand. "Word is that your brother is now safely back with the AIS," he says.

"Thank you for keeping your word," I reply.

"Do you know why I'm here right now?" he asks me.

I just stare warily at him. "Why?"

He reaches into the pocket of his suit jacket, then pulls out what looks like a heavy purse. With a careless gesture, he tosses it in my direction.

I fumble with it as it lands against my chest with a chunky clink of metal. "What's this?" I say.

"Your payment, of course," Hann replies. He nods at me. "I only pay in real gold corras. Soon, this place's virtual currency will be useless after the Level system is disabled. I figure you'll want real money instead."

I glare at him, then peek once inside the purse.

There are hundreds—thousands—of gold coins in here. Each is worth a thousand corras. This entire purse must contain at least a million.

I look sharply back up at him. He'd promised a handsome pay for what I did, but this level of money is an amount that I hadn't guessed at.

Hann smiles at me. "Surprised?" he says. "I've made enough of a fortune doing what I do. It's a worthy investment for me to spend that money on talent like you."

This kind of money is beyond what even most of the Sky Floor citizens can earn. It's money that could pull Pressa and her father completely out of the Undercity. It's money that could buy you the kind of Level that would make you safe forever.

It's also the kind of money that's dipped in the blood of people who have paid dearly for crossing someone like Hann.

I close the purse back up and toss it to the floor between us. "How long are you going to keep me down here?" I ask quietly. "Until my brother comes to find me? Until the AIS descend on you? Just because you disable the Level system doesn't mean they don't have a way to hunt you down."

Hann smiles, unconcerned about the way I've rejected his money.

"I'm not going to keep you anywhere," he replies, nodding toward the door. "You're free to go, whenever you wish. My guards are ready and waiting to escort you back to the surface of the Undercity whenever you want."

Now I know he's messing with me. I laugh, shaking my head at him. "What kind of game do you want me to play?" I say.

"I don't play games with people I respect," Hann replies. "Or have you just lived in a gamified society for so long that you don't even know how to react to people outside of its system?"

"Why would you let me go?" I demand. "I've been a proven asset to you. I know where this place is. I've *seen* you, and I could go straight to the AIS the instant you release me."

He shrugs. "I know."

I spread my hands wide. "So—that's it? You're setting me free?" As if to test him, I stand up from my chair and walk toward the door. Everything in me tells me that this is a trap, that the instant I try to step out into the hall, they'll clap me in chains or shoot me dead.

But Hann just watches me. "Go."

When I still don't budge, he leans forward in the chair and regards me with a focused expression. "Do you want to know why I'm letting you go? Do you want to know why I'm willing to give you millions?" He smiles. "Because you'll be back."

"What?"

"You'll return to find me again. I can see the fire in your eyes, the way you try to hide the satisfaction of seeing that machine work with your engine attached to it. I know that you believe in the same things I believe in." He narrows his eyes. "It's haunted you the entire time you've lived in Antarctica, hasn't it? The way this place runs its

Undercity? The way the government handles the poor? The Level system that is as corrupt as it is innovative? You hate it all, just like I do."

I shake my head. "Once I step out of here, I'm never coming back."

Hann leans back in his chair and heaves a sigh. "Yes, you are," he replies. "You will, because when you see the chaos that will reign in this city after the Level system is disabled, when you see the change it can bring about in the upper-class people you loathe . . . you'll realize that what I do here is the noble cause. You want to be a part of something significant, don't you? All people with your talent desire to make a difference. And I can help you get there. You can go from obscurity in your brother's shadow to becoming one of the most prominent disrupters of change that the world has ever seen." He nods at the purse on the floor. "And think of your friend Pressa. You can change her life forever with that. With a new job at my side."

I start to shake. "You're offering me a job," I repeat incredulously.

He nods. "Yes. I'm offering you the chance to come work for me, permanently. Think of the things you could do, Eden, without restrictions placed on you. Think of not having to cater to anyone else when it comes to your schedule and your life." Hann laces his fingers together. "You're free to come and go as you wish. Should you need to contact me again, you can use this."

A series of six numbers appears in front of my view. I stare at it for a second, memorizing it, before it vanishes.

Hann smiles briefly at me. "I never intended for you to be my prisoner, Eden, and now I want to prove that to you in the most obvious way."

I don't trust him. I don't believe him.

And yet, I think he's telling me the truth. Somehow, this killer—the most-wanted criminal in all of Ross City, someone whom Daniel fears and hates, a person who has ruled the Undercity with an iron fist—is the only person I've ever known who seems to see me straight to my core.

Now he's offering me a chance to work with him.

"I can't do this," I tell him. "We aren't the same person. We don't have the same beliefs."

Hann stays even-tempered. "You can tell yourself whatever you want," he replies. "I understand that it would be difficult to do this, because you would be separating yourself completely from your brother. But I know this is what's in your heart. You want to change things, just like I do. And you're tired of other people getting in your way. Tired of being unable to help the ones you care about the most. Tired of being unseen."

I stay where I am, my mind whirling with confusion. On a surface level, he's someone I'd need to avoid at all costs. But this . . .

"What if I choose not to work for you?" I say. "Will you still let me go?"

Hann nods. "If you choose not to, then what's the point of keeping you here? Life is too exhausting to hold someone hostage every time I need something to get done." He waves at the door. "Go. Confide in your friends. Find your brother. Never see me again. I won't hunt you down at races; I won't have my guards stalk what you do. All I can tell you is that you're about to see what Ross City should actually be like, once it rises from its ashes. It's time for someone else to run this place." He leans forward on his knees. "Then you'll soon ask yourself . . . who are you helping, exactly, by refusing my offer?"

I don't know what to say to him. I don't know how to prove him wrong. I don't know what's going to happen to Ross City.

All I do is step toward the door. I go through the entrance and into the hall. Just like he'd said, his guards are waiting to take me wherever I want to go. And Hann is still behind me, sitting in my chamber.

I turn my back on the estate. Hann's words ring in my mind, lingering, haunting.

*Who are you helping, exactly, by refusing my offer?*

And right as I consider those words, a high-pitched sound crackles around us.

I press my hands to my ears. The chip implanted near my temple seems to grow warm. My heart jumps into my throat.

Then everything goes silent.

It's over as quickly as it happened, like an electric shock that blitzed right through the walls and floors and us. The guards, too, felt it—they hunch for a second, flinching, then look at one another in bewilderment before everything settles back down.

But something is missing. I open my eyes and see nothing virtual hovering in my view. No numbers, no account, not even the persistent warning that I'm unable to connect down here. There's a weight to the silence, like the kind of quiet that you hear when you're truly severed from civilization. The buzz and hum of technology. It's all just *gone*.

He's done it. It worked.

Dominic Hann has ordered the real signal to trigger. And he has just eliminated Ross City's entire system.

# DANIEL

IT HAPPENS THE NEXT MORNING, RIGHT AS JUNE AND I reach the AIS headquarters.

I'm awake by dawn, pulling my shirt and trousers on and tugging smooth my suit. Beside me, June's already ready, as impeccably neat as any soldier trained in the Republic.

I don't know what to say about what happened between us last night. Neither does she, I think. All we can do is glance occasionally at each other as we get ready. When I do speak, it's about Eden.

"AIS messaged," I tell her as we step out of the apartment and into the hall. "No luck hunting down Eden's location. But my description of the underground has narrowed it down to a rough patch of the city."

"What part?" June asks.

I bring up a map between us as we enter an elevator station, then point to a section of the grid. "This area was once in development to expand the Undercity to floors beneath the surface," I explain. "They were going to house Undercity folks down there, in cramped spaces underground. It turned out to be a disaster, though—not enough escape routes up to the surface in case of fire or flood, not enough emergency ventilation. There was a huge fire that ripped through the space. After that, no one bothered with the maze of tunnels."

"And it sounds like what you saw when you were down there?"

I nod. "The kind of building I saw, the construction site . . . it had the kind of infrastructure that reminded me of that story."

June looks down at the city through the elevator's glass windows. "We're going down there, then, aren't we?" She glances skeptically at me. "Are you sure you can do this?"

"I have to," I reply. "I'm not going to keep lying around up here, waiting for AIS to find something." In desperation, I bring up Eden's account again and try one more time to track his location.

That's when I feel it.

There's a spark of something electric, as if every particle in the air were suddenly charged—followed by a sharp crack in my ears. It's so loud that I flinch. June does the same in unison.

"What was that?" she exclaims.

But as soon as she says it, every single one of our Levels flickers out. June's name and Level vanishes from over her head. The faint glow on the handles of her glasses disappears. The numbers and bars in my view fade into nothing. The elevator shudders to a stop on one of the middle floors of the building. When I glance up at the ceiling, I notice that the power's out. None of the elevator's panels are lit.

*What happened? A short circuit in the system?*

My first reaction is to turn on my grid lines—but there are none. Nothing about my system works at all. It's as if it turned off.

June glances at me with a frown. "It looks like it's not limited to our building," she says, nodding out at the city.

Sure enough, she's right—every building close to us also looks blacked out, with no hovering virtual info on any part of them.

June glances at me. "AIS? Can you contact them?"

I shake my head. "No. Everything about my system is disabled. Come on." I step off the elevator, then motion for us to head down to the walkways. We start sprinting along the halls. Here and there, we run into a few other people also coming out of the elevators, looking bewildered.

One of them shouts at us as we pass. "Your systems working?" she asks.

I shake my head. "No," I call back. So it's not limited to our accounts, either. A heavy feeling starts creeping into my chest. Something has gone severely wrong—and a part of me knows it must be somehow tied to what Hann was doing.

What he had stolen my brother for.

As we sprint down the stairs, I almost run right into Jessan and the director, right as they exit into the stairwells from the headquarters.

"Wing!" Director Min exclaims. "You're not supposed to be up—"

I ignore her comment and keep going. "Your systems?" I ask. "Anything working?"

She looks pale as she shakes her head back. "Our Levels—everything—our data—all the info that the government displays and tracks and keeps. All of it's gone—not just reset, or flattened, but *gone*. Wiped."

A cold fist tightens around my chest. *It's impossible*, I want to say—because everything I know about the infrastructure of the system, how spread out across the city and how decentralized everything is. But I've seen too many goddy impossible things come true to believe those words.

"It's citywide?" June asks.

Jessan nods grimly. "As far as we can tell. We can't reach anyone. No calls going in or coming out."

If the entire city's system is down . . . the pandemonium on the streets in the Undercity must be unimaginable. My heart seizes at the idea of Eden still being trapped somewhere underground there.

"I've seen what happens when you have a complete blackout in a city as divided as this one," June says as we run. Her face turns grimmer. "When people who have been held down for decades suddenly realize that their chains have been removed, things unravel quickly. It can take less than an hour for a society to destabilize."

Jessan looks sharply at June. "What do you mean?" she asks.

"I mean, you'd better make sure your military is down in the Undercity right now, before things get out of hand," June replies.

I think of the constant outages we had in Lake, the unrest that would take over the streets. June's right. There had been one particular outage that once affected the entirety of Los Angeles—and within the hour, fires had broken out all over the city as the poor sectors clashed with the Gem ones. I remember seeing the tanks rolling down the streets to bring order back. My mother had forced us to stay inside for two weeks as police swarmed through the neighborhoods.

"Ross City is not the Republic," the director says stiffly to June.

"No," June replies, just as severely. "It's worse. This is a far more concentrated place, and the effect will be swifter. As far as I can tell, without your system in place, the Undercity will crumble, and it will happen soon if you can't get your system back up."

Damn, I've missed hearing her talk when she's breaking down a situation. Min scowls at the bluntness in June's voice, but she doesn't argue back this time. Instead, she returns to trying to place a call out to the President.

"Emergency power's still not up," she swears under her breath after a moment.

"Head northeast as soon as we reach the ground," I say to June. "We'll go in the general direction where we've been hunting for Eden."

She nods without hesitation. I have no idea what we'll do after that, or how we'll find our way down, but it's the best bet for finding my brother.

We finally reach the bottom floor. The stairs lead out to a tall set of heavy, barred metal doors, and when we slide them open, they reveal the streets of the Undercity.

We step out into a scene of chaos.

All around us, the names and data hovering over each street stall, each shop, each person, are gone. When I look up, I notice that virtual overlays have vanished from over the elevator stations too. There's nothing we look at that isn't already real.

My eyes go to June, but she's looking down the street. Some are taking advantage of the moment already, and the space in front of a station is starting to flood with people. My first, fleeting thought is that all the stations have also powered down instantaneously—if everyone's Levels have been flattened, then everyone is trapped wherever they happen to be.

But that's replaced almost instantly by my second thought: Our Levels haven't just been flattened, they've been *deleted*. In one fell swoop, Ross City's Level system—the class system I've always argued about with AIS, the same system that Eden rebelled against by constantly coming down here—has been cleared.

People are now able to enter the stations and stairwells, no matter their Level. Local police patrolling the streets struggle in vain to control the flood of people. Small, isolated scuffles have already started to break out between the authorities and the citizens.

Behind us come several other AIS agents. The director hurries over. "Coordinate the police in this district!" she shouts at me, pointing down the street. "Tell them we're calling for reinforcements. Emergency martial law, immediately. Understand, Wing? We have no time to lose."

I nod at her. "Yes, ma'am," I reply. Then she's off like a bullet, running with her other agents toward the nearest police headquarters to try to get the emergency lines up and running.

Shattered glass already litters the concrete, and not far from us, people are pushing into a store and eagerly starting to haul things out. Carts full of food they would never have been able to buy with their Levels, armfuls of clothing, appliances, and furniture. Around them, others are starting to get the hint too. I can hear the shouts rising up and down the street.

"Quick!" someone yells. "Before they get the system back up!"

I keep running in the direction that my brother might be in. How the hell am I ever going to find him in this mess? I reach a busy intersection and halt in the middle of it, looking in despair down both streets to see masses of people crowding out into the road. Beside me, June takes my hand and squeezes it once. I look at her, hating the feeling of helplessness that washes over me.

Suddenly, I feel like I'm back in the heat of the war with the Colonies, searching frantically for my brother in enemy territory.

And then, I see something familiar.

There. In the middle of the street. A flash of familiar, wavy blond hair and the glint of his metal glasses. A miracle in the midst of absolute chaos.

At first, I think I'm hallucinating. There's no way Eden is here.

But I blink, and he doesn't disappear. There's his hair again. June also tightens her grip on my hand and points in his direction. "Is that him?" she calls out.

I don't know how he got away from Hann. I don't know how he found his way back here to the surface of the Undercity. I don't know anything except that maybe he was heading back in the direction of our home too, so that our paths crossed.

But I raise my voice, and in it, I can hear my own terror. "Eden!" I shout. "*Eden!*"

His head snaps over to us. His gaze falls on me. From his distance, I see the recognition click on his face. "Daniel!" he calls back, and it's as if I were seeing him as a child again.

Everything in me floods with adrenaline. I suddenly start pushing my way over to him. Beside me, June follows. I have to get to my brother before something happens to him. The fear in my heart reaches a bursting point.

Eden shoves his way toward us. It seems to take an eternity for him to fight his way through the throngs. For an instant, I think we'll never reach each other. *This is it*, I think. I'm lost in one of my nightmares. I'm running and running toward my brother and I will never reach him.

But then he's suddenly standing before me. And I'm not dreaming. And I'm sweeping him into a fierce hug. He embraces me tightly back.

It's Eden, and he's out of Hann's clutches.

# EDEN

I'VE NEVER SEEN ROSS CITY WITHOUT ITS LAYERS
of augmented-reality before. I don't think it was ever meant to be seen
this way.

There are no signs or street names, no hovering messages, no grid
lines. Most of all, there are no Levels over anyone's head. It is as if
everything that holds a city together—streetlights, traffic laws, police
enforcement—has vanished in the blink of an eye.

Riots are triggered so quickly that—from the AIS headquarters in
the Sky Floors—we can see the chaos happening in real time on their
screens. At first, people stand around out on sidewalks, puzzled,
muttering to one another as they ask others if their Levels had suddenly vanished. Auto-cars and trucks stop in the middle of the roads.
The traffic starts to pile up.

Slowly, I see the realization start to hit the Undercity. It ripples
through the streets in a wave. Murmurs turn into exclamations, and
then into shouts.

*The system is down.*

*The Levels are gone!*

And just like that, the ripple becomes a tidal wave. *The system is down, the Levels are gone, the system is down, the Levels are gone.*

After the scene in the Undercity, the Sky Floors seem eerily quiet. It's midnight now, and even though we're at least a hundred floors high, I can see the orange glow of fire coming from the Undercity far below. Smoke rises in plumes as the city brings in the military to try to contain the chaos.

Even the AIS headquarters itself is struggling to stay operational, running on limited backup power. Here in the main lobby, a large screen plays live footage from the Undercity as a newscaster talks rapidly over the scene. It's weird to see video like this without our Level systems in place.

"Why would Hann just let you go?" Daniel asks me as I pace restlessly by the windows. "Did he hurt you?"

"No," I reply, distracted. I'm trying to place a call manually on a phone to Pressa, but nothing's getting through. On my dozenth try, I swear under my breath and turn to my brother. "He didn't do anything to me," I reply. "He told me that he would release you if I helped him install my drone's engine into his machine."

"And then?"

"And then . . ." I hesitate, wondering whether I should tell Daniel about Hann's history. My eyes go to my brother's bandaged finger. Hann had promised he wouldn't hurt Daniel at all—but his promise had only been partly true. Daniel was apparently hospitalized for dehydration. The guards broke one of his fingers.

Because of me, he'd hurt my brother. The thought makes me so sick to my stomach that I have to pause for a moment to fight down the nausea.

"After I finished installing the engine," I say, "Hann told me that he would let me go, as a gesture of goodwill. But he said that I'd be back." *He knew, fundamentally, that Daniel and I would find ourselves at a crossroads again. That I'm not like my brother.*

Daniel frowns at me. "It makes no sense," he mutters.

"Hann said he has no interest in forcing me to work for him. Besides, he's already got what he wanted." I turn back to the windows, where we can see plumes of smoke rising from the streets below.

Daniel narrows his eyes at me. "He's playing a game with you," he finally says. "It's what he's known for. I've seen several cases of him winning over loan victims by giving them the illusion of safety with him."

Something about the way Daniel just assumes that Hann's playing a game with me makes me feel wary. It's true that he's a dangerous man—he kidnapped us both, after all, and held us hostage. Just the fact that he let us go on a whim . . . well, it's something only a confident criminal would do.

But I can't help thinking about what he'd said to me. What had happened to his son and wife. The genuine grief that had been etched onto his face. The way he seemed to know exactly what was going on in my mind, better even than what Daniel knew.

The call I'm trying to place fails again. I grit my teeth in frustration and toss the phone onto a nearby couch. Then I turn to look at the elevators leading out of the AIS headquarters.

"You're not going down there," Daniel says automatically as he watches me.

"I have to," I reply. "I can't call through to Pressa at all. If the AIS headquarters is this stripped down in terms of tech, the Undercity is probably completely cut off."

Daniel's lips tighten. "No." He nods at the screen, where they're showing the streets down below. Barricades have been put up in some parts of the Undercity, but they're doing little to stop people from hopping over them and organizing into furious crowds. Some are marching down the streets, shouting. Others are breaking windows and flooding into shops.

"See that?" he says, glancing sternly at me. "The President himself is flying out tomorrow for his safety, and he's taking his security detail with him."

"Anden has offered to host him in the Republic," June finishes. "He has invited us to evacuate with him too."

Even the President's leaving this behind. The thought of us all flying out sends fear rippling through me. What about Pressa and her father? I can't just leave them here and run like a coward. And even then, tomorrow is far away. Daniel's heading down to the Undercity in a few hours with the rest of AIS to get things under control.

I turn determined eyes on my brother. "Isn't your shift next, down in the Undercity?"

"It's my job to contain this mess," he replies.

"Your job. Always your job." I throw up my hands. "You think I don't worry about what'll happen to *you* every time you head out into that? You put yourself in danger's way every day. But you won't let me in. You won't let me join you."

"I do it so that you don't have to," he snaps.

"*I have to!*" I suddenly burst out. The anger burns in my throat. "When you head out there and don't come home until late, when you're captured by a dangerous criminal, *I have to deal with it. I* have to bear the idea of losing you. You can't let me just leave Pressa to fend for herself down there. That's not what you would do." I take a deep breath and glare at him. "If June were down there, you would tear every street of the Undercity apart to find her. You would keep going until you were dead, and you wouldn't care what the hell I said."

June clears her throat uncomfortably at my words. Across from me, Daniel's quiet. His face has turned pale, as if he's remembering something from his past.

"It's going to get worse down there," June says after a while. I can't tell if she's siding with me or not. "People who have suffered for that long, who don't have the ability to attack higher powers, turn on one another instead. They'll destroy every shop and stall and home down there, and they'll do it quickly. So if we're going to get anyone out of the Undercity, we have to do it now. It's about to become impassible."

Daniel's gaze goes from me back to the dark windows. When he finally speaks, his voice is pulled tight. "Fine. But you're not going alone. I'm coming with you."

"Same," June says.

Even with this compromise, I can feel the chasm widening between us. No matter what Daniel says, he makes me feel small, like a little brother asking for permission to do anything and everything. I turn away, disgusted with myself, and start heading toward the elevators.

\* \* \*

Even though it's past midnight, the streets of the Undercity are fully lit tonight—with lights from the backup electric system; with handheld lamps, glowsticks, torches, and portable screens held up by protestors; and with floodlights set up along the streets' barricades, monitored by police and soldiers alike.

Now I run through the streets with Daniel and June at my side. Shouts come at us in all directions. The streets, always narrow, are crammed full of people in every form of celebration and confusion. Some are uncertain, standing outside the front of their stalls or shops and wringing their hands, looking meekly at the police that rush by. Others hang out the open windows of the floors above, squinting at the buildings in disbelief at the lack of any augmented layering. Others take photos with old-school cameras, now that their systems are disabled.

Still others are furious, delighted to unleash their anger by attacking their neighbors with the kind of violence that'd normally get your Levels flattened. There are some taking advantage of the system's disappearance to break into shops and stock up on all the things they've never been able to buy. We pass several young people who are simply wrecking the street for no reason, crushing scooters and boards and auto-buses and spraying them with buckets of paint. In the night, their figures cast long shadows against the wall.

"Things are deteriorating quickly," June calls to us as we run. "Eden, we won't have long before this situation makes it unreasonable for us to stay down here. Can we get to your friend before that?"

*Pressa.* Her name rings through me over and over. Her father's apothecary is deep in the heart of the Undercity, right in the thick of everything. "We'll reach her," I call back as we hit an intersection and make a sharp turn. "We have to."

A flipped auto-car in the street stops us dead in our tracks. People have already crowded around it so tightly that there's no easy way around it. Nearby, flames burn gold against the night.

I spit out a curse. "We can't get through," I say.

Daniel looks overhead and nods for me to follow. "There's a way," he replies. He reaches the end of the street and then darts into a narrow alley between two blocks. His movements are steady and sure, like he's been down these roads a dozen times before.

We hit a dead end stopped by a locked gate. But Daniel doesn't stop moving. He kicks off against the wall and shimmies up to the second floor in a matter of seconds, then leaps off the ledge to climb onto the top of the gate. He drops out of sight. June runs up to the gate right as Daniel emerges from the other side of it, opening the gate from the inside.

"Hurry," he gasps as he ushers us through. We dart down a private walkway before emerging back out into the streets.

Two blocks down, I see it. The apothecary.

There's a mob of people that have surrounded the shop, and the front window is already smashed. Standing in the entrance is Pressa's father, his frail body gamely pressed in the doorway as he pleads with the people to keep order. Beside him, Pressa and her father's assistant, Marren, are shoving back anyone who gets too aggressive.

"Get away!" she shouts. "Get back in the street! You can't come in here!"

There are others trying to help them, too. I recognize a few of the store's frequent customers. Several of the larger men have formed a human barricade on one side of the shop, while two others are boarding up the broken window on the other side.

My heart lifts a little at the sight, even though the situation looks like it's about to tip over into something dangerous.

"Pressa!" I shout at the top of my lungs as we approach. My hands wave high in the air.

Her head whips around in my direction, and her dark eyes search the crowd for me. They finally settle on where we are.

"Eden?" she says incredulously. Her entire demeanor brightens at the sight of me.

I don't hesitate. I just start pushing through the crowd to reach where she's standing with her dad. She grabs my arm in a viselike grip. Her eyes are wide and frantic.

"Everything's falling apart," she tells me in a rush. "People are trying to steal our medicine."

Behind me, Daniel and June have pushed their way up to the top of the steps too. When one man trying to get into the shop suddenly shoves Pressa's dad, June whips out an elbow so fast that she breaks the man's nose before he can even react. He cries out in pain and shrinks back.

June narrows her eyes at him and raises her voice at the crowd. "Police!" she shouts. "Get back, *now!*"

The authority in her voice is so militaristic that, at least for the moment, everyone listens. Beside her, Daniel shoves two people away from the entrance.

I turn back to Pressa. "You and your dad have to get out of here," I say. "Leave the shop. Dominic Hann destroyed the Level system—it's not coming back up anytime soon. This situation's going to boil over."

Pressa looks desperately to where her father is standing guard at the entrance. "There's no way in hell we're leaving," she replies. "I can't just let him stay behind, and he's not going to give up on his entire life's work."

I grit my teeth and start pulling her with me. "Do you get how dangerous this is?" I urge her. "I'm talking about your lives here!"

She yanks herself out of my grip. Her eyes flash with anger and fear. "You think I'm stupid?" she snaps. "This is everything we have, Eden! *Everything!*"

"It's a *shop*, Pressa—not your lives!"

"This shop is something that Dad has built all his life. It's all that keeps us from being homeless. He's not going to run, so I'm not going to leave his side." She gives me a bitter glare. "Not that I expect a skyboy like you to understand."

I release her arm, and she goes hurrying back to her father. Mr. Yu's now pleading with the people who are trying to shove their way past him.

"Please!" he calls out. "I've known many of you for years!"

But the hunger and chaos is building to a breaking point. I see two men suddenly crash through one of the side windows. They stumble into the shop, then start dumping any and every herb and canister they can find into a bag. Others start stepping in.

I curse at the sight. Daniel's struggling to keep the tide of people from entering through the broken side window, while June stands determined at the front entrance. I shove back a woman clawing her way through another open window.

Pressa shields her father, and together with Marren, they pull him back. Her father's sobbing now—rivulets run down his face as he tries in vain to tell people to stop taking his medicines. "Please!" he calls over and over again, grabbing a passing sleeve and arm and pant leg whenever he can. "Stop! Please!"

*This is going to go wrong.* The thought amplifies until it becomes a scream in my head. My heartbeat speeds up until I think it's going to explode. It's the feeling of being tied down in a gurney in the seconds right before a soldier shoots my mother.

*This is going to go very, very wrong.*

I see it happen in slow motion.

A young, bone-thin man with hollow cheeks makes a beeline toward the shop's entrance, trying to pass underneath Mr. Yu's outstretched arms. He stumbles in his rush, falls, and hits his face hard against the edge of the doorframe. It cuts a deep gash across his cheeks.

Mr. Yu turns to him. I see a flash of worry cross his eyes—and instead of shoving the young man back out of the store, he bends down to help him.

"Steady," Mr. Yu says to the young man on the ground as he clutches his face and moans. "That's a nasty gash. I'll help you bandage it—"

But the young man whirls on Mr. Yu in a blind fury. Pressa sees the glint in the air at the same time I do. She screams and grabs her father to yank him away, even as he holds the bandages in his hand. I open my mouth and lunge in their direction.

Neither of us reaches him in time. The young man's knife plunges deep into her father's stomach. Once. Twice.

Then I slam hard into the man and knock the knife from his hand. The weapon goes spinning to the floor as he and I both fall.

Above me, Pressa grabs her father as he clutches his stomach, his watery eyes wide with shock.

The young man struggles with me. He's surprisingly strong for his size, as if he were fighting for his life. Finally, I kick him off me hard enough to send him skidding against the wall. He hits his head and shakes it, dazed for a moment.

Daniel sees the commotion and rushes over, but it's already too late. Pressa's father drops to his knees in the middle of his floor as people stream all around him, running to grab everything from his shelves. Mr. Yu's face has gone paper white, and he's shaking uncontrollably. Between his fingers clutching his stomach seeps dark blood.

"Dad!" Pressa's shouting at him as she helps him lean against the wall of his shop. She presses her hand against his leaking wounds too. Blood runs across her skin. "*Dad!*" She looks helplessly up at me. "Call an ambulance! Now!"

But without the Level system, there's no way to make a proper call to anyone. I dash out into the street in an attempt to grab the nearest police officer I can see—but there are so many people in the streets, some shoving their way into other shops, others trying in vain to stop them. I run back in, bend down beside Mr. Yu, and strip off my thin jacket.

Mr. Yu's eyes flutter weakly at me before they go to Pressa. His breaths come in irregular beats. He whispers something to her that sounds like he's telling her to get out of here. She ignores him and keeps trying to stop the flow of blood.

I take Mr. Yu's hand and hold it tight. Before either of us can do any more, his eyes fade, the light in them dimming to nothing. His trembling stops. One of his hands clutches the bandages that he'd been ready to use to help his killer. They're stained red now.

Pressa's hands are still pressed against her father's wounds. Around us, people stumble forward to the shelves to grab handfuls of herbs and powders, stepping over his body as if he were nothing more than an obstacle.

I realize I'm tugging on Pressa's arm, telling her we have to leave. She tries to shake me off and go back to what she's doing. Only when June and Daniel join me do we finally manage to snap Pressa out of her reverie and start pulling her away from the store. Marren flees into the street and turns to watch helplessly as people overrun the store. Only then does Pressa break down in tears against me.

I force my eyes away from the scene around us. No matter how strong the country, no matter how invincible one might seem . . . there is always a tipping point. Always something that can pull the entire house down.

# DANIEL

I KNOW WHAT IT FEELS LIKE TO BE FORCED TO LEAVE your home behind. I know what it's like to lose your parent. To feel helpless as the world around you burns.

The girl named Pressa is quiet as we leave the hospital the following morning, where they've already covered her father's body. She doesn't look at me. She barely speaks to Eden, who has his arm around her in a protective grip.

I feel sorry for her. In her eyes, I can see a mirror of my own grief from the past. I can hear the echo of my screams and the blood on the ground.

"The Elector's plane takes off in half an hour," June says in a low voice to me as we walk toward the elevators. "We need to hurry. Your President is heading out soon too."

I nod at June, then look back again at my brother and his friend. In this moment, it's as if we're back on the streets of the Republic, evacuating as the Colonies closed in. But this is no battle from an outside force. This is the consequence of a flawed system, something that had been rotting underneath a glistening exterior.

From the screens in the AIS lobby, we can see the police pushing the Undercity crowds back, clubs out, guns sparking. People falling.

I tear my gaze away from the sight and keep going. My job is to keep Eden safe. And right now, the only path to safety is to get out of this country.

We enter the elevator, now functioning only on emergency backup power.

As we rise toward the top floor, the Elector's private jet comes into view. I stare at it, the red and black paint streaking the sides of the plane, the angled nose, the lights dotting the platform around it. The entire scene feels surreal.

I fall into step behind June, my brother and Pressa silent at my side. What thoughts must be running through his head? What were his last moments with Dominic Hann like? But I don't have time to dwell on him before we are inside the jet and seated across from Anden.

As the engines start and the jet lifts into the air, I look out my window and down at the city below us. Smoke rises from the lowest streets, hazing the still-glittering lights on the higher floors. Without the colorful overlays on the city, the place looks more vulnerable than I ever imagined—the buildings stark white, empty of substance. Tiny dots of people run back and forth on the pathways that connect each of the buildings like a web.

It looks like war. It looks like something I've seen all too much of in my life. As we rise higher and the scene below fades behind the clouds, I find myself wondering if there is ever a time in history of peace, if we can ever find a way to escape the cycle of destruction we bring upon ourselves.

If there is, I sure as hell haven't seen it.

# LOS ANGELES

REPUBLIC OF AMERICA

# EDEN

**I SPEND THE ENTIRE TWELVE HOURS ON THE PLANE**
sketching one schematic after another.

It's the same habit that emerges every time I'm trying to distract
myself from my anxieties. My drawings are of what I remember from
working on Dominic Hann's device, but they're not enough—I hadn't
gotten access to everything, and as a result all I end up with is an unfinished idea of how he managed to take down the entire Antarctican
system in Ross City in one fell swoop.

*"Eden."*

It takes me a while to realize that Pressa is saying my name. I
startle out of my sketching to see her staring pointedly at me, a cup of
steaming tea in her hands. She puts it on the table before me.

"Thanks," I mutter, forcing myself to sit back in my seat and wrap
my hands around the cup. The heat of it scalds my skin, but the sudden
shock feels nice too.

Pressa turns her dark eyes toward the window. She tucks her hair
behind her ears. "Thanks for taking me with you," she says in a low
voice.

She's been quiet for most of the trip, her eyes hollow and red with grief. Now she glances uncomfortably around the Elector's jet. It's a luxurious space, its rounded ceiling high and its sides lined with smooth couches and chairs. Behind us, two full-length beds with thick curtains draped over them bookend the back of the plane, along with a bathroom that rivals the one in our apartment.

Her gaze settles again and again on the Elector, who sits at the other end near the front of the plane and talks in low voices with June. Daniel lounges beside her, his face trained idly on the scene outside the windows. Despite his attempts to look like he's not paying attention to what they're saying, I can tell he's taking in every bit of it. Just like how he's noticing where I am right now and what I'm doing, even though he'd never show it.

Pressa's eyes dart briefly to my schematics, then up to me. "You're gonna need to rest if you want to make any more progress, you know," she finally murmurs. "You've been at it nonstop for the entire flight."

"I know." I rub my bleary eyes. "I just . . . The Level system was destroyed because of me. My own engine powered that machine, and I just let it happen. I have to figure this out."

Her eyes soften at me. "This wasn't your fault."

"Wasn't it, though?" I put my cup down in disgust.

"I never should have taken you to the drone race."

"What choice did you have?" I say gently. "You were trying to help your father. And instead, I gave Hann the last piece of the puzzle that he needed."

And now Mr. Yu was gone. I see fresh pain cross Pressa's face and bury my head in my hands. Numbers and blueprints crowd my exhausted mind.

Finally, Pressa shakes her head. "Hann would've gotten it somehow, with or without you. He couldn't have moved as fast as he did otherwise." She leans her elbows against the table between us. "How long must it have taken him to set that up? Months? Years?"

I flip incessantly through my useless sketches. "Long enough that no one noticed him building up that kind of infrastructure." The only consolation I have is that at least he *did* use a part of something I'd created. It gives me some starting point to try to figure out the rest of his puzzle, at least. But there isn't much time for that.

As I think about Hann, I feel a strange tug in my chest of something uncertain. The memory of the man's grave eyes comes back to me, along with the story he'd told me about what had happened to his family.

*You remind me of my son.*

Those words of his shouldn't stick with me. For all I know, they could be a lie. But the grief in his eyes as he'd said them . . .

He'd let my brother go. He'd let *me* go.

He'd taken down the very system that Daniel had argued against to his superiors, that I'd hated and defied every chance I could get.

*It's his fault that Pressa's father is dead,* I try to remind myself.

But was it Hann who had killed him, or Ross City's system?

The plane dips slightly, and an announcement from our captain comes on the speakers. I pause to glance out the window and see a familiar outline of land emerging beneath the clouds. The curve of California's coast.

Suddenly, thoughts of Hann dull as I realize that we are now officially over the waters of the Republic.

On the other side of the plane, Daniel stiffens at the sight and straightens in his seat. For a brief moment, his eyes flicker to mine. I remember the last time we'd visited, how uncomfortable he'd been to return to our homeland.

Now we're back.

And the Republic is strangely our savior.

\* \* \*

Half an hour later, we've emerged from the plane and are headed down the ramparts. I follow quietly behind June and the Elector. Beside me, Pressa clings tightly to my arm as she studies the entrance into Los Angeles's airport. Everything looks so different here, as if we'd gone back in time to a different era. Towering, brutal columns draped with bold banners of red and black heralding the Elector's return to his country. Tall, harsh rectangular windows. No augmented overlays or hovering digital images.

Daniel is also unusually silent, his head lowered and his hands shoved into his pockets. Republic soldiers in familiar, formal red-and-black uniforms snap to attention as we pass by. I can see my brother flinch slightly when they move. Even when we'd been here weeks ago for my interview, he was quieter than usual. Every instinct in him must be telling him that these guards are here to kill us, to arrest him, to take away his family.

Suddenly, I feel a rush of guilt at his days spent constantly wandering the Undercity. It's one thing to hear him tell me how much he wants to leave our past behind. It's another to see the past haunting every line of his body.

As we're ushered into the airport, a throng of waiting reporters flock to the railings holding them back. A barrage of cameras clicks into overdrive, and we're engulfed in a sea of blinding lights and roaring voices.

"Mr. Wing! Mr. Wing! Daniel!"

"Commander Iparis!"

"Elector! Elector, over here!"

I blink, taken aback by the onslaught. Ahead of me, Daniel stiffens even more beside June, keeping his head down as the news crews push forward toward us. I put an arm instinctively around Pressa, who has gone wide-eyed at the mess of a scene.

June looks the calmest of all of us. She lifts her head and snaps her fingers at the other guards walking alongside the Elector, and they tighten their formation protectively. Then she presses herself beside Daniel enough for their shoulders to come together. When an overly eager reporter sticks his camera too close to Daniel's face, June shoves him unceremoniously back.

"Make way! Keep this area clear!" Her voice is unwavering and efficient. The reporters part obediently, but then keep trailing us in a constant tide.

"Daniel! *Eden!* Over here!"

I turn at the familiar voice.

There, in the midst of the crowds gathered to see the Elector's— and Daniel's—arrival, is Tess, her face as bright as ever and her arm waving high over others' heads.

She doesn't try going up to June, who's technically still in formation and guarding the Elector, but I do see the two exchange a grin and wink. Then Tess darts away from the Elector's entourage and makes a beeline for us.

I'd first seen her again a month ago, when we'd returned to the Republic for my interview. I hadn't recognized much in her then of the little girl I remembered—small, uncertain, with hunched shoulders and wide eyes, always wringing her hands. She'd grown tall and straight-backed, her hair cut into a short brown bob, her movements confident and precise to match her surgeon demeanor. But the glint in her eyes, the bright echo in her voice . . . *that* stayed. And it's still here now.

She waits until we've emerged and the guards allow her through, then steps toward us and throws her arms around Daniel's neck.

My brother doesn't hesitate. He wraps his arms around her and hugs her so tightly that he lifts her slightly off the ground. Cameras around us click wildly. As he puts her back down, he tweaks her nose the same way he used to do to me as a child. She protests, shoving him in the shoulder. Like his second sibling. He just laughs.

It makes me realize how long it's been since I've heard such a lighthearted sound come from him.

"Welcome back," she exclaims, beaming at him, then looking over to Pressa and me. Her hand comes up to pat my cheek. "You haven't been sleeping well since the last time I saw you."

"I'm fine now," I say, trying not to let my embarrassment show. Nearby, Pressa watches with an uncertain look on her face.

Tess smiles shyly at her before she holds out her hand. Pressa takes it, and Tess shakes it once.

"This is Pressa," I tell her. "A friend of mine."

What I *want* to say is *my best friend, my confidante, the girl who makes me bolder than I think I can be.* But *a friend of mine* just comes out. It sounds careless, even cold.

"Nice to meet you," Tess says to her, and she manages a smile back.

"Likewise," Pressa answers. But I can see a slight tension in the way she steps away from me.

Several cars are waiting for us at the airport's loading zone. Pressa and I follow Daniel into a second car. June and Tess climb into the seats in front of us. The doors shut, and the din from outside fades to a hum of noise. Here, Daniel's shoulders relax and he leans back against the leather headrests. The Republic may not have the high tech of Antarctica—there aren't auto-cars or rails running every-where here—but it's kind of comforting. Our driver, a Republic sol-dier, gives us all a terse nod before he follows the Elector's train of cars as they pull onto the road ahead.

"News about Antarctica has been all over the news here," Tess says as she swivels around in her seat to look back at us. "Is it true, what happened to their Level system? I thought that was supposed to be completely secure."

"Nothing's completely secure," Daniel says in the silence after-ward. "We didn't know how fast it could go down, though. Every-thing works until it doesn't."

"Now what?" June looks from Daniel to me, her eyes quicksilver as bars of sunlight and shadow slide through the car's interior. "What is this man's plan?"

Daniel shakes his head. "You crumble a place's foundation, crack its walls, and anything can get in. There are fires in the streets—everything's chaos. And chaos is exactly what someone like Dominic Hann likes best."

There's real anger in his voice. With this blow, Hann is going to take advantage of this mask of liberation to seize power for himself. In chaos, monsters rise quickly.

Whether or not Hann actually *is* a monster . . . I'm still not sure.

Tess frowns at us, then shakes her head. "We all know what chaos can do," she says impatiently, waving a hand at us. "But I think what June's asking is what he wants to do with that chaos. Specifically."

At that, Pressa straightens beside me, shaken out of her daze at the overwhelming introduction to the Republic. She tilts her head at Tess. "I hadn't thought about that," she says. "Hann's taken down the entire system. What if he knows enough about it to bring it back up? Put it back in place and change it to suit him?"

Tess nods back at her. "It's what a dictator would do," she replies. "Pure anarchy is never what they're going for."

A thought snaps into place. Sometimes I forget that Tess is a girl who had scraped by on the streets and barely survived the same revolution we had. She's no stranger to understanding how a society falls apart.

It seems like an obvious next step. Why would Hann go as far as taking down a system of control just to throw it away?

And suddenly, I find myself thinking about my schematic doodles in a different light. I dig into my pocket and bring all the papers out in a crinkly mess. Then I straighten them in my lap. Pressa looks over my shoulder as I do.

No wonder there were so many parts of the machine that felt to me like they didn't need to exist. Maybe it's because the machine was never meant to just take down the Level system. Maybe Hann's invention is also designed to bring it back up.

When I glance up, I see Daniel's eyes locked on mine. This, at least, is something he recognizes in me—when he sees the flash of an idea on my face.

"What are you thinking, Eden?" he asks.

*It's time for someone else to run this place.* Hann's last words to me flash through my thoughts, searing and clear.

"What if Hann is going to rebuild it?" I say automatically. "The Level system, I mean?" I point to several parts of the machine that I hadn't figured out. "What if he's going to implement a new system, one that has him at the helm?"

The pause that follows is thick and ominous.

June finally nods at me. "How much do you know about his device?" she asks.

"Not enough," I reply.

"Any is better than none." She raises an eyebrow at me. "I hate to say it, but your meddling might be just the thing that takes Hann down."

# DANIEL

**EVERYTHING ABOUT THE REPUBLIC FEELS FAMILIAR** and strange.

I'm quiet as I walk with June during sunset through the streets of inner Los Angeles, where we'd met so long ago. When I'd first come back here with Eden, I hadn't had the time or guts to wander through my old haunts. Now that I do, I remember why I'd hesitated.

June walks with me, content to let me take it all in. Antarctica's slick high-rises and chaotic, jumbled floors are a distant world compared with this place. The red-gold haze hovering over the lake in downtown Los Angeles, iron waterwheels churning in the water. The smell of fried dough and boiled goose eggs and pygmy-pig hot dogs filling the streets. The divide between the rich and poor, the Gem districts and the other districts, still stark. These images are clear between the holes in my memory, and with them, I think I can piece together the rest of what my childhood had been on these streets.

But there are things I don't recognize. No more Xs spray-painted against doors. No more plague patrols haunting the streets of my own neighborhood. There are vegetable gardens now, patches of green striping the ground here and there, the result of people being allowed to create and sell products. And most of all . . .

Scaffolding. Everywhere. Buildings—crumbling towers, subpar housing—are being torn down and built back up again, and the bones of steel construction sites line the horizon. Plans for parks, private shops, safer neighborhoods.

"It's been a decade," June says as she notices my gaze lingering on the horizon's cranes. As always, she is breaking down my thoughts. "But change is still slow to come. Anden has been trying to bridge this gap with some new work projects. We can't afford any of this, but Anden's confident he can get international investments to keep our pace going. I hope he's right."

My thoughts waver from the Republic to the feeling of June's smooth hand sliding into mine. She edges closer to me as we near the water. The awkwardness between us is still there, lingering, but at least it's been dulled. I savor her touch. The memory of her in my arms several nights earlier comes back to me now in a wave of warmth. Somehow, beside her, this whirlwind of lost memories and dark places stills in me, and I can remember things better.

I pause at an intersection marked with the edge of the lake on one side and a pair of towers rising up on the other. One of the towers is old, just as I remember it—ramshackle layers of concrete long streaked by water and grime, the lowest floor a barely lit entrance to a bar and the upper floors made colorful with lines of drying clothes and plants draping haphazardly down rusted balcony ledges.

The other tower is new, a structure of straight lines and polished stone, its sides draped with crimson-and-black Republic banners. Over the steps leading up to the entrance are words I've never seen engraved on a building here: REPUBLIC HISTORY MUSEUM.

I look at June, and she gives me a terse nod. "Come on." She tugs slightly on my hand and starts making her way up the stairs. "They just finished it this year."

I nod wordlessly and follow her. It's better than standing in the middle of the street, lost in memories I don't want. Trying to keep the fear of my past at bay.

Inside, curators in red and black stand at the entrances of the museum's many rooms. They bow their heads in recognition at the sight of us. Our boots echo against the stone floors.

We stare at the exhibits in silence. This is a memorial to the horrors of the past. The child-size outfit of a Trial taker, plain and white, now framed and hanging. A plague patrol uniform encased within glass, its gas mask rusted and faceless. Portraits of the late Elector and those who came before him, all lining the back wall. Anden had banned his portrait being hung everywhere not long after the end of the war with the Colonies. I guess one of them ended up in here.

We step between the rooms without speaking. There are old videos from the JumboTrons, the pledge that we used to recite every morning, giant maps hanging by steel cables from the ceiling, indicating how and where the borders of America had changed over the years. There are even rooms dedicated to America before the Republic, when we were unified with the Colonies. I stare, overwhelmed, at placards describing the events that led up to the war that divided us. They've named it Coranda's War, after the young general who first staged a coup and became the first Elector Primo of the Republic.

They don't call it the Civil War. There had already been one that split the nation before, hundreds of years ago, during a time when the enslavement of human beings was legal based on nothing but the color of one's skin. There is an entire room dedicated to that, to the unified, sinister America before we existed.

We linger in this room so long that the curators have to ask us to leave as they close for the night. I don't say a word. Maybe the United States was only ever united for some. Maybe this place has always been a dystopia.

The sun is dipping below the clouds as we step out of the museum's entrance again, and the light against the haze on the lake casts the sky and water in gold. I stand there with June for a moment, taking in the intersection.

"There used to be a row of pawn shops and food stalls where this museum now is," I finally say, then point to the bar across the street. "I first met Kaede there." The memories are scattered and broken—a faded image of a dim interior, an Asian girl with a vine tattoo on her neck leaning over the bar counter to give me a clue. Then, a narrow alley, a crowd gathered in dirty, dingy rings, their voices hoarse from yelling. Me, watching a young Tess cut her way through the throngs to place a bet for us.

"This is where I first saw you," I say in a low voice, my eyes lingering on the narrow street between the two towers. The space is empty now, the shouts of those Skiz duel gamblers nothing more than an echo from the past.

June's face is serious. She doesn't turn in the direction of the alley, and I realize with a jolt that it's because it reminds her of the darkest time in her life, because I recognize the same grim look in her eyes as I'd seen back then. The memory sparks in me, clear and in focus, another piece of her puzzle coming back to me.

"I don't like coming here," she finally says in a quiet voice. "It reminds me too much of his death. Of everything that happened after."

She doesn't need to say her brother's name. Metias. I try to remember the first time I'd seen *him*, and I can't. To me, he's nothing but a blur of a Republic uniform in the night. Instead, I see an image of John, his jacket thrown over his shoulder as he heads home wearily from a long shift at the factory. I recall him reading by candlelight, one word, slowly and steadily, after another.

June has adjusted better than any of us. But even so, she's afraid of the past. Just like I am. We may not be the same people we used to be. Maybe we'll never find our way back to that place. But we bear the same scars from the same old wounds.

I reach out and touch her hand. "You're here," I reply, pulling her close. "Living in the future, changing the world around you. He'll always be a part of your story."

She leans into me, and I close my eyes as she rests her chin against my shoulders, her straight, confident body suddenly tired. She doesn't answer. She knows I understand what it's like to love a brother, to hurt for one's absence, and to worry for the one who's still here.

"You need to talk to him," she says, pulling away too soon. Her eyes turn up to me. "Eden. He is you now, in the position you were once in."

I put my hands in my pockets again and look out at the shining water.

"He's the only one of us who has any understanding at all of Dominic Hann's work. It's not the first time a nation has suddenly come to rest on his shoulders. He needs to know that you *get* him, Daniel. That you can see the past like he does, not like we do. That you'll be there for him now. He can't move forward and figure this out without you."

*See the past like he does.*

I look in the direction of where our current residence is, a sleek condo far off in a Gem district. I think of Eden's faraway look, his haunted expression when the house is quiet and he thinks no one is around. I think of the defiant anger in his gaze whenever we argue. He had learned that from both his older brothers, from John and from me. And maybe, in my singular drive to protect him, I've never acknowledged that he can use his defiance in the same way John and I once had. To change things.

Some pasts can't be left behind. They must be fought.

* * *

When the sun finally goes down, Los Angeles transforms back into the evening view I know so well—the dark, grungy streets, pockets of the city grid dark as some sectors have scheduled blackouts in order to conserve electricity.

I'm perched on a ledge overlooking our place when Eden heads into the entrance. He expects me, because he automatically turns his head up without me even moving a muscle.

"Spying again?" he calls up at me with a raised brow.

I shrug, turning my eyes up to the sprinkle of city lights leading toward the horizon. "Just idling until you came home. Not like there isn't a precedent for you being in trouble when you go missing."

I hop down from the ledge and lean against the apartment entrance. He's pale, and I can tell that behind his hesitant exterior is a deep undercurrent of guilt over everything that had happened. Deep, dark circles rim the bottom of his eyes.

A flicker of pain washes over me. Hann had done this to him. But so had I.

"Hey," I say quietly, nodding toward the Lake sector's skyline. Just studying the familiar cityscape sends another current of fear and dread through me. But this time, I force it away. I have to do this for him. "I'm going out for a run. Come join me?"

Eden's eyes widen slightly in surprise. He knows I've never really trusted his physical capabilities, and the invitation catches him off guard. It only twists the knife deeper in my chest. Had I tried protecting him every chance I could, only to turn into yet another person who has hurt him?

Then, to my relief, Eden nods. A faint smile hovers on his lips. "Sure. But you're gonna have to lead the way."

# EDEN

DANIEL'S DEFINITION OF A RUN, OF COURSE, IS different from everyone else's. In all the years he's spent darting across roofs and shimmying slick as oil between balconies and railings, he has never asked me to come with him or taught me how he does it or even mentioned where he goes. The one time when I was fourteen and tried to follow him up the side of a wall, I fell on my back and hit my tailbone hard enough to limp for several days.

"Where are we going?" I ask him now as we head out of our complex. We're dressed in comfortable clothes—loose pants scrunched at the ankles, soft hooded jackets, shoes with good traction. Nervous energy buzzes in my head.

Daniel doesn't seem bothered. He walks in front of me with the absolute assurance of someone who knows where he's going. His mess of blond hair bounces with each step he takes. I try to keep pace with his strides.

"How well do you think you know the Lake District?" he says to me over his shoulder.

I shrug. It's hard to think about our old neighborhood when we're staying in the middle of this Gem district. "I remember our street," I reply. "John's factory. Mom's workplace. The alleys where we used to play street hockey. Why?"

In the night, shadows cut across Daniel's face and hide his expression from view. He casts me a sidelong glance as he turns us in the direction of the humbler districts. It's easy to see them from this hilltop view, the areas of the city where lights turn sparse.

"Just follow me," he says, turning into a narrow street that leads to a set of tracks. "I figure it's time I show you what my memory of our past looks like."

It's an old subway stop, the concrete thick with layers of graffiti. My brother nods down the track to where the first glimmers of a train's light flicker in the darkness.

"Keep close to me," he says. "We're going to take it easy today, but over time, I'll show you how I make my way through tougher areas of the city."

Over time. "You mean, you're going to take me with you on some of your outings in Ross City?"

He gives me a brief smile as the subway pulls up to a stop. "I'll *think* about it," he replies. "If there's a Ross City to return to." Then he ushers us into the train, and the glass doors close behind us.

Half an hour later, we emerge onto the cracked, humble streets of Lake.

I have a vague recollection of this intersection—it's where I used to walk through on my way to school, at least before everything happened. I look curiously on as Daniel walks up to the building wall of an alley and tests his boot against the crumbling brick. Then he steps back and points up to show me.

"See this?" he says, touching the cracks in the brick. "If you step up on something at this height, you should be able to grab on to the second floor's ledge." Before I can respond, he backs up a bit, then darts at the wall and kicks off against the brick. He reaches up and swings himself onto the ledge, then shimmies over to the closest balcony he sees. I look on, stunned, as he swings his legs over the balcony railings and then hops up to perch against them.

"Okay," I say slowly, eyeing the brick. "Just give me a sec."

On my first try, my boot slips against the brick and I fall on my back. It takes me four more tries before I finally grip on well enough to grab the second-floor ledge. Then I pull myself up laboriously, inching carefully along the wall until I reach the balcony. Daniel grabs my arm and helps me climb over it.

I eye him, waiting for him to scold me for being careless, for that worried light to appear in his eyes. But he just shrugs. "The more you practice, the easier it'll get," he replies. "If you end up in trouble in the Undercity again, you'll know how to make a quick escape."

I look at him in surprise. "You'd actually be okay with me going down to the Undercity by myself?"

He gives me a withering look. "After everything we've already been through with Hann? You wandering the Undercity sounds like day care." He nods to the side of the building, where a thick pair of cables crisscrosses between the alley's two buildings. "Come on. I'll show you where I used to stay."

I follow him gingerly onto the cables. He steps rapidly along them, as sure-footed as if he were walking on the street. *Where he used to stay.* "John always said you never strayed far from the house," I call to him as I try to keep my balance.

"I never told John about all the places I went," he replies. "It was safer that way."

Daniel waits patiently as I take an extra few minutes to cross the wires. Then we make our way onto a flat rooftop, and from there, take a metal ladder up another floor. With each step, we go deeper into the heart of Lake, until I can see the vast, dark shoreline, the water lapping idly below us. I'm drenched in sweat by now, and my breath comes shallow as I try to keep pace with Daniel.

Finally, he stops us on a street crowded with crooked sheds and shuttered stalls, all closed for the night. I've never been this way before. Trash piles in heaps on the sides of the streets, and tattered clothes line the sides of each stall. It looks like some kind of market-place.

Daniel nods up at the second story of stalls stacked on top of the first. He points to an empty one, then the shadows behind it. I follow him up the side of the first-floor stalls until our boots clang against the tin metal sheets of the roofs. The second level of stalls is low enough that we have to duck our heads. Daniel leads us into the shadows where the stalls are stacked against the wall.

Here, the wall itself is crumbling away, so that there are tiny con-cave pockets of loose brick hidden behind the second-story stalls' cloth drapes. It's just enough space for a person to curl up without being seen.

Daniel crouches here for a moment, his eyes distant. His entire body is tense, and his hands fiddle restlessly. He swallows hard. It looks like it's taking everything in him to be back here.

"When I first started roaming the streets," he says, "I'd end up looking for these crumbling pockets in the markets. They were high and dry, for the most part, and the street police wouldn't bother you if they did a sweep through the neighborhood. You could get a decent night's sleep and no one would ever know you were in there."

I stare in disbelief at the tiny pocket of space. It's filthy and dark, littered with brick and dirt. "You'd sleep here?" I whisper.

He nods. "For years. It wasn't so bad. I liked that it was right in the markets. Made it easier to steal food."

His lips have tightened now. I look at him, wondering what kind of effort it takes for him to dredge these memories up. He has never talked about the details of his street life with me before. I knew nothing about how he survived, what he had to do, where he had to live. Now I try to picture my brother—the legend of the Republic, the star of Ross City—curled into a tight ball in this pitiful place, scrounging for a meal.

And I'd never understood. I'd never *bothered* to understand his abhorrence of this kind of surrounding.

He shakes his head at me, then starts climbing back down the side of the stalls. I follow him.

He leads me to the back alleys behind the markets, pointing out the trash bins. They are overflowing, with heaps of garbage piled around them. "This hasn't changed much since I lived here," he tells me as we walk. "Another place you could get food, albeit during more desperate nights. Sometimes Tess and I would camp in alleys like this one. The street police only did their sweeps through here every other night, you know. Lack of funding and manpower."

He pauses at the end of the alley, then points out to the water. "See that?" he says.

I look closely. Rising out of the water some fifty yards from the shoreline is an old, abandoned skyscraper, hollowed out and long gutted for parts, its skeleton towering dark and foreboding against the night. These structures litter the entire lake.

Daniel hops onto the end of a dilapidated, abandoned pier leading out into the water. He nods for me to follow. I do. Together, we make our way along the pier's rotting floorboards, hopping over parts where it's all caved into the lake. As we reach the end of it, Daniel jumps onto the lowest floor of the skyscraper rising out of the water.

I take a running start, then collapse to my knees beside him. He gives me a grim smile as we settle against the edge of the building.

"John always told us to stay away from the lake when we were kids," I finally say through my gasps of breath. "He said these skyscrapers were full of dangerous folk."

Daniel nods. "He wasn't wrong. You had to be careful which towers you chose to stay in, which floors you ventured on. Gangs would rotate in and out on these structures. I had to make sure I stayed out of their way and remembered what the schedules were. But it's the nicest place that me and Tess were able to find. Whenever we had a chance to stay on these towers on the lake, we considered that a lucky day."

A stone sinks to the bottom of my chest. I've always known, to some extent, why he's never told me his stories—why he doesn't seem like he wants to remember our home, or seems so eager to stay in the Sky Floors of Ross City. I knew, and yet I didn't know at all. I've never walked these streets like he has, never understood what he faced out here every day, a child with a family he could never contact.

I was always drawn to the humble streets of Lake, always despised the luxurious ignorance of our current home.

But I never had to fend for myself in Lake, either.

*The screaming, the blur of soldiers in our home. The sound of a shot to our mother's head.* The past crowds into my head, loud and relentless.

Daniel watches me quietly. What he sees in my expression, he doesn't say, but after a while, he looks away and leans back on one arm. "How much do you remember of John?" he asks.

An old, rusty memory appears of Daniel and me waiting around our dining table, impatient for John to come home from his work shift so that we could eat. My oldest brother's weary smile, his cheeks still red from heat and exhaustion, his arms outstretched as I'd dash from the table to greet him.

Enough nights pass now when I forget that we had another brother. The realization makes me flush with shame. "Not as much as I wish I did," I reply.

Daniel smiles. "John was the one who taught me how to change your diapers, you know."

Now it's my turn to smile. "That's not where I thought this conversation would go."

"Who do you think was in charge of you as a baby when Mom had to work late shifts?" Daniel raises an eyebrow at me. "John would drag me over to the table where he'd change you, and the two of us would hover over you, arguing about the best way to pin a fresh cloth diaper on you while you screamed your head off. It was the worst goddy chore in the world. He taught me how to put you to sleep and how to tell if you were sick. I almost burned down our house once when I was trying to boil you some mashed carrots. John almost killed me for that one."

I try to picture two young boys bickering with each other while an infant version of me looked on. I try to imagine Daniel frantically putting out a kitchen fire while John watched in horror. The thought is so ridiculous that I can't help a laugh from escaping my throat.

Daniel laughs once, too, and shakes his head. "I used to fight with him even more than I do with you. Everything was a battle. He hated how impulsive I was, how sometimes I'd stand in the street and complain about the police loud enough for everyone to hear. How many questions I'd ask about why Republic soldiers had roughed up our father or where he'd gone. I lost count of the number of times he had to drag me home after I'd gotten in some argument about Republic history with the kids at school. He was convinced I'd get myself killed someday with my carelessness, or that you'd pick up my bad habits." He sighs. "I guess he wasn't wrong."

A breeze sweeps past us, bringing with it the scent of a Lake night—fried street food, smoke, briny water. I cross my legs and try to ignore the sudden lump that rises in my throat. "I should have listened to you," I finally say, my voice so quiet that I can barely hear myself.

"I couldn't protect you any more than John could protect me. You've seen the wrong in this world, powerful forces that no brother could ever hope to hide from you. And no matter what John did—or what I do—those things stay with us forever."

I start shaking my head. "John shouldn't have had that burden. *You* shouldn't have."

"Keeping you from the truth of the world only made it worse for you." Daniel gives me a sad smile. "This place was your home too. Every single one of these rotting streets, these back alleys. This is where we were all raised, yeah? But I'm so afraid of this place, Eden. I'm afraid, even now. I wanted to hide it from you, like somehow that would keep you from being drawn back to it, so that you'd never have to know what it was like." He shakes his head and stares out at the water. "Like somehow, us leaving this all behind meant that it didn't exist anymore."

I look out into the darkness, the voices crowding in my head. As always, I can feel myself pulling away, trying to shield the jumbled mess in my mind from Daniel, to turn it inward and let it churn there until it all fades again into the background. But it doesn't fade.

Daniel's looking at me now, and I realize it's because there are tears streaming down my cheeks. I hadn't even noticed when I started crying. Embarrassed, I wipe them angrily away and try to force myself back into a state of calm. But the tears keep coming. I can't stop them.

Daniel reaches out and seizes both of my wrists in his hands. "Look at me," he says, his eyes locking on to mine. They are fierce in the night, and in them I see the same brother who had once stood up to an entire nation. "It is not weakness to open your heart. It does not make you less of a man to ask for help. To turn to someone when you're vulnerable. To need a shoulder to cry on. You don't have to bear the weight of anything by yourself. Do you understand me? I know what it's like to be forced to go it alone. I never want you to feel that way."

I find myself nodding through my tears, wishing I could have turned to him sooner, wishing I could be more like him in every way. "I see them every night," I say to him, my words breaking. "They're there every time I close my eyes. I jump at every sound. I see a soldier in every person standing at a corner. I thought—I thought if I could just drown it all out in the Undercity, if I could replace it with something else so loud and overwhelming, that it might go away—I thought if I could just see the Republic again, return home and understand my past . . ."

The pain in Daniel's eyes is raw and real. The fear of this was what had kept me silent for so long. He nods once, his hands firmly on my shoulders. "I see them too," he says quietly. "I should have talked to you about my nightmares. I can't expect you to open up to me if I don't do the same."

I nod again. "I'm sorry. I—"

"Don't be." His eyes soften, and he pulls me into a hug. "You didn't do anything wrong."

It is his embrace that finally breaks my last barrier. I cry and cry and cry. I cry because I'd never let myself truly understand my own brother, because I'd never understood myself. I cry for all the lives that our pasts have set on different paths—for June's loss of her family, for Tess's loss of her childhood, for Daniel becoming a parent when he was himself just a boy. I cry because I'm grateful that we still, in spite of everything, have all found each other.

Because sometimes, broken pieces find a way to make a new whole.

# DANIEL

WHEN WE FINALLY RETURN TO OUR APARTMENT IN
the dark hours of the morning, Eden showers and collapses into
a deep sleep. He doesn't stir again until the sun has already risen
high in the sky. At least he doesn't seem to be dreaming.

I spend most of the time awake, leaning against our balcony
railing, watching the headlines and videos rotate on the city's Jumbo-
Trons. News about what's happening in Antarctica comes out in a
steady stream. I watch the screens and see tanks roll through the
Undercity, making their way down streets full of bonfires and angry
people. There are police struggling to contain the chaos.

ROSS CITY IN FLAMES AS TROOPS,
BROKEN VIRTUAL SYSTEM STRUGGLE

The President has called for an emergency meeting today in
Batalla. But while all the politicians try to hash out a plan, time
is ticking by. My lips tighten in frustration. The advantage that
Hann has always had is the ability to ignore laws entirely. It was

my advantage on the streets too. When you aren't accountable to anything, you can move pretty goddy fast.

I look away, sick, as police surround a protester and swing their batons down at her body. The rest of the crowds raise their fists, cheering for Hann. He had wanted to make his point about the city's corrupt system. He's just willing to sacrifice all the people he claims to be fighting for in the process.

By the time my brother gets up, the sun has started to paint the sky gold.

I glance at him with a wry smile. "You look awful," I say.

Eden lets out a single laugh as he limps over to join me. He's holding his drone in one hand, its engine glowing with a faint blue light. "I don't know how you climb all over the city like that without being completely useless the next day. My legs are killing me."

I offer him a sip of my coffee. He takes it, cupping the hot mug between his hands, and we're silent for a moment while the light turns steadily stronger. Eden tosses the drone in the air, and we watch as it hovers in place, steady and straight. Eden seems lost in thought, but I don't push him. There's a new ease in the quiet between us.

Finally, he straightens and nods out at the horizon, in the direction of Antarctica.

"I saw the news," he says. "The Antarctican military has imposed martial law on Ross City."

I shake my head. "No call signals are getting out of the city right now. It's like no one knows how to function without the Level system in place."

For us, who came from the humble streets of Lake, functioning on days when the power grid died was something we were used to dealing with. But a place like Ross City suddenly stripped of its technology?

Eden moves his fingers idly in the air, and his drone shifts to match his gesture, swerving right and then left. He frowns thought-fully. "Hann said that his device would wipe the entire Level system clean," he says. "But something about what Pressa said yesterday stuck with me. She mentioned that Hann might have taken down the entire system so that he could bring it back up again. Replace it with something to suit him."

I nod. "But?"

He shakes his head. His fingers move again, and the drone obeys, flipping once in the air. "It's stupid to dismantle the entire system only to rebuild it all over again. I don't think he wiped it all clean. I think it's just suppressed somehow, that he did something to dis-rupt the implementation of the system, but that it's all still there somewhere. Intact. It's much easier for him to work with something like that." He shrugs. "I wouldn't dismantle my drone completely if I wanted to change it. I'd just revise it."

I look on, marveling at the invention of his drone as it turns this way and that, its power source strong and stable. "Are you saying you might know how he did that?"

There's a long pause, but when Eden finally nods, I note the light in his eyes. "I'm saying I can find a way to reverse it. He's using the engine that I built to power it. If I can get back into his circle, I can find a way to shut the whole thing down and get the Level system back up."

To prove his point, he waves his drone back into the balcony and lets it hover between us. Then he reaches for it, sliding his finger underneath the glowing engine. The engine gives a sudden, strange noise, and then it shuts abruptly down, clattering to the balcony floor.

I look back at my brother. The old fear rises in my chest, and images flash through my mind of him captured in the Undercity, his face pale and frightened. "But you'd need to be back in his good graces to do it," I say, echoing his words. "You have to find him, yeah?"

He nods. "The machine needs a physical chip installed on it. I have to do it physically."

The terror of not knowing where the Republic had taken him; the uncertainty of what was being done to him; the paranoia of ever letting him go again. It all rises back up in my chest. Eden can see it on my face, because he leans toward me and fixes his steady gaze on mine.

"You told me last night that I don't ever have to go it alone," he says. "Well, that goes for you too. I can do this, if you let me. But I'm going to need your help. June's too."

Everything in me wants to pull him back, tell him to stay here, stay safe. But I know he's right. His silhouette is long and lanky now, no longer the small boy I once carried through a war-torn street. There are no guarantees that he'll come out of this safely— that any of us will. But I also know, without a doubt, that he's the only one who can do this.

At last, I nod. "What do you need from us?"

"A diversion. I need to convince Hann that I've decided to go rogue from what you and the others are planning to do, that I want in on his plans. Come back to Ross City with me. Find ways to slow him down. If you and June then go after his device with what little we do know, if you're acting from the outside, then maybe I can convince Hann that I'm helping him keep it safe from you."

It's ridiculous. Too dangerous to play this kind of game with a mobster who has survived his entire life on tricks and double crosses. Hann is going to figure this out, and then my brother will be completely at his mercy.

But I still find myself nodding at him. "I'm in," I say.

He blinks, and I realize that he'd been expecting me to push back. "Do we go to the President with this plan today? Do you think they'll agree to this?"

I shrug. "There's no way in hell any of them will—not in a meeting, anyway. But that doesn't change anything we're planning to do. We don't have time to wait around watching them debate issues."

He looks at me in confusion. "You mean you're going to go behind the AIS's back on this? On the government?"

His words bring a smile to my face. My brother—the rulebreaker who has made me panic more times than I can count—has never actually rebelled on the world stage. The old part of me, the wildling from the streets, the boy who'd spent his life running the city and dodging the Republic, stirs.

I shake my head. "I'm such a bad influence on you."

At that, a grin creeps onto his lips too. "You mean, we're just going to go?"

"As soon as we can sneak out of this country. By the time we discuss it with them, they'll have no choice but to agree."

"They're going to kill you for this."

I give him a sidelong grin. "They can try."

We laugh a little at that, then fall back into silence. "What if we're doing the wrong thing, Daniel?" Eden asks me. His voice is grave again. "What if restoring the entire system is exactly what shouldn't happen?"

I look at my brother and take a deep breath. "Then maybe we don't restore it to exactly what it was," I finally reply.

I study his face, taking in how serious he is. "What are you planning?" I say.

"I can add a chip to the machine that tweaks how it handles the Level system." He digs papers out of his pocket and waves me over to the desk. There, we bend over it as he points out where his engine is installed. "The machine pulses a signal through the city's entire Level system," he explains as he scribbles. "So we pulse a new signal through it that tells the Level system what to do." He glances up at me. "Maybe we add some things to that signal that changes how the Level system judges people hooked up to it."

I frown at him. "And you can do this before we leave?" he asks.

"It's the machine that's complicated to put together. Not the signal. Once you understand how it works, you can run another signal through easily. I watched them test one, and it took a matter of minutes."

I think of the late nights I'd seen him up before, as a small boy and as a young man. The light of creation is bright in his eyes now, and as I consider his words, my emotions gradually alternate from uncertainty to wary hope. "A rebellion within a rebellion," I murmur.

Eden smiles a little. "Never let it be said that we take the easy way out."

* * *

June seems even less enthusiastic about the plan than I am. But she still shows up at our apartment late in the afternoon, her outfit simple and black, her voice hushed. Beside her, Pressa has a backpack that makes her look even more petite than she is, but she stands tall and confident, the grief in her gaze now replaced with resolution.

"If they come after our plane and we're forced to stop, let me handle it," June says. "I swear, somehow these things only ever happen when I'm with you two."

I lean against the doorway and smile down at her. "You're the one who agreed to help us."

"I didn't say I wouldn't come." She shrugs. "Anden will forgive me. It has to be done."

I reach for her hand and brush her fingers with mine. "Thank you," I murmur. My eyes skip to Pressa, who has unzipped her backpack and is handing something over to Eden. It looks like a small package of glass vials.

"This is a serum for Hann's lung infection," she says. "The way Eden describes his hoarse voice reminds me of the later stages of my dad's illness. So I used to make this serum for him out of some of the herbs we carried. It's not a cure, so don't tell him that it is. He won't believe you. But it should improve how he feels if he takes it every day." She replaces the vials and gives the backpack to Eden.

"And it's swallowed?" Eden asks.

"Swallowed." Pressa nods. "But I did make one change. Hann's serum contains a powerful sleeping drug. It'll knock him out pretty hard and give him a slight fever that will throw off his judgment and strength. Give him a heavy enough dose of the serum, and it'll stop his heart entirely."

Trying to poison Hann will be a risky move. I bet he's survived dozens of such attempts. Still, Eden gives Pressa a grim nod. My brother's feelings for her are on full display here. I can see it in the way he pulls her in for a hug and how tightly he holds her, the faint blush on his cheeks as she smiles and hugs him back. In them, I see the early signs of how, despite our backgrounds, June and I had first come together.

Finally, we're ready to head out. "Your signal?" I say to Eden.

He nods. His face is paler than it should be, and his hands are trembling slightly. But he seems calm enough as he holds up a tiny chip, so small that it could sit on the tip of his smallest finger. "Got it," he replies.

As the President prepares to host his political meeting with the Elector, we take an unmarked military car to the airfield and into a plane that June has somehow gotten for us. The soldier who salutes us as we board is sweating up a storm. He doesn't meet our eyes. June stops, though, to put a reassuring hand on his shoulder.

"I'll vouch for you," she says. "Thank you for your help. The Elector himself will pardon you—I give you my word."

He shuffles his feet. "Of course, Commander," he replies to June.

We take off in silence. The plane has been airborne for only a half hour before a call comes in, right as we clear the waters of the Republic. The pilot's voice flickers on overhead, and we all tilt our heads up as her apologetic words fill the air.

"Commander Iparis," she says regretfully. "The Elector Primo has ordered me to patch him through. He would like a word with you."

June doesn't even blink. "Of course, ma'am," she replies. I find myself marveling, yet again, at how cool and calm she can be even in the most stressful circumstances.

There's a pause, followed by Anden's deep, familiar voice. He sounds more weary than furious. "Hello, Commander," he says, addressing June. "I assume, as usual, that you have a good reason for leaving the country without notifying me?"

June looks a little guilty at his tone. "As always," she agrees. "It has everything to do with the emergency that you are currently discussing with President Ikari. We thought it best to discuss it with you while the plan is in action. There's no time to waste."

"Is Daniel Wing with you, then?" Another voice comes on—and this time, it's Director Min's. She sounds less formal than Anden, and much more livid.

"I'm here," I say, glancing at my brother. "With Eden."

"And do you have an explanation for this? Or should I have you all court-martialed the instant you land in Ross City?" She sighs. "I'll have you know that the President is sitting with us as we speak. He would like to know why I can't seem to wrangle one of my agents into line."

"You know it has nothing to do with you, Director," I reply evenly. "President Ikari, sir, the director has been nothing but gracious to me. But there are policies in place in Ross City that have her hands tied, and in turn, they tie my hands. With deepest respect, sir, the best way we have right now of confronting this crisis is for us to act against those policies you have in place." I smile a little, even though I know they can't see us. "Of course, we can discuss it now. If you like."

There's a pause, then the sigh of a man that I've never communicated directly with before. "Enlighten us, then, Mr. Wing," he says. It's a voice I've only ever heard in broadcasts or on screens. Now he's addressing me by name. Suddenly, I feel the audacity of what we're doing—of going against the leader of Antarctica.

*Doesn't mean he knows what the hell he's doing*, I remind myself. So I take a deep breath and straighten in my chair. "My brother, Eden, has had personal contact with Dominic Hann before," I say. "So have I. We've seen a glimpse of how Hann's operation works. Eden thinks that, contrary to what we think happened, Hann did not completely erase the Level system. It's only been temporarily disabled. Unless we act quickly, Hann may have plans to revise it to work in his favor. I don't know what the hell that might do. I only know that we have to find a way to stop him before he does it and disrupts the capital of our entire country."

I look meaningfully at my brother then, and Eden nods. "I think I can find a way in," he says. "If I can get close to Hann again."

There's an incredulous laugh from the President. "Is that the boy talking?" he says. "Eden? You're going to take on Hann alone?"

"Not alone," he replies. His voice is so confident and calm that I can't help but feel a surge of pride.

The director stays silent. When she speaks again, her voice

sounds thoughtful. "What do you plan to do when you arrive?" she asks.

Eden hesitates, exchanging a quick glance with Pressa. "I'll find a way to make contact with Hann," he says. "He's using the engine design that I'd made—it's not a stretch to think that he might still want to recruit me onto his team. He'd told me himself that he expected me to come back under his fold. And Pressa knows enough about the layout of the Undercity to take us somewhere where we can get his attention."

"And Daniel? June?"

"We'll be staging a diversion," June says. "We'll be trying to break Hann's system from the outside, staging an obvious attack to draw his attention. When Eden warns him about what we're doing, we're hoping it'll persuade Hann to let Eden into his circle again."

"Of course," I add, "it'd be helpful to have the AIS and the military at our back during all this. Getting arrested by our own the instant we land won't be much help. So our fate's ultimately in your hands."

I pause, abruptly nervous that maybe they won't go along with this after all. That we've all just signed our own prison sentences. The irony of it, after everything we've been though, almost makes me laugh. Across from me, June's eyes are fixed on mine, dark and logical. I feel a tingle of nostalgia, the feeling of fighting at her side, of once again working together toward something.

There's a silence, followed by a few murmurs that none of us can make out.

Min speaks first. "You are, by far, the worst agent I've ever recruited," she says. "After this is all done, you *will* stand trial, as well as your brother and those working around you."

"It won't be the first time I've been on trial," I say stiffly.

"*After* this is all done. The President will issue a temporary pardon for you. When you land, the military will be there to greet you and assist, *as is practical*, with what you need. You will have AIS resources." She sighs. "And I hope, for your sake, that your plan works. I'm not holding my breath, though. Don't make me pay for your funerals out of the AIS budget, Wing. I don't have the balance for it."

"You won't have to," I reply. "You might want to set aside a fund for our parade, though."

"I hate you, Wing."

"And I love you, Director."

Anden's voice comes on again. "Commander," he says. "I expect you to be careful. I don't want to appoint someone new. Understood?"

June bows her head. "Of course, Elector."

And that's it. The call ends, and far below our plane, the clouds close in.

# EDEN

MY THOUGHTS ARE A JUMBLED MESS WHEN WE land. Through the airplane window, I can see the skyscrapers of Ross City piercing the view below us as we hover over the landing pad on the top floor of one complex.

Looking at the cityscape sends chills along my spine. Plumes of smoke billow from the Undercity all the way up to the sky, cutting the air into light and dark streaks. The enormous virtual markers that usually hover over the city, names of buildings and cumulative scores of its residents, the lights that would wash the buildings in bright colors . . . that's all turned off. What's replaced it are troops lined up in battalions on several of the higher floors, monitoring the elevators.

I remember scenes like this from the Republic, from the days when we couldn't be sure if the nation would still be standing at the end of its war. But to see Ross City—*Antarctica*—without its blanket of technology, is to see a superpower suddenly vulnerable and exposed.

I lean back in my seat and close my eyes for a second as we start to land. Hann's face swims in the darkness, grave and deadly.

"Hey."

I open my eyes to see Pressa beside at me. Her hand is warm against my upper arm.

"You're not going to be alone down there," she reminds me.

Alone, this would be overwhelming. With Pressa here, though, maybe, *maybe*, we can do this. Still, as I watch her dig in my backpack to double-check the supplies she's brought with her, I feel a pang of fear. This is no longer a game I'm playing with my own life.

Daniel leans closer to us both, but when he fixes his eyes on me, he doesn't mention how pale I look. Instead, he holds out a small, flat phone and a tiny, insectlike drone. "The phone's for you to contact Hann," he says in a low voice that only he and I can hear. "He'll probably confiscate it from you as soon as you're in, so there's nothing else on it." He nods at the drone. "And once you're in, we're not going to be communicating via any type of signal."

I study the drone he hands me. On it is a nail-size chip. It's the patch that I'm going to install on the Level system when I try to bring it back online. A patch that will alter the system to something different from what it originally was. *A revolution within a revolution.*

"So hold out your wrist," Daniel tells me now.

I do. He takes a wet cloth, swabs my wrist with it, and then wipes it on the drone. It instantly lights up with a faint green mark, then fades back into its black color.

"This will track you down and deliver any message we need to send to you. Use it to send a message back. It'll only deliver one round before it self-destructs. Anyone who isn't you or me and tries to tamper with it will get a nasty surprise when it simulates a bug bite and then erase its drive. Got it?"

Already, my attention has shifted to how the insect drone functions.

It's solar-powered—I can tell from the sheen of its shell—and its metal body looks so much like a real cockroach body that I want to recoil from the way it flicks its antennae.

"Got it," I repeat. "I won't be able to transmit back to you, not until I figure out what our options are if we get to Hann."

"*When* you do," Daniel corrects me firmly. Uncertainty flashes in his eyes, but he just looks away and leans back.

AIS agents are waiting for us when we step off the plane. Their uniform black suits blend into one as they line up at the base of the steps, giving respectful nods to June. They greet Daniel too, albeit warily. There are several soldiers here too, in their gray and green uniforms.

I fall into step behind them as we make our way down the elevator. Through the glass windows, we get a better view of the chaos that has engulfed the city.

"Things have calmed a bit," one of the agents tells us as we go. "Martial law is firmly in place. Curfews are set for nine at night."

"And the Undercity?" Daniel asks.

His skeptical tone makes the agent turn slightly red. "It's under control," he says, as if to defend himself. "We've rounded up and jailed a lot of the protesters."

I frown, mirroring my brother's expression. "That's not going to keep people in check," he says. "The last we saw, the entire Undercity was in open rebellion. You're telling me you locked up everyone?"

The man reddens again. "We're containing it," he insists again. It's all I need to hear to know that things down there aren't really in control. Even a city like this place is going to have trouble quelling a lifetime of abuse against an entire population.

"The President has given explicit orders about you all," he goes on, impatient to shift the subject. He eyes me. "You're the brother?"

"I'm the brother," I reply, used to the question, but beside me, Daniel narrows his eyes.

"His name's Eden. *I'm* the brother."

I glance at Daniel, surprised, but he's not looking at me. Instead, his attention has shifted to the floors appearing one by one below us as our elevator gradually slows. The closer we get to the Undercity, the more of the chaos we can see. There are heavy barricades set up at intersections everywhere, and many of the lower floors are barred from entry, guards present in front of every elevator entrance.

Finally, we reach the floor where our escorts will get off to join the rest of the Antarctican troops. This is where Daniel and June will leave too. Where Pressa and I will go on alone.

June and I exchange a steady look, one borne from a lifetime of surviving together. Then she turns to squeeze my shoulder. "See you soon," she says. "We'll be right here, listening for you."

I nod, trying to mimic her calmness. When she was young, when she was going through the worst of the Republic's war, did she ever feel terrified? It seems impossible, looking into her level eyes.

While June gives Pressa an encouraging nod, Daniel and I hesitate before each other. As a kid, I used to throw myself into his arms without thinking twice. I'd grab for his hand whenever I had the chance. I'd wrap my arms around his neck and babble affections until he'd shove me off.

But now, we don't quite know how to say goodbye. We stand there for a moment, feet shuffling, expressions awkward. In the end, we don't. He just pats my arm once before giving me his crooked smile. "Don't be late," he tells me.

I nod, searching for something to say, but Daniel has already turned back around and is walking out of the elevator. At first, I think it's because he didn't want to linger any longer. Then I realize that it's because he can't bear to see me go.

Too soon, Pressa and I are alone in the elevator. We head down to the Undercity. Through the glass, I can hear the sirens coming from below, the shouts of an officer through a megaphone.

It's too much like the Republic. The sounds surround me like a blanket, and I suddenly wonder if I'm in one of my nightmares, that maybe all of this has been my subconscious, trapping me. My palms break out in a sweat. I look to my side. Pressa is pale, too, her shoulders trembling slightly.

Her presence gives me the strength I need. I reach out to touch her arm, then give her a small smile. "I'm glad you're here," I say.

It startles her out of whatever thoughts she had. She turns to me with a smile of her own, relieved, and presses herself closer to me as we reach the last floor and step out into the chaos of the Undercity.

The path toward Pressa's shop is completely shut off. We wander past police barricades and troops lining the streets, of wary Undercity civilians eyeing the soldiers or grouped behind barriers, shouting angrily.

Pressa tightens her grip on my wrist. "This way," she whispers, nodding us down a narrow alley away from the main streets.

We make our way along until we've gone past where most of the soldiers have set up. Here, the streets are more shaded by skyscraper shadows, the roads more cracked and broken.

I finally stop near where Pressa and I used to make our way down to the Undercity. The streets are quieter here, eerily so. We're in uncertain territory now. I stop in the middle of the path, then place a call on my phone to Hann with the number he'd given me.

For a moment, I think no one will answer. Maybe he changed it by now, or never meant for me to use it at all.

Then a voice comes on. It's not Hann, of course, but one of his associates. Her words fill my ears.

"Step out of the shadows, so we can have a better look at you," she says. "The boss would like to know why you're back in his neighborhood."

Every hair on my neck stands on end. They're already watching us. I look at Pressa, then motion for us to step into the light.

"Who's the girl beside you?"

"A friend," I answer. As if in response, Pressa reaches into her pack and holds up a box of vials. "Hann will remember her from the drone races. She's here to give him something for his condition."

I guess the associate wasn't prepared to hear that. She pauses for a long time. When she finally does speak again, she's still addressing me. "And what do you want?"

"I'm here to help him," I reply. "If he'll still have me. Tell him he was right about everything." I hope he can't hear the lie in my words. "And I'm here to warn him. The AIS is planning an attack on his system soon."

The phone goes silent. I wait a few seconds longer. "Hello?" I ask, but she's gone already.

Pressa stares sidelong at me. "Do you think she'll relay this to Hann?" she whispers.

My lips tighten. "We'll know soon enough."

We stay where we are for what feels like an eternity. My eyes turn up. The skyscrapers overhead disappear into the air, and if I look for too long, the sheer endlessness makes me dizzy. What if Hann has people watching and waiting everywhere up there, their eyes turned toward us in case this deal goes wrong. I glance around us. We are as vulnerable as we can be now. If he wanted to, he could shoot us down right here. And for a moment, I think that's exactly what he'll do.

A new call comes on. I answer it. My hand trembles against my ear.

Even before he speaks, I know it's him. His presence hangs in the air. "Your brother is already calling for me to meet with him," he says. "Does he know you're down here?"

So Daniel and June have already made their move. I tilt my head up, listening for their voices being broadcast. It's faint, coming from the heart of the city where the advertisements jumble the closest on the skyscrapers.

"No," I reply.

I can't tell if he believes me or not. "And why is that? A change of heart?" he asks, a touch of amusement in his voice.

I will never be able to fool him. This will all go terribly wrong. But I still take a deep breath and answer. "I just want to meet again," I say.

He's silent for a moment. My eyes lock on a silhouette that appears at the entrance of the shuttered bar ahead of us. It's one of his men; I recognize him as one of the people who had held me hostage in the Undercity. Beside me, Pressa stiffens.

He approaches us. His eyes are expressionless. "Come with me," he says.

# DANIEL

THE MAIN DIFFERENCE BETWEEN THE ANTARCTICAN military and the Republic one is that, back in the Republic, we knew exactly who we were fighting. The Colonies were pushing on our border, and their airships filled our skies.

Here, though, they hide in the shadows. Our enemies are ourselves. And it makes it that much harder to fight back.

I frown as we survey an area where we are to try to make an announcement to catch Hann's attention. Ross City used to be filled with virtual billboards that stretch all the way across the entire sides of skyscrapers. Their 3-D advertisements wandered around on each floor, all the way to the ground. Now though, with the Level system shut down, only a few screens still work, ones that were physically installed and operated before the Level system was implemented. Old-fashioned tech.

June holds out a device to me. "Here," she says, tapping its screen once so that it lights up with a blue glow.

I study it with a thoughtful frown. "What's this?"

"When we send our message out to Hann, let's send out different versions on different frequencies." She nods down at the device. "With all of Ross City's systems down, Hann will be using more primitive communication tech, just like we are. This will tell us whether or not he's listening in on one of our frequencies."

I look at her. "So we run a different message on each frequency," I reply, puzzling out what she's saying, "and based on how he responds, we get an idea of roughly where he might be in the city."

She blushes a little at me. "It's how I first tracked you down in Lake."

A dark figure standing in the middle of a midnight street, holding up vials of plague cure. Me, crouched in the shadows of a second-story ledge, talking into a crackling speaker. The memory wavers in my thoughts. "So that was how you did it," I murmur.

She looks away toward the city, as if sorry to bring it up. I wait a moment before I reach out to touch her hand. Her skin is cool to the touch.

Our beat of silence ends as an officer comes up to us to set the frequencies on the device. She nods toward the platform where we will be playing my statements. "We're ready to start, whenever you are," she says.

I nod back, then get up and head with June over to the platform. There, we run through several of the alternate statements we'll be releasing. Finally, I clear my throat, and as they start recording my voice, I begin the first statement.

"We have a deal we're ready to cut with you," I say, forcing myself to stay calm and my chin to stay up. "I know there's something you want from this city that we can offer you. But we want a meeting with you, face-to-face."

My voice reverberates into the mike. It's jarring to hear the silence around me as I record. Has Eden already found his way back to Hann? Has the man even responded to him?

"We are prepared to give you a good offer," I go on. "But the city can't go on like this. Both you and I know that. So let's find a way to negotiate, unless you want to continue this stalemate. We will meet you in two hours in the Undercity, at the intersection that divides the four quadrants of Ross City. If you choose not to come, we'll have to force you out. Let's do what we can to avoid a bloody end to this."

I finish. The message starts to play from the beginning again, looping endlessly until the meeting time. I listen to it several times. When we're all sure that it sounds right, we move on to the next statement.

A half hour passes before I record every single variation. There are differences in the locations where we're asking Hann to meet us, with the kind of deal we're offering him. I feel a sense of hollowness as we go about it. He could easily not be listening at all—or he might have figured out what we're doing in the first place. But it doesn't matter if this works or not.

All we're doing is buying Eden time.

June gives me a nod when we're done and begins broadcasting out the different messages on each frequency.

"Place a call to Eden," she says quietly. In order to give a realistic illusion that Eden and I are at odds, I need to try to contact him.

I call Eden. As expected, he doesn't answer. Even though I know he isn't supposed to, a part of my chest still tightens in fear.

I call several more times, then stop. It's a good sign that Eden isn't picking up, I tell myself. It most likely means that he and Pressa are in, and that he's no longer on the grid.

June is already checking the harnesses on her waist and legs. She's going to lead a small team into one of the intersections we requested Hann to show up in, to watch for where he might appear. I'm wearing a similar getup—hooks, harnesses, and an assortment of knives and weapons. My team will head to the opposite side of hers. Still other teams are on their way to the other locations.

I watch as she works. She may not be with her Republic teams, but even here, with a patrol of foreign soldiers at her beck and call, she exudes a natural leadership that makes them wait respectfully for her command.

A sudden sliver of a memory returns to me at that. I remember the swing of her dark ponytail as she stood in an alley, her hand on her hip and her chin tilted up, the light in her eyes invincible, calling out a challenge for a Skiz fight. *The first time I saw her. The first moment she caught my eye.* How could I not have known then, immediately, who she was?

June notices me looking at her. A curious smile touches the edge of her lips, and she tilts her head at me. "What?"

"Nothing." I shake my head, embarrassed to be caught. "I was just making sure you looked like you have everything, yeah?" I point out the gun at her hip and the climbing hooks hanging from her belt. "If, for some reason, Hann does show his face—"

"—then our teams are ready on the ground, hiding in our zones on every side of the intersection." June nods down at the street. It's desolate right now, the usual rows of cluttered shops and neon signs shuttered and fenced off. "And if he doesn't show—"

"Then we hope that it's because he listened to Eden's warning and has taken him into his circle." I take a deep breath, run through the elements of the plan in my head, and look down at my watch. "We should hear from him in several hours."

June walks up to me. She reaches out to touch my wrist with her hand, gently coaxing me to lower my arm. "We'll hear from them before then," she promises. "I've seen Eden in worse situations."

"I know." I run a hand through my hair, trying to keep my eyes on the horizon instead of on her so that she can't see my worry. "I'm just thinking everything through."

June hesitates, then edges close to me. Her lips brush mine in a light kiss. For an instant, it's as if she has created a small, sheltered space for us—even here, on a tower overlooking a standoff. I close my eyes and let myself lean into her, savoring this small moment of peace.

Finally, we pull away.

"You'd better make sure you're careful," June says.

I smile back. "You know I always am."

Then she pulls away, and the moment's over. We straighten, step back from each other, and go to our teams. I do stop, though, to glance one more time at her over my shoulder. You rarely regret the things you do, but always the things you don't. A last glimpse of June walking away. Then she's with her cluster of soldiers, and I keep walking.

Lara and Jessan are here, along with two other AIS agents. Then there are a handful of Antarctican soldiers. They give me wary looks as I join them. Guess they must've heard enough about my reputation to be nervous. Good.

"There are a number of supplies missing from one of the factories on the city outskirts," Jessan says to me.

"Weapons?"

She nods grimly. "I don't think this is just an operation to destabilize the city. Hann is ready to start a war with us."

*That's where Eden and Pressa are right now.* I grit my teeth, pushing the thought back, and nod down toward the intersection. "I know wars," I reply. "He should be careful what he wants."

Moving stealthily with all these gadgets strapped to me is always a strange feeling. I'm used to finding my footing on my own— running and hiding with the help of nothing but a sturdy pair of boots. If I'd had all this equipment with me on the streets of Lake, the Republic might never have caught me at all.

It's the work of a moment for me to scale the top of a shuttered shop and slide my way inside its second story, then weave in and out between the windows until I'm perched at the vantage point I need. From here, I get the perfect view of the street. Down below, the others are slowly getting into position—crouched in the shadows of alleys that branch off down the street, hiding behind parked buses and stations.

June should be in position now too. I look at my watch. It's almost time. My heart thuds. My head feels light. I keep imagining Hann's cold, lean figure walking up the street, using Eden again as his hostage. What if we'd overestimated his desire for Eden's work on his project? What if he's already guessed what we're doing?

The seconds drag by. The time comes for Hann to show up.

No one appears.

I hold my breath. He shouldn't appear. If all goes well, he should stay put. Maybe he'll send out a broadcast to us, just as we did to him. My hands are sweating, and I press them idly against the wall. We should receive an insect drone from Eden later, telling us that they're in. Telling us what he's doing.

The silence continues. Over the city, my repeated message continues to play. I start to let myself believe that Eden has made his way in.

But I'm not ready for what happens next. Because just as the thought occurs to me—I hear a loud pop come from the opposite side of the street. My head jerks to where June and her team should be waiting.

It's all I have time to do before an explosion engulfs their building.

# EDEN

**THE FIRST THING THEY DO IS BLINDFOLD US. I STAY** quiet, trying to remember every stair and turn we take. My shoes clank against metal floor, then clip against wood. All I hear beside me is the flutter of Pressa's breath, soft and rapid. She doesn't say anything.

I have no idea how long we walk, but finally we come to an abrupt halt. I stay still, listening intently as our guards murmur to each other in low voices. Their words are too hard to make out.

Then rough hands are undoing my blindfold, and I squint in the sudden, artificial light.

This isn't where I'd been held the first time. Instead of the estate-like property where Hann had first taken me, we're now standing on a balcony overlooking what seems like a series of walled compounds. I realize that this is right near the border of Ross City, where the bio-dome ends. When I look out beyond it, I can see the expanse of frozen tundra that still makes up the vast majority of Antarctica's terrain.

"You're back. Just as I thought."

His calm, smooth voice is like a knife scraping against my skin. I whirl around and find myself face-to-face with Hann.

He looks paler than when I last saw him. His skin appears almost entirely drained of color, nearly milky white, and new circles of exhaustion seem to drag underneath his eyes. But his gaze is as sharp and cold as ever, and his smile is the same: confident, secretive, and intimidating.

Pressa stiffens. I reach out instinctively to touch her hand, and she startles at my gesture.

At my hesitation, Hann takes a step closer to us and tucks his hands behind his back. "You took longer than I would have guessed, though," he continues. "You have a high tolerance for watching chaos unfold. I should have known that, given your past."

*Remember why you're here.* The words clank through me, and I force myself to swallow and open my mouth. When I speak, my voice comes out hoarse. "Where are we?" I ask. "And what are you doing out here?"

He shrugs, glancing out at the frozen wasteland. "The chaos in the city won't last forever. But while it does, this is the best place for us to be. Now is that something you're transmitting to the military, or are you genuinely here for a reason that matters to me?"

I hold my hands up. Already, my heartbeat has jolted up to a feverish rhythm. "No one else knows I'm here. Or, at least, they don't know where I've gone."

Hann doesn't look like he believes me. He nods at two of the guards behind him, and they head over to pat us down. I hold my arms up. Pressa does the same.

"I know you left the city with your brother," he says as we're inspected. "What did you spend the last few days talking with him about?"

"We didn't talk so much as fight." I hope the bitterness in my voice is convincing enough. Beside me, Pressa snaps at the woman searching her—the woman shoves her roughly against the glass wall. I take a step toward them. "Hey, how about telling your folks to cool it?"

Hann's smile turns amused. "What's this? You've brought your friend with you? Maybe you're serious after all, if you're willing to risk her life." He tilts his head at me. "What are you doing back here, Eden?"

The two guards finally step away from us. Pressa straightens her shirt, still mumbling under her breath, and comes to join me again. If she's putting on an act of bewildered innocence, she's doing a good job of it.

"I came to find you without my brother knowing. Right now, he's probably sending out search parties for me." I take a deep breath. "When I last saw you, you told me that you wanted my help on your plans for restructuring the way Ross City's system works. I'm back here because I'm wondering if you still need me."

At that, Hann narrows his eyes. "Why the change of heart?"

I hesitate. We may be here because we're trying to fool Hann, but suddenly I feel like I'm here of my own free will. Hann studies me with the same concern and interest he had on the first night of the drone races. And even now, knowing what kind of person he is, I feel the urge to impress him.

"I did what you said," I end up muttering, forcing myself to go on with my lie. "I had an audience with my brother and the AIS. They're studying the chaos happening in the city right now."

"And what did they say?"

"Their solution to fixing it all is to just—sacrifice the people in the Undercity." I pause here and look at the floor. "I told Daniel he couldn't let that happen. I thought that he would understand, of all people."

When I trail off, Dominic Hann studies my face carefully. "But he sided with the AIS, didn't he?"

I look up to meet his eyes. They're still studying me, and I wonder if I remind him of his son right now. "They're trying to lure you out with a deal," I say. "They might even have broadcasted it by now—that they're willing to meet you somewhere and negotiate a truce, in exchange for you disabling your system."

I'm not sure whether Daniel and June have already made their move, but when a glimmer of recognition appears in Hann's gaze, I get my confirmation.

"They're setting up a trap for you," I go on, my words speeding up in my urgency. "So I came here to tell you that, as a gesture of goodwill. I can give you the details of what they're planning as far as their operations go."

"A gesture of goodwill." Hann is still watching me with that lethal stare, and a shiver runs through me. He doesn't look convinced.

I glance at Pressa, and on cue, she pulls out the glass vials that she'd carefully packed for us. "My name is Pressa," she says, slightly bashful. "I was the one who had the counterfeit money at the drone race."

Hann nods once at her. "I remember you," he replies.

Pressa's voice is small but clear, more secure than mine, and I find myself admiring her calmness. "Eden told me about your condition, so I got these from the apothecary where my father used to work."

"Used to?" Hann raises an eyebrow at her.

Pressa trembles for a moment. Hann sees it, and to my surprise, sympathy flickers in his eyes at her. "I'm sorry," Hann says to her, gently now.

In spite of everything, I can feel Pressa want to take his pity. Is that what I look like when I feel drawn in by Hann's charisma too? My anger flares suddenly. Mr. Yu had suffered under the Level system, but he'd died because Hann had caused this chaos in the Undercity.

Hann may be a father figure, a man with a painful past. But he's also a master manipulator.

Pressa doesn't answer Hann's words. She tightens her lips instead and holds up the vials. "This is a serum that's supposed to ease the symptoms of your lung infection. I used to make it for my father, when he was suffering from his condition. It's not a cure. But it's the next best thing."

Hann doesn't seem to expect this. His eyes widen slightly, and he blinks once. He glances at me before returning his focus on Pressa. "And why would you offer that?" he says.

His piercing stare doesn't faze her. Pressa lifts her chin. "I spent a lot of years helping my dad run our apothecary. His failing health was the reason I started gambling in the drone races in the first place. I know what it's like to struggle like you did. And while I don't agree with your plans, I do believe in your cause. So here we are, helping you out. The question is, will you return the favor?"

Whatever hesitation Pressa might have had earlier, I see none of it in her response. She's cool and calm. It's as if this reminder of the death of her father has given her new strength.

Hann doesn't move, but I can tell that Pressa's boldness has brushed past some vulnerability hidden in him, however small. His eyes linger on the vials. I might be promising him my skill set—but Pressa is promising him his life back.

Hann frowns at me. "You think this is enough to bring you both into my fold," he says. "You dare to dangle my own life in front of me?"

Maybe we've stepped too far; maybe we've overreached. The fear coursing through me starts to make way for anger. "Fine," I snap. "You want to know the real reason why we're here—why we're offering all this? It's because I'm sick to death of watching both you and the Antarctican government play your games with the Undercity, while the people there are the ones who suffer from your antics. I've had it. You've seen the riots, haven't you? I watched Pressa's apothecary get destroyed and her father . . . There's nothing left of it. She had to flee. Is that what you're fighting for? Is that you championing the rights of the lower classes—turning their home into a battleground? We're here right now, offering all we got, because I can't stand watching you do this for another second. Stop hurting the people you claim to be helping. Stop all this—and I swear I'll serve you however you need. I'll help you build a system that upends everything Antarctica had. Whatever you want. Just put an end to all this."

When I finally stop, I realize that I'm shaking. My words must have come out convincing. Even though everything spilled out in a mess, and all I remember is a blur, I can still hear the anger in my voice ringing in the air.

Hann is quiet. His face is serious now, his eyes thoughtful.

Pressa speaks up now, in her clear, steady voice. "You may think you're taking a huge risk, putting your trust in us like this. But we're risking everything here too. Our friendships. The people we love. Our lives."

I don't know what Hann might be thinking. He might kill us on the spot now, furious with us for having brought his personal problems into this. Or he might toy with us, capture me to use me again as his pawn. Or maybe, *maybe*, we've managed to strike him in just the right way.

Hann takes a few more steps toward us. His head is bent down, as if in deep thought. He stops right in front of us.

"Luckily for you both," he says, "the AIS and your brother did indeed try to make a deal with us an hour ago. They announced it in the central city, then set up their people to trap me." He holds out his hands. "As you can see, I'm still here, and they failed. But it looks like your information was good."

So the false trap had already been triggered. I let out my breath, hoping my relief looks like it's directed at being right about what I told Hann.

He extends a gloved hand in my direction. "You're not in the clear yet, Eden," he says. "I'll be watching you very carefully, as well as your friend here. But if you do as you say, then I'll agree to shift my tactics. I'll hold you to it." He gives me a tight smile. There's something there that resembles trust. Something sincere. And even now, I feel like I want to believe it.

I nod and shake his hand. Pressa does the same. But the look in his eyes makes me afraid even as I feel a twinge of sympathy for him. My words had sounded so real and true to him because a part of me had believed what I was saying. Because I'm still convinced, even a little bit, that Hann's mission is a good one.

What does that mean? When the time comes for us to move against him, will I be able to do it? And what will happen when he figures out that we've betrayed him?

I tremble at the thought as Hann turns away and motions for us to follow him.

*If he figures us out, he'll kill us.*

# DANIEL

**MY VISION BLURS. I CAN'T EVEN FEEL MY HANDS. A** shout bursts from my chest. Before I can even register what I'm doing, I'm running, heading toward the stairwell and down to the street toward where the explosion had gone off.

*June. She had been there. Right there, right where the explosion happened.*

A thousand images, each more horrible than the last, flash through my thoughts. I readjust the mike on my ear and keep calling into it, even as police dart around me in a chaotic scene.

"June! June? Can you hear me? What happened down there?"

No answer. I spit out a swear and reach the stairwell. I don't even bother taking any of the steps—with one leap, I'm on the railing and hopping from one turn of the stairwell down to the next, grabbing hold with my hands and swinging down to each lower floor until I land lightly on my feet at the bottom floor of the building. I race out into the street.

Rubble and white dust obscure the air. I squint as I race through it. Already, a patrol of soldiers is down here and directing others from June's squad back to the main building. None of them look injured yet, but their faces look bewildered and coated in ash.

"June!" I call out again as I stop before the pile of broken concrete that used to be the building where she was supposed to be staked out. It's a twisted mess of broken stone and metal now. A wave of light-headedness sweeps through me, and I sway. She must be in there somewhere, trapped underneath all the debris, she must be injured, dead—

A hand suddenly materializes out of the white dust and seizes my wrist. My head jerks to one side.

It's her.

June has a grim smile on her face. "You don't think that could take me out, did you?" she says.

Every bone in my body turns weak at the sight of June. Her hair's rumpled and dirty, and ash smears her cheeks, but otherwise, she looks unharmed.

"You're the goddy worst," I snap at her. "What the hell happened? I saw you there, and then I saw the explosion—"

She's already pulling away and tugging me along with her back toward the tower where I came from. Her eyes are dark and serious. "You *thought* you saw me there," she corrects me. "I had a decoy team stationed instead, fully aware of the risk of a potential attack from Hann." She squeezes my hand in apology. "I'm sorry I didn't tell you. I wanted Hann to think that he'd succeeded, and he would if he noticed your shocked reaction."

I'm so relieved to see her safe that I have no strength to be angry. "You play some dangerous games," I say instead, shaking my head.

June holds out the device from earlier, then brings up a

transmission that looks like it came from somewhere underground. "Obviously, he heard this transmission," she says. "And with that display, he's going to think he struck a blow against us. It should also make Eden look trustworthy enough to him, that he came to warn him about a plan that actually happened, that clearly you didn't want to happen."

We walk in silence for a moment before we return to the command center. There, the other transmissions are being analyzed. None of them had seen a similar explosion go off.

I point to an area underneath the eastern border of the city. It's near the outskirts, where the biodome ends and the Antarctican tundra begins. "This general area," I muse. "It's likely all his people are stationed near there—otherwise we might have seen more reactions to the other transmissions."

"And it looks like Eden's successfully made contact with him," June adds.

Eden. My heart seizes again at the thought of my brother back under Hann's control. I look to where June points at the footage of the explosion looping on one of the screens in the room. "It was what Eden said he would suggest Hann do, as a reaction to our offer."

"Any word from him yet?"

June shakes her head. "Nothing yet. But we should get something tonight."

I nod, trying not to let my fear show through. I push away from the table, then go to stand in front of the window looking out over the city. Over the speakers in the center, I can hear Director Min talking with their officers, getting updates on what's happening.

The sooner this is all over, the sooner things can return to normal. But as I look out at the city, at the chaos that has filled the Under-city's streets, I wonder if that normalcy is even possible.

A revolution within a revolution.

June isn't the only one working without telling everyone every detail. Change never happens unless you force it.

# EDEN

**THE ONLY WAY I CAN TELL THAT NIGHT HAS FALLEN** is by the blackness of the skylights in the building. Outside, beyond Ross City's biodome, the open tundra must look like nothing more than a pitch-dark sea. Even from inside, I can hear the roar of the wind across the empty plains.

Pressa and I are alone with Hann now, in a room that looks like it's operating as his office. Outside the doors stand his guards. Inside, it's just him, seated wearily against a chair, and for the first time, he looks like a vulnerable man.

Pressa stands over him and holds out a single vial. "These may make you cough a little at first," she warns as she presses one into the palm of his hand. "But they'll start to kick in soon after you swallow it. You're supposed to take one a day."

Hann gives her a wary look, but doesn't move to stop her. His guards outside aren't looking out at the rest of the building, but inside at us. Their guns are hoisted. If they sniff even the slightest hint of us trying to poison or sabotage Hann, they'll fill us with bullets faster than we'll ever be able to explain ourselves. So Pressa moves slowly, emphasizing each of her words.

I find myself marveling yet again at how calm she can stay.

"How long has your family lived in the Undercity?" Dominic Hann asks her as she pours the contents of the vial into a cup and mixes it with hot water.

Pressa doesn't say anything for a second. Her concentration stays on the mixture she's preparing. "As long as I can remember," she replies. "My grandparents came to Ross City when they were fleeing chaos in their own country. They ended up in the Undercity. My dad says the apothecary first belonged to them."

"I see," he says.

He's testing her, I realize, with the way he watches her as she stirs the concoction. He's looking for something unusual in her gaze, the secret of why we must really be here.

But he doesn't stop her as she works. I realize that, maybe, he's genuinely hopeful this will work.

As she works, I speak up. I clear my throat and lean forward from the desk I'm seated on. "Like you said," I tell Hann, "the military's not going to stay back forever. We don't have much time. What do you need done on your system?"

Hann tilts his chin at me. "You'll be in charge of installing a hack on the system that redirects all Leveling to be under my control," he replies.

A chill courses through my veins, as cold as winter wind outside. Our assumptions had been right, after all. He's going to make himself the sole dictator of what's legal and illegal. I blink, feigning shock instead at the scope of the hack. "A program that can do that?" I ask. "It'll take far too long."

Hann observes me with his penetrating stare. "Not if you're working on it," he replies. "I'm told it's a simple matter of installing a new chip on the system. You'll take a look at it tomorrow night."

Tomorrow night. It's too late. If I'm going to keep with our plan, I need to dismantle things and install our own chip sooner than that. I frown at Hann. "Show me the system tonight. If it needs to be done manually, I'm going to need all the time I can get."

Hann studies the liquid in his mug. Nearby, Pressa holds her breath. "You're going to do it when I tell you," he replies. The command in his voice is cool and detached, so used to being obeyed that he doesn't even bother questioning whether or not I will.

"But—" I start to protest again.

In the blink of an eye, he whips a hand out at Pressa and seizes her wrist right as she starts to pull away.

She gasps. I freeze.

Hann looks at her with an unblinking gaze—and then finally releases her. There's an unspoken threat in his words as he turns his eyes back to me. He's suspicious of why I want access so soon to his system, why I'm not questioning his ambition. He's telling me that he could easily snap Pressa's wrists, that he could slit my throat and leave our bodies in the streets like he's done with so many others.

It's easy to forget that Hann is known for being a cold-blooded killer. The sudden flip between this and his vulnerable, exhausted self leaves me reeling.

"After you," he says to her, as he holds out the mug that she's handed him.

To my amazement, Pressa doesn't falter. Instead, she nods and holds the mug up. She takes a long sip. I have to stop myself from reacting as she does and giving us all away, but my muscles feel weak with tension at her move. Does this mean the effects will hit her too? Did she guess this might happen?

"You might feel a little weak tonight," she says to Hann when she's swallowed some of the drink. Her voice has a slight tremor in it, but she manages to keep her words slow and measured. "Some clear liquid may come up in your coughs, but it's a good sign that the medication is working. If the liquid looks dark, we'll need to give you some antibiotics."

Hann waits, watching her. But she just meets his gaze with her own calm one, and if I didn't know what we were doing, I'd think she was genuine, nothing more than someone following through with what she's promised him.

For a moment, I don't think we'll get away with it.

Then his cold gaze disappears. He leans back, looking more satisfied now that Pressa has drunk enough of the serum herself.

"I'll show you the system tonight," he says to me. "Tomorrow morning, I expect you to have an efficient solution for implementing what I want. I should be able to tell that you're the top student in all of Ross City." He gives me a brief smile at that.

I nod back and let out a slow breath as Hann rises to his feet. He straightens his jacket, looks once at Pressa, and gives her a terse nod. "Tomorrow, we'll talk again. I appreciate your help."

It's not spoken with gratitude. There's a promise in there, a confirmation that tomorrow we're going to have to face him again. I just follow Pressa and murmur in agreement, then head out of the room behind him. My eyes stay lowered, but I keep my attention on Pressa beside me.

If we can survive the night, we just might make it out of here. But if things go wrong, I may just have overreached for the last time.

* * *

Pressa and I are allowed to stay in the same room, with a set of twin bunks stacked on top of each other. Guards are stationed right outside the entrance. We're to take our dinner in here, and I'm going to be shown where the system is kept.

The instant we close the door, Pressa reaches into her pocket and puts a pill in her mouth.

"What's that?" I ask her.

"The antidote," she murmurs to me before she swallows it. She makes a face. "Ugh, so bitter."

"The antidote?" I shake my head in disbelief. "You'd planned for him to ask you to do something like that."

She blinks. "Of course," she replies. "You always have an antidote for every concoction you make. We feed our customers this stuff."

I realize with a pang that she still talks about the apothecary as if her father were alive. "You handled that like you've always known how to do it," I say.

She shakes her head, then motions for me to sit down on the bed beside her. "With any luck, he's going to be down and feverish all night, tossing and turning in bed. I don't expect him to wake up until late morning."

I nod. "It should give us enough time to work," I reply.

She looks at me. That lopsided smile I know so well from her appears on her lips, and for a second, it looks like she's going to lean

313

forward and kiss me. My heart leaps in terror and excitement at the thought.

I don't know if Pressa saw something in my expression, because she abruptly backs away and clears her throat. "Remember the first drone race I ever took you to?" she says instead. "You were shaking so bad, I thought you were going to pass out."

I laugh along with her nervously. It had only been a couple of years ago, but I felt ages younger then. "It was the first time I'd ever been to the Undercity, period," I reply. "You didn't even give me a heads-up. You just tossed me right into the fray with the bets and the crowds."

"I was saving you some time. It's better to jump into cold water all at once, instead of painfully edging yourself in."

"Right."

We're silent for a moment. "Let's say we succeed in all of this," I say in a low voice. "Let's say everything just resets back to how it used to be. Are you going to be okay? Your father? . . . His shop?"

Pressa shrugs, trying to play it cooler than I know she feels. "If we make it out of here in one piece, maybe the AIS will help out Dad's apothecary, give me a stipend that lets me pay for the repairs." Her words trail off, and for a moment, we sit in silence, the weight of her father's death pressing down on us.

"I mean, I might have some connections," I say to her. But I feel a pang in my chest. If for some reason our plan to interfere with the Level system doesn't work, Pressa's going to go back to her life in the Undercity, battling her way through the Levels just like everyone else. I can see the struggle in her eyes as she thinks the same thing.

Finally, she looks down and says, "If we make it out of all this, I'd like to leave the Undercity," she says. "Go somewhere new. Find an adventure." She's silent for another beat. "I stayed for my father. Now he's gone, and I don't know what to do."

Then she laughs and shakes her head, as if this is an impossible dream forever out of her reach.

I touch her hand. "You'll know," I tell her. "You always have."

Pressa gives me a tired smile. We sit without speaking for a moment before she looks at me again. "Do you feel sorry for Hann?" she asks, her voice softer now. "I mean—I'm not saying that he's someone we should sympathize with, but . . ."

Do I feel sorry for him? I'm about to say no, of course not . . . but something makes me stop. I think of the way Hann has to have his medicine tested. "A little," I end up replying. And I realize that maybe she's asking because she does.

Pressa nods down at the medicine bag she tossed onto the bunk bed between us. "I think he might have been trustworthy, a long time ago. He has the characteristics of someone from the Undercity, you know? You always find a way to make things work, until the world makes it impossible. And even then, you have to hang on."

I'm quiet at her words. The world had thrown Pressa out, and yet she somehow still managed to hold on to the goodness in herself, had never truly wavered from what was right. And I found myself wondering about the fine lines in our lives that turn us one way or the other—that the hardships my brother or June faced twisted them in one direction, while Hann went in another.

"When this is all over," I finally say, "I'm going back to the Republic."

Pressa smiles again. It's a sadder expression this time, like she'd known all along, and the sadness twists my heart into a knot. "I never thought you were going to stay here in Antarctica," she replies.

I look at her. "You didn't?"

"Eden, you've lived your whole life with your shoes pointed in the direction of the Republic. That glint's in your eyes every time I see you. It's where you belong." She puts a hand on my arm, and I think back to when she'd helped me up after the others in the university had shoved me to the ground. I think about what she's doing right now, with me. If I head back to the Republic, I won't get to lean on Pressa anymore.

"I . . ." I don't know how to finish my sentence. I'll miss her? I've liked her ever since we first became friends? That when we hang out late at night, I love watching her beautiful eyes flash in the dim light, reflecting the glow of everything around her?

She just smiles at me and leans closer. "Just visit me sometimes, okay?" she whispers. "So I can see how you're doing."

I swallow, searching for a good way to tell her how I feel. And in the middle of that search, I realize that what I've wanted to do all along was just to show her.

I lean toward her in the silence. Then I kiss her.

It's a light kiss, my lips gentle against hers. She stiffens in surprise at my gesture, enough for me to pull away and give her a hesitant look. Maybe I shouldn't have been so forward about it.

But before I can apologize, Pressa wraps her arms around me and pulls me back. She kisses me again, harder this time.

Every thought I have scatters. I can't believe that I never knew this is what should have happened between us, that I never made a move earlier. There's a bitterness in our kiss that reminds me how little time we might have left. I pull her close, wanting more, regretting that I'd held back so long.

At last we pull apart, our breaths shallow. Pressa looks down, a rare moment of fragility coming across her face. She laughs a little. "I've always wanted you to do that," she murmurs, peering up at me through her canopy of lashes.

"Well," I murmur back, "thank goodness I did something about it."

Our conversation's interrupted by an abrupt knock on the door. We dart apart as one of the guards comes in. He doesn't smile at us. Instead, his eyes lock, cold and unfeeling, on mine. "Hurry up, both of you," he tells us. "Hann doesn't have all day to waste showing you the system facilities."

I stand back up and give the man a firm look. Beside me, Pressa rises and lifts her chin, steadying herself back into calmness.

"Right behind you," I say to the guard.

He glares at me again, casts an ugly glance at Pressa, and turns around, motioning for us to follow him. It won't be long now before all our plans come to a head. Pressa and I exchange a quick glance before I follow the man out the door.

That's when I realize that the tiny insect drone Daniel gave me is no longer in my pocket.

A jolt of panic rushes through me even as I try to keep my expression calm behind the man. But Pressa senses my sudden fear. She gives me a questioning look before she realizes what happened. Her eyes widen.

Maybe the drone fell out of my pocket.

But a feeling of dread swells in my chest. Somehow, I know that it wasn't an accident. Somehow, I *know*.

Dominic Hann took it.

# DANIEL

**ANOTHER FITFUL SLEEP.**

This time it's a dream of my past, another series of memory fragments I'm struggling to piece together. Some of it doesn't make
sense at all—a bundle of sea daisies floating in the middle of the
ocean, a lone figure struggling through a frozen tundra. But when
my dream finally settles, it lands on a memory from childhood.

It's of when I'd already been living on the streets for a year.
Tess is nowhere in sight; I haven't even met her yet. I'm still limping
badly at this age, and when I finally make my way past the rooftops
and stop behind a chimney near my mother's house, I'm drenched in
sweat.

My hands are bloody and raw from pulling myself up onto ledges.
The hollow in my stomach feels like a cavern. All damn day, I struggled
to find enough food to fill up that emptiness—but the day was difficult. No trash to be found. Guards patrolling the newly docked
supply ships. I barely escaped the clutches of a street stall mer-
chant selling pygmy-pig entrails strung on sticks. The smell was so
intoxicating that I forgot myself for a moment and lingered too

long. He lunged at me with a butcher knife. I got away, but not before he managed to catch me with the edge of the blade and sliced clean through my side.

I sway weakly. My hand stays pressed against my skin, but blood is still leaking out of the wound, staining everything black. I look desperately down at my mother's home. The candles are lit inside. She's home, and probably so are my brothers. As if on cue, I see John's silhouette walk past the window.

They don't know I'm alive. If I reveal myself to them, how will they react? What will the Republic do to them if they somehow make my family talk?

Another stab of pain lances its way up my side, and a soft groan escapes me. I lean my head back against the chimney and close my eyes. I can't stay like this. If I do, I'll die. In the morning, someone will find my lifeless body up on the roof, and a car will come to drag me away to some unmarked mass grave.

The side door to our home swings open, and a rectangle of golden light momentarily beams across the alley. John emerges with a bag of trash. The screen door claps shut behind him as he heads down the block to toss the bag into one of the bins.

I hesitate again, blinking sweat out of my eyes. My world is spinning now, my head dizzy from the loss of blood. Still, I find myself holding back.

Another wave of nausea hits me. I grit my teeth and swear. Then I finally begin making my way painstakingly down the side of the building. My hands cling desperately to the gutter running along the wall. The cold, slick metal is tricky, and I nearly fall several times.

At last, I reach the ground and collapse with a grunt. I pull myself up laboriously, then stagger toward my house right as John starts making his way back to the door. He steps inside, turning away from me.

I open my mouth to call out for him, but I'm too weak. As the screen shuts behind him and he locks the inside door, I crawl up to the steps. One, two, three. I reach the closed door, gather the last of my strength, and knock.

For a moment, I don't think the sound is strong enough to be heard. I wait a few seconds, listening for my brother, and then try knocking again. Still nothing.

I sink against the steps and close my eyes, savoring the cold of the stone. They might find me dead here in the morning. My mother will scream. John will furrow his brows in grief. And Eden . . .

Then the door suddenly opens a crack. I look up and find myself staring into the blue eyes of my older brother.

He doesn't recognize me, at least not at first. His mouth curves down into a frown I'm all too familiar with, and for an instant, I feel like I never left home at all. I crack a feeble smile at him.

"It's me," I manage to croak out. My hands move aside from my wound to show him the blood soaking my shirt. "Could use some help, John."

That's when the realization hits him. He knows my voice, remembers the way I screamed for him when my train pulled away after I failed my Trials. His face drains of color, and his eyes widen in shock.

"Daniel?" he whispers.

But I'm too weak to answer now. I slump against the steps, trying hard to focus on them. I feel arms wrap around me and scoop me up. I shiver in the cold. Then I'm lying on a dining table lit by a flickering light, and staring up into the bewildered face of my brother.

"It's impossible," he's saying over and over again. He runs a hand through his hair even as he takes a knife and cuts my shirt open. "I saw them take you away—they told us you were—you were—"

"Don't tell Mom," I whisper. "Don't tell Eden." A hoarse cry escapes from my lips as he wraps something tightly around my wounded waist. "I had no choice but to come to you. But if they know I'm here, they'll kill all of you."

John pauses in his work for a moment. He leans his head down toward me and rests it against my shoulder. It takes me a moment, through my delirium, to realize that he's crying. I try to put my arm around his shoulders, tell him I'll be all right. But even here, something cuts through my dream.

*This isn't real.* Because John is dead.

I try to focus on the ceiling. It twists and morphs, and then somehow I turn into the one standing by the dining table. John isn't here anymore—I've replaced him. And the figure on the table isn't me, but Eden, a child version of him, chubby-cheeked and wide-eyed, in shock as blood seeps from his chest.

I frantically try to stanch my little brother's bleeding, but it's no use.

"Eden?" I call his name. "Eden. Look at me." My hands are covered with scarlet. No matter how tightly I bandage his injury, the blood continues to pour. What has he done? He's gone to save others—as always. But now he's dying, and there's nothing I can do about it. I look up and scream for help.

There's no one here, though. It's just the two of us.

\* \* \*

I jolt awake with a shudder. There are smooth hands on my face, but it takes me a moment to realize that they belong to June. In the darkness, I can barely make out her eyes. She's looking at me in concern.

"Hey, hey," she says gently. "You're okay. You're right here."

My body's drenched in sweat and trembling all over. Apparently, I collapsed on the couch and drifted off to sleep while waiting for Eden's message to come in, for him to tell us that he's securely in Hann's circle. The image of young Eden bleeding to death on the table is still fresh in my mind. I close my eyes in an attempt to blink it away, but it lingers like a stain against my eyes.

"I'm okay," I finally whisper, nodding at June. "Just a nightmare. It's fine."

From her expression, I can tell June knows instinctively that my nightmare must have been about Eden. But she doesn't press it. Instead, she nods and looks away toward the window. The metal of her epaulettes clinks softly.

I didn't realize she was dressed in her full uniform. Her eyes are alert, glittering in the night.

"What's going on?" I say, gradually shaking off my dream's fog of terror. The room comes into sharper focus. Through the window,

I can see the silhouette of Ross City's outskirts. "Eden—did we hear from him yet?"

June shakes her head, and before she even starts talking, I feel the ominous pit stretch in my stomach. "Nothing. It's zero-three-hundred hours. He should have responded hours ago."

No sugarcoating. There's no use in doing it, and June knows. I fight to keep my fears at bay, but she can see it spilling out onto my expression. I sit up straighter on the couch. "Any signals at all coming from the drone Eden has? Is he still in the same location?"

June looks at me with a grave face. "Daniel, there's no more location signal."

No more location signal. It can only mean three things: Eden chose to remove it, for his and Pressa's safety. The drone itself doesn't work anymore. Or . . .

Hann has discovered and disabled it.

# EDEN

**MY MIND WHIRLS FRANTICALLY AS THE GUARD** motions for us to follow him.

Hann had taken the drone. He must have.

For an instant, I think we're done. They've caught us, and there's nothing we can do to stop Hann from killing us.

In front of us, the guard gives us an impatient wave of his hand. "Hann's waiting," he says.

Pressa glances once at the door and mouths a single word at me. *Go.*

I don't know where our surge of courage comes from. Desperation, probably.

Pressa's hand shoots out and seizes the guard's wrist. Before he even has time to utter a shout of surprise, she yanks him hard inside the room and shoves him against the wall.

He gasps, then snarls at Pressa as he moves to grab her throat.

I strike him hard in the jaw before he can touch her.

If there's anything I've learned from my brother, it's how to throw a punch after getting jumped.

My hit lands true. The guard's knees buckle, and everything in him goes limp as he slides slowly down to the floor.

Pressa gives me an impressed look. "Nice one," she says.

I shrug. "The benefit of a brother who's an AIS agent," I reply.

We waste no time stealing out of the room and locking it behind us. Our clock is ticking now. There's no going back. My steps quicken across the metal stairs leading to the upper levels of the building.

Here, I recognize the cavernous space that houses Hann's construction site. Everything is cloaked halfway in shadows, as if silhouettes of guards are standing in every corner. We move slowly, startling at every stairway.

Finally, we arrive at the construction site I remember from when I'd first been held captive. The mazelike cavern full of rows of blinking machine lights is as ominous and mesmerizing as ever, the glow casting everything in the space in a dim blue hue.

I pull Pressa down beside me before she can reach the top landing of the steps. There, we crouch in the shadows, watching the two guards standing along the metal railing leading down to the main floor.

Pressa's gaze sweeps the endless corridors of computers, her mouth slightly open at the sight. Then she glances at me. "How do we get down there?" she whispers, emphasizing the words soundlessly.

I glance at the guards. Their eyes are turned down toward the rest of the floor space. If we can just get past them, we'll be able to lose ourselves in the maze of halls and make our way to the control platform located at the other end of the building.

I study the railings of the steps. If Daniel were here, he'd avoid the guards altogether and shimmy down the side of this railing, dropping quietly from floor to floor until he reached the ground below. They'd never even know he was here.

Before my brother took me on his run through the Lake district, I'd have even laughed at the idea of even attempting to do this. Now, though, I find myself looking at the landing, wondering if there's a way I could at least get us one floor lower and bypass the guards. I may not have Daniel's agility—but maybe I could find a way with my own tricks.

I begin shrugging off my jacket. Pressa glances curiously at me.

I gesture at her jacket, telling her to do the same, and then point at the railings beside us and then at the ground below.

Pressa blinks at me. "Are you out of your mind?" she whispers.

"If you want to fight those guards, be my guest," I whisper back. Then I slide over to the metal bars of the railing and loop my jacket through the holes. The bottom of the railing is open just wide enough for me to slide through. It's a tight squeeze, though.

Pressa watches me go for a moment before she comes over to join me.

I lie flat on my back and push through the bottom of the railing, then lower myself gingerly, the sleeves of my jacket wrapped tightly around my left fist. I dangle over the edge, a silhouette lost in the shadows. Up above, the guards don't move.

I let myself swing a little back and forth. Then I let go. I catch myself against the lower floor's railings and manage to land in a soft crouch. There I stay for a second, breathless, listening for the guards above to notice and mutter to each other. Nothing.

Pressa comes shortly after me. She hangs in midair for a beat too, before doing the same and crouching beside me. Her landing is quieter than mine, but one of her bootlaces clinks against the metal railing. The sound makes a tiny echo.

We freeze. For a second, we don't hear anything.

Then one of the guards shifts above us. "That came from downstairs," she says.

"Are you sure?" the second one answers. "It just sounded like the building shifting."

"Probably." The first guard starts to move. "I'll take a quick look in case."

We have to move, now. I grab Pressa's hand and we start running as quickly as we can down the walkway toward the next flight of steps. Up above, the guard's footsteps clank loudly on the stairs. If she reaches us before we can get to the lower floor, she'll see us and sound the alarm.

We race on quiet feet down the flight of stairs. We make it to the ground floor just as the guard above us starts walking across the second-floor walkway. I look around. The maze of halls now stretches out all around in every direction.

"This way," I whisper, then choose one of the halls that seems to head toward where the control platform will be. Pressa darts silently behind me.

Behind us, the guard reaches the bottom floor too. She stops there for a moment but then continues, searching for the source of the sound.

My palms are drenched in sweat. All I want in this moment is for Daniel to be here, but I push the thought away immediately. Focus on the task at hand. That's all I can do. We make our way down the hall. Somewhere behind us, the guard begins to turn into our hall.

We reach the end of the corridor. Pressa yanks me along as she turns us sharply right, down another corridor. There we crouch, sucking in lungfuls of air.

The guard walks halfway down the hall we just came from. I get ready for us to sprint again. But then the guard halts, silently, for a moment. We wait, two tense, frozen figures.

Finally, the guard sighs and begins walking the way she came. Her footsteps grow more distant, until I hear the familiar clang of her walking back up the stairs to join her partner again.

Pressa lets out a shaky breath. I glance to our side, then pull us to our feet. "We're not far now," I whisper.

We race down the halls. There's no time. Hann is probably delirious with fever right now. It's our only chance.

The hall stretches so long, the computers on either side so endless with their blinking lights, that I start to think I'd taken us the wrong way—when finally, up ahead, I see the corridors abruptly open up.

There, ahead of us, is the circular control platform.

I skid to a halt before it. Then I reach down with trembling fingers and pull the chip from the side of my ankle. Beside me, Pressa gapes at the space.

I power the system on. The virtual circle expands out in an arc around us, followed shortly by the burst of glowing white nodes. I kneel in the circle, trying to remember how Hann had shown me to access the main system. *Almost there.* Pressa stands guard nearby, looking out at the corridors in anticipation of guards.

Finally, I find it. The system initiates, showing me Hann's profile. I'm so relieved that I almost let out a shout. The chip holding the signal I created is in the palm of my hand. I touch it once, and the data on it suddenly appears to hover over my hand.

Now all I have to do is download it into the system.

But I don't get to. Because the instant the system comes on, I hear a familiar voice behind me. It's Pressa, but her words are tight with fear. "Eden," she says.

I know he's here without even turning around. The hairs rise on the back of my neck. I look over my shoulder to see Hann standing there, his eyes fixed on me. He doesn't look sick at all. There's a faint smile on his face.

"I was wondering when you'd make your move," he says. His eyes flicker calmly to Pressa. "And the little doctor. You're looking very awake, miss."

Pressa freezes beside me. She doesn't say anything back to him. Hann's referring to the fact that she hasn't reacted as she should have to the concoction she'd fed him. I shift slightly toward her as if to protect her.

At her expression, Hann just smiles coolly and turns his attention to me.

My heart lodges in my throat. I glance long enough at his face to gauge how he must be feeling right now. His face is pale, and there's a very faint sheen of sweat on his brow. But otherwise, he seems to be alert. He must have figured out Pressa's serum in time to give himself an antidote of some sort, or he hadn't drunk enough of it.

Behind him are at least a half-dozen guards, their weapons drawn and pointed in our direction. Hann snaps his fingers once. The virtual system that had hovered around me now shifts to encircle him.

"This was once a part of the grid that Ross City used to store the Level system's data," Hann tells me. "Now it's part of my system."

I wait for him to mention the drone he must have taken off me. He doesn't. Everything he's doing seems natural right now, as if he knows nothing about my and Pressa's plans at all. It makes me shiver.

"You always wanted something greater than just disabling the Level system," I say. "You wanted to control it for yourself."

"Exactly," he tells me. He waves a hand once before me—and when he does, I suddenly am able to shift the floating nodes around. "And once you start behaving yourself as part of my crew, you'll have access to all this as you help to rebuild it for its new purpose."

*Once you start behaving yourself.* Now when I look at Hann, I can see the dangerous glint in his eyes. Gone is the grieving father I once saw, the man who had lost his wife and son. This is the killer, the criminal.

"I found your clever little drone," Hann says softly to me. "Or were you going to tell me at some point?"

I step slowly around the circle, my attention still partly fixated on the nodes. Every single one is a marker of how you level up—at least, in Hann's new world.

"What's the point of doing this?" I say suddenly. "Corrupting it all, destroying the Level system, and then replacing it with your own? What about everything you said against the city, that you didn't believe in people being treated like this? Now *you're* just going to do the same thing?"

Hann smiles. "Sometimes it isn't the idea that's corrupt, but the one operating it," he replies. "Would you want the entire Level system deleted? You've seen what kind of chaos can reign in the streets without it."

It's almost as if he knows about the chip I planned to install into the Level system too. I hate him for the gray zone that he keeps challenging me to think in.

"Think about how many people in this city must be terrified right now, without the Level system in place," he continues. "The Undercity's civilians have suffered, been suppressed, and been beaten back into line by the city. Now imagine that *I* replace this city's government. *I* return the Level system to its place—only now, it runs how I desire. The Sky Floor citizens lose their power. I hand it to the Undercity's population. People hate chaos, you know. If you hand them back control over their lives, they will fall to their knees before you and shower you with gratitude."

I scowl at him. "So you want the people to look up to you instead as their savior, after they've suffered through the chaos that you inflicted in the first place."

Hann nods. For a second, the fatherly side of him returns, and his gaze softens. "My son, Erick, was as sharp as you are," he says, shaking his head. "I wish you could have met him. He was such an intelligent boy, so full of potential. He was as promising as you."

Even though I'm standing here as his captive and enemy, I can tell that when he looks at me, there's someone else he imagines in my place.

Then the moment's gone, and his eyes harden again. "You think I let you back in here without suspecting anything?" he says. "That you suddenly had a change of heart, that you really chose to turn your back on your brother?" He shakes his head, looking almost sad. "You really think I believed that you wanted to cure my condition?"

Pressa scowls at him. "That medication was real," she interrupts.

"Oh, I know." He raises an eyebrow at her. "And I appreciate your administration of it. You'll have to forgive me for emptying the contents of my stomach afterward, though. I've heard those herbs will cause terrible fevers. Or were you already aware of that?"

Pressa's jaw tightens. She opens her mouth to say something back at him—but before she can, Dominic Hann has a gun in his hand, the shiny barrel pointed in her direction.

I move toward Pressa, but he's too fast.

He fires straight at her.

# DANIEL

**"DANIEL—WAIT!"**

I can barely hear June calling to me as I hurry out of the building's waiting rooms and out into the main control area, yanking my jacket on as I go. The air outside is crisp and cold, and the simulated night is heavy, broken by a smattering of screens playing advertisements.

*"Day."*

It's only the sound of my street name that makes me pause long enough to turn around. June catches up to me, her hair bobbing in the wind, and grabs my arm with one hand.

"You're not going down there alone," she says firmly.

"I have to."

"We have no idea why Eden didn't send his message. He could just be late for some reason, or trying to fix his device. There are a dozen possibilities. If you just go down there now, you could be blowing his cover."

"And what if he's in trouble?"

"Then Hann will let you know soon, without a doubt." June

crosses her arms. "You think he won't pass up an opportunity to use Eden against you, if he figured out this whole plan?"

I hold up both hands. "That all makes sense—I get it. But if he's preparing to use Eden against me, then we're already too late. He's not going to let Eden go again. And if he knows that we're aware of what he's doing, that we're coming for him, he'll be ready for us." I shake my head. "I can't just sit around here and wait."

June sighs and looks away for a second. Her eyes flash in frustration. I'm reminded suddenly of the way we used to argue when the Republic was in the thick of its war, and a part of my heart twists in guilt. "You know me, yeah?" I say, taking a step closer and leaning down toward her. "You know I can do this. I've been at it my whole life. Let me go alone. It'll be easier for me to hide if I'm on my own. Stay up here and watch my back. Keep track of my location. And if you see us on our way out, tell the AIS to be ready for us."

She turns to me now. The frustration on her face has given way to fear, and within that fear, I see the same worry I have every time she risks her life.

"Then hurry up," she finally says, leaning toward me. Her voice is soft and steady. "We'll be ready for you. I promise."

I think of the night we shared, all our moments of awkwardness, the slow dance of getting to know each other again. The potential of a lifetime with June. If there's any reason to make it back up to the surface, it's for that—and I'll be damned if Dominic Hann takes that chance away from me. I have lived through revolutions and war, massacres and illness. I'm going to survive this too, and so will my brother.

I bend toward her. My lips gently touch hers, and for a moment in time, we stay locked together. Then I pull away. "I'll be back before you know it," I say.

* * *

The cool night air bites at my cheeks. The tracker June put on me, a patch of metal at the middle of my back, feels cold against my skin. There's a cap pulled down securely over my eyes, and a black half-mask covering the bottom of my face. As I head deeper into the quiet outskirts of Ross City, the familiar sense of being alone on the streets comes back to me. There's something oddly comforting about it. I pull my cap lower on my head, then pick up my pace and dart through the shadows.

With the city's system offline, I can't bring up a map before me like I usually could. All I'm relying on is the memory of the location that June showed me on a map back at central control, the last location we'd received from Eden when he went down with Hann's men. I won't have anyone guiding me to where they happen to be. I'll have to find my own way there.

Finally, I stop at an intersection nearest to where I remember the location dot was. This street corner looks abandoned, but Hann's guards could be hiding in some building, watching for anything suspicious.

I pause in the shadows of one of the buildings, pull myself up to the second-floor ledge, and then take out a small metal sphere from my pocket. The AIS has a number of weapons that remind me of the

Republic's. This one is like a homemade smoke bomb, what I used to make back in Lake—except it's much stronger, and the smoke spreads over a wider area.

I glance up at the buildings around me, looking for any telltale signs—a glint of light, the flash of a mirror—anything indicating someone lying in wait.

For a while, I don't see anything.

Then, the slightest movement in one of the windows. Someone's up there.

I smile a little. Then I edge along the side of the second floor until I reach a balcony. I crouch in the shadows and lift the smoke bomb. Then I fling it as far from the intersection as I can.

It clinks once as it hits the ground. Then it explodes.

Smoke bursts in every direction, filling every crevice and alley in its wake.

I turn to look back at the window where I'd seen movement. Sure enough, there's another flicker—and an instant later, shadows shudder through the darkness on the street below me. Hann's minions, off to check what's happened.

I push my mask higher. When the coast seems clear, I drop back down to the first floor without a sound and dart toward the last building, where the location marker had been.

The space looks like a factory sitting on the edge of the city. It's enormous. Its exterior is almost completely solid, except for a row of glass windows wrapping around the very top of the building, reflecting the lights of the city.

Behind me, the guards' shouts are already starting to echo in my direction. They're heading back. I rush to the building and scan it for any easy entryways. Everything looks locked down, though. My eyes turn skyward to the glass windows again. Then I step onto the hinges of a metal gutter and start pulling myself up the wall.

I'm making my way to the third floor by the time two of the guards return to their stations. They're clearly agitated, their voices sharp and harsh. No doubt someone has already alerted Hann about the smoke bomb. But there's no time to dwell on what they might do next. If Eden's not contacting us, he's already in trouble.

I freeze on the fourth floor, right below the glass windows, as one of the guards shines a flashlight in my general direction. The sweeping light barely misses me. Sweat drips down my brow. If I can just leap up to grab the window ledge, I can pull myself up out of his angle. As he steps closer below, I edge around the side of the wall until I've turned the corner. Then I jump and stretch out my arm, seeking the ledge.

I catch it. With all my strength, I pull myself up and shove the window slightly. It slides open by a sliver.

Inside the building, dim light filters through the glass to illuminate a seemingly endless maze of computers. Their blue sensors blink in unison.

This is the construction site that I'd glimpsed when I was first captured.

An instant later, I notice a circular platform in the center of it all. The disc of metal on the floor glows with a faint light, and virtual holograms—a web of white nodes—hover over it.

I take one last look over my shoulder, toward the guards approaching the outside of the building below. Then I swing inside the building, pull the window shut behind me, and lower myself carefully into the shadows that slant against the wall. There I cling, barely gripping the hand- and footholds I can find.

A noise from the center of the space makes me turn in its direction. Three figures silhouetted by the light have stepped onto the circular platform. When I recognize them, my chest tightens into a knot.

It's Eden and Pressa, their bodies turned to face a man who is unmistakably Hann. Guards are already approaching them from the shadows of the halls.

They've been caught.

# EDEN

**PRESSA JERKS BACK WITH A GASP OF SHOCK.** Blood sprays the floor as the bullet hits her hard in her left shoulder. She falls to her knees.

I'm stepping in front of her before I realize what I'm doing. "You know I was the one behind all this," I snap at Hann. The iron smell of blood penetrates the air. Behind me, Pressa bites back a choked cry.

Hann doesn't look moved at all. Instead, he aims his gun toward Pressa's leg. "You can keep talking while I work," he says. "I'll let you know when it's your turn."

He readies to fire again. I lunge between them. "*Wait!*" I shout out, holding my hands up. "Please! Wait a second. I—"

But he's no longer interested in talking. He shifts his gun slightly, aiming instead at her left arm.

My mind spins frantically. "Let her go, and I'll do whatever you want. Use me as ransom, kill me, anything."

He gives me a cool look. "I already plan on ransoming you out," he replies with a shrug.

"And what would your son think of all this?" I demand.

"He would think you're stalling me for time," Hann says. There's no sympathy in his eyes now, nothing but a low-burning fire at the audacity I have for bringing up his family. He points his gun at Pressa's head this time. I stand in front of her, but it's a helpless gesture.

"Is this what you imagined for yourself, if your son and your wife were alive?" I finally snap. "You think you're the only one who's ever suffered? You think this is the solution to everything that's gone wrong for you?"

This time, a flash of anger darts across his features. He shifts his gun so that it's now pointing at me instead. "I wouldn't know, would I? Because they're gone. And that's the last time you will mention my family to me again."

A surge of adrenaline floods my veins. He's going to shoot me. I think of my own family—of my brother, all I have left, waiting alone for my signal. There's no way I'm going to let this man kill me here. I'm walking out alive, one way or another.

As if something in the universe has aligned at my thought, I'm compelled to look behind Hann, toward the glass windows lining the top of the building. There, silhouetted against the shadows, is the shape of a young man crouched on top of one of the towering computer shelves.

Daniel is here.

It's all I need to see.

I suddenly lunge toward Hann.

He doesn't expect me to do this—all he's known of me is the awkward brother, the shy one, the one who still has to wear glasses in the dark. I duck low as I reach him. Before he can fire at me, I barrel into his legs and throw him off balance. *Remember what Daniel taught you.* The words flow through me like a current of electricity. In one move, I seize the gun from his hand and hold it up to his temple.

His guards all still at the sight.

"Back away from her!" I shout at them as I nod toward Pressa's kneeling figure. "Drop your weapons!"

In my grasp, Hann laughs. Only now can I tell that he's noticeably weaker than I remember him from the last time I saw him. Either he didn't avoid Pressa's serum as well as he claimed, or his illness has worsened significantly. Perhaps it's both.

"Well," he says. "Thank goodness you've got some surprises left in you."

A sharp elbow strikes me hard in the chin. Stars burst in my vision—I'm forced to release him. He still moves faster than I can. He whirls around, seizes my arm, and locks it into a hold. I barely manage to twist out of his grasp, but he knocks the gun from my hand. It clatters to the floor.

He reaches down for it. In the same moment, I take the chip and swipe all its data onto the platform's system.

The entire web of nodes flashes in a ripple of scarlet. I allow myself a grim, satisfied smile. Hann's system shudders, corrupted, then deletes. Almost immediately, I see virtual markers reappear over Pressa's head, over Dominic Hann himself, over his guards—the city's original system has reset.

This is the only thing that buys me some time. Dominic Hann freezes, shocked at the sight of his system undone. I don't wait for his reaction beyond that. I'm already sprinting toward Pressa, who has managed to struggle to her feet. In the chaos of the moment, I grab her hand and yank her forward with me. I chance a single glance over my shoulder.

Daniel's no longer where he was crouched by the window. If he's here, then he might have already alerted the AIS as to where we are. The troops should be arriving soon. Hann's eyes are trained on me now, and the fury in them sends a wave of terror through me. I turn around and run faster.

"Hang in there," I say breathlessly to Pressa.

She just clenches her jaw and fights to keep pace with me. "I've had worse," she replies.

A bullet pings behind us. I duck instinctively as we round a corner of one hall. Behind us come the shouts of Hann's guards. I stoop for a second, frantically gathering my thoughts. We have to hold out until the reinforcements arrive.

Suddenly, a popping sound comes from the ceiling. I glance up to see artificial misters all turn on in unison, filling the space with a thick fog. It's the building's original fire retardant, meant to put out fires in this maze of computers without damaging the systems with water. The mist is so dense that it settles onto us like a blanket. I can barely see Pressa beside me. Around us, the guards shout in frustration. An alarm begins to blare.

I smile a little. Daniel must have set it off.

Pressa taps me. In the thick fog, an emergency light has turned on, its searing green light cutting through the veil of mist at the far end of the building. "An exit," she whispers to me.

I nod. "Come on," I urge, taking her hand again. Where's Daniel? Can he see us through all this?

We dash through the gray mist, keeping our hands out against the computers to guide us. I feel a surge of panic at how blind we are—the murky surroundings, the shouts in the air—it all reminds me of the Colonies' final attack. Of my stumbling through the mist, calling out my brother's name. My heart pounds against my chest. I force it down, trying to tell myself that I'm not back there.

Another bullet sparks against a computer near us. We both cringe, falling to our knees. They're getting closer to us.

Then suddenly—I hear a startled yell, followed by a sharp crack that must be to someone's head. *Daniel.* Had they gotten him? I look behind us, trying to see through the fog, but can't make anything out. Another loud crack, followed by a scuffle.

Then, out of the mist, materializes a familiar face covered in a black half-mask and a cap. My brother's blue eyes meet ours.

"They're on their way," he says to me before he bends down and helps me hoist Pressa back onto her feet. She hisses in pain.

It's all I can do to not break down in front of Daniel. He's here. He's come for me. I start to say something back, but a ripple of gunfire behind us forces all of us to drop again to our knees. The bullets ping hard against the computers.

"They're coming from the side," Daniel says to us in a rush. "They're cutting us off from the exit."

"Where do we go?" Pressa gasps out.

Daniel glances up, where a lattice of steps snakes upward onto a metal walkway. "Up," he replies. "We're going to draw them away from you. Make a run for it. Do you understand?"

She looks ready to argue, but Daniel's eyes are the color of steel. She decides against it, then folds her lips into a grim line and nods.

Daniel looks at me. "Remember our climb?" he asks.

I nod without a word.

"Good." With one leap, he pulls himself onto the top of the computer shelves, then reaches down for me with a hand. "Then let's go."

I take his hand and haul myself up. Down below, Pressa crouches, facing the direction of the exit. Daniel glances toward where the shadows of guards can be seen darting through the fog. He nods at me and forms a foothold with his hands.

I take a few steps, then step up with his help and reach for the first stair railing I can. My fingers close around one of the metal banisters. I haul myself up. As I go, Daniel comes beside me, moving easily through the fog.

Bullets spark below us. I hope they're not aiming for Pressa. She's already invisible to me in the mist.

I pull myself over the first railing and hop up for the next one. Daniel's up before me and reaching down to help me. I climb up and over the second stair railing. Now we can look out at the shrouded warehouse. Above us is the walkway that leads along the top of the building before curving back down toward the exit.

We're almost there. On the other side, beyond the exit door, is the Antarctican army. June.

"Come on," Daniel urges me. We rush up the last flight of stairs until we reach the edge of the walkway suspended above the rest of the building.

That's where I freeze.

Standing at the other end of the walkway is Dominic Hann. He must have seen where we were headed, even through the fog—he knew we were heading for that exit. Now he's blocking our way. His eyes glint dark and furious through the haze.

Behind us, I hear the clatter of his guards' footsteps on the lowest staircase. We're trapped.

Daniel's arm shoots out to protect me. "Stay back," he whispers, his gaze locked on Hann.

"No," I reply. This has always been my fight, the beginning of my haunted trips down here to the Undercity, the struggle to understand who I am. So I push my brother's arm away and shake my head. When he resists, I turn to look him directly in the eyes. "I can do this."

Something about my expression seems to click with him. He searches my face, hesitating, and then forces himself to take a step back. "Fair enough," he says. "But hell if I'll let you go alone."

A small smile touches the edge of my mouth. "Never said I didn't want your help," I reply.

Hann walks toward us. A red light—probably turned on with the alarm—has started sweeping across the building, and it washes the man in scarlet, as if he were drenched in blood. His lips curl into a snarl.

"Where do you think you'll end up?" he calls out to me. Even now, in his anguish, his voice is smooth and deep. "Where do you think that exit leads to?"

"A place you don't control," I answer.

He laughs bitterly. "Does it make a difference? You'll be under the thumb of someone else. And I could have shown you something so much better."

He draws something in his hand—a glint of metal flashes in the fog. Then he lunges for me.

He's so fast that I barely have time to throw myself to the floor of the walkway. Daniel leaps up onto the railing with a single jump, spins, and ends up on Hann's other side. But the man keeps coming. He swipes at me once, twice. I scramble backward. As the blade flashes again in the light, I kick my leg up. My boot catches his hand. It's not enough to make him drop the knife, but it stops him long enough for me to get up and throw myself at him.

He stumbles backward. I twist around in his arms before he can stab at me with the knife, then force his wrist to one side. Behind him, Daniel shoots out a leg and trips the man. He goes down, taking me with him.

But he's back on his feet in an instant. Another dagger appears in his other hand. He strikes at my brother. Daniel arcs backward—but one of the blades catches him on his shirt and slices clean through. Daniel winces. A touch of red stains the fabric.

Everything around me fades at the sight. My teeth clench. The muscles in my arms tense.

"You asked me if I thought this was the solution for everything gone wrong in my life," Hann calls out. He strikes at me and I jump backward. The guards are making their way up the stairs behind me—they'll be here any moment now. "Nothing can fix the past, Eden. Don't you know that by now? Where is your mother? Your brother?"

I lunge at him again. This time, in my rage, I kick out at his hand and manage to knock one of the knives from his grasp. It clatters to the walkway floor. He's starting to tire. Beads of sweat line his brow.

"This isn't about fixing the past!" I shout back. "It's about repairing the future! And all you're doing is—"

"—making it better!" Hann finishes, striking at me again. His knife slashes through my sleeve. I feel the bite of the blade as I duck low, seeking the knife he'd dropped. Daniel, still clutching his chest, whirls around to face the first guard that reaches the end of the walkway. He dodges a blow from the man and kicks him hard against the railing.

Hann is breathing heavily now. I can hear the rasp of his lungs. "Do you think the city is going to change what they're doing? Now that you've erased our chances of fixing things—do you think the city will do what's right? That they'll listen to you?" He nods down toward the exit. "Think your young friend will get to do anything other than go back to suffering in the Undercity?"

Even now, even here, his words have a way of seeping into me. I remember the way he shot Pressa, that he would have put a bullet through her head if I hadn't stepped in. "The city wasn't the one who tried to kill her," I snap, and throw another punch at him. "Or who killed her father."

He dodges my blow and hits back, hard. His fist catches me on my jaw. Stars burst in my vision. I collapse onto the walkway. Somewhere in the distance comes a shout from Daniel. And—am I hearing it right? A shout from *outside* the building, through a megaphone. A searingly bright light shines into the warehouse through the glass windows. The AIS has arrived.

Then a boot kicks me hard in the stomach. Pain lances through me. I gasp, curling into a ball.

"You think she's better off living?" Hann's voice is hoarse with anger now, as if he's no longer talking about Pressa, but about someone else. "So that she can struggle to get by, day after day, on her rigged Level? You think you'll keep in touch with her after your elite internship? You'll return to your life in the Sky Floors while she gets to crumple a little more with each passing year." He seizes me by my collar and drags me up. My face is so close to him that I can see the film of tears against his eyes. "I see all this because I've seen it before. Call me whatever you want. I'm not the villain you seek."

"You're right," I spit back in his face. And I'm telling the truth. He's not. "But you've got your eyes set on the wrong villain too." I lunge up with my boots and kick him as hard as I can. He releases me. "If you have to sell your soul in your quest to make things better," I say through gritted teeth, "then you'll never succeed."

He slams me back against the railing. Behind him, I glimpse Daniel leaping over the side of the banister and swinging out of the grasp of one of the guards. There are more and more of them now.

Hann stares me dead in the eyes. "Be their puppet, then," he snarls. "Let them animate your broken limbs." Then he grabs me and shoves me over the side of the balcony.

Daniel shrieks my name. As I fall, I grapple for a handhold and barely manage to cling to the side of the railing, trying not to tumble down three floors.

Below, the exit finally bursts open. A swarm of shouts suddenly echoes through the space. *The troops. The agents.* Their guns are held up, pointing at us.

I struggle to hang on. Above me, Hann gets ready to dislodge my grip and send me falling.

I stare up at him with a look not of anger but of grim determination. "This isn't what they would've wanted," I say to him.

Then I twist up. Daniel's lesson comes to me in a flash. I swing to one side, grasp the banister with my other hand, and then use my momentum to kick high enough for my boot to grip the railing where my hands are. I shimmy up with a final burst of strength.

I don't know if what I said made Hann hesitate for an instant. Maybe the faces of his lost family appeared to him. Maybe what froze him for that fraction of a second was the thought of those he'd once loved.

Whatever the reason, Hann doesn't get a chance to strike me down before I swing over the railing's edge.

My boots connect directly with his chest. The force of the impact sends him careening backward. He stumbles, hits the railing, and flips over it. For an instant, it looks like he might catch himself. But then he tumbles over.

I have a sudden instinct to catch him and pull him back. A surge of panic rushes through me. But it's too late now. For a moment, he looks like he's frozen in a state of falling. Then he hits the shelves below and crumples to the floor.

Agents swarm around his body, their guns all pointed down at him. Hann's guards have already backed away from Daniel—their hands are up, their weapons on the ground as soldiers head up to our walkway. Among them, I see a young woman with a lean figure, her shoulder-length hair swinging as she races up the steps toward us. *June*.

I sink to my knees. I look at my brother, who staggers toward me, still bleeding from his chest. He crouches down beside me with a weary look. We're both bruised and battered, but we're alive. How long ago it seemed that Pressa and I joined in on the drone races, when I couldn't bear to stay away from the Undercity, where I could still see echoes of my past. Maybe not much has changed since then. Tonight, after I go to bed, will I still be haunted by my nightmares? Will I see Pressa crumpling to the ground, bleeding—will Hann's final gaze lock on to mine as he falls from the railings?

I don't know if he's dead. I still don't even know if he was entirely wrong.

Daniel puts his hand on my neck. The sudden surge of adrenaline is waning now, and we lean against each other in exhaustion. Our lives have always been a war. Maybe that war won't ever be over. But at the end of it all, we still have each other. It's this thought that keeps me whole.

As Antarctican soldiers approach us, I pull back to give my brother a tired smile. "Still here," I say.

He smiles back. "Still here," he echoes. "And not leaving anytime soon."

# DANIEL

JUNE TELLS US THAT DOMINIC HANN ULTIMATELY survived his injuries. I can tell you from personal experience that it's possible to live through a four-story fall if you know what you're doing and learn how to land right. Hann's not the kind of man you kill easily. But his days of terrorizing Ross City have come to an end. He won't be leaving prison anytime soon, not with the level of security they have on him.

It doesn't mean things in Ross City have been resolved.

Eden and I get the update as we sit at the hospital, where doctors are tending to our injuries. My brother hasn't said much since we were escorted from the outskirts and brought back to the center of the city. Already, most of the Level system has been restored, and with it, everything else: signs hovering over the buildings, virtual banks and stores, the elevators that restrict people to the floors where their Levels allow them to go. It's all back up and running, as if nothing happened.

*Almost* as if.

Now I sit in the waiting area alone, looking out at Ross City while Eden is visiting Pressa in her hospital room. From here, I'm so high up that I can't make out the Undercity. Before everything happened with Hann, I'd let myself believe I was relieved to not have to see the troubles down there all the time. Now I feel uneasy that it's invisible from this vantage point.

Eden's past arguments with me echo in my mind. How had I let myself become so far removed from that world? Why had it taken everything falling apart here for me to understand what Eden had been trying to tell me for years?

I look down at my hands and trace the faint scars here and there. Old scratches from my days running buildings. Cuts from the fights I used to get into. They are memories of a past I thought I wanted nothing to do with anymore. After all, Hann had been consumed by his past, had let it twist him further and further until he withered away into nothing but rage.

But I can't just pretend that my past never happened, either. The comfort of not remembering is an artificial thing. I rub my hands together, then sigh and lean against my knees. The scars are still there, long since healed over.

"Hey."

I shift instinctively at the touch of her hand on my arm. It's June. Today she's not in her formal military uniform, but in a breezy collar shirt tied casually at her waist, her hair pulled loosely back into a low, messy braid. She smiles at me, then takes a seat beside me.

"I head back to the Republic tomorrow," she says.

I try to keep the disappointment from my face. "So soon," I reply.

Her expression wavers. "Anden's currently talking to your

President, figuring out the details of us resuming our trade routes."
There's a slight pause as she glances at me. Loose strands of her
hair fall from her braid, and I pull back the urge to tuck them behind her ear. "I heard the Level system is back in place."

She says it with a question hanging at the end. I don't answer
right away, either. I nod out toward the city. "More or less," I reply.

Except it isn't really the same. Eden's chip installed something
else onto the system, a few alterations to what it had once been.
June knows it too, and when I meet her gaze again, she doesn't seem
surprised.

"I hear there's a protest planned in the Undercity tomorrow,"
she says.

In the old Level system, a protest would have been too hard for
Undercity citizens, those with lowly, single-digit Levels, to partic-
ipate. The penalty for going against the government is having your
Levels halved, and your future Leveling severely punished.

But with Eden's new chip and our alterations, that won't be the
case any longer. Across Ross City, people will gradually find out
that they won't be penalized for protesting. Or marching. They
won't be punished for doing what Pressa had been doing for her
father—trying to transfer her own points to help him reach a Level
where he could buy the medications he needed. There are a dozen
differences we'd secretly implemented onto the Level system.

Whether or not the city will let it all stay in place, though, is
another question. I'm going to have to explain it all before the AIS.

"When are you going to let them know what you did?" June says
after a while.

"They want to see us this afternoon, as soon as Eden and I are out of this hospital." I clear my throat.

She nods. "If you need me to vouch for anything . . ."

I smile at her, then reach over to touch her hand. "I know," I reply.

Her hand lingers, holding gently on to mine. "We can't save the world," she says softly.

"But we still try anyway," I say. "One day at a time."

Her hand squeezes tighter. I wonder if we'd ever had this kind of ease around each other, where we could show our love for one another without a dark cloud perpetually hanging over our heads. It's a strange new feeling, this freedom.

"Eden's internship at Batalla starts soon," I say. "I'll be headed your way."

She smiles. "Are you ready?"

I don't think so. Maybe I never will be. Still, my heartbeat quickens at the thought of being back in the same country with her, and I look away, suddenly nervous. "I've never belonged here," I say instead. "Maybe the Republic has always been my home. It's about time, yeah? It just took Eden giving me the nudge to do it."

A glint of disappointment flits across June's expression, and I can only hope I know why.

I keep my hand around hers and pull her toward me. Then I kiss her, our lips barely touching, as tenderly as I can.

"My home is where you are," I murmur.

Her expression softens, and she leans against me, her body warm. It feels, as always, right.

"Come home soon, then," she whispers back.

\* \* \*

When the AIS sends for us, they call for us both. Eden and me. We find ourselves standing in the center of a circle on the top floor of the AIS headquarters, surrounded by an arc of politicians and agency directors.

It's not just the AIS we're answering to. It's the President and his council as well. The whole thing looks like a goddy trial.

Beside me, Eden is calm, his face steady and chin up. I look for signs of his usual anxieties—his hands wringing, his jaw tight, his back stiff. But he's not doing any of that today.

President Ikari frowns at our calm state. He leans forward on his elevated dais and weaves his fingers together. His eyes fix on me. "Four days ago, the man known as Dominic Hann corrupted the Level system and led a riot that left Ross City on fire and in ruins. As I understand from what Director Min has told me, you and your brother acted on your own discretion to stop what he was doing. Is this all correct?"

Eden nods. "Yes, sir."

"Yes, sir," I echo him.

President Ikari frowns. "I've been informed, however, that instead of restoring the Level system to what it once was, you've altered other parts of the system to suit yourself. Have you done this, Mr. Daniel Altan Wing?"

"It was me, sir," Eden speaks up first. "I implemented the new system when I deleted Dominic Hann's hack."

Everyone shifts in their chairs. A chorus of murmurs fills the chamber. I glance quickly to where Director Min is sitting. She nods quietly at us to continue. Whether or not she'll stand up for us, I'm still not sure, but I return an imperceptible nod to her and look back at the President.

President Ikari sighs. "And why would you do such a thing?" he says.

Eden hesitates. In the silence, I take over.

"Because sometimes, sir, the only way to make your government listen is to force them to," I say.

There's another round of whispers and gasps. I'm reminded of the Republic's Senate, of when June had once been so unhappy trying to maneuver through their ranks. It's a special kind of hell, speaking frankly in a system that doesn't reward honesty at all.

"With all due respect, President Ikari," I go on, "I know what it's like to live in a place where people have no choices. What happens in a world like that, when you're unable to speak out against something you think is wrong?"

Ikari frowns at me. "Are you trying to compare Antarctica to the Republic of America, Mr. Wing?"

I hold my hands up. "I know how different the two are. But the Republic was founded on a system of fear. People allowed the first Elector to come to power because they were afraid of everything and everyone else. They turned in on themselves, closed their borders, and gave up their freedoms in exchange for security. And then, one day, we woke up realizing that we'd handed over so much that we'd given ourselves up too. I know what that feels like all too well. It's part of the reason why we left the Republic to come here in the first place."

I'm not sure if my words are sinking in with the council, but hearing what the Republic did wrong seems to make them sit up straighter. As if they know that their country is better. The President studies me for a moment, then nods at Eden. "You're the top student of Ross City. Why don't you tell us your thinking behind all this, and whether or not you align with your brother?"

I think of the way Eden always left early for university in the mornings—with that tense look on his face, bracing himself for another difficult day. But he doesn't hesitate now. He just looks the President square in the eye and answers.

"Antarctica was founded on the principle of innovation. Wasn't it?" He looks around at the council, and to my satisfaction, they look happy with his words. Eden knows how to play this game, too. "I learned it when I came here for school. You teach it to all your citizens. This country was built on the idea of progress and experimentation. All of this—the Levels, the biodome—came from young people who created big, bold, new things that took the world by storm. So many came here in the hopes that this would be where they could find the freedom to be who they wanted to be. They flocked to this unknown, barren land because they were excited by what it could become. They were dazzled by the brilliant and the frightening, the technology that was changing things day by day here. That's how Antarctica became what it is today. It's still so young, barely a country, and yet it holds so much power."

He shakes his head and points out at the windows, where the glass separates us from the sky beyond. "This isn't the Antarctica of the past anymore. Ross City no longer rewards the very principles it was founded on. It's a place where people are forced to conform to what this council thinks is right or wrong. They can't speak up about their frustrations and hardships. The Level system was supposed to be a system that encouraged good behavior and success. Now it's just a system that holds half of the city's population back. There's no hope for people in the Undercity. How can there be?"

"So you took it upon yourself to change what you thought was wrong." The President narrows his eyes at my brother.

Eden takes a deep breath. "So I made some adjustments," he says with a slight shrug. In that gesture, I recognize a glimmer of myself. "Isn't that how all change happens? Someone just has to do it first?"

The head of the police unit snorts at his words and looks at the President. "The boy put in a stop to Levels deducted for rioting against the government. There's already a march scheduled for dawn tomorrow. They halted points associated with health care and welfare. They've altered points deducted for crimes."

"For crimes of what?" Eden interrupts. "Not having a home? Taking away their Levels if they can't afford something? Let people protest without punishment. Let them have a chance to help their families. Let people struggling in the lowest floors of the city know that you still care about them, too."

The President's stare on Eden is ice-cold. "What you've done is the height of arrogance, boy."

"Maybe." He steps forward this time. "But it's because I care. Because, sometimes, being patriotic means calling out the problems rotting away your country. I'm not saying we don't want to work with you. But we represent millions of voices you're not hearing right now. If you want to preserve the spirit of what made

Antarctica a world leader to begin with, you should take a look at your blind spots."

Murmurs rumble among the council members. I look over to Eden. He's pale, and frightened, but he stands his ground with his fists clenched at his sides, and all I can think about is the memory that comes to me now—the moment he had volunteered himself, without hesitation, to help the Republic find a cure for the plague. I think of the determined light in his eyes, the resolve he'd had to save a country that had taken everything from him. I think of his plans now for the Republic, his architectural suggestions for what to do with the old Trial stadiums and the old military halls.

No matter the demons that haunt him, he has still remained a light. And I find myself feeling prouder of him in this moment than I ever have. When he glances at me, searching for approval, I give him a nod and a smile.

"You will stay in Ross City," the President finally says. The murmurs around him die down. "Until we have decided the appropriate course of punishment for you both for your actions. The Level system will be reset to its original state."

I never expected the city to approve of what we'd done. Neither had Eden. But even now, as the President speaks, I see some uncomfortable shifting around the room. There isn't unanimous agreement on this.

President Ikari sighs, then continues. "Meanwhile, I will also convene a special council to discuss possible solutions to some of what you have brought up. You'll be notified if your services are needed again."

It's not much. Change never happens quickly, anyway. But

something in his tone lifts a burden off my chest, and I exchange a look with my brother. He had done this. However things go in the future here, he was the one who planted the seed.

I half expect Eden to hesitate when he speaks again. But he doesn't. His voice is clear, and his shoulders are straight. He bows his head slightly at the President, as if this is something he's used to doing every day.

"Of course, sir," he says.

# EDEN

**OUR FINAL SENTENCE COMES A WEEK LATER.**

Two counts each of insubordination—one for heading back to
Ross City without notifying anyone, and the second for installing
changes onto the original Level system. Our own Levels are halved.
Daniel is released from the AIS.

Prison time, however, is pardoned by the President himself. He
has permitted us to return to the Republic on schedule, in time for
my internship with Batalla Hall. Returning to Antarctica at any time
will require his personal consent.

It all works out in the end. I think our time in Antarctica has
come to a close.

\* \* \*

A month later, on our last day in Ross City, I head back to the Undercity. My system is tracking my every movement now—Daniel
knows exactly where I'm going, as does the entire government. But

I'd gotten permission for today. Today is when I'm seeing Pressa, who has been released from the hospital for her shoulder injury.

Things already look different by the time I arrive in the Undercity. The street's still grungy, of course, the tightly packed stands still billowing smoke from their grills, the half-working neon signs still hanging over the crammed storefronts. There are still zero-level folks huddled against the walls, trying to sleep in the midst of all the bustle.

But I also see a newly appointed task force at work. President Ikari had kept his word, at least—people with blue armbands are surveying Undercity civilians, interviewing them and listening to their grievances. Here and there, I see scattered groups of people gathered to hear someone giving a speech, or pockets of protesters waving signs in the air. The Levels hovering over their heads aren't being deducted for their protesting.

The shop that Pressa's father owned is still being repaired. One of their neighbors is nailing a new windowpane in, while two others are hoisting a new neon sign over the store. I pause to smile at the sight.

Pressa is standing outside the shop and calling directions up at the two working on the sign. Her left arm's still in a cast, but she seems like she's moving around pretty easily with it as she directs them.

When she sees me, she pauses to pat me on the shoulder. "Glad you came by today," she says.

"Glad to see you smiling," I reply, and she grins that familiar little grin of hers, leaning subtly against my shoulder as she does. It sends a warm current through my chest.

"I brought you something," I tell her, then reach into my backpack and take out a frame encasing a delicate arrangement of dried flowers. It's the first time I've ever given her something like this, and I blush as I hold it up for her. "I thought it might look nice in your father's shop, you know, herbs and everything."

Pressa holds the frame before her with a look of wonder. Her eyes shine with moisture. "Oh, Eden," she breathes, tapping a finger gently against the glass. "It's beautiful. Thank you."

I beam, feeling my heart lift at her words. Then I reach into my pocket and take out a fresh flower, a small yellow bud that I hadn't pressed into the frame. "And one for you," I add, tucking it neatly behind her ear.

She looks up at me with a smile that brightens everything around us. She seems happier than the last time I saw her—and even though the death of her father still haunts her eyes, there's also a sense of purpose there, that she can still find him if she preserves her father's store here. I smile at her, taking in her beauty, and feel the sharp stab of leaving her behind.

I clear my throat and try not to think about it. "How's Marren doing, managing the store?" I ask her.

"Good," she says, squinting inside the shop's windows, where her father's assistant is now leaning over the counter and measuring out several spoonfuls of herbs for a customer. "You should've seen him the first few days. He was running around like a headless chicken. But I think he's settled into a groove."

We look on as Marren searches the shelves in vain, scratching his head as he tries to figure out where he has stocked all the new medicine the shop now carries. I can't help laughing a little.

"Good groove," I say.

Pressa smiles. "He's always had it."

Daniel, in his final AIS act, spoke up for Mr. Yu's shop. Director Min legalized it after the city ran an inspection, giving it a permit to sell the higher-quality medications that had previously only been available to the Sky Floors. Without the fear of arrest hanging over everyone's head, and with the new medicines, people have been flocking here from all over the Undercity. The shop's bigger than it used to be, too, thanks to the compensation package that the city gave them for their reconstruction.

It doesn't fix everything wrong with the system down here, of course—there are still too many others who can't afford the luxury of healthcare. But at least the memory of her father will be preserved here.

Now Pressa looks at me. "You got a haircut," she replies, running a hand playfully through my newly trimmed locks. "All set to make an impression in the Republic, aren't you?"

She's trying her best to cover up the strain in her voice, but I can hear it. It mirrors my own reluctance to leave. I run a hand absently through my curls and try to smile at her. "We'll see about an impression," I reply. "They're starting me as early as next week."

She shuffles her feet and glances down at the framed flowers, then back to me. "Are you nervous?"

"After what we went through? Nah, I'm feeling pretty calm." I hesitate. "I'm going to miss you, though."

She winces at my words, and it's all I can do to not wrap my arms around her right now and pull her into a kiss. "You have to leave so soon?"

I nod.

We both fall into an awkward silence. "Thank you," Pressa finally says. "For putting in a good word for my father's shop and making sure the community stays intact."

"What are you going to do here?" I ask her. "Now that you've got Marren running the store?"

She shrugs, looking uncertainly around at the Undercity's streets. "I don't know. I'll figure something out," she answers with a shrug. There is something lost in her gaze. "They said I can apply to the university, even with my Level. They might give me a scholarship. But . . ."

"But?" I ask.

She looks at me, and then down. "I don't know." And in her gaze, I see that same restlessness I've always felt, the feeling of not fitting in, the same need to do something bigger, to find myself in this strange world. The same thing that drew us together as friends from the beginning. "I'm ready to leave the Undercity," she finally says. "I just don't know where to go next."

"Come with me," I say.

The words spill out of my mouth without warning. Pressa looks at me in surprise.

"Come . . . with you?" she murmurs.

I hadn't thought any of that through at all. But when I speak again, I find myself taking her by her hands and pulling her closer. "Come with me," I repeat, my voice more eager this time. It's so obvious now. "You've always said you never felt like you belonged in the Undercity—like there was an adventure out there, waiting for you to make it happen. Come to Los Angeles, to the Republic. Please. You could change everything there for the better. You could do everything you've ever wanted to do. And I could be there with you, we could . . ."

I trail off, too shy to ask her to be with me. But I can see the spark lighting in Pressa's eyes, that addictive sense of life in her that I'd always admired. Her lips curve up. This is the adventure that had been waiting for her.

"Okay," she says quietly, as if to herself, and then breaks into a wide grin. "Okay!"

Then she throws her uninjured arm around me without warning, hand still clutching the framed flowers, and I find myself hugging her in return, and we're both laughing at the awkward angle of her one-armed embrace. She feels so good in my arms that I can't imagine ever letting go.

On an impulse, I kiss her.

She leans into me and kisses me back, fully and firmly. It's the most perfect kiss in the world. I hug her tight. Somewhere around us, I hear whistles, then the workers on the ladder teasing us gently before bursting into friendly laughter. I don't move away. I just keep my arms around Pressa, holding her tight, feeling sure of our future for the first time, feeling *happier* than I've been in a long time.

The world shifts, tilts, sometimes collapses. But sometimes, it bends toward you, and everything feels right.

* * *

By the time I return home that night, our apartment's already filled with packing boxes. Daniel is walking around in a restless state, double-checking our things and making sure everything is put away.

When he sees me, he straightens and tries to hide his anxiety. "Are you ready to go back tomorrow?" he asks me instead.

I walk over to our couch and plop down on it one last time. "Ready enough," I reply as he comes over to join me.

Immediately, he smiles.

"What?" I say.

"Something really good happened to you," he says, studying my face. "It's Pressa, yeah?"

I laugh a little. How good it feels to have a brother who can read my emotions again, who knows me. I nod. "Pressa's going to come to the Republic too. She's figuring out all the logistics for herself now."

Daniel grins at that and nudges my shoulder. "Good," he says. "I always thought she was meant for more than the Undercity. Glad you'll have each other."

My eyes settle on a small, square box in one of his pockets. "What's that?" I ask.

He hesitates, and his smile wavers. He leans his head against the back of the couch and closes his eyes. "It's nothing. I don't know."

Now it's my turn to read his mind. It's that look he gets only when he thinks about June. I wonder if he has an entire life laid out in front of him, if he sees glimmers of her at his side, of him holding her hand. I wonder if he's afraid of that vision of a life, how easily it could shift depending on the directions that the present will shift him. On how the next few weeks will go.

"Daniel," I say gently, so that he turns back to me. "She's nuts about you. And you've been obsessed with her since as far back as I can remember. It's obvious to everyone."

He looks down at his hands. They fidget nervously, the fingers weaving together and then pulling apart. Even now, he can't seem to bring himself to shake off his past, the feeling that maybe he was never meant to be with someone as high-ranking as June.

I wonder if we'll ever fully escape our history. But every step forward takes us to a better place.

"If you need help with anything related to June," I add, "you know you have a brother that you can count on." I shrug a little. "Just in case you had something specific in mind."

He looks at me, then smiles a little. There's hope in his gaze—but even better than that, there's trust. We may always struggle with our pasts, but we can rest assured that we'll always have someone else who can pull us forward. In this moment, at least, the fear of going to bed and confronting my nightmares again seems distant.

"Glad you said it," he finally answers. "I think I *will* need your help."

# DANIEL

THERE WAS A TIME WHEN MY WANTED POSTER WAS
scattered on the JumboTrons all over Los Angeles. It's still strange
to be in the Republic without seeing those ads, to know that I'm not
walking down the streets as a criminal anymore. Hell, it's strange
to walk down these streets and know that I'm not going to sleep
huddled against an alley wall, that I'm not constantly searching for
my next meal.

Eden and I have been back in the Republic for a little over two
weeks. Behind us and across the oceans, Antarctica has begun the
first experimental phase of revising its Level system. Although the
President doesn't want to admit it, they've incorporated a lot of
the changes that Eden had originally put in. Ways for people in the
Undercity to redeem themselves, Level exemptions for things like
medicine and food and shelter. More freedom and less punishment
for what you can say and express.

They're small steps, of course, just like the Republic's progress. All
around the world, everyone's just gradually trying to move forward.

The streets are still slick tonight from a gentle rain earlier in the afternoon, and the air smells crisp and clean, the breeze cooling my cheeks. I take my time strolling toward the complex where June lives, counting out steps of my own. My fingers brush against a small box tucked in one of my pockets. I haven't opened it since I packed it away. I'm too afraid to.

I reach the main entrance of her complex and exchange a familiar nod with the security guard. June and I have had several dates since I arrived. We've caught up over quiet dinners in the corners of restaurants and drinks in the dim recesses of her living room, our faces turned out toward the lights of the city. I've talked to her every day. She's told me about how Anden is securing funding for the Republic's rebuilding. I've told her about how quickly Eden has adapted to his internship and life back in the Republic.

I go over everything I want to say again in my head. Maybe she'll tell me that I'm rushing things too much. The thought sends a shiver of uncertainty through me as I head up the elevator to her floor. June is a practical person, after all. How long has it been since we were reunited, anyway? Only several months, with a lot of chaos in between.

\* \* \*

I reach her door. There, I press her doorbell and then linger for a moment, trying to stop my fidgeting.

I'm still debating with myself when the door swings open to reveal June.

The sight of her cuts through the train of nervous questions engulfing my thoughts. Her hair is down to her shoulders tonight, dark and wavy, and she has pinned one side with a delicate floral pin. She's wearing a pale dress that shimmers slightly in the light. Seeing her in full military gear is always breathtaking, but it's when she's like this—off duty, her guard down and smile on, her eyes relaxed—that I find myself barely able to handle how stunning she is. She looks so gorgeous in this moment that I just end up staring at her in disbelief.

She laughs at me, then takes a step toward me and kisses me once. "Good evening," she says, raising an eyebrow at me. "Nice to see you too."

Does she suspect anything? I smile at her, trying to stay casual, then offer her my arm. "Just so you know," I say as we start heading back down the hall, "I wasn't completely overwhelmed at how beautiful you look. That would be stupid."

"Right." She tilts her head at me. "Then why were you staring off into space?"

"You had a spider in your hair."

She laughs again, and I realize that I'll never get enough of the sound. "Thanks for not telling me," she says.

We banter as we head out of her complex and into the freshly washed night. I guide her around the puddles still on the sidewalk and watch as the light dances against her hair. Our conversations come more easily now, and somehow, I almost feel like we've gone back in time to when we'd first met.

"You said you found a new café that opened near the train station?" she asks curiously as I lead her down the street. "How come I've never heard of this place?"

I smile a little. "Eden told me about it. I think they just opened their doors today, and haven't really publicized it. He said it looks perfect for a quiet night."

June just frowns and concentrates harder on figuring it out. "I usually know about all the openings in this area. Their permits need to go through a strict check, and if they were able to get it approved, I would have heard and sent someone to inspect it."

I sigh at her and laugh. Keeping a secret from June is just as hard as it's always been. "Just trust me," I say before she digs too much deeper.

The train station I take her toward is the same one that I saw her walk by several months ago, for the first time in ten years. I'm quiet as we head through the space. It's serene right now, the newly paved area empty as no more trains are running here for the night. Patches of grass decorate the gates around the station. The area is dimly lit, only a few streetlights dotting the night.

The memory of that meeting plays sharply in my mind. Eden walking beside me after his first internship interview, his spirits high as he tells me what he wants to do for the Republic, my hands in my pockets, a smile on my face as I listen to him. The sight of June walking toward me from the opposite side of this walkway. The way I had stopped as she passed me by, how everything about her—her eyes, her walk, the sense of her there—had seized me like a hook. I think of how I'd caught up to her, how we'd introduced ourselves to each other again after so much time apart.

*Hi, I'm Daniel.*

*Hi, I'm June.*

Now I've taken her back here. I look at her as we walk, a lump forming in my throat. Is she thinking about that moment, too? She's quiet, and her eyes seem far away.

Eden should be in position, ready to do his part of my surprise. I glance toward the ledge of the train station's second floor. He should be up there somewhere. My heart pounds in anticipation.

It's now or never.

Suddenly, as we go, strings of tiny lights illuminate overhead. There are thousands of them strung in arcs along the trees and poles, guiding our way.

June looks up at them in surprise. A soft gasp escapes her.

I tighten my hand around hers and pull her forward. As we walk, more strings of lights turn on to guide our path, one round after another, their golden, twinkling glow reflected against the wet sidewalk until it looks like we're walking through a fairyland.

June looks at me, the lights gleaming in her eyes. A curious, puzzled smile is on her face. "Is this your doing?" she asks me, nodding up in wonder at the lights.

I smile and lean down toward her. "Just follow me," I whisper.

The lights continue to illuminate for us, one row after another, guiding us toward the end of the walkway, where a small park surrounded by shaded trees sits around the corner. As we reach it, I feel a tremble go through June. Her steps falter for a moment.

The walkway leading all around the square space is lit with candles. Thousands of tiny fairy lights glow in the trees overhead. Delicate glass orbs hang from the branches, filled with intricate bouquets of dried flowers, and baskets of roses blanket the grass all around us in a breathtaking pattern, their scent sweetening the air.

I lead her to the center of the space, then turn to face her, my eyes meeting her dark ones. A faint breeze whispers through the leaves. I'm trembling now too, unsure if I'm going to be able to do this.

"Each memory I have of you, I keep in a treasured place in my heart," I say. "This place holds one of my favorites. You remember it too, yeah? Where we saw each other again, for the first time in a decade?"

June's eyes are wide now, full of love and fear and expectation. "Of course," she whispers.

I turn my eyes down for a moment, too shy to hold the gaze between us. My smile edges one side of my mouth up. "I've thought about that meeting every day for the past few months. That in this big world, somehow, I found my way back to this city, to this place, and somehow, after everything, the world still chose to put us back in each other's lives."

I turn my eyes back up to hers. "The Republic is a place that holds some of our darkest memories, for both you and me. You've been through so much, and so have I. We went through it together, and somehow we emerged from it to be here again, at each other's sides."

She smiles at me. There is a sheen of tears in her eyes now, and within them are a million stars. "Is that why you brought us here?" she murmurs.

I step closer to her and look down at our intertwined hands. "June," I whisper hoarsely, "I'm in love with you. I've always been, since the first moment I knew you. There's nothing that feels more right to me than to be by your side. And I realized that I could never get that feeling if I stayed in Antarctica. So I came back to find you."

She leans toward me, searching my gaze. "Thank you for coming back," she whispers.

I glance up at the twinkling lights. "I wanted to bring you here because I think this place holds my favorite memory of us. Of the fact that we're still here." Then I reach into my pocket and pull out a small, polished box. I'd spent so long preparing for this moment, overthinking every second of it—but now, I can only keep going. "I . . . wanted to bring you here because I'd like to stay here, at your side, no matter what happens. I thought this place might be a good beginning for the next chapter of our lives." I hesitate, bashful now. "That is, if you'd like to be here with me too."

Her hands tremble against mine as I kneel down before her and open the box to show her a ring.

It's a clean, silver band studded with tiny, evenly spaced sparkles of diamonds, designed with an intricate twisting pattern reminiscent of the paper clip ring I gave her years ago, and of the one she'd given me. I'd worked with a craftsman on it years ago, had kept it in my possessions in the hopes that one day I'd be able to gift it. It looks like ten lost years aching to be made up for by a lifetime together.

"A long time ago, I gave you a ring that held my entire heart," I tell her. "But it represents a past. I want to give you something that is a future. A possibility."

June looks at me with eyes full of hope and fear. "And what is that future?" she asks.

I gather all my courage.

And I ask her the question I've been thinking about for so long, the one that my life has been leading up to since the moment I first met her, when we were still so young, unsure what the next day would bring, clinging to each other in desperation, finding ourselves together, the question that has drawn me back here to her, heart bared, vulnerable, afraid and hopeful.

"Will you marry me?" I say to her.

And for an instant, I think I'm dreaming. I'm going to wake up and this is all going to disappear. Or maybe we aren't meant to be—she will turn away, or she will shake her head, and this particular future will never come to pass.

But then June's tears finally spill down her face, and her smile is the brightest light I have ever seen, and she is wrapping her arms around my neck, crying and laughing and shaking, and I am so overwhelmed with joy that for a moment all I can do is embrace her. I take the new ring and slide it onto the finger where she'd once worn a twist of paper clips that represented our history.

A past. A future. Something that can be ours.

I realize I'm crying too, because the final puzzle piece of my heart has fallen into place.

June's answer drifts up into the night air and echoes across the cityscape, one of millions of things happening in each of our lives, the small steps you take that are invisible to everyone else in the world. The steps that, nevertheless, matter the most.

*Yes.*

*Always.*

*Forever.*

# ACKNOWLEDGMENTS

The idea for *Rebel* first came to me while I was still writing *Champion*, but it arrived in fragments—a gamified society, an augmented reality, and a pair of brothers healing in the aftermath of a war. I had to write an entirely separate duology (Warcross) before I understood what I wanted for this final story set in Legend's timeline, and for a while, I didn't think I'd ever get to it. During all those years, the reason I kept revisiting this idea was because of readers who wanted to know what happened after the end to the original trilogy. So thank you firstly to my wonderful audience. You all always inspire me.

To Jen Besser, who has been my editor, champion, and friend from the very beginning. I can't tell you how happy I am that I got to work on all four of the Legend novels with you. You are one in a million.

To the entire team at Macmillan Children's who have welcomed me and my stories with so much warmth and enthusiasm. I'm incredibly honored to be working with you all.

Kristin, I don't know where I'd be without you. You're the best agent a writer could hope for, and I'm excited for all the stories we'll continue to work on together.

Legend couldn't have found its legs without the support of so many school librarians and teachers. I am endlessly grateful to you all for bringing my books into your classrooms and libraries, and hearing

## ACKNOWLEDGMENTS

stories from you about students reading the series is such an honor. Thank you.

To my wonderful friends, for letting me lean on you as I talked this one out. Tahereh, Leigh, Amie, Dianne, Sabaa, and Renée: I'm so lucky to have you in my life.

Finally, to Primo, my forever confidante and best friend. Love you, always.